Friends of the Dusk

Phil Rickman

Friends of the Dusk

CORVUS

Published in hardback in Great Britain in 2015 by Corvus,
an imprint of Atlantic Books Ltd.

10 9 8 7 6 5 4 3 2 1

A CIP catalogue record for this book is available from the British Library.

Hardback ISBN: 978 1 78239 694 9
E-book ISBN: 978 1 78239 696 3

Printed and bound by CPI Group (UK) Ltd, Croydon, CR0 4YY

Corvus
An imprint of Atlantic Books Ltd
Ormond House
26–27 Boswell Street
London
WC1N 3JZ

www.corvus-books.co.uk

Part One

I was much disturbed by the unhealthy and near-hysterical publicity given by the national press to the question of exorcisms in the Church of England. I was also disturbed by the number of requests for help and advice about the exorcizing of places or persons which I was receiving...

The general attitude in the Church of England seemed to be to regard exorcism as an exercise in white magic or a survival of medieval superstition.

The findings of a commission convened by the Right
Reverend Robert Mortimer, Bishop of Exeter.
'Exorcism' (SPCK, 1972)

Castle Green is the hidden gem of Hereford. To find it, behind the streetscape and beyond the Cathedral, it has to be stalked...

David Whitehead,
The Castle Green at Hereford, a Landscape of Ritual,
Royalty and Recreation.
(Logaston Press, 2007)

1

Touch the darkness

WAS IT REALLY a good thing visiting the old woman ahead of a much-foreboded late-October storm?

Was it, in fact, a good thing to be visiting her at all?

The room at The Glades, a Victorian greystone home for the elderly, had expanded into a whole suite after the deaths – eerily timely – of Anthea White's immediate neighbours on the second landing. Two new doorways had been made in the partition walls. Miss White had paid for all this from a recent bequest. She could have bought herself a nice, period cottage down in Hay, but she claimed The Glades suited her lifestyle.

The new living room had floor-to-ceiling bookcases and a view of the bell tower of Hardwicke Church. Miss White was curled into her wide, multi-cushioned swivel chair, a black widow spider biding its time. Were people who'd recently had hip surgery supposed to sit like that?

'Oh, now, you'll never believe this, Watkins…' The old girl leaning forward. '… Cardelow's woman was apparently *refusing to dust the books.*'

'Actually,' Merrily said from the piano stool – no piano, just the stool, 'I think I *would* believe it. Especially if you were sitting there watching her. Even with her back turned, the malevolence would be palpable.'

Miss White smiled modestly. Mrs Cardelow, proprietor of The Glades, had brought them tea and cakes herself, asking Merrily if she'd mind bringing back the tray when she came down. *Save my legs*, Mrs Cardelow had said wearily. *And possibly a little of my sanity.*

'Cardelow's daughter was married the other weekend, did I tell you?' Miss White said in her tiny, kitteny voice. 'Some awful junior canon at the Cathedral.'

'Really? What's his name?'

'Didn't ask. Couldn't be arsed, but I expect you'll know him by his receding chin. All change, I hear, at the dicky heart of the Hereford Diocese.'

'Just a new bishop.'

'Is he charismatic, like the delicious Hunter?'

'I hope not, with all my heart; I haven't met him yet. Next week, apparently.'

Merrily became aware of an oak side table to the left of Miss White's chair, a white mat on top holding something covered with a black velvet cloth, like a very small catafalque. Miss White peered at Merrily, eyes darker than the caked mascara.

'Why are you here, Watkins?'

A trapped, tawny leaf flapped irritably outside the window. Merrily shrugged.

'Just passing.'

'Bollocks!'

'I was on the way back from Hay, where I visit the Thorogoods occasionally, and I, erm… thought I'd drop in and, you know, see if you were still breathing?'

Miss White scowled.

'Don't trivialize breathing. I enjoy my breathing, in all its infinite varieties. Along with occasional astral tourism, it's all I have left.'

Merrily smiled. OK, she'd called in because Betty Thorogood had said the word in the bookshop was that Miss White was *not well*. At her age, often a euphemism for *may not see the weekend*. She'd been surprised at how hard this had hit her. Exchanging banter with Miss White had become almost like a spiritual exercise, a test of faith. Reaching out a hand to touch the darkness just to prove you could still draw it back.

She glanced at the nearest shelves where a whole row of books had the name Crowley on the spine.

'And it's Hallowe'en next week, of course. Your official birthday, Anthea.'

Moments of quiet. The leaf escaped from the window and fluttered away like a timid soul. Miss White was leaning lazily back into her nest of cushions. She might be dying, but it didn't look imminent.

'And are things going well for you?'

'Things are fine. My daughter, Jane, she's due back from her gap-year archaeological dig in a week or so. Sooner than expected, but I'm quite glad.'

'And Robinson?'

'Lol is also finally coming home. Been touring all summer, for the first time in years, then he was asked to do some studio work. Good for his self-esteem.'

Miss White pondered this.

'He's never been frightened of me. Odd, that.'

'Unlike me, huh?'

'I love the way you come here simply because you *are* frightened.'

'Oh, come—'

Merrily leaned back then had to steady herself on the piano stool. Miss White raised her eyes

'Come on, then, little clergyperson. Out with it. Don't be annoying.'

'I'm sorry?'

'Thinking of packing it in, are we?'

'*What?*'

'Snipping off the dog collar? Depositing the cassock in the Oxfam bank in the vain hope it might reach some impoverished African priestess?'

The old woman seemed to be rearing in her chair, without

5

moving; she could play tricks with your head. Wasn't bloody dying at all, was she? Merrily coughed.

'Makes you ask that?'

Miss White was smiling sweetly again, bending to the tray on the Victorian Gothic table between them to pour more tea. Then she stopped, looking up.

'Oh, but I never thought…'

Putting down the teapot and leaning back to the side table, she pulled away the black velvet cloth to reveal a small, rectangular cardboard box, with gold sides. On the top, it said:

Ordo Templi Orientis
Thoth Tarot Cards

Merrily had seen the pack before. Exquisitely painted by Lady Frieda Harris, designed by A. Crowley.

'*Would* you like me to read for you, Watkins?'

The window rattled, and the first raindrops plopped on the glass. The impending high winds were supposed to be the residue of some Atlantic hurricane with a pretty name.

'No, I would not,' Merrily said.

2

A date with Hurricane Lorna

DRIVING BACK TO Hereford from Annie's place, his mood as crazy as the night, Bliss got pulled over by the cops four miles short of the city.

Bugger.

Brakes on as the traffic car's headlights turned near-horizontal rain into tracer fire, he lowered the glass minimally, sat and waited, engine running. The road was a causeway through a war zone of waterlogged fields. No lights in the farmhouses.

'… assuming, sir, that you didn't see the sign back there?'

This big, sarky face swimming up in the side window, all pink and runny like the inside of a freshly sliced tomato: Darryl Mills, ex-CID, gone back into uniform for a more exciting life in a powerful car. Bliss cut his engine, leaned back out of the spray.

'You know, Darryl, I don't believe I did. Maybe it got blown away?'

'One second.' Up came the flashlight to confirm that Bliss's face matched the only Scouse accent in Gaol Street. 'Ah. Sorry, boss.'

'If you want a whiff of me breath,' Bliss said wearily, 'you'll have to hop in the other side. Buggered if I'm gerrin out in this.'

'Only the sign you missed, look, that was a diversion.'

'Darryl, this is Herefordshire, where they leave the friggin' flood signs up in a drought.'

Darryl Mills shrugged his sodden shoulders.

'Just telling you, boss. Road's well blocked up ahead. Trees down everywhere.'

A blast of weather had Darryl hanging on to the wing mirror to stay on his feet, his partner billowing up behind him, waterproofs flapping: Big Patti Calder, mother of four.

'If you're going into town, Frannie, it's gonna take you a while. Five B-roads closed. A49 north of Ross. Flash flood at Letton. Might be more, all we know. Rough ole night.'

'Bastard of a night,' Bliss said.

In all kinds of ways. The last thing he'd planned was a date with Hurricane Lorna. His day off. He should be warm and dry at Annie's flat in Malvern. And would be if her old man hadn't rung around teatime to check she was at home – Charlie thinking he'd drop in for a coffee on his way back from some meeting in Worcester. Bliss getting the gist and throwing his jacket on before Annie was off the phone. He had bad memories of a rainy night with Charlie Howe in it.

Annie had been wearing the famous old stripy sweater from the night the God of Policing had thrown them together. The sweater had holes in both elbows now. Worn these days only as a kind of talisman against evil fate.

Yeh, right. Putting down the phone, Annie had finally told him the real reason Charlie was coming round. What she'd already known about the old bastard but had kept to herself in the hope he'd come to his senses. Bliss had just stared at Annie, and she'd looked down at her slippers. It was like a bad joke. Except Annie didn't do jokes.

'—OK, boss?' Patti Calder said through the blast. 'You look—'

'Just recovering from a bit of awkward news, Patti. Not your problem.' Though it could be a problem for all of them, soon enough. 'Listen, how bad is it, really? I'm assuming nobody's actually been *under* a fallen tree?'

Darryl Mills laughed, and the rest got blown away. Bliss thrust his head into the weather.

'What?'

Maybe too much to hope that a ten-ton oak had come down on Charlie Howe's car with Charlie inside.

Darryl bent to Bliss's window.

'We almost got excited, boss, but it was nothing.'

'No, go on,' Bliss said. 'What?'

When he left his car on a double yellow in East Street, the rain had stopped and the wind was dying back. Not yet seven p.m., and Hurricane Lorna was already over the hill, an old prozzie parading what was left of her in the brick alleyways accessing Castle Green and the River Wye.

Driving into the city, it had looked surreal, out of time: hardly anybody on the streets, whole areas blacked out except for the lonely flickering of candles and lamps behind fogged glass. The Cathedral tower was a grey smudge in the gaps between buildings.

Bliss was in jeans and beanie and a fleece he didn't need – under the wind, it was weirdly warm for the time of year. When he saw lights up ahead, they were actually on Castle Green, lights in a huddle, like a small camp or a party for the homeless. He felt his way along the rails by the long duck pond that used to be part of the castle moat in the days when there was a castle on the Green. Just a spread of parkland, now, with a Nelson's column in the middle, and then the River Wye.

Bliss paused on the path above the Green, dead leaves spinning around him like moths on steroids. It was hardly unusual for a body to be uncovered here. This being an historical site, it was almost certainly going to be an historic body, nothing in this for him. But still he kept on walking towards the lights. If he went home he'd just be sitting in the dark, listening to the last of the storm and the slithery sound of shit rising to the surface.

Nothing to say he'll get it.

Annie's voice in his head, parched with uncertainty.

Equally, Annie, there's nothing to say he won't. I've actually met people who love the fucker and not all of them criminals.

They actually liked that about Charlie Howe. Bit of a maverick, law unto himself, Jack the lad. And *a local boy*, see. Always important.

He gets it, I'm out of here, Bliss had told Annie. *Obviously.*

Not thinking, until he'd left, about the weight of what he'd said there and what it would mean to her. One way or another this was going to cause all kinds of—

'Boss?'

A hand-lamp's broad beam swung past his face before tilting back to light up DC David Vaynor, striding towards him across the grass, cutting through the wind like a long blade.

'Didn't know you were coming out.' Vaynor shining the light down the Green. 'Something and nothing, boss. Anywhere else it'd be something, here it's nothing.'

'Just passing, Darth,' Bliss said, and then the beam landed on something massive and unexpected, writhing and clicking in the wind. 'Bloody hell.'

'Ripped clean out,' Vaynor said. 'Roots and all.'

Behind the roots, a jungle of clashing branches, pale and bloated in the lamplight.

'Nobody heard it coming down, with the wind,' Vaynor said. 'Nobody saw it happening with all the lights out. Heavy enough to flatten a Land Rover. Anybody been walking past at the time… no chance.'

'Sure there's nobody underneath, are we?'

'Only our friend. And he's well out of it. Assuming it's a bloke.'

By the time they'd reached the fallen tree, the lamp had found a pick up truck and people erecting an orange barrier fence, plastic mesh, not easy in this wind. Bliss stopped next to a wooden bench.

'So where is he?'

'Just there.'

The torch lighting yellow plastic sheeting and disturbed

earth that looked like a plundered badger sett. Vaynor telling Bliss somebody from the Cathedral had come over, spotted bones down there and rung a mate from the county archaeologist's department. If you lived around Castle Green you could get to know a lot of archaeologists.

'Neil Cooper,' Vaynor said. 'He's around, somewhere.'

'Yeh, I know him.'

'Those are the council blokes, with the fencing. They'll probably take the opportunity to excavate properly when the tree's removed. Get him over, shall I?'

'No, finish the story.'

Darth said Cooper had gone into the hole, confirmed they weren't animal bones and then followed established procedure, getting word to Gaol Street. Hence Big Patti and Darryl Mills getting diverted to Castle Green at the start of their shift.

'And they're definitely old bones?'

'Looked old to me, boss. And with a tree that big on top? Cooper's thinking medieval.'

'So what you doing here then, Darth?'

'Just a slight complication, boss.'

They had one of these ten zillion candlepower lamps running from the truck. On the edge of its savage beam, Cooper, under his yellow hard hat, looked a bag of nerves. Kept rubbing his jaw, leaving mud-scrapes.

'Can't believe this. You turn your back for... five minutes?'

Nice-enough lad, a few years younger than Bliss, youthful-looking, just about, like a member of a boy band, now retired. Cooper had been with the county archaeologist's department as long as Bliss had been in Hereford and now, apparently, was running the show while the top guy was recovering from some injury.

'Let me get this right, Neil. This was when you'd come out of the hole to call the police, right? That was when you reckon it happened.'

11

'Possibly then, or could've been earlier. Very dark and really noisy with the wind in the branches. That's why I went to make the call from the top of the bank. Couldn't hear a thing down here.'

No more than half a dozen people around now. Novelty over. Bliss looked down at the plastic sheeting covering the hole, stones weighting it down.

'How many people would've been left around the tree while you were on the phone?'

'Not sure. More by the time I got back.'

'Who were they?'

'Nobody I knew. I imagine word was spreading. Shops not long closed. I was trying to be polite and tell them there was nothing to see, but it was clear it had got out about the bones. People love bones, don't they?'

'You reckon?'

Neil Cooper bent, lifted a brick so he could draw back a corner of the plastic sheet, plywood slats underneath. He lifted one, beckoning Vaynor to shine his lamp down. In the earth, Bliss made out what might have been part of a ribcage, flattened like old rubber. Interesting but hard to love.

'Not exactly the first bones found here, right?'

'What? Oh no. Good God, no. And the nearer you get to the Cathedral… it's like one big charnel house under there. Bones upon bones, upon bones. Thousands of skeletons, men, women, children discovered in The Close. And people were buried here – on what became Castle Green – before there *was* a cathedral. Hundreds of bodies found.'

'So how come they missed this feller?'

'Just that we don't make a habit of destroying mature trees to see what might be underneath. But when one happens to blow down…'

'Was it a full skeleton? When it was first revealed?'

Cooper winced. Behind him, the dying wind was wheezing like an old Hoover.

'What I'm asking, Neil, is are you absolutely sure it originally *had* a head?'

'Francis, leaning over the hole I was this….' Cooper opened his muddied hands to the width of a brick, '*this* far away from it. I was staring into its eye-sockets. Amazingly, the roots had not become entangled in the skeleton, or the bones would've been dragged up and they'd be all over the place. The roots stopped *just* above the bones, so it was virtually all exposed.'

'So when did it *not* have a head?'

'All right.' Cooper nodding hard, drawing breath. 'It was still raining so I covered it over lightly with some soil before I went to call the police.'

'Having already phoned your colleagues to come and assist?'

'By the time I got back they were here with the truck.'

'So who was here while you were on the phone?'

'You've asked me that before. I don't know. It was very dark.'

'And when the police came… did *they* see the head, the skull?'

Vaynor tapped Bliss's arm, shaking his head. Figured. On a night like this Mills and Calder would've lost interest rapidly when they learned the corpse wasn't exactly fresh. Called in, cleared off.

'And you've looked all around?' Bliss said.

'Best we could, with all this mess. We're not really going to get anywhere without chainsaws, and that's not going to happen till tomorrow. Yes, I suppose it's possible somebody might've picked up the skull and then thrown it down somewhere.'

'Or even in the river.'

'*Don't.*'

Cooper turning away.

'It's really not your fault, mate,' Bliss said. 'Bloody chaos here, these conditions.'

'Couldn't just have got mislaid, kicked away, I'm sure of that. Somebody had to have gone down in the hole and lifted it out. Now who would want to do that?'

'Neil…' Bliss exchanged a lamplit glance with Darth Vaynor. 'I'm not saying that's a naive question exactly, but… Were there any kids here? Teenagers?'

'Kids?'

The team erecting the head-high protective fence had nearly finished and were waiting, a respectful distance away, with the last section at their feet and a sign saying DANGER.

Neil Cooper sank his hands into his jacket pockets.

'If it *is* kids, it'll be in pieces by now.'

'Maybe not,' Bliss said. 'Could be on a shelf in a teenager's bedroom. A ciggy between its teeth.'

'Thanks for that, Francis.'

Cooper didn't look at him. Well, what did he think – that they'd be doing house-to-house, putting out a photofit of some bugger who'd passed on eight centuries ago? Was body-snatching still an offence? *Was* this body-snatching, or just petty theft? And from whom? Who owned rotting old bones?

Police life was too short for this. And yet…

'Nothing else you want to tell me, is there, Neil? Something that might not be obvious to dumb coppers?'

Lifting an apologetic hand to Vaynor, who had some totally unnecessary posh degree from Oxford.

'I don't know what you mean,' Cooper said.

'Well, if you think of anything, Neil,' Bliss said, 'you know where I am.'

For a while, anyway.

Till he was forced to leave Hereford due to the resurrection of something old but recent enough to stink.

Bliss turned back into the wind, gritting his teeth, firming up his beanie.

14

3

Hallowe'en. Normal,
irrational anxieties

HUW OWEN'S PHONE voice always brought up the same portrait, in the style of Whistler's Mother only sloppier. Spiritual director in repose in a severe rectory in the Brecon Beacons. Sitting back, stretching out his legs in frayed jeans, no shoes. Rag-haired Welshman with a Yorkshire accent and holes in his socks.

'Just my annual Hallowe'en call, lass,' he said.

Merrily said nothing. She didn't recall him ever phoning her at Hallowe'en before. More likely, he'd just sat down, examined his mental agenda and noticed the word *Merrily* had found its way to the top.

Sitting at her desk in the old scullery, in a circle of light from the Anglepoise lamp, she sipped tea and winced: too hot, too strong, no sugar.

'Well, come on,' Huw said. 'How'd it go?'

'How did what go?'

'Him. Him in the Bishop's Palace.'

'I haven't met him yet.'

'I thought it were today.'

'It's tomorrow.'

'Oh.'

They'd not spoken for a couple of weeks. Not since she'd run the name of the new Bishop of Hereford past him and his reaction had been fast and… the word was probably *forthright*. And then he'd calmed down, said maybe he'd overreacted, ignore him, he had a lot of work on. So she'd ignored him, put it out of her head that there might be dark history between Huw Owen and the new Bishop of Hereford, who'd replaced poor old Bernie Dunmore with unusual speed.

It was too warm, the warmest Hallowe'en she could remember. Rain had blown through, leaving the roads faintly steaming. The neck of her clerical shirt was undone, the dog collar on the desk by the phone. The last day of October. It was unnatural.

'You've been quiet,' Huw said.

'Well... domestic stuff. Jane came back yesterday. Lol's coming back tomorrow. Getting organized. All that.'

A silence.

'That woman sorted? Her in the hairdresser's house?'

'Hopefully.'

A few weeks ago she'd expected to be summoned to give evidence at crown court where a woman was being tried for murder. Knowing that, when the case was reported in the media, *she* would be the defendant, forced to explain to a jury exactly what she did, as a so-called exorcist, and why she thought it was necessary and relevant. All the time knowing she'd only been put in the witness box to be taken apart, bit by bit, in front of a roomful of sceptics so that the defence could show how an already disturbed woman had been pushed over the edge by the belief that her home was still occupied by a dead previous occupant.

A belief that the so-called diocesan deliverance minister had done nothing to discourage.

But the woman had pleaded guilty. No trial.

Salvation. For now.

'Still getting the anxiety dreams, mind,' Merrily said.

'Aye.'

More silence, several heartbeats' worth. Then his voice was louder in the old Bakelite phone.

'I'm always here, you know. Might be a miserable old bugger, but I'm not going anywhere. Yet.'

'Good. I'm glad.'

'What about you?'

'What?' She swallowed too much tea and burned her tongue. 'Why does everybody suddenly think I want out?'

'Who else thinks you want out?'

'I dunno, I— You remember Anthea White?'

'Athena?'

'As she prefers to be known. Athena, yes.' She didn't think Huw had met Miss White. If they ever did, it would be epic, gladiatorial. 'I dropped in on her, last week.'

'She's a witch.'

'Actually, she despises witches.'

'In the original sense. How come you keep putting yourself through it?'

'I dunno. She's been helpful to me, as you know, even though I feel it would be wrong to tell her that. She knows all the places… *all* the places angels fear to tread. Because of what they might pick up on their sandals.'

'So I've heard.'

'Also I know she's never going to admit how lonely she is. And so, occasionally, I… expose myself to it. I'd hate to think we're two halves of something, but… Anyway she looks at me in that knowing, baleful way, like some evil granny, and she asks me if I'm thinking of packing it in.'

'The Night Job.'

The Night Job. Jane had been the first to call it that. Huw loved it, had added it to his lexicon of secret-service style euphemisms for this madness.

'The lot, actually. The whole fancy-dress party. Cassock in the Oxfam bank, as she put it. Which was odd because I'd just been thinking about that, in quite a level, realistic kind of way. I'd been over to Hay, to look in on the Thorogoods in their shop. See how things are now.'

'Aftercare.'

'Mmm.'

17

Part of the deliverance programme; in the end, she'd done a minor exorcism of place in the shop in Back Fold. Betty Thorogood had phoned, Merrily asking her what they'd be doing tonight, for Samhain, the Celtic Feast of the Dead. *Nothing*, Betty had said. *It doesn't matter any more.*

And Merrily had found that disturbing because she'd thought it did matter. They'd followed a spiritual path, believing in something bigger, albeit pagan, and now, because they felt it had rebounded on them...

Supporting the heavy old phone with both hands, she stared into the empty dog collar on the desk. She could hear Jane coming downstairs, home prematurely from Pembrokeshire. After so many weeks alone in the house, it sounded like burglars. Jane had once delighted in paganism, too. A couple of years ago, the kid would be galvanized by Samhain. This morning, she hadn't mentioned it, perhaps hadn't even noticed the date.

'It's a secular society, Huw. Comparatively few of us will now admit to believing in anything unscientific. I can accept that half the world thinks I'm fooling myself. What's harder to take is that a proportion of the other half think I'm trying to fool *them*.'

'You're grasping at straws, thinking any kind of spirituality – paganism, whatever – is better than nowt?'

'And how far the night job is conditioning my own faith. No, of course, I don't want out. It's just that sometimes you examine your reasons for carrying on.'

'Ah,' he said.

Like he knew what was coming, and maybe he did.

'Bottom line, I've even asked myself if I could do one without the other now. And that's not good at all. The Night Job's become a touchstone.'

'Touchstone,' Huw said. 'What a lovely word that is.'

'Like I'm starting to measure everything against whatever evidence of transcendence – or an afterlife or *something else*

18

– that I've collected through working as an exorcist. Like I'm using the woo-woo stuff as support for an increasingly unstable belief system.'

'Highlighting a failure of faith?'

'Isn't it?'

The phone felt damp against her skin. She scrabbled around for her cigarettes and then remembered. *Bugger.*

'Listen,' Huw said, '*I* can't tell you how strong your faith is. That's summat between you and Him. Or Her, depending. Or it might be faith's just a device to enable us to carry on in the face of all the shit, and some of us need that bit of extra hands-on to top it up. For which—'

'Yeah, but if we *need* that—'

'—for *which*, if you hadn't realized this, we bloody suffer. We get *extra* shit.'

'We can't win?'

His laughter crackled in the heavy old phone, multiple creaks suggesting he was coming to his feet.

'Jesus Christ, you want to be seen to *win* now?'

She was silent. The whole house was silent. Last night, she and Jane had crouched over an open fire in the sitting room, and she'd sensed an uncertainty in Jane about the future, about what kind of adult she wanted to be. She'd been working with real archaeologists in West Wales to get an idea of whether she wanted to become one, whether real archaeology would support her fascination with ancient myths in the landscape or crush it.

'You still there, lass?'

'Sorry. I try to be open to possibilities while, at the same time, sceptical and impervious to people like Anthea White who undoubtedly know how to mess with minds. But I don't know what kind of person this is turning me into.'

And was she going to be the same person Lol had loved?

He was coming home tomorrow after a long summer of touring, session work, production work. All of it good for him. Maybe *too* good. So good he'd be restless. So good that

Ledwardine, the village he'd once been almost agoraphobically reluctant to leave, would probably seem tame and restrictive.

Normal, irrational anxieties. Hints of an early menopause? God, don't start that again. Merrily found the e-cig in her bag. It had run out of charge. She had a packet of cigarettes in a drawer in the kitchen, but if Jane smelled smoke…

'So, it's tomorrow.'

'Huh? Oh… yeah, the Bishop. He's coming over to the gate-house. Sophie says he wants to see the set-up.'

'Sophie's staying on as Bishop's secretary?'

'And mine. I hope. And probably whoever comes after me.'

'She said owt to you?'

'No.'

It had all happened with unexpected haste. They'd thought at first that Bernie Dunmore's stroke would be less disabling. Hadn't expected him to call it a day so rapidly. And suddenly he'd gone and there was a new Bishop of Hereford.

Huw said, 'What's the word in the cloisters? About the new regime.'

'I've no idea. I don't spend time in the cloisters.'

'Happen you should. Them Cathedral lads always hear the whispers.'

'Huw—'

'Course, he might've changed.'

'You keep *saying* that… When I first hung his name on you, you asked me to pardon your French and then you called him—'

'I know what I called him. And it were thoughtless of me to burden you, wi' my prejudices.'

'Might've been less thoughtless if you'd gone on to tell me what they were. No! Sorry. I don't want to know. I'll make up my own—'

'Quite right.' Huw paused. 'So what time are you scheduled to meet the cunt?'

'Two-thirty tomorrow afternoon. You want me to give you a call afterwards?'

'If you want. I'll happen send up a prayer for you, lass.'

4

Win-win

FOR A FEW moments, it looked to Lol like the old days. Car lights on the square warped in ancient glass, the shifting of apple logs in the hearth. Familiar cider taps on the bar top. Except that Barry was wearing a raffish black eye patch and, against the Jacobean oak of the pillars, the smoke pluming around Gomer Parry was Vatican-white.

It couldn't be…

He pulled out a stool under the long mullioned window, next to Gomer, who glanced at him, nodding.

'Ow're you, boy.'

Lol registered that it wasn't smoke.

'*Gomer?*'

The old guy looked down, through his glasses, at the device in his hand, smiled.

'Janey, this is.'

'Gave you that?'

'Present from Pembroke.'

'And you're… getting on OK with it?'

'En't bad,' Gomer said.

God, you really had to hand it to Jane. The old guy must've been doing roll-ups for well over sixty years.

Barry was watching from behind the bar, formally attired with it being Friday night: black suit, black eye patch. In no time at all, the patch had become part of his legend, another ex-SAS emblem, except it was more recent. Lol felt close to tears, all they'd gone through together, these guys and him.

He never wanted to leave this village for so long again. Maybe wouldn't have to.

He nodded at Gomer's cider glass.

'Another one?'

Whole weeks had passed over the summer and early autumn with Lol only occasionally getting back to Ledwardine, each time having to leave after less than two days. No half measures with touring. He hadn't liked it one bit, but he'd done it.

Proving he could.

And then, just as it was coming to an end, Prof Levin had called to say Belladonna was demanding his services as session man – *sole* session man – on the comeback album nobody other than Bell was going to describe as long-awaited. It had taken the best part of a month at Knight's Frome studio. Another month away. With Bell, you couldn't snatch days off, couldn't even count on a full night's sleep. A woman that age with so much latent creative energy, it was scary.

But he was a professional again. Hell, not even *again*, this was probably the first time. He'd earned the right to return, look guys like Barry in the eye when he walked into the Black Swan.

And then, as he was preparing to leave this morning, job done, Prof, instead of just handing him an envelope, had taken him into the office to write a cheque.

But that wasn't the half of it.

Bloody *hell*.

'Thing is,' Gomer said, 'I can do it in yere and *he* can't say nothin', see.'

'Not yet, anyway,' Barry said. 'Government'll doubtless find a way of screwing it. Or taxing it bigtime. It's what those bastards live for.'

Gomer wafted the vapour at him as the e-cig lit up green. The tube looked like a combination of opium pipe and hypodermic.

22

'En't giving up proper ciggies, mind. Rollin' a ciggy quiets your mind, see, gives you a bit o' time to think summat over.' Gomer turned to Lol. 'Where's the vicar?'

Lol nodded at the e-cig.

'Did Jane, er…?'

'Oh hell, aye. Brung one for the vicar, too.'

'Blimey.'

'En't seen her with it yet, mind.'

Lol gazed around the bar to see if anything else had changed in the dimness between the mullioned windows and the smouldering logs. No candles, no pumpkins, no concessions to Hallowe'en; this was England. Barry brought over Lol's half of cider and one for Gomer, picked up Lol's tenner from the mat.

'Merrily said you wasn't coming back till tomorrow.'

'Yeah, well, we worked all last night in the studio. In case there were going to be power cuts tonight. Finished mid morning. So I came back early. And the storm didn't last. Win-win.'

Lol shivered. Not a phrase he'd ever used before. The night was mild, but the logs in the big ingle were alive. Dry, fragrant apple logs, and a stack of them. Barry was no longer having to economize. Might only have one eye but at least he now owned half the Swan – something to rebuild.

Back at the bar, he'd offered Lol a fee to do a gig here in a couple of weeks' time. Lol had said yes but thought he might not take the money. He didn't really need to take money from Barry.

Didn't need…

He drank some cider, feeling the strangeness of it, looked up at Barry.

'I was thinking… Merrily doesn't know I'm back. Thinking maybe I could surprise her, and we could come back and have dinner in the restaurant?'

'Dinner?' Barry said.

'You got a table free, about nine? Maybe Jane, too?'

23

Neither he nor Merrily had ever actually dined at the Swan except for the celebration night when Barry had acquired half the pub. Sandwiches. On a good week, they did sandwiches.

Barry looked uncertain.

'She might've eaten already. Not used to… late dinner. You know?'

'No. No, you're right. I didn't think.'

'You better ring her, mate.'

'Right.'

'You all right, Laurence?'

'Think so.'

Lol brought out his phone then he turned at the sound of laughter outside, saw Barry frown.

'Here we go.'

Through the old glass, torchlight brought up chalky face-masks in the market square.

'Not even dark yet,' Barry said, 'and out they come. Demands, with menaces. Worst thing to cross the Atlantic since McDonald's. Let's show little kids how to prey on pensioners.'

5

… or treat

MUM SAID, 'GET that, would you, flower?'

Calling down the stairs. She'd been in the bathroom, doing her face, actually singing to herself. She'd got out the new black and silvery knitted dress, from the summer sale at Ross Labels.

For Lol, this was. Lol had rung. Lol was back early and inviting Mum to dinner at the Swan, for heaven's sake. Jane had absolutely refused to join them. She wasn't *stupid*. Whoever was at the door, she'd tell them the vicar was out or in the bath or something.

The bell rang again, too soon, conveying impatience. It annoyed the hell out of Jane, how people thought vicarage hours were like 24/7 for any kind of trivia. For the kind of money Mum collected.

She waited. In the Holman-Hunt print by the side of the front door, Jesus was limply dangling his lantern over a few Mars bars lying on the table underneath.

Oh, *right*. Of course.

Jane hung on a while longer then opened the door to four kids, all male, packed into the open porch under the light. One was mumbling *trick or treat*, in a nonchalant way, like he was here to read the meter. You expected them to flash their ID: *We are accredited children, give us stuff.*

Jane checked them out, recognizing one as Jude Wall, Dean Wall's little brother, though not little any more – close to sixteen and even closer to clinically obese. He was the only one

25

of them not ghouled-up, probably figuring his normal face was scarier. His mask was pushed back on his head. He wore an old black overcoat. Two of the others carried rucksacks for the loot, which was all that the Celtic feast of the dead meant to these little bastards.

A car drew up in the street outside, headlights brushing the vicarage hedge.

'Trick,' Jane said.

A kid said, 'You what?'

Jane shrugged.

'Go on. Spook me.'

Just as she'd figured: nobody had ever said *trick* to them before. Probably not ever. They didn't even have a trick. They *were* the trick.

Actually it might not have been the wisest thing to say. One of them had a hand moving inside a pocket of his hoodie. What if he had a knife down there? In *Ledwardine*? Oh yeah, after a gap of a century or so, people had been stabbed in Ledwardine again. And the vicarage was well screened from the village, with only the empty church on one side. People were always getting stabbed at vicarages.

The kids were swapping glances, ghoul-mask to ghoul-mask. If they did anything remotely funny or original, she'd hand over the Mars bars, get rid of them. If they didn't… well, she couldn't back down now.

Actually, under the light, they *all* looked too old for this. Maybe they were just accumulating stuff they could trade for pills down the Ox. According to Mum, Jude Wall's older brother was on bail, having finally been found with a stash that merited more than the police cautions he'd been collecting since before his balls dropped.

'I mean, "trick or treat"?' Jane said reasonably. 'What's it mean? Why?'

She waited, watching the hand in the pocket. The air was sweet with applewood smoke from the chimneys of the Black

Swan across the square. The night was far too warm for the end of the old Celtic year. The storm had made sense, but it had faded. Which was so wrong. Like these kids, climate change had no respect for tradition.

'I mean, any of you guys even know what Hallowe'en's *about*?'

They looked at one another again, and then the reply came back, boxy from behind a mask.

'*Horror.*'

'Oh. *Right.* And what's that mean?'

'You really wanner find out?' a thin kid said.

The boy next to him giggled. Jane said nothing. She became aware that they'd divided, two standing either side of Jane so she couldn't keep them all in focus. Jude Wall had pulled his mask down over his face. It was a zombie mask, corpse-white with black radial lines through its thin lips. He drew a long, hissing breath and, one by one, the others joined in, and then the applewood scent was soured by beer-breath, which was…

… coming from behind. Jane saw, turning, that one of them was now between her and the door to the house.

'All right,' she said, maybe too sharply. 'Back over there.'

The kid laughed.

'Getting scared, now, is it?'

Jane stared at him, hands on her hips. He had a vampire mask, blood bubbles down its chin. He lifted his arms, raising long shadows under the porch light.

'Yeah, I'm trembling,' Jane said. 'Now piss off over there, before I—'

She stopped. They were silent, all looking behind them towards the sound of footsteps on the drive. She saw a slender man, wearing a suit, the pool of porch light bringing up a sheen on his shoes.

'I do hope these children aren't bothering you, Mrs Watkins.'

His voice was quite low, a purr.

One of the kids hissed, 'Children? *Children?*'

But they were still edging out of the porch.

The guy didn't even look at them. He wore a long Edwardian kind of jacket, and his hair was swept back from his forehead, hanging behind to his shoulders. He wasn't very tall but his back was straight, his head held high and, somehow, there was more of Hallowe'en about him than any of them.

'Oh, I'm sorry,' he said. 'You're obviously not Mrs Watkins.'

Jane stepped out.

'I'm her daughter. She's—'

'It's OK, flower.'

A hand closed around her arm. Mum was behind her in the porch, all made up, aglow. Mum could still be quite something when she shed the vicar kit. She slid alongside Jane. Perfume. Wow.

'Oh,' Mum said quietly. 'Mr Khan.'

She knew him?

'My apologies.' His voice was like satin. 'I would've phoned first, but I'd been to visit my cousin, found I was passing and it occurred to me that I should call in.'

Mum said nothing. She let go of Jane's arm. Jane scowled. One of the fundamentals of being a vicar: you thought you had to let every bastard in, like that was how God would want it.

'You're going out?' He appraised her. 'Or expecting a guest? If this is inconvenient, I can come back.'

Jane saw the kids had slunk away into shadows. Mum evidently hadn't noticed them. She put an arm lightly around Jane's shoulders.

'Flower... could you just pop over to the Swan for me, and tell Lol I'll be over as soon as I can? You stay and have a drink with him.'

'You'll be OK?'

Asking because it had just occurred to her who this guy might be. *Mr Khan.* Bloody hell. Flashback to a summer night out in Eirion's car. A traditional-looking pub which, inside, had proved to be anything but. Actually a good night. Cool music.

28

And this guy in a white suit, periodically passing through the crowd like a spectre.

The next time she'd seen him had been in a picture in the *Hereford Times*, with a group of local dignitaries outside some derelict building down by the river that they were redeveloping as a bar and restaurant. Mr Hereford Nightlife.

'I'll be fine,' Mum said.

Because, of course, she did know him. Raji Khan. Bloody hell.

'Well… OK.'

Under the light of the street lamp outside the vicarage gates, Jane saw Jude Wall leaning over from the other side, was pretty sure he let go a gob of spit. Halfway down the drive, she turned and saw Mum following the guy into the house. The porch light went out and the vicarage faded back into the seventeenth century. Jane slipped between the trees and out through the gates where a single street lamp overhung the guy's posh car. She wanted to kick it. Like what if Lol planned to talk to Mum about… well, about the future?

On the square, the council had reduced the street lighting to save money. The fake gaslamps were unlit and the black and white buildings were grey and greyer in the moonless early night. Only the Black Swan was a beacon, its sunken old windows like lanterns. She didn't think Jude Wall and his mates would be too far away, but she only had to cross the street to the cobbles where cars were parked outside the Swan.

She didn't run and she didn't look behind her until she reached the front of the pub where she stood with her back to the wall, aware of breathing too hard.

Seemed ridiculous being scared of children, and yet it really wasn't any more. In Pembrokeshire, a couple of the archaeologists had talked about having to work mob-handed these days because kids would nick anything, and if you got in their way… One of the guys had a mate who'd once been kicked into a trench and stoned with his own rubble.

Not that this neo-Biblical stuff had put her off archaeology, exactly, so much as how futile the job seemed to have become in other respects. Jane surveyed the shadowed centre of what was still called The Village in the Orchard, although most of the orchard was long gone. A lot of serious archaeology under here, possibly including the remains of a Neolithic henge that might only be discovered if some unsightly development got planning permission and the developers were forced to finance a dig to find out. And then they'd flatten it and build on top.

This was mostly what archaeology was about now – drawing a memory map of a Britain nobody was ever going to see again. Britain before it got turned into a shithole. As for rediscovering the magic in the land… She'd gone to Pembs, eyes open, with no mystical baggage. Determined that the phrases like *ancient energy* would never pass her lips in front of anyone with a degree in archaeology. And then one of them had said, *More things, Horatio, more things.* And something changed. Her face was burning now as she recalled waking up on that last morning not knowing who or what she was any more.

Jane took a couple of breaths, walked up the steps to the front door of the Swan. Most people these days went in through the alleyway, with its bracket lamps and disabled access, but Jane liked the old, worn steps. On the top one, an eruption of giggling sent her spinning round, and she glimpsed shady movement across the road, below the vicarage. Where the car was parked. Khan's car, something smooth and bronze, maybe one of those compact Jags.

The little *bastards*. Were they using the car as cover for something or trying to break into it?

She heard rapid footsteps coming up from Church Lane, where Lol lived, so she knew she wasn't alone. She slipped back down the steps, moved quietly onto the square, keeping close to the parked cars there. A man came out of Church Street, ran across the road. She heard a cry from behind Khan's car, saw shadows rising, and then something was flung out like a rag.

She saw hands clawing at the air, recognized Jude Wall as the zombie mask came off. The big kid was sprawling in the wet road, the man standing over him as Jane took hesitant steps, pulling her phone from a hip pocket of her jeans. Stopping well short of the action, ready to run back.

When the man looked directly at her, even a scrappy beard couldn't disguise Jude's older brother, Dean Wall. Didn't seem that long since they'd been at school together. First time she'd thought of him as a man as distinct from a bully and a slob.

Jude Wall tried to get up, and Dean glanced down and kicked him hard in the back. Jude yelped.

'Shut the fuck up, boy,' Dean said calmly, 'else you'll get one in the teeth.' He looked up at Jane again. 'Do my brother a favour he don't deserve, Jane. Don't tell *him*.'

'Him?'

'Don't tell him who done it. Don't want no trouble.'

Dean nodded at the car and then bent down.

Jane said, 'Trouble?'

She saw he'd picked up a knife from the kerb. He shut the blade, zipped it into a pocket of his cargo trousers, Jude squirming crablike out of the road, tripping over his long coat.

'All right, Jane?' Dean said. 'Not a word?'

This was like weird, dreamlike. Needing to keep a modicum of cool, Jane told him she'd think about it, and Dean Wall nodded. He'd lost weight, maybe donated it to his brother. He stood looking down at the boot of Khan's car. Under the lone street lamp, you could see the number plate.

SUF 1

Personalized, obviously. What did it mean? She ought to know, but she didn't ask Dean, having just seen what his brother's knife had done to the Jag's paintwork. One word scratched in. Almost.

childre

'He called them children,' Jane said. Her own voice sounded hollow. 'And they were offended?'

Respect was all, especially if you were never going to deserve any. She felt sick, dislocated. Jude Wall was whimpering, gutter-dirt mingling with the syrupy blood on his face. Dean made a contemptuous, snorty noise.

'Got no brains at all, this boy,' he said.

6

Nightlife

MERRILY FED A log into the kitchen wood-stove and the one below it collapsed into pink and orange flakes. She closed the cast-iron door, and the new log flared in the glass. Mr Khan wandered over.

'Not as simple as it appears, wood-burning.'

His voice unrolling like an expensive carpet. Long black hair flopping over his forehead as he bowed. He did things like that, all these period-English flourishes. She recalled the one other time she'd met him, in his office at the Royal Oak near Wychehill in the Malvern Hills, all velvety Victorian, like Sherlock Holmes's sitting room.

Rajab Ali Khan, owner of nightclubs. Elegant, educated and barely thirty.

'Quite astonishing,' he said, 'the amount of wood needed to fuel one of these things over the winter months. One of the peculiarly *rural* problems my cousin is having to cope with. Not a rural person, my cousin.'

Not the first time tonight that he'd mentioned his cousin. Been to visit this cousin, he'd said, and decided to call in on his way home.

Except his cousin lived down in the Golden Valley and if Mr Khan was still based in Worcestershire this was not his way home. *Get him out*, Frannie Bliss would say, if he knew. *Get rid of the little shit.*

Rajab Ali Khan, sometimes philanthropist and co-opted member of various diversity advisory committees. The young entrepreneur who'd converted a rambling country pub into a venue for loud music. Unpopular with its neighbours, but you couldn't be everybody's friend. She'd once watched Frannie Bliss's fingers actually curling with the need to feel Khan's collar.

Due to him being a significant link in the West Midlands cocaine chain. Allegedly.

His smile was apologetic.

'Actually we're not so closely related. I just call him that.'

'Sorry?'

'Cousin.' He turned away from the stove. 'Mrs Watkins, I am *so* sorry. I had absolutely forgotten what night this was.'

'Well, that's…'

'No, no. It's unforgivably stupid of me. I arrive on All-Hallows' Eve to consult you about a series of… anomalous occurrences. *So* embarrassing. Crass. Unsubtle. Not my style.'

'Really, it's… not a problem, Mr Khan,' Merrily said, although of course it bloody was. 'Good a night as any, and…' Motioning him towards the refectory table. 'I didn't really imagine you'd come to book a wedding.'

Jane said, 'I just… I can't believe that *happened*. Any of it. One minute she's getting all dolled up, singing in the bathroom, and then…'

It was like somebody had lit a slow fuse and there was no stopping it until there'd been an explosion.

Lol was half out of his seat.

'So where is she?'

'In the vicarage. With him. But…' She reached out to his arm. 'No… Honestly, she's fine. Like, what's he going to do? She *knows* him. She told me to come and have a drink with you and she'd be along later. There's not going to be any more trouble. Not till he finds out what the little bastards did to his car, and even then… I don't know.'

Her thoughts were swimming in the white noise of bar chat. Lol had been with Gomer and Barry, glasses on his nose, head turning as the door opened. Excusing himself quickly when he'd seen her face, guiding her to the little niche behind an oak pillar.

'But Wall was scared?' Lol said.

'It was weird. You know what he's like, all mouth and bullshit and phoney bravado. I thought he was going to give the kid a serious kicking.'

She sank back, head against the oak pillar. Bloody hell, you went away for a few weeks and it was like the whole climate had altered. Kids at the door, too old for what they were doing – trick or treat becoming a protection scam with menaces.

'Dean Wall… he was always just a thick yob. But still a kid. Like when *I* was a kid. And now he's a man. Facing charges for dealing, according to Mum.'

'You don't know if there's history here. If Wall is on bail and the stories about Khan and the drug trade are true… I'm not sure what I'm saying here, Jane, I'm just a jobbing guitarist.'

He'd never expressed much of an opinion on drug use one way or the other. Probably a legacy of his unwarranted stretch in a psychiatric hospital on a diet of orange-coloured pills.

'Remind me,' Jane said. 'Mum met Khan at Wychehill, in the course of the job?'

'When Syd Spicer was vicar there. I went over with her a couple of times, as you know, but I never met Khan.'

'Thing is, Lol, the dealers and the fences and all that in Hereford, they all live on the Plascarreg and everybody knows that. But Khan's in another league. He has this respectable side. You see his picture in the paper with councillors.'

'But he also has a respectable side?' Lol said.

Jane laughed. She'd really missed Lol. Realized she hadn't seen him for nearly two months. He was wearing a dark jacket over a sea-green T-shirt. Looking tired, but in a good way. His hair was shorter. Since he and Mum had become an item, she'd had to concentrate on not fancying him any more, counting every new grey hair, that kind of thing.

But now…

She felt queasy. In the mullioned window above their table, the panes of thick, scarred glass had dulled to near-opaque.

She dug out a smile.

'You had this planned? Dinner?'

'Not really, it was just a spur of the moment thing. With getting back early.'

'Romantic.'

'We've never actually done it before. Seemed like extravagance.'

'Special occasion?'

'Not really. Just that I'm home. Properly home.'

'And, like… you have a little box in your pocket? With a ring in it?'

He looked worried.

'You think I should have? You think she—?'

'No.' Jane patted his hand. 'Bound to be the wrong kind. In the movies it can be like a curtain ring or a keyring. Real life, always more complicated. But hey…'

'We *have* talked about it,' Lol said.

'Yeah, well, keep talking. If you ever get another chance.'

She wondered if *she* could talk to him properly. About some things she really would not like to tell Mum. She'd noticed how Lol had kept looking at her, puzzled, like he thought she'd changed.

God, what a mess she was.

Too warm in the glittery dress, too informal, too girly. *God.* Merrily had offered Mr Khan coffee, which he'd declined, then tea, which he'd accepted – did she *have* Earl Grey? She'd had to go down on her knees to a rarely opened cupboard under the worktop. The Earl Grey packet had been embarrassingly dusty.

'As I recall,' Mr Khan said, 'when we met, you were investigating, on behalf of your diocese, a series of road accidents in the Malvern hills, prior to which the drivers experienced either the same hallucination or… something else.'

He paused, as if giving her a chance to finish the story, which she didn't plan to do. It had no happy ending, they both knew that.

'The job title is Diocesan Exorcist?' he said. 'Is that correct?'

'Tends to operate under different names nowadays. Deliverance Consultant, Adviser on the Paranormal. I think the Church is hoping it'll get lost in a scattering of inexact terminology.'

'But you're still doing that?' he said.

'Far as I know.'

'The casting out of devils.'

'Well, that's a bit…'

'Extreme?'

'A bit.'

He nodded solemnly, leaning back in the cane chair, hands in his lap, the pot of Earl Grey between them on the refectory table. How long had he been feigning this absurd young-fogey gentility? What did he think it conveyed, apart from that he was someone you'd be a little crazy to trust?

'OK, devils,' Merrily said carefully. 'Some of my colleagues would tell you that was all in the movies. I wouldn't be quite so dismissive. Never had to carry out a major exorcism – that is, an attempt to release someone from alleged demonic possession. Never easy to distinguish from mental illness. Apparently.'

Raji Khan was nodding. He had his sinister side, but how much of that was theatre? He looked down and bent to pick up something from the flags.

Ethel, the cat. He sat her on his knees.

'What about houses, Mrs Watkins?'

'In what respect?'

'Houses that might appear to be inhabited by… what you might call non-human…' He fondled Ethel's ears. '… presences.'

Mr Khan and Ethel waited, both golden-eyed in the lamplight. Merrily sat and thought for a moment.

'A surprising number of people do come to believe something is sharing their homes.'

'The dead? Or something else?'

'In many cases, it's simply a question of things getting moved around. Disarranged. Possibly linked with the extreme emotions – or hormones – of living people.'

'Poltergeists.'

'It's word we're stuck with, I'm afraid.'

'And you can deal with that?'

'Pest control? We do what we can. With…' She raised her eyes briefly to the beams. '… whatever help we can get.'

It never got easier explaining to people what probably was not meant to be understood. Assuring them that they weren't alone. Weren't mentally ill. Unless, of course, they were.

'I recall…' Raji Khan was stroking Ethel now, long and luxuriant motions, one hand after the other. '… when we met at Wychehill you were considering holding a service. A Requiem for the dead. Which you thought I might like to attend.'

'Seemed logical at the time. Your… venue was being accused of putting too many dangerous drivers on the local roads, and that was getting mixed up with the other problems. A death's an awful catalyst. A Requiem – we believe – can calm a situation. Bring people together. I thought maybe you wouldn't be against that.'

'It would have been a very public occasion.'

'Intentionally so, but that's not—'

'My cousin's difficulty, you see,' Mr Khan said, 'is something that he and his family would very much prefer to be kept *out* of the public domain. And not only because of his faith.'

'You're both Muslim?'

He was, she recalled, a Sufi, a follower of the more mystic side of Islam. He opened his hands, leaving Ethel balanced for a moment before dropping to the flags.

'In which case,' Merrily said, 'wouldn't your cousin talk to his imam? Wherever he is.'

'Worcester.'

At least an hour's drive. Hereford didn't have a mosque, or many Muslims for that matter. The ones here in the north usually went to Kidderminster.

'And here we come to the problem, the reason for my visit,' Mr Khan said. 'It was actually my cousin's imam who suggested he might discuss the situation with *you*.'

'Erm… why?'

Mr Khan drank some Earl Grey then set his mug down.

'He didn't want to touch it, Mrs Watkins. Wouldn't go near.'

7

Not one of ours

'HAVE I ALARMED you?'

The dapper Khan was leaning back in his chair, his head tilted oddly, like a puppet's, a wing of black hair over one eye.

'I— No.'

Yes.

'It is, I suppose, a political barrier rather than a spiritual one.'

'Mr Khan, that's even more frightening.'

He laughed.

There were supposed to be over two hundred Muslims in and around Hereford. Which, compared with almost every city east of the county, was minimal. In theory, the C of E was still almost uniquely dominant in this part of the country, more Anglican churchgoers per head of population in Herefordshire than any other English county, according to census figures. No mosque. You occasionally saw a woman in a face-hugging scarf, though rarely a burka. Merrily didn't know any imams.

She drank some Earl Grey: too sweet, too scented, never liked it much. Raji Khan sighed.

'It is a cause of the greatest sorrow to me, Mrs Watkins, the way the merest mention of Islam provokes apprehension. My cousin wanted to be a suicide bomber but failed the intelligence test. So had to become an orthopaedic surgeon.'

He looked concerned to the point of stricken. A lightbulb was buzzing somewhere. Merrily glanced from lamp to lamp then back to Raji Khan.

'You see… you're afraid even to laugh, Mrs Watkins.'

'Was that an Islamic joke?'

'A Sufi joke. We're famous for them.' He waved a dismissive hand. 'But let's put all that aside for the moment. Let me tell you about my cousin's house.'

She traced the failing bulb to the converted oil lamp on the dresser, went to switch it off, leaving the big kitchen ochre-lit and full of sepia shadows.

The Golden Valley was in the extreme west of the county, green pillows under the headboard of the Black Mountains. An area of hidden villages, its nearest towns in Wales.

Adam Malik had never intended to live there. Certainly not in a crumbling medieval farmhouse where the only neighbours were sheep.

'We grew up in the same industrial area of the west Midlands,' Khan said. 'I am… what you'd think of as godfather to his daughter. At university, he took up with a woman of white, English stock. Nicole. Now Nadya.'

'She converted to Islam?'

'Oh, yes. Her father is a Herefordshire heritage builder… Dennis Kellow?'

Merrily shook her head. At one time, the Welsh border seemed to have more heritage builders than heritage.

'I do realize,' Khan said, 'that many of these chaps are well-spoken cowboys. Claiming to have worked extensively for the National Trust and numbering the wealthier estate agents among their drinking companions. Choose your heritage builder with care. Kellow, however, has been one of the exceptions – painstaking, not cheap, and impatient with clients who expected quick and cosmetic results. He'd been working, on and off, for several years, on an ancient farmhouse owned by the scholar Selwyn Kindley-Pryce.'

'I must be sounding very ignorant, here, Mr Khan, but…'

'I wouldn't worry. Eminent but not terribly well known.

Pryce's income fluctuated. He'd have restoration work done when he could afford it, until ill-health forced him to move out, with the work far from finished. And when its sale to a film director fell through, Kellow saw his chance. I think he'd been planning for some time to sell his business and retire, but he wasn't the kind of man to buy himself an expensive armchair, if you see what I mean. He wanted to retire into a project – a labour of love.'

Khan described it: large, rambling, six bedrooms, barns and a hundred acres of land. More than just a house, far more, and even during the property slump it had been beyond the resources of Dennis Kellow. However, it failed to sell to anyone else and he'd ended up renting it, in the hope of buying at a future date.

'The opportunity eventually presented itself when his son-in-law obtained a senior consultancy at Hereford Hospital, and was in need of a home.'

'Ah.'

'I'm not sure of the details – indeed, it's none of my business – but I believe they agreed to buy the house between them and share the renovation costs. The house would eventually pass to the Maliks.' Khan raised his eyes to the beams. 'After my experiences at Wychehill, I would have urged Adam to run a mile, but he's more of a romantic than me. Even more of an *Englishman* than me.'

Was that possible? Merrily said nothing.

'The thought of becoming a country gentleman... you know? Madness. However, an element of urgency crept in when Dennis Kellow had a stroke.'

'Oh God. Serious?'

'Caught quite early. He's recovered and wants to continue with his *life project*. Promising to take it slowly, calm down, improve his diet... and, of course, with a doctor in the house...'

'No better safety net than that. That mean they've moved in now, the Maliks?'

'Some months ago.'

'OK.' Merrily fired up her e-cig. 'So we have an old house, a man with health problems and… did you say there was a baby?'

'A teenage girl. Aisha.'

'Right. And, erm…'

'Something else. Another, unwanted, member of the household. Which the Maliks thought their imam in Worcester might deal with. Until he informed them that he was unable to assist.'

'Because? Can we spell this out?'

'Because this is an old house. A *very* old house. And whatever is happening there is almost certainly linked to its history. Which is not *our* history, do you see what I mean?'

'Not Islamic?'

Mr Khan sipped his tea, his feline eyes finding hers over the cup.

'How to put this. In large areas of the Middle East, the heritage is Islam, and other faiths are considered interlopers. At the same time, we accept that in other places, here in the West, it's *we* who are the newcomers and must tread carefully.'

'I see.'

'There are… let's say fundamental theological differences pertaining to what you might call paranormal phenomena. The imam tells my cousin his problems relate to lower spiritual forces emanating from something entirely British. That if he wants the problem addressed he needs to approach a Christian priest.'

'Is he Sufi, too? Adam?'

'Oh, heavens, no. We both grew up in the more orthodox, Sunni tradition. I felt the need to move on… and move inwards, if you like. Most members of my family have nothing to do with me now. Never been an issue for Adam, and so when I told him I'd actually encountered the Hereford diocesan exorcist…'

Already she was foreseeing problems. She poured herself more of the stewed tea.

'So… what exactly are we looking at? And please don't go all elliptical on me.'

'I think you should hear it from the people concerned.'

She folded her arms on the tabletop.

'There are going to be formalities. I've never dealt with an inter-faith situation before, so I'll have to get some kind of clearance from—'

'No, no.' He sat up. 'I don't think so.'

She stared at him.

'I don't know what level of bureaucracy you have in the Anglican Church pertaining to this kind of situation, but we'd feel better if you were… shall we say operating below its threshold.'

'*What?*'

'Adam Malik is a quiet man, a good man in a very public occupation. His daughter's settling in at a local secondary school. He doesn't want to draw attention to himself or his family, doesn't want talk around the hospital. Or amongst his new neighbours – not that there are many of those.'

'There's always a strong element of privacy in deliverance. Everything kept mainly between me, my bishop and our mutual secretary.'

'Mrs Watkins, with all respect, I doubt you have any control at all over your bishop and who *he* consults. He might, for example, want to discuss it with a senior Muslim cleric. He might even want to make a "thing" of it. Publicity.'

'He wouldn't.'

'Islam itself has no great foundation in Hereford. There's a meeting room and embryonic plans for a mosque. It's at a delicate stage. No one wants controversy of any kind.'

'This is already getting too complicated for me.'

'No, no.' Khan was shaking his head. 'It's not complicated at all. We're simply asking for a modicum of discretion.'

Merrily poured herself some more of the awful Earl Grey.

'It might take a while. It's never a quick fix. It can involve several visits.'

'I realize that.' Khan's fingertips tapping softly on the table. 'Look, if you were to say now, go away, Khan, leave me alone, this is not *my* problem… well then, I should do that. Walk away and that would be an end to it.'

'Except it wouldn't be, would it?'

He thought for a few moments, fingers steepled.

'I'll tell you one aspect of this. Which you can accept or reject, according to your beliefs. The situation had been escalating, from minor what you would call poltergeist phenomena… to more extensive damage and disruption. And then… an apparition. And Kellow's stroke.'

'They think there's a connection?'

'You ask Adam Malik if he thinks there's evil here,' Khan said, 'and he'll become subdued, reticent, embarrassed even. He's a doctor, a scientist.'

'But he sees a link between paranormal activity in this house and his father-in-law's illness?'

'He agreed to discuss it with the imam. I offered to make an approach to someone who I thought would handle it all with discretion. His wife Nadya was, I have to say, averse to having a Christian priest in the house.'

'This is Dennis Kellow's daughter…'

'Converts,' Khan said, 'can sometimes be more… extreme than most people born into a faith.'

That was true enough. Born-again Christians could be hard going. She drew slowly on the e-cig. Health issues were a minefield. Faith issues a wasps' nest.

'I'm assuming,' Khan said, 'that the disturbances have resumed. To what extent I don't know. I had another call this morning, and this time it was from Dennis Kellow. I do know him, he did some work for me at Wychehill. He asked me if I was still in touch with the priest. Used to be a jolly, exuberant man. A man who loved his job. Hardly recognized his voice.'

Oh God.

'I can't— I mean, it would be difficult tomorrow. Meeting with the new Bishop in the afternoon, and I don't really like going at night, in the first instance.'

'The following day would be fine,' Mr Khan said. 'That will be Saturday. I'll provide you with the address and directions.'

She saw he was eyeing the vial between her fingers, the light brown fluid in it.

'I see nicotine remains your drug of choice,' he said. 'Splendid.'

8

Lawful and justified

AT LUNCHTIME, ANNIE HOWE was waiting for Bliss in the Gaol Street car park, wearing her buttermilk trench coat, a red woollen scarf and a scowl.

'Francis, I really don't have too much time…'

'I'm coming now,' Bliss said. '*Ma-am.*'

Making a show of muttering as he pulled on his beanie in the CID doorway, aware of plump, smirking Terry Stagg watching him. Holding the smirk on his way into CID. *Giving the DI a hard time again. Poor bastard can't put a foot right with Howe. Taken him off for another private policy-briefing – translate as bollocking.*

Staggie playing his usual double-game. He'd slag off Howe in front of Bliss, who knew he was secretly on her side, for obvious reasons – principally the question of succession if Bliss were to crack and leave town. What was funniest, if he ever told Terry Stagg the absolute truth about him and Annie, Stagg would think he was taking the piss.

This had been amusing Bliss for months, but not today.

Outside, he pulled out his car fob.

'Mine?'

Annie nodding, tightening her scarf. Colder this morning, the sky sepia over Hereford, as if it had sucked all the autumn colours out of the leaves. They climbed into Bliss's Honda, didn't say much until they were out of the city on the Brecon road, coming up to White Cross, Bliss slowing for the zebra.

'What did you tell Stagg, about why you were looking for me?'

'I didn't,' Annie said. 'Just made sure I didn't appear happy.'

'Yeh, that usually works.'

'Wasn't hard,' Annie said. 'Today.'

Bliss put on a sigh.

'Tell me.'

He drove slowly along suburban Kingsacre, many of its trees prematurely stripped by the gales, fields exposed behind the houses. Pretty obvious what was coming.

'Charlie rang me about an hour ago.'

'So it's official, is it?' Bliss kept an even speed. No surprise to him, but still a gut-punch to hear it confirmed. 'Tossed his name into the hat.'

'Not yet, but he's decided to. Just wanted to sound me out the other night. See how I felt about it.'

'And you really think that would influence him one way or another?'

'Look,' Annie said wearily. 'Do you think I *like* this?'

Bliss said nothing. Annie was back in Hereford full-time, heading up CID, Iain Twatface Brent having returned to Worcester to stab a few backs at headquarters. And get promoted for it. Unbelievable.

'I checked the regulations again last night,' Annie said. 'Thinking there might just be a chance Charlie would be too old.'

'I'd guess not.'

'Far as I can make out, the only rule is that a candidate needs to be over eighteen. No seniority limit. He's eminently quali-fied. Ex senior police officer, county councillor, served for years on the police authority. He's also fairly fit, after his hip replace-ment. And he doesn't, of course, look his age.'

'One of the benefits of having no conscience,' Bliss said.

He didn't think Annie smiled. Well, who would? The thought of this man returning to policing, in his dotage, to become their ultimate boss because the blindingly stupid fucking govern-ment had altered a system that didn't need altering...

'He has to obtain supportive signatures from a hundred citizens registered to vote,' Annie said. 'I didn't ask him if he'd done that yet.'

'Bastard could collect them in one morning, Annie, door to door. "*How're you, my dear. You remember me. Local boy?*"'

He'd perfected the accent long ago, Charlie's oily, popular-market-trader jollity riff. Once rang Annie as Charlie and it worked for nearly a minute.

On election day, the bastard would pick up votes because he was local and he had a friendly smile on a recognizable face. That was one of the big jokes in replacing the old local police committees with a single, elected Police and Crime Commissioner. People – the few who bothered – would vote local and they'd vote friendly smile: all it took to replace a wonky kind of democracy with a dangerous autocracy. At least the old police committees, made up mainly of councillors, generally recognized they weren't much more than a formality and had very little impact on actual policing.

'How long's he there for, if he gets elected?'

'Four years.'

'Mother of God, you imagine the damage Charlie could do in four years?'

'To you, you mean?'

'That, too.'

The housing thinned, and Bliss turned right into the Wyevale Garden Centre, driving straight through to the field behind that was used for overflow parking. It wasn't summer and it wasn't Christmas, so they were alone here, behind the hedge, looking out to the hills. He stopped the car, brought out his phone, scrolled down to the oath that the Police and Crime Commissioner would have to swear, which included…

I will not seek to influence or prevent any lawful and reasonable investigation or arrest, nor encourage any police action save that which is lawful and justified within the bounds of this office.

Handed it to Annie and watched her face tighten, registering for the first time that, in the couple of days since he'd seen her last, she'd had her pale hair cut shorter. Her make-up was minimal, her skin almost translucent. She looked five years younger and innocent, as if she'd been scrubbing away at an ancestral skin rash.

'Strictly speaking,' Annie said, 'this is less about what he might have done in the past than what he agrees *not* to do in the future.'

'Annie, he took bribes to suppress evidence. When he was a young DC, he covered up a major landowner's… *involvement* in a murder. By the time he was running CID, it was second friggin' nature. The way things were done. Cheaper, more expedient. He was saving the country time and money.'

'But none of it was *proved*,' Annie said very quietly. 'He's never even been publicly—'

'Because he's clever. And he's local. And he's been in the Masons and every other friggin'—'

'All *right*.'

'Sorry.'

'I'm not disagreeing with you, Francis, I'm telling you that yes, I think he did these things … of which he hasn't been accused.'

'*I've* accused him.'

Tried to, anyway. Bliss couldn't even think about Charlie without feeling again the pissing rain on the night in Christmas week when he'd confronted the bastard on his doorstep in Leominster, Charlie entirely unintimidated. *You en't going no higher and you know it.* Bliss reduced to screaming through the downpour as the door slammed in his face. Forced to accept he really didn't have what it took to bring down somebody as practised in bare-faced deceit as Charlie Howe.

But then… the unimaginable happened. A night of sublime irony just before Christmas, which had ended with the woman they called the Ice Maiden defrosting in Bliss's bed.

50

Till that night, it had never occurred to him that he might actually fancy her. *Metal coat-hanger with tits*, Terry Stagg would say, knowing he was on safe ground with Bliss, who, everybody agreed, was never going to be Annie Howe's kind of copper, not in any sense.

The strangest, most gratifying part had been how it had happened. The catalyst: working together, out of hours, at the sharp end for the first time, to craft an exceptional result. Feeding the mutual craving for a collar. Finding one another professionally.

They'd still lie in bed talking Job, and all this had made him so insanely happy. And he understood, now, why she played everything by the book, by a whole fusty library. Why she was so tight and proper, so politically correct, cold and humourless in the workplace, diligent to a fault. Why she was such a pain in the arse.

You couldn't hope to understand Annie, or even like her a bit, until you knew where she'd come from, and where she'd come from was Charlie Howe, a man so bent for so long that the sinister kinks in his history were invisible to him now.

Bliss had sometimes wondered what it would do to Charlie, if he ever discovered who his daughter was spending quality time with. Sometimes he thought of how good it would be to arrange for Charlie to find out accidentally. Then he'd start wondering what Charlie might do to smash them apart, and it really hadn't been worth the risk.

Only now… now it looked like Charlie was about to achieve that anyway without even knowing. Charlie who hated Bliss because he'd been developing an interest in history. *Bitter, twisted, sick little man. I know about you, Brother Bliss.*

Bliss picked up Annie's right hand, and it felt cold and rigid.

9

Overpowering

BISHOPS CAME AND bishops went; Sophie Hill, like the Cathedral, remained. Same pearls, same crisp white hair, same silver chain on the half-glasses. Same watchful expression, an emotional temperature control set to frost.

'So how long have you been doing *that*?'

Nodding at the black leatherette case Jane had brought back from Pembrokeshire. Merrily had boldly placed it in the centre of her desk by the window overlooking Broad Street. Start out how you meant to go on.

'Just over a day.' She lifted the little glass tube up to the light. 'Still looks slightly sinister to me, compared to tobacco and paper. Every time I bring it out, it reminds me I'm feeding an addiction.'

'And does it?'

'Does, actually. Surprisingly. Didn't think it was going to work. And I can do it in here and it causes no more pollution than the kettle. That *is* OK, isn't it Sophie?'

'I suppose.'

Sophie looked unconvinced. Merrily expelled vapour, very close to telling her about Raji Khan and his cousin. All deliverance cases had been filed by Sophie from the start: each visit, the measures taken, the aftercare. Keeping this one to herself felt like a step into the worst kind of dark.

But she'd given her word. As a Christian. To a Muslim. She'd actually wound up doing that, with a certain formality, after Khan confided that Dennis Kellow's wife had been reluctant to approach their local parish priest because the woman was too helpful and effusive. Which meant nosy, Raji Khan had said, not having met her. Helpful to the point of intrusive.

As distinct from me, Merrily had thought. Cautious to the point of timidity.

'Why are you smiling?'

Sophie observing her, over the half-glasses.

'Was I? Sorry. Nerves, perhaps. I've only met two new bishops of Hereford, and one of them—'

'Let's not talk about Michael Hunter.' Sophie frowned and then lightened. 'It won't be an ordeal, Merrily. He might seem a little overpowering at first, but that probably conceals his own insecurity. Most new bishops go through a short period of—'

'How do you mean "overpowering"?'

'Wrong word, perhaps. He's... emphatic. He knows what he wants. A phase, probably. It'll pass.'

'It's just that Huw Owen appeared to be... slightly uncertain about him.'

'Doesn't surprise me greatly,' Sophie said. 'He's rather like Huw Owen in reverse – in that Huw was born in Wales and brought up in England, whereas Bishop Craig was born in England into a military family. His father having been an army officer in Brecon, so that was where he went to school: Christ College.'

Private school.

'So, where Huw Owen has a Yorkshire accent,' Sophie said, 'Bishop Craig sounds rather Welsh.'

According to the *Hereford Times*, Craig Innes had been at Oxford, where he'd stayed on as an academic for a couple of years before becoming a curate in Banbury. Then he was a vicar somewhere in the Thames Valley, returning to Brecon as a junior canon at the Cathedral and then, for a short time, a rector and rural dean in the Usk Valley. A suggestion of fast-track?

'What's he like, really?'

You had to accept the possibility of split loyalties here. The deliverance side of Sophie's work had expanded probably four

fold since Merrily had taken over from the granite-faced tradi-
tionalist, Canon Dobbs. Sophie had never complained and
would even, if pushed, admit to finding it fascinating. But her
principal role was still as the Bishop's lay secretary.

'What do you want me to say? He's quite large, rather
imposing...'

'I know what he *looks* like.'

'Ebullient. Tends to fill a room.' Sophie walked across to the
second window, overlooking Gwynne Street, where Dobbs had
lived. 'I'm not yet sure how he works. He's still setting out his
stall. I don't know how much he delegates.'

Merrily leaned her chair back against the wall and drew on
her e-cig. This wasn't a hard room to fill. It always felt intimate
but active, like a hayloft or a granary. It was her second home.
Through the vapour, she noticed for the first time that it had
been very subtly tidied. No visible personal items – scarves,
gloves, library books, packets of mints. Even the florid calendar
from Sophie's sister in Tuscany had gone. Was the new Bishop
some kind of minimalist?

'Sense of humour?' Merrily said.

'Good-humoured, certainly.'

Not always the same thing.

'And played rugby, of course,' Sophie said. 'But you knew
that.'

Merrily put down the e-cig.

'Sophie, do you happen to know what dealings he had with
Huw? Both were in the Brecon diocese, but is there any obvious
history between them?'

'What has Huw said?'

'Not much.'

'Parish priests and bishops...' Had Sophie's eyes become
guarded? 'We both know that parish clergy and bishops... it's a
different career path, and they rarely see eye to—'

'A parish isn't usually a career path at all,' Merrily said.

Bishops were admin. Bishops were chosen for their managerial and social skills. Spirituality rarely came into it. Or that was how vicars tended to see it.

'It's inevitable,' Sophie said carefully, 'that all bishops will have encountered some animosity on their way to the top.'

You had to smile. The higher clergy could fight like rats in a sack.

'But to answer your question,' Sophie continued, 'I imagine Bishop Craig first encountered Huw Owen the same way you did. He completed one of Huw's deliverance courses.'

Merrily sat up slowly.

'When?'

'During his time in the Usk Valley, I assume.' Sophie's eyes flickered. 'Huw didn't mention that?'

'No. No, he bloody didn't.'

'Interesting,' Sophie said.

'So – let me get this right – that means Innes was actually in the deliverance ministry? For how long?'

'I don't know how long. But you don't do it unless you have some interest, do you?'

You didn't just have *some interest*. It became part of you, altered your awareness of everything. And then, before you knew it, it had become your touchstone.

On one level, having a bishop with exorcism experience could be helpful. Might save a lot of explanation and justification. But a bishop sometimes could be *too* close to it. The rules decreed that anyone in purple could no longer do hands-on deliverance, but that didn't stop a Bishop from adopting a director's role.

'Anyway, we have all that to find out.' Sophie uncapped her fountain pen, made a small note on her pad, looked up. 'And is Laurence back?'

'Oh yes. I feel awful. We were supposed to have a small celebration dinner last night, at the Black Swan, but… something came up. As usual. So we ended up just having a sandwich. As usual.'

In the end, Jane had stayed with them in the Swan, but neither she nor Lol had asked, in this too-public place, about Raji Khan. And then they'd gone back to their separate houses, separate beds, with too much unsaid, a sense of too much in the air. Jane had come with her to Hereford this morning with the intention of pestering Neil Cooper, of the county archaeologist's department, for some gap-year work. They'd had lunch at All Saints, another too-public place, again not much said. Why did she have the feeling that something had occurred during the foreshortened Pembrokeshire dig to take the edge off Jane's enthusiasm for a future in archaeology?

Sophie said, 'Do you never think about a holiday?'

'Never been able to afford one. Not much of one anyway. And no time, really.'

'I meant you and Laurence. You had a chance when Jane was away.'

'Not much of one. With Lol away as well, much of the summer.'

'If you don't,' Sophie said, 'you might regret it. One day. Maybe sooner than you think.'

She blinked, as if slightly appalled at what she might have said.

Merrily heard the door opening at the bottom of the stairs.

Footsteps. Big footsteps.

10

Trashy world

THERE WAS NO sign of a grave or excavation, just the Green.

Castle Green. All green, no castle. The norm in Herefordshire. If it hadn't been for the widespread destruction during the Glyndwr warfare of the fifteenth century, you wouldn't be able to stand anywhere in this county without seeing a stone tower. Today, the term *castle* usually referred to nothing more than a green mound in a field that you wouldn't even notice unless, like Jane, you were obsessed with bulges in the landscape.

No bulges here. Just a park now, Castle Green, featureless under a grey foil sky.

'That's where it was,' Tris said, pointing. 'Where Neil's standing. They had the tree sawn up and cleared away within a day.'

'And the bones?'

'Safely removed. Couple of days. Wasn't a proper excavation, though it doesn't mean there won't be one in the future. For now, they've just filled it in and returfed.

'So what's Coops doing?'

'Dreaming, I suppose,' Tris said.

When she'd asked for Neil Cooper at his office, Tris had insisted on bringing her over here. She'd never seen Tris before; he'd introduced himself as Neil's assistant, and he was very charming, lithe and fit and floppy-haired and, like, incredibly good-looking. Even if you could've found Castle Green with your eyes shut, how could you not let Tris take you?

Pack it in. Stop testing your responses, it's not going to change anything.

'Sadly, he probably won't be able to offer you anything,' Tris said. 'Things are really, really tight. We're just a planning footnote nowadays. Way things are going, there might not even be a county archaeologist's department in a year or so. Everything else has gone to the private sector.'

'Are you… permanent?'

'Thought I might be. I understood the county archaeologist might not return when his leg was out of plaster, and if he took early retirement, Neil might get his job, leaving a vacancy.'

'He's coming back?'

'So it seems.'

He sounded quite bitter, and she might have asked him more if Coops hadn't seen them and come over.

'Jane.' He didn't sound excited to see her. 'You get days off?'

'All over,' Jane said. 'The work ran out. The Pembrokeshire highways department were doing this road improvement scheme close to an Iron Age camp. One of those situations where the archaeologists get to go in first to see if there's anything interesting. And if there is, the council still builds the road.'

'It's called Rescue Archaeology, Jane.'

'I know. Anyway, we found signs of a couple of hut circles, but no strong reason to hold off the bulldozers. We had like twenty-eight days before the road-building guys moved in? And that was it. Nothing. Anticlimax. So I'm home.'

'Oh dear.'

'Hoping I can get something local. I mean, sooner or later they're going to have to check out the Ledwardine Henge – either it is or it isn't.'

'Sooner rather than later, Jane, only if the supermarket scheme goes through.'

'I thought those bastards were going bust.'

'If that happens, it might actually slow things up for you.'

'What a trashy world,' Jane said.

Coops didn't seem like the same guy. Certainly not standing next to Tris. Not so long ago, he'd still seemed fairly young and cool; now he had that family-man look, his hair too cleanly cut, his jeans too functional.

Nothing lasted. Jane felt this unexpected tear-pressure. You went away and everything changed. It was like the space she'd made for herself over the years had closed up behind her and wouldn't reopen for her now.

'Well, then,' Tris said. 'See you around, Jane.'

As if he knew he wouldn't. She watched him walk away, up the bank to where part of the moat remained as an extended duckpond below the Castle House Hotel.

'Tris is temporary,' Neil Cooper said.

'Too good-looking to last?'

'Nothing lasts. Although everything does. In some form.'

'There's philosophical.'

'There's experience. Sorry, Jane, don't mean to be depressing.'

'You found some bones, then.'

'Who told you that?'

'Should he have kept quiet about it?'

'Tris? No reason to.' But his expression had darkened. 'Anyway… you enjoyed it while it lasted.'

'Well, I got to do bits. Under supervision, obviously.'

Second week in Pembrokeshire, she'd found this metal artefact and they'd let her excavate it herself. Took an hour of intimate trowelling to bring up what could have been part of a gold torque. If it hadn't been the end of a towing chain from a tractor. She'd still kept it – gap-year souvenir.

Coops said, 'And you're still committed to becoming one of us?'

Jane was gazing across Castle Green, this grassy space bordered by the river and the benches where people sat in summer to eat sandwiches and check their phones, or just get pissed. In Pembs, she'd been reading this thick book by the archaeologist Francis

Pryor, who could walk into a modern landscape and tell you in minutes what used to be there, by the colour and texture of the soil, the positioning and content of hedges, field boundaries, ditches and field drains, the stones under your feet. A touch of the visionary about Francis Pryor, who had written that walking into a strange landscape was like meeting someone for the first time. Asking yourself if this was a place you could trust.

This place must've been seriously trusted to get the castle and the Cathedral. The castle was all gone, every stone of it, but if you half closed your eyes you could almost see cold, etheric walls. And underneath…

'You *have* found some bones, right?'

'Some old human remains were exposed, yes,' Coops said. 'When the tree came up.'

'A tree had grown on top of an old grave?'

'So it seems.'

'So you put a quick trench in.' Which she could see, over the temporary fencing, had now been filled in. 'How old *were* they?'

'Probably medieval. Look, Jane, I—'

'Well preserved?'

'Not bad.'

'What do they suggest?'

'Suggest someone was buried here.'

'Just the one person?'

He had his phone out, body language for *bugger off, Jane*.

'No, like, grave goods or anything?'

Coops shook his head, finger-scrolling on the phone.

'Jane, I need to get back.'

'Got pictures of the bones on there, Coops?'

'No, I haven't. He palmed the phone. 'I've a meeting that's been brought forward, OK?'

'Could it be someone important?'

'What?'

'The bones.'

'Jane—'

'Well, obviously not *that* important. Sorry. Just some monk, then.'

'Look.' He lowered his phone. 'It's not exactly unusual for bones to be found here. It's an historic place – castle, ancient churches, holy well, et cetera. Behind the Cathedral we've turned up graveyard on top of graveyard. It would be wonderful to have a huge, definitive excavation, but that's not going to happen any sooner than digging up your village to see if it was built inside a neolithic henge.'

'Can I see them?'

'No! We've put them into store. In our… municipal ossuary.' Probably meaning some old shed. 'Jane, this is *routine*. It's not… not the start of something. I'm sorry.'

If it was routine, what was *he* doing here, the head guy, when it was all over bar the chainsaw massacre?

'So no jobs here then,' Jane said. 'No making tea for archaeologists, emptying barrows, sieving soil. Listening to them moaning about all the false starts, lack of money, backbiting, constant competition for work…'

'Are you *sure* this is what you want to do?'

'I *want*…' Jane's fists were tightening in frustration. '… to have seen enough sides of the job to make a firm decision about whether that's how I want to spend my working life till I'm too stricken with arthritis to pick up a bloody trowel.'

He smiled.

'You mean until you settle down and have kids.'

'Piss off, Coops, I'm never going to have kids. Overpopulation – biggest problem facing the world. Which the short-sighted pondlife we call politicians never seem to notice. Can't be long before they lower the voting age to ten.'

'OK.' He nodded. 'I'll ask around. I take it you got on with them OK? The guys at the dig?'

'They were… fine.'

'Tend to drink a lot of beer. Probably just as well your boyfriend…?'

'Eirion.'

'Of course. Just as well he was with you.'

'Yes.'

For the first month, anyway, until he had to go back to uni. Which was when she'd started going to the pub with the guys who really knew how to put away the booze. Not all of it happy booze. Maybe it was seeing so many dead bodies, evidence of cheap life. They were like, *Fuck it, this is how we all wind up, so let's just get hammered.*

And have sex, *oh God.*

'You OK, Jane?'

'Fine.'

Jane turned away.

'Anyway, leave it with me,' Coops said. 'No promises, and if you do get something there might not be much money in it.'

'No. Whatever. Thanks.'

Coops walked away up the bank to the path that led to the huddle of narrow old murky-brick streets below the Cathedral. The sky was turning salmon, the sun coming out only to set. The atmosphere was all wrong.

Blinking back tears, she walked up the bank on to the footpath, looking down over the filled-in, empty grave. A chainsaw started up somewhere, then another, echoes multiplying across the Castle Green, sounding airborne, like a dogfight from one of those ancient Battle of Britain movies. Jane thought she'd shuddered, but it was the mobile in her jeans.

She pulled it out – still nervous every time the phone went, scared the screen might say SAM.

It said EIRION.

Jane switched off the phone, walked rapidly away towards what used to be the centre of the city. Coming out of narrow Quay Street, she saw Mum in her best coat, pale blue silk scarf wrapped across the dog collar. On her face an expression Jane had seen before, but not often.

Christ…

11

Purple haze

OUT THROUGH THE Cathedral's back entrance, past the school buildings into old Hereford: the quiet grey-brown streets of offices and terraced houses. The direction you walked if you didn't want to bump into anyone you might know. Or anyone at all.

Thinking, *Bloody hell... bloody hell, bloody hell.*

But this was a small city and Merrily almost walked into Jane, in her green Gomer Parry Plant Hire T-shirt, fleece over an arm, looking desolate. A job-seeker on the barren streets.

They'd arranged to meet around half-four in the Cathedral café; they were both early.

'I thought you were over at the council,' Merrily said. 'Looking for Neil Cooper.'

'Got redirected to Castle Green. They found some— Anyway, I've seen him. Says he'll find out if there are any openings. Not holding my breath.'

Evidently not. Oh God, there really was something wrong here. You spent so much time worrying about your own problems you could miss the obvious. She looked into Jane's eyes. Please God, don't let her be pregnant.

'Jane, you really don't have to rush into anything, you have lots of—'

'I do, actually. Have to cram in everything I can get. Have to collect experience. Any kind. And money.' Eyes glittering with something bafflingly close to anger, Jane nodded towards the hidden river. 'And you're going...?

'Nowhere.'

God, that sounded… not as she'd intended. Jane's eyes came back slitted.

'I meant I was just walking,' Merrily said. 'To think about things.'

There was suddenly quite a few people about. The Cathedral School was letting kids out. They were in a public place, looking at one another in dismay.

Jane said, 'You met the Bishop?'

'Kind of.'

Certainly been in his presence. Like Sophie said, he tended to fill a room.

'Bishop, this is Merrily Watkins.'

'Ah yes. Vicar of….'

'Ledwardine.'

'Of course. Ledwardine. "Heart of the New Cotswolds". Didn't I read that somewhere?'

Merrily nodding. Everybody had read that somewhere.

'Though not entirely true,' she'd said.

Wanting to say something halfway eloquent. Failing, through nerves; she hadn't realized, until the moment came, how nervous she'd be. Now, trying to recall Bishop Craig Innes, what he looked like… she couldn't. Just a strong, square face, high forehead with hair like curls of grey fuse wire, above a purple cassock. Purple haze. Nothing clear. Except she realized she'd seen him before and not just in photos. Just couldn't think where. Not then.

'Merrily's your Deliverance Consultant,' Sophie had said helpfully.

'So I understand,' Bishop Craig Innes said.

And never mentioned the D word again.

Just other things.

She said desperately to Jane, 'You want to get a cup of tea? Cakes? Anything?'

'Not particularly. You?'

'Think I'd rather get out of town.'

'OK.'

They walked back towards the Cathedral, side by side. There was a time when it had looked as if Jane was going to be quite a bit taller, but the height difference had settled, mercifully, at just an inch or two. They were growing more alike, but was that good?

She'd left the car in the Bishop's Palace yard, as usual. When they reached the gatehouse, Merrily didn't look up at the office. The sky over the red-brick palace had a dull sheen, like tin. Maybe she'd call Sophie at home tonight. Meanwhile, she had a notelet in her bag, with an address and postcode.

Why not?

'Why don't we take the long way back?'

'Which way's that?'

'It's the one that goes via the Golden Valley.'

Merrily unlocked the black Freelander, Jane staring at her over the bonnet.

'Correct me if I'm wrong, Mum, but isn't that totally the wrong direction for home?'

'Probably.'

She and Jane didn't speak again until she was driving down King Street with the Cathedral in the rear-view mirror. Jane sat with her hands crossed over the fleece crumpled in her lap and stared through the windscreen.

'You were, like, spitting nails.'

'Me? When?'

'Back there. I saw you before you saw me.'

'Oh God.'

Merrily turned out of Bridge Street, heading for the permanent traffic tangle caused by a desire to access Asda. It required concentration until you were through and crawling up to Belmont.

Jane said mildly, 'Do you think there's a possibility we might actually reach the stage where we can communicate directly with one another? Like adults?'

12

Cutting edge

SOMEONE – IT MIGHT'VE been Gomer Parry – had once said to Merrily that, in the old days, people used to look west from the city and say, *That en't Herefordshire, that's Wales.*

Maybe it was, once. Now, apart from the broken nose of the Skirrid mountain to the south, there was nothing of today's Wales to be seen. Even the flank of the Black Mountains, lying like grounded cloud on the western horizon, that was still England. A half-forgotten England of hybrid place names, of wooded hills and hidden villages of rusty stone and crouching churches. A dark, poacher's pocket of England.

Merrily followed a tractor and trailer into the potholed B-road that was the valley's main thoroughfare. No hope of overtaking, and you knew from experience that when two big container lorries met on this road it was rural gridlock.

'I'm still never quite sure why they call this the Golden Valley.'

'More to the point,' Jane said, 'what are we doing here?'

'Some people say it's from the name of the river. The River Dore. Like French. *D'Or.* River of gold?'

'Mum, the Dore is a ditch. Makes the Wye look like the Mississippi.'

Merrily slowed for a small signpost.

'I'd try the satnav but Mr Khan said that, in these parts, it adds an hour to your journey.'

'Ah,' Jane said. 'So you're finally going to tell me what you were cooking up with a guy who frightens Dean Wall.'

It had come out in the pub, over the sandwiches, about what Jude Wall had done to Khan's car and Dean Wall had done to Jude. Jane telling it like a funny story, but you could see how badly it had shocked her, happening in Ledwardine. Strange, strange night. Merrily had felt strange in her posh glittery frock. Men had kept looking at her. At one stage she'd fooled herself into thinking Lol's eyes were moist with longing and she'd wished they were alone. At the top of Church Street, they'd gone their separate ways.

'Have you seen Dean since?'

'He's probably in the river attached to a concrete block,' Jane said. 'Not this river, obviously.' She turned to look out of her side window at a stocky church next to a loaded barn. 'It does sometimes look golden in the sunset, the valley. A proper sunset, not like this. But so much of it's…'

'In shadow.'

'Yeah. Eirion says—'

'Sorry, flower? Eirion?'

This was the first time since she'd come home that she'd spontaneously mentioned him. Eirion's family lived near Abergavenny. To get there you often passed through the Golden Valley. It was how she knew so much about it.

'Eirion…' Jane took a breath, as if she'd needed help to get the name out. Another thing – normally she'd call him *Irene*. 'Eirion says that's bollocks about the Dore, it's probably from *dwr*, Welsh for water. There you go. That was kind of adult, wasn't it?'

'You heard from him since you got back?'

'Don't like to bother him at the start of a university year.'

It came out a mumble, Jane was huddled into her fleece, arms folded. Definitely something amiss. When she was first in Pembrokeshire she'd phoned every couple of days, full of stories about what she'd been doing, the people she was working with. The other night, during the storm, she'd just talked, a touch bitterly, about how they struggled to find enough paid work, much of it coming from local authorities obliged to fund the examination of landscapes they hoped to despoil. But she'd known all this before, surely?

'Is there something you haven't told me, flower?'

'Lots I haven't told you.'

'Something else that might affect… the future?'

'There *is* a future in it. Though it's all hand-to-mouth, even according to Coops. Not that I *mind* that. I never really want, you know, security and all that crap.'

Merrily nodded. What could you say? Nobody wanted security at Jane's age. At Jane's age, she'd been listening to vintage goth rock and wearing black lipstick. No, actually that was when she'd been a few years younger than Jane. At Jane's age she'd been about to get herself…

She stopped to let another tractor haul its trailer into a field.

'I'm not pregnant,' Jane said.

'I didn't—'

'You were working up to it. I keep telling you, I'm never going to get bloody pregnant. We're choking the planet.'

'Right,' Merrily said.

You got this increasingly from Jane who was even cooling on her beloved paganism because so much of it was based on rituals to promote the kind of fertility we didn't need any more.

She was peering out at a tilting signpost.

'What's the name of this place you're looking for?'

'Cwmarrow.'

'Valley of the Arrow? Are you *sure* it's round here? Because, obviously, the River Arrow—'

'Is miles away, yes.'

She'd wondered about this herself. The River Arrow was one of their own rivers, to the north. It didn't come anywhere near this far down.

'And this is from Raji Khan, right?' Jane said.

Merrily leaned back, loosened her grip on the wheel. Adults. Communicate like adults.

'A long-time friend of Khan's – so close he likes to call him his cousin – lives at Cwmarrow in a house he believes is badly haunted. The guy, like Khan, is a Muslim, but imams don't mess with infidel ghosts. So they've come to me. That's it.'

'Wow. Cutting edge, or what?'

'And, because I don't want to go there tomorrow entirely unprepared, I'd like to see where the house is, before it goes dark. How old, et cetera. Essentially, I don't want to be surprised by something I ought to have known.'

'A recce?'

'Something like that.'

'And, erm…' Jane's arms had unfolded. 'What's happening there?'

'I don't really know. Khan was being reticent. I mean, all this work needs to be fairly discreet, but this, for various reasons, is more so. So, no I was *not* to tell the new Bishop of Hereford. And you know what, flower? Suddenly I'm quite *glad*.'

Glancing sideways, she saw eyebrows going up.

Adults.

Sod it. She told Jane about this afternoon and felt better.

Turning left into the village of Vowchurch, they passed a little church with a squat-spired timbered tower, and then, in the adjacent hamlet of Turnastone, another church. She remembered an old story explaining why these two had been built so close together: two sisters, rivals, one saying, *I vow to build my church first*, and the second one sniffing. *I'll have mine built before you can turn a stone of yours.* Something like that. In this area it was hard to find a church without a foundation myth.

They also passed a shop with ancient petrol pumps outside, the kind that needed someone to work them for you. Sloping fields, sheep, the carcass of a pickup truck with bricks instead of back wheels, all below a lowering sun, light bleeding between fleshy clouds.

'Obviously, I've no right to expect him to pay me any more attention than any parish priest. It was just that Sophie had told me he'd done a deliverance course, so I thought maybe… you know, I *was* asked to *be* there when he called in at the office. Which he said, by the way, that he loved because he could look out of the window and see his flock milling around on Broad Street. He's sitting in my chair, I'm perched on the side of a table near the other window, nodding and smiling, the way you do, and waiting for him to talk about… something he wasn't going to talk about.'

He laughed a lot, the Bishop. He went *haw, haw*. He actually did that. But it was raucous, something thrown out. Not a laugh you shared.

'He said he must visit Ledwardine one day. And then he said he had some letters for Sophie to do, and he opened his brief-case, and began to dictate. I thought maybe it was something urgent and he'd stop after one letter, but it was just an accept-ance of an invitation to lunch with the chairman and cabinet members of Herefordshire Council. And then he started another and… that was it. I realized I was expected to leave.'

'But he'd arranged a meeting with *you*.' Jane sitting up, straining her seat belt. 'That was what you said.'

'Evidently I was wrong. According to Sophie, he'd said he was coming to see her office, and she assumed he knew it was also the deliverance office, and she'd asked him if he wanted to see me, and he appeared to nod. But… he was coming to see his lay secretary. In *her* office.'

When she'd left the gatehouse, Innes had been sitting at her desk, his back to the window, dictating a letter to Sophie. Not interrupting his thread to say goodbye, not really looking at her. Just raising a hand while consulting the notes on his iPad.

'So when *is* he coming to see you? *Don't* sound like you don't care. I saw your face when you came out.'

'Maybe I was remembering something. Like, when he said he must visit Ledwardine, as if he'd never been… well, he had. I'd been trying to think where I'd seen him, and it was in Ledwardine. On a bank holiday. August? With his wife and two or three kids, on the square. I noticed him because he was wearing some kind of Hawaiian shirt. And looking across at the vicarage. Which is not that unusual. People do, it's a nice old house. Jane, I'm a bit lost. I thought I was still following Khan's directions, but...'

The way forward was far from obvious. And the road was getting narrower and the day was dimming. Farms and cottages you could only half see behind trees and swellings in the land, the Black Mountains so close you couldn't see them at all.

'We could ask somebody,' Jane said. 'If there was anybody to ask.'

She glared out at the sunken lane, its unruly hedges. Merrily slowed. The dipped headlights had found a ridge of hard grass growing down the middle of the lane like a Mohawk haircut. Usually an indication that this would end in a farmyard.

'Actually, I really like it round here,' Jane said. 'Lots of archaeology. Most of it hidden. Overgrown castle mounds and tumps. And hill forts. No official history – like no National Trust stuff, but it's all around you, unlabelled. You need to know what you're looking for. I like that.'

It was growing dark so quickly that you could almost watch it happening, like speeded-up video with the soundtrack dropping away. Merrily's window was down. No birds, no wind. Only the sun's last watery discharge between the clouds.

Then lights ahead. Jane turned to look behind them.

'Didn't that sign say Cwmarrow?'

'Think so.'

The lane widened into a clearing; at the end of it the headlights found a gated field and then close-packed, mixed woodland to either side. Dead end, apart from a track curving uphill towards a sprawling farmhouse with lights in downstairs rooms, and the lump of a hill behind.

'What's that?' Jane was sitting up. 'What is *that*?'

'Where?'

'There!'

The hill was clearer now, and also what was jutting from a wooded ridge like a smashed tooth.

Merrily said, 'Castle? Bits of.'

'You didn't say there was a castle.'

'I didn't know. Khan… ah, he said there was "a significant outbuilding".'

'I've never heard of a castle, anywhere near here. I mean, there are castle *mounds*, maybe one or two stones, but *that…*'

'There's not much left.'

'There *is*, Mum. That's a serious ruin. Why don't I know about it? Is it a nineteenth-century folly or something?'

'In this area? Wouldn't think so.'

The road was deeply rutted, the car bouncing. In the dancing headlights two wooden gateposts came up, and one carried a sign: *Cwmarrow Court*.

'Go on.' Jane was feeling for the door handle. 'Drive up.'

'No way.' Merrily swung the wheel. 'I just wanted to see it, that's all.'

'If it's a castle, there must be a footpath, at least. Bloody hell, Mum…'

'Too dark. You could break a leg up there. But it's not exactly a disappointment, is it?'

'It's an enchanted landscape. You know what I mean?'

It was good to see the kid's mood change so rapidly. Good to know the diminishing world could still excite her. Merrily smiled in the gloom of the cab.

'Before you left for Pembrokeshire, it was like all that was behind you. Then, when we were talking on the phone once, you said you'd been surprised to find you weren't the only one turned on by the mysterious.'

'Did I?'

'You were rabbiting on about it all again, for the first time in ages, getting excited. Alignments of ancient sites, the importance of myths and legends. As if you were, I dunno, suddenly amongst friends?'

'I may have got that wrong,' Jane said quietly. 'Maybe I was just being... humoured.'

Spell broken. Merrily reversed to the field gate at the end of the clearing. In the rear-view mirror, the sky had scabbed over.

13

Big voice

SOMETIMES SOPHIE WOULD sound annoyed or affronted, seldom anything more intense. Her emotions lived on a short leash. Which tonight, on the phone from home, was evidently fraying.

'He asked to see the deliverance files. He wanted to know what you'd been working on.'

'When was this?'

'About half an hour after you'd left.'

'Why didn't he ask me?'

Merrily nodded thanks to Jane for a mug of tea. Jane left. The desk lamp in the scullery lit a folded 1:25,000 Ordnance Survey map. At its centre, inside a circle, the word *castle* in gothic script.

'Merrily, I don't know what's happening,' Sophie said, sounding almost querulous, sounding her age. 'I wish I did.'

'What did you tell him? About what I was working on. If you don't mind me asking?'

'That you were keeping an eye on the New House on Aylestone Hill, staying in regular touch with people there. Aftercare. And also acting in an advisory capacity with local ministers on two bereavement issues. Why would you think I might mind?'

'I suppose because you're the Bishop's lay secretary, and your primary allegiance should be to him. I'm just a...'

'Just someone I've known for several years and grown to care about.'

'I'm sorry.'

Silence. Sophie had rung twice while they were in the Golden Valley, leaving messages on the machine. This was not sounding good. Merrily kept trying to picture the new Bishop and couldn't. He was just somebody big and bland and purple.

'He was looking back over the past couple of years. On the computer and in the filing cabinet. He went through the related press cuttings. He went through the contacts list. He'd occasionally ask a question.'

'Like?'

'Like how often did you work with the police? Were you consulted by them or was it sometimes the other way round? Seemed he'd had lunch recently with the chief constable accompanied by DCI Howe. In the way that new bishops do. I pointed out that his predecessor thought that careful interaction with police and some social services was a positive thing. Knowing that Bishop Craig is keen on the Church being relevant.'

'What did he say to that?'

'He asked how many parishes you had. I said just the one. But covering quite a large area. He expressed surprise. I pointed out how the deliverance role had expanded significantly since you took over from Canon Dobbs. And that his predecessor, recognizing this, had tried to avoid overloading you in other areas. He… said nothing.'

'Well…'

'I tried to explain that you rarely managed a day off and hadn't had a holiday since you started. He didn't comment on that either. And then… then he went on to ask about someone he said he found in the contacts file. Anthea White.'

'She's not *in* the contacts file.'

'I didn't think she was either.'

'He asked if she was a personal friend of yours. I said she was not.'

'Dear God.' Merrily took a hit from the e-cig. 'What's happening?'

'I thought I should explain something about Miss White. I told him she was a former senior civil servant with considerable knowledge of… I used the phrase 'spiritual byways'. He said, do you mean occultism? It was immediately clear to me that he already knew who and what Anthea White was.'

'He actually asked you that?'

'Not directly. I said that the explosion in religious activity of a kind that was once illegal meant you felt you had to keep abreast of what was happening. He laughed.'

Haw haw.

'I took the opportunity to tell him again how hard you'd had to work in quite a short time, and how – possibly because you were the first woman to undertake the deliverance role – you'd been approached far more often than your predecessor, Canon Dobbs. In retrospect, I regret saying that. He said you looked tired.'.

'I do?'

'He—' Sophie's voice had grown parched; she cleared her throat. 'He asked me if I thought it might be a good idea for you to be relieved, as he put it, of some of your burden.'

'Oh.'

'Like… putting extra people into deliverance?'

This had happened before. A deliverance panel. Some of it still remained, but nothing formal. There were people she could call on. Not all of them inside the Church.

'I don't think that was what he meant,' Sophie said.

Huw's phone wasn't answered. There was no machine functioning, only the BT message telling you the unnamed person was not available.

She sat under the Anglepoise, the only light in the room, and tried to concentrate on the map. It was one of Jane's old ones. Ley lines had been drawn in. Jane's once-beloved leys. She'd encircled the word

castle

76

Probably thinking it was just a mound. The word Cwmarrow wasn't on the map, which was slightly odd because there were a couple more houses, a stream or river and something with dots around it, identified only as

earthworks

She kept staring at the map as if it might tell her something – which occasionally they did, with their dots and symbols and arcane lettering – and because she wanted to concentrate on something that didn't involve an emotional response. All the map told her was why an imam might feel inappropriate. This was olde England, verging on olde Wales.

As soon as they got in, Jane had found Cwmarrow Castle on the Net. Believed to have been built in the reign of King Stephen – late eleventh century? Stone keep and bailey walls. It had been held by the de Chandos family, major landowners in the area and then passed into the hands of the Louduns, whoever they were. By the fifteenth century it was already half-ruined. Now it wasn't even on a right of way and...

had lunch with the chief constable accompanied by DCI Howe.

Merrily closed her eyes on the map. What had Howe told Innes? A year ago, that would have explained a lot. Annie Howe hadn't liked her, she hadn't liked Annie Howe. Now, while they weren't exactly mates, an understanding, of sorts, had been reached.

Hadn't it?

When she opened her eyes, the map was blurred. And the phone was ringing.

'You didn't tell me you'd had him on a course.'

Trying to keep her voice steady.

'Thought he might tell you himself,' Huw said. 'I were interested to hear what he might have to say about it.'

'Sophie told me. The Bishop didn't mention it. Or anything, much.'

'And what else did Sophie tell you? That he had a big pulpit voice?'

'No, she didn't say that.'

'Preacher from an early age. Too early. He could make people listen. In Wales that's always counted, a big voice. Open your mouth, shit comes out, but it comes out loud. Except he's English and his old man were a Scot. Anyroad, he still got taken under the wing of a local minister who became a canon at Brecon. The legend is that Innes came to believe God had chosen him.'

'And you think?'

'I think God sometimes likes to take the piss.'

'Huw, I…'

Her voice fell away. She was seeing Craig Innes before he was Bishop, the vision clear as day. Ledwardine Square. Innes with a blonde woman, presumably his wife, and some kids. All brandishing ice-cream cornets in the sunshine. His shirt not quite Hawaiian but certainly loud, his face far more distinct in this particular memory than it had been this afternoon in the gatehouse office.

'Craig Innes, the Deliverance Years,' Huw said. 'Except it weren't years. Months, more like. He didn't say owt about it?'

'The subject didn't arise, and I didn't think I knew him well enough to bring it up.'

'When he were on the course, he said virtually nowt, either. I'm thinking, you even listening, lad? He went through the motions.'

'Box-ticking? Been there, done that?'

Craig Innes smiling over his ice cream. On the square at Ledwardine last summer. Looking across at the vicarage.

Merrily looked up at a familiar sound from outside the window: *tock, tock, tock.* The old, old briar she'd never liked to cut tapping thoughtfully at the glass.

'All right, I'll tell you,' Huw said. 'I'll tell you about Craigie's finest moment as a deliverance minister. Don't put t'lights out.'

14

Bridgework

THERE WERE CERTAIN things Bliss had never asked. No need. This element of the unspoken-about between Annie and him, sometimes he'd even felt it was essential to their survival as an item.

But it was different now.

'I don't think I've ever asked you this before,' Bliss said. 'But do you actually still like him?'

They were in Dyfed-Powys Police country, north of Hay. A scruffy darts and pool pub, Bliss in jeans and his baseball sweater with the big numbers on the front, Annie with the stripy top under her jacket.

Very occasionally, they allowed themselves to go out together like this, for a drink or a meal in some obscure pub outside the West Mercia boundary. Yeh, there was always a remote possibility of some off-duty cop lurking in one of them, but they could explain it. Sometimes senior plod met out of hours to iron out some admin issue; if they were spotted, Annie would be able to handle it. Annie scared policemen.

'Is it possible to like him as a man,' she said, 'and hate him as a police officer?'

'He isn't a police officer, Annie, he's something worse. Or could be very soon.'

They'd tried talking about other things, but everything kept coming back to Charlie. It was like he was watching them from the bar, giving his daughter the occasional friendly wink over his pint, pretending he hadn't seen Bliss. As he would.

'I wish he'd been something else in the first place,' Annie said. 'Dentist or something.'

'He'd still be bent. Pull out a few healthy teeth and then offer you bridgework for five grand.'

Annie said nothing. Bliss was already sorry he'd said that. Charlie was her dad. She worried a lot about bent genes. There was silence for what seemed to Bliss like a long time. His head was feeling numb. Another reason for frequenting dark pubs was that bright lights could still push a spike into his brain stem. Made him think that maybe he should've owned up to this problem, taken a lump sum and got the hell out. Joined his old bagman Andy Mumford in the private inquiry business.

Nah, that'd be like an ante-room to old age.

'It means, of course, that I have to go,' Annie said. 'Probably sooner rather than later.'

Bliss looked down into his grapefruit juice – teetotal now; one pint and he couldn't walk a straight line. She was right. He heard her swallow.

'He rang just before I left.'

'*Did* he?'

Taken a while for this to come out.

'He said there was no reason at all for me to seek a transfer if he's elected.'

'And *he* brought that up, did he?'

Annie faded back into a wonky old settle with initials carved into the varnish. Her voice came back tired.

'He's planting the idea, isn't he? Giving me time to find something, elsewhere. That's the real reason he rang, isn't it? A little reminder.'

'That would be like him,' Bliss said.

He'd been online again, hoping there was some small-print clause indicating that a candidate for the still comparatively new position of Crime Commissioner for West Mercia should not be related to a serving police officer in that force.

There wasn't.

'He sees it as the summit of his achievements,' Annie said dully. 'The natural high point of his career.'

'And a last chance of real power in his sunset years. He'll be like some redneck sheriff. He can probably see the good old days reforming around him, only better. And I mean, Christ, he might be right. All this talk of regional devolution, so we wind up run by a West Midlands parliament made up of every dirty councillor who ever collected a brown envelope. Twats in Westminster like to talk about real local democracy, but it's...'

Something throbbed over Bliss's left eye.

'Like selling the country into organized crime?' Annie said. 'Possibly. Central government might be considered remote, but at least it's always under press scrutiny. The regional media, what's left of it, doesn't have the resources.'

'Or the balls in most cases, if there's advertising at stake. Yeh, Charlie's the tip of a black iceberg.'

On the face of it, this was not particularly his problem. He was hardly the only cop in town who knew Charlie Howe's history, or some of it, anyway.

But then, if Annie transferred to South Wales or Thames Valley or somewhere, it wouldn't be her problem either.

'And what about us?' he said.

His feelings for Annie continued to surprise him. They'd been coppers first and he suspected they always would be. It was a key part of what made them work – he kept telling himself this – but it wasn't everything, not any more, not for him.

You're a sick little man, Brother Bliss. Charlie's voice like static through the crashing rain, the night of the big confrontation. *Come down yere thinking you were God's gift to West Mercia. Smart young city copper... show the country boys how it's done... you en't going no higher and you know it.*

Not now, certainly. Not here.

'He'll have me at some stage, Annie. There'll be so many snares out that one day I'll step into one, and that'll be that.'

But if Annie was gone, how much would he care? He noticed she hadn't answered his question. *What about us?* Meaning, was there any chance of them ever becoming more important than the sum of their careers?

His phone went ding-dong in his jacket pocket. He didn't touch it. He'd always had this little fantasy of one day sending to Charlie's mobile a selfie of him and Annie in bed.

He felt long, cool, slightly bony fingers on his right hand.

'Francis, the whole Crime Commissioner thing's so flawed they could scrap it anytime.'

'When did flaws ever get anything dumped?'

Thing was, he probably knew enough to hang Charlie out to dry. He'd need to work on it a bit more, get all his ducks in a row, and then take it to... who? Who did he know who was both powerful and clean, out of reach of Charlie's tentacles? If Charlie didn't go down, *he* would.

And what would it mean for Annie, either way?

Her phone was playing something by Vivaldi. The two phones going off at once only ever meant one thing. Annie already had hers out.

'What's the problem, Terry?'

Bliss sighed and slid his answer bar across.

'Darth,' he said heavily.

'Boss, we have a suspicious death. In town.'

'How suspicious?'

'Well... he might've fallen over and cracked his head on a coffee table.'

'Yeh?'

'And then picked himself up and fallen on it again from the other side. And then done terrible things to his face.'

Does the DCI know?'

'DS Stagg seems to be telling her as we speak.'

'You're not there now?'

'DS Dowell's there. Meadow Grove – that's the left turning before the Plascarreg, coming out of town.'

'All right, I'm about half an hour away. I'll come now. Perhaps you can get Terry to point this out to the DCI in case she's washing her hair?'

'I'll pass him a note,' Vaynor said.

15

A sense of betrayal

HUW SAID CRAIG INNES had been working deliverance for no more than a couple of months when he was consulted by one of his own deacons, a hesitant, unmarried middle-aged woman. Huw called her Ann Evans, Merrily guessing he'd changed the name.

Ann was the only daughter of the Rev. Alwyn Evans, a low-church minister of the old school. Not exactly a hellfire preacher, Huw said, possibly due to lacking the necessary warmth, but a man who thought he was most certainly not in the business of offering comfort.

'Made R.S. Thomas look a bit cosy,' Huw said.

Merrily recalled once spotting the Rev. Thomas's *The Echoes Return Slow*, at the end of a shelf above Huw's fireside chair. Poems of a uniquely Welsh starkness, a sense of drab resignation. Beauty beyond despair. It made a certain sense. She asked when Ann Evans had become a deacon. You didn't have to think too hard for an answer.

'She were thirty before he allowed her to teach Sunday school. Course, by then, there were only about four kids going, and happen he were blaming her for that, for not dragging them off the streets by their collars.'

'No mother around?'

'Alwyn's wife? More like a live-in housekeeper. Never allowed to spend a penny on the house, in all its Victorian drabness. Worked set hours as rector's wife and given a week's holiday a year, when she'd go away with her sister to a boarding house in Porthcawl.'

The Rev. Alwyn Evans never moved away from his church in the Usk Valley and was perhaps unaware of the wider Church moving inexorably away from *him*. Huw said Evans had thought that the very idea of women priests was so risible that it would never happen in his time, nor even his daughter's.

'Not in Wales, anyroad,' Huw said. 'Not till the End of Days were in view.'

The End of Days came, appropriately enough, in the 1990s. When the worst happened, Evans said nothing to anybody, would never discuss it or rail against it from his pulpit. In his world, nothing had changed.

Except that Evans had begun to fade away. No other words for it. Literally faded into the grey fabric of the village, walking its streets before the milkmen were up, rarely speaking to anybody, resistant to approaches, oblivious.

'Like there were a dark, resentful mist around him,' Huw said. 'He'd stand in the pulpit when there were no service on, sometimes at night. Fully robed, staring out down the nave in complete silence. The very air were toxic wi' his sense of betrayal. Got so the parishioners didn't like to enter in the hours of darkness, not even the cleaners, in case he were there.'

'Like a ghost?' Merrily said.

'Not yet.'

The dust had built up on the pew ends and the book rests.

And then the rector died.

'Whatever it said on the medical certificate di'n't matter. You might've said it were a broken heart if the bugger'd had one to break. If you were looking for a cause of death, you'd have to say he died of malcontentedness, if that's the right word. Silent, suppressed outrage poisoning his system.'

'Not in the church?'

'Most likely in his own bed. Don't matter. Wherever he were found, nobody could tell the difference, his face had been in rigor that long.'

His wife had gone to live with her sister. His daughter, Ann, stayed in the village.

'Living in a little terraced cottage and making a living doing accounts for farmers as couldn't be mithered wi' calculators, let alone computers. And meanwhile, owd Alwyn's church had became part of a cluster of parishes run by a young lad based five miles away.'

It had taken the new rector six years to persuade Ann Evans to become a deacon, by which time the rector wasn't a young lad any more and she was in her forties. It was a role at which he knew that Ann, in her quiet way, would excel: a sympathetic ear, a caring nature. Without the old man to stifle her spirit, her personality had flowered. She could talk to people and she did.

Deacon – that was just the start, Huw said. She'd taken services in the smaller churches and was a natural for the priest-hood, everybody said that. Everybody but Ann who, mindful of her father's unequivocal if undeclared opinion on the ordin-ation of women, had kept very quiet. Which everybody thought was respect, though in fact, it was fear.

For the new rector, Ann had become a special project. He'd told the story to Huw a couple of years later. Telling him how it had ended. About the churchwarden who'd found Ann Evans in the graveyard. The warden, a widower, had been drawn to Ann, looking out for her, thinking there might be a chance for him.

Huw's voice had slowed, his descriptions becoming more deliberate. He was on firmer ground now, having actually been to the village and its church, making a point of sitting on his own at the bottom of the nave, observing the pulpit, eighteenth century with nineteenth-century additions, too much dark varnish, a heavy overhead sounding board.

He said he still didn't know what Ann Evans looked like, could only see her in his mind, from behind as she entered the nave at twilight, padded towards the chancel, the big, dark pulpit like a cliff face on her left.

It was the third evening in a row that Ann had done this. Coming to pray for an answer, a sign. One more time. Should she put her name forward? *Should she?*

Huw said he could imagine her walking away from him towards the chancel, almost trembling but finding, from somewhere, the determination. Looking directly ahead of her towards the unlit altar where, it was said, no candles ever burned lest it cause offence to the spirit of the Rev. Alwyn Evans.

'And at that moment,' Huw said, 'by God, I felt it. The pressure. The pressure to turn your head and look up. Did she think that were *meant*? That if she gave into it and turned her head to the left, she'd get the sign she was looking for?'

Both Merrily's hands were clammy around the phone.

'The instant she turns,' Huw said, 'the cold's settling around her like cement.'

Anyone else, you might've thought he was making this up, sitting there beside his open fire, his imagination following Ann's turning head to the pulpit.

Where *he* stood.

Dear God.

Merrily could see the old rector. Arms raised high in the winged sleeves of his surplice, and his face like a cracked memorial, giving off stone dust, radiating malice.

'When the warden found her in the churchyard, she weren't dead. That would have been too easy, too pat. She'd kept going back, after she saw him. Still went back. Can you imagine that? Going in, along the dark nave, knowing he were there but *not looking*. Eyes focused on the altar ahead of her, refusing to turn her head. Managing, finally, to kneel on the chancel steps. But she couldn't pray.'

This happened. Merrily knew that. The ability to pray would desert you when you needed it most.

'Couldn't get the words out,' Huw said. 'Couldn't get the words into her head.'

'I know that feeling. Terrifying. Deadening pressure. The only way out of it is to relax. But in some situations that's next to impossible.'

'In the end she were running out into the churchyard, thinking he were coming after her. Outside, she trips over a grave-kerb. Scrapes her head on the edge of a headstone. Happen slightly concussed when the churchwarden finds her. Takes her home, makes her some tea, wi' brandy. Story comes out. Next day he goes to the rector. Rector doesn't bugger about. He consults his local deliverance minister, one Craig Innes—'

'Just... slow down, Huw. *Was* there something in the church?'

'Don't matter, lass. Pretty much the same either way. Imagination, if you want to call it that, can be just as damaging. But if you apply the same balm...'

'A Requiem Eucharist.'

'*Exactly.* Either way, Requiem's likely to work. The rector had the right idea. Best way to get shut of the ole bugger. Send him to his rest, whether it's the image in the church or Ann's head. Or both. Give him the full Requiem.'

Merrily nodding.

'It involves clergy, and a church. What else would you do?'

'The lad could've done it himself. His church, his responsibility. But he wanted a second opinion, and that were the right thing, too. He had the right idea, just went to the wrong man. Innes told the rector he'd deal with it himself. Which he did. He didn't go to see Ann Evans, he simply phoned her. He phoned her that same night. He gave her his considered advice.'

Merrily sighed, her mental landscape falling into shadow.

'Go on.'

'Advised her to go and see her GP,' Huw said. 'Wi' a view to referral to a psychiatrist.'

16

Claw

THE FACT THAT the ground-floor flat was in a small block only a short walk from the Plascarreg Estate took away a whole level of mystery. From the ill-lit road outside, Bliss could point to the steel-reinforced doors of at least two dope-dealers' dwellings.

But this was not what dope dealers did.

He got out of there as soon as he could, standing outside the doorway breathing harder than a man of his experience should ever be seen to breathe.

There'd been a small hallway, but one of its walls had been taken out so the front door opened directly into the living room, where there was enough blood for a multiple stabbing. But it wasn't a stabbing.

Billy Grace, the Home Office Dr Death, had been and gone. Karen Dowell had been here a while with the crime-scene crew, watching everything, inspecting everybody. Karen could get possessive about crime scenes. She joined Bliss outside, pushing back the hood of her Durex suit.

'OK, boss?'

'Course I'm OK. We know him?'

'We do now. But not in the way *you* mean. I don't think we're looking at what you might call a Plascarreg neighbour dispute.'

'We're not actually on the Plas, are we?'

'These flats were here before all that was even thought of. I remember them as a kid. Quite bijou at one time but, when something like the Plas goes up next door, your property value goes into a steep slide and it all gets a bit scruffy.'

'Robbery?'

'Don't think so. But look...'

Bliss pulled in a quick breath and turned to the room. The body was face down next to a small Shaker-style table. There was a wall-mounted TV and a packed bookcase. All quite tidy in here, in fact, if you ignored the spatter, some of it so liberal that it looked like the furniture itself had been bleeding.

An investigation was assembling around the body with no sadness, only the excitement that cops had become so good at hiding from the public. An excitement, Bliss was thinking, that was only heightened by the horror. Despicable, really. He was forcing himself to look, if only so as not to come over as a wuss in front of Karen, who was famous for taking a bag of chips and a kebab into a post-mortem.

'While I wouldn't think robbery as a motive,' Karen said, 'I reckon something's been taken. There's a printer on the desk, see? But no computer. Where's the computer?'

'Somebody killed him and walked out of here with their arms full of computer?'

'Maybe a laptop. I don't know, I'm just speculating.'

Bliss tweaked a smile. Speculation? Was that still allowed?

'So who is he, Karen?'

'Tristram Greenaway. Thirty-five. Employed by the council. Lived here on his own. There was a girlfriend, but she's said to have moved out a few weeks ago.'

'Mind your back, Francis.'

Slim Fiddler was shooting video, trying to frame the whole room. Slim was Chief CSI. They liked to call themselves CSIs now, sounded sexier than SOCO. Before long, the ambitious bastards would be using American TV words like *exsanguination* and *directionality*. Bliss edged gratefully away from the action. Slim Fiddler hadn't lost any weight; there were whole crime-scene teams who took up less room.

'What's Billy say, Karen?'

'Well, obviously blunt instrument, that's how he was killed. Blows to the head. Bang, bang, bang. Something like a hammer. But not *that* blunt because of the messy stuff. Probably done afterwards, Dr Grace thinks, and that's more than just a blunt instrument. Lot of ripping here. So we could be looking at a claw hammer or some similar tool, and it was the claw that did most of *that*. Unless he had something else.'

'Killer's not gonna come in with a friggin' toolkit, Karen.'

'If it *was* a claw hammer, the claw end was well used.'

'Or even sharpened,' Slim Fiddler said. 'See the way the right eye's almost been prised out, and the nose and mouth ripped, and the teeth—'

'Yeh, yeh.'

God, what was that bit, looked like a chicken nugget? Bliss turned away, swallowed. This was more than savagery.

'Sort of thing that's done to obscure identity,' Karen said. 'But that would hardly apply here. More like uncontrollable rage.'

'Who knows?' Bliss said. Needing to get out of here, the stench at work on his guts. 'No sign of the weapon?'

'Probably put it in a bag, walked across the road and tossed it…' Karen walked out through the front door, Bliss following, thank you, Karen. 'See, the river's only down there, across the road. Could've tossed it in there.'

'He'd be covered in blood and gunge.'

'I reckon he would.'

Bliss following her out, starting to breathe slowly. He looked across the strip of grass separating the flats from the main road where city-bound traffic sighed as the signals changed to red. Three uniforms were poking around in the stunted bushes. Not many onlookers. Get too close to cops on the Plas and one of them might recognize your face from an outstanding warrant.

Not much in the way of CCTV round here. Cameras got smashed on the Plas.

'So no signs of a struggle,' Karen said. 'Unless he's gone round tidying up afterwards. Is this a surprise attack? Somebody he didn't expect to get attacked by? Could be somebody he knew and invited in. No reason to be afraid, turned his back on whoever it was and…'

'Splat. How long since?'

'You know Dr Grace. Earlier today. Probably. Unlikely to be last week.'

'Neighbours?'

'We're still on the door-to-doors. Nothing significant so far. Always a lot of coming and going round here.'

Most of it by people the neighbours would try not to notice, in case they caused offence. Never good to cause offence on the Plas. Crap street lighting back here, too, in the one residential part of town where powerful lights wouldn't exactly be inappropriate.

'What was his job with the council, Karen?'

'County archaeologist's department. Though only temporary. The county archaeologist fell into a trench or something and broke a leg. Likely to be off work some time, which left his assistant, Neil…?'

'Cooper. Ran into him the other night.'

'Tristram Greenaway seems to have been a freelance archaeologist – i.e. jobless – who'd been taken on for a few months to help Cooper until the boss comes back.'

'Who told you that?'

'Woman in the flat above. Greenaway talked about it. We haven't talked to Cooper yet. Vaynor's still trying to track him down.'

Neil Cooper. The lad who had his skull nicked.

'Perhaps *I'll* have a word,' Bliss said, thoughtful. 'When he surfaces.'

Maybe this wasn't as simple as the address would lead you to expect.

'Tell you one thing,' Karen said. 'Some murders you can be dispassionate. Or, some of them, you feel nearly as sorry for the

92

killer as the victim. But this killer… even I don't feel safe with him out here.'

'Or her?'

'No way.' Karen fiercely shaking her head. 'Not even a human being any more, Frannie, he's just… lost it.'

17

Get over it

SINCE LOL WAS last home for any length of time, the council had cut back on public lighting. New shadows had grown like night foliage. The narrow street between Lucy's old house, where he lived, and the vicarage seemed, in the hours of darkness, like a deep river. Small lights blinked on the other side, on an island between the trees.

Always something to be crossed. Ledwardine, which always looked peaceful, was a cluster of small worlds in torment, the vicarage its unresting conscience.

Like a deep river... island in the trees... worlds in torment...

Lol spun away from the window. Bloody hell, there were days when it seemed like his whole existence had been reduced to scraps of material for possible lyrics. When all he was was something that served songs.

As distinct from Merrily Watkins, who served people and also something else that could seem as distant, amorphous and unapproachable as a cold sun.

She'd phoned earlier to see if it was OK if she came over.

Like she had to *ask*. For God's *sake*, she had her own key to the house that used to be Lucy's house. He'd had it made for her. She used it when he was away, to come in and check everything was OK, do a little dusting, pick up his mail from behind the door to see if there was anything crucial. But when he was at home, she almost never used that key; she'd always knock when all he wanted was for her to let herself in, any time of the day or night, be presumptuous, feel free. It wasn't as if the whole village didn't know. It wasn't like anybody in Ledwardine sat in judgement or even cared.

He bent to the wood-stove in the ingle. It hadn't been active for most of the four months he'd been away – relearning how to make a living wage out of music, a summer of small-venue and pub gigs across Britain, indoor busking for people who carried on drinking and talking. Funny how you learned not to mind this as long as the songs were out there and the pennies kept dropping into the hat, so to speak.

And then the unexpected. The warming of the distant sun. One of those half-heard songs had sneaked off quietly on its own, done some business, and was sitting waiting for him when he got back.

The song was smoking a fat cigar.

In the stove, the new flames were pale and vaporous, the kindling wouldn't catch. He wondered if the house's last owner was annoyed with him for spending too much time away, neglecting things, leaving her alone here and dead.

'Lucy,' he murmured, kneeling on the rug, messing with the vents, 'this *will* be OK, won't it?'

He'd really thought it was finally going to be OK. Couldn't wait to share the news with Merrily, who'd sat there in the Swan last night, looking glittery and lovely…

… and out of it. Preoccupied. The distant sun receding.

Behind the glass of the cast-iron stove, the kindling flared, all at once, almost explosively. At the same time, he heard quick but clunky footsteps on the cobbles at the end of Church Street.

Clogs. The clogs she wore in the house? *Clack, clack* on the stone flags in the kitchen, but never before *clack, clack* across the street.

He didn't wait for the knock. When he opened the door she was standing there like a waif in the dark, and he was sensing something on the other side of tears.

*

There'd been a big picture of this new Bishop in the Hereford Times. Large guy, fit-looking, solid and beaming. You'd have to say he looked honest, upfront, approachable.

Lol was firing the wood-stove hard. Inevitably, he was thinking of the last but one Hereford bishop, smooth, handsome Mick Hunter, who had also been approachable and fit – went running in a purple tracksuit. Please, not again, not another one.

'God, no,' Merrily said from the sofa. 'Nothing at all like Hunter. Twenty years married. Six kids.'

'*Six?* Jane know?'

The stove glass was rattling, bright orange radiance in the room. He'd switched off the lamps, for intimacy. Possibly.

Merrily salvaged a smile. She was wearing jeans and an old grey cardigan. No dog collar, no cross. Lol was calmer now. Now that he knew, more or less, what this was about. Where it was coming from and that it didn't seem to be connected with Khan, the dealer. Only the Church.

Only. Yeah, right. He wanted to say it was OK, she didn't need to take any of this crap. That things had changed, they could go away... somewhere... anywhere they wanted. And they could. Anything seemed possible now.

... except neither of them wanted to. Certainly not him, after spending most of the summer fantasizing Ledwardine sunsets, Ledwardine dawns, his own bed, Merrily in it.

'OK.' He moved over to sit at her feet. 'Why is he doing this?'

Why is this big, beaming bastard pissing on my picnic?

Merrily leaned forward, the stovelight in her eyes hinting at an anger which had to be better than the fog of mute desperation she'd brought in.

'I'm sorry.' She flopped down, her arms draped loosely over Lol's shoulders. 'This is really not what I'd planned. Neither tonight nor last night. Last thing I wanted was to be sitting here talking about bloody theology. I wanted you to tell me... whatever it is.'

He looked up into her eyes.

'What?'

'What you were going to tell me last night,' she said. 'Over the dinner we didn't have?'

'Oh...'

'What you probably didn't want to say in front of Jane?'

'It wasn't that. I can say almost anything in front of Jane. I just thought you should... Anyway, it'll wait.' Lol crawled away to the hearth to slip the vent, lower the flames. Wood-stoves were like women. 'What else did Huw say?'

She told him instead how the Bishop had avoided her in the office. What Sophie had said later on the phone about the relieving of her *burden.* Lol looked up at her, shocked.

'What does he *want?*'

'He's a modernizer. Represents a movement inside the Church that... I don't know what he wants. Just what he clearly doesn't want.'

She told him the story of a woman called Ann Evans, who believed she was being menaced by her father's spirit and was advised by Innes to see a psychiatrist.

'Did she?'

'No. Nor did she go back to the Church. Any church. Just carried on helping farmers with their accounts and then moved in with one for a while, but Huw doesn't think it worked out. He talked to her on the phone as well, but she wouldn't see him.'

'Huw talk to Innes about it?'

'Yes, well, he would, wouldn't he? Innes shrugged it off. Needed to pull herself together. Be strong in the Lord. If she can't deal with her own psychological phantoms, she isn't fit to be ordained. No room for neurotics in the pulpit.'

'So, in other words, he shafted her entire—'

'See, I didn't want to *think* that!' Merrily throwing up her arms. 'All the times I've been warned about people only to find they've been bad-mouthed by someone with an axe to grind.

I mean, even Huw… even Huw's not a saint. He has an ego, kind of.'

'Has Innes done that to anyone else?'

'I don't know.' Her arms flopped. 'Presumably. He wasn't a deliverance minister for long. I think he just wanted to find out about the more primitive aspects of the Church, maybe with a view to… I don't *know*. Huw sent me a link to several articles Innes wrote that you can find on the Net. One supporting the removal of references to the devil in the baptism service. Can't have primitive superstition inflicted on babies. The Devil is a medieval term beyond which we've progressed. He likes that word "medieval". Or rather *doesn't* like it.'

'They did that, didn't they. Dropped the devil from baptism.'

'He was surfing a tide. Riding the zeitgeist. The Devil had to go. Well, I'm not some kind of throwback, I hope, but I was unhappy about that. Were you here then, I can't remember?'

'I was still on tour. You talked about it on the phone. I probably didn't realize the significance.'

'It's the fact that a baptism is also an exorcism. The old services reject the Devil and the deceit and corruption of evil. Now all we do is we "turn away from sin". Hey, kids, let's just look the other bloody way. Don't worry your little heads about all that crap.'

'Oh.' Hadn't seen her like this in a while. 'So this is symbolic of how Innes feels about exorcism.'

'We assume.'

'And can he… if he wants to, can he actually wind it down, in his diocese? Or even…'

She shrugged.

'Somebody has to do it until they actually persuade some wimpy synod to abolish the whole thing.'

'But that…' Lol took a long breath. '… that means not necessarily you, right? He might want someone who thinks the Devil should be pensioned off.'

'Mmm.'

'Can he do that? Fire you?'

She leaned back with her hands behind her head.

'Firing a vicar is not easy. Even with good reason. An exorcist, however… See, I'm not licenced to be an exorcist. Nobody is. There's nothing on paper. I'm doing a job for the Bishop.'

'What's that mean?'

'Means that if you're not officially there, then…' Snap of the fingers. 'Gone. Like that. Whenever he wants. He can replace me tomorrow, if he wants, with someone who thinks people convinced they've seen images of the dead are in need of Prozac.'

'Shit,' Lol said. 'After everything you've been through?'

'I've made mistakes, a whole pile of mistakes.'

'Sure, but— How else do you get experience?'

'Sorry?'

'Without making mistakes.'

He stared down at the rag rug. Merrily's extra job, what Jane had called the Night Job… he hadn't known her all that well when she'd first accepted it but he knew it wasn't something she'd welcomed. He remembered that first winter, shock upon shock. Merrily, who knew nothing compared with what she knew now, having repeatedly to find the demarcation line between the rational and psychological and the stuff that even the clergy didn't have to accept.

Baptism of ice.

'Everything you've learned, all the knowledge you've acquired,' Lol said. 'If he sacks you as his exorcist, he'll just be throwing all that away.'

'Lol, you're not getting it, are you?'

'That's what he wants?'

'Bin it.' Merrily sagged into the sofa. 'Anachronistic crap. Turn away. Turn the page.'

Lol sat on the hearth next to the stove.

'I've never seen you look so gutted.'

The walls were furnace orange, stabbed by shadows, like a

naive, picture-book hell. He'd wanted to ask her if she knew what was wrong with Jane, but he could hardly do that now.

'I'm not very good company tonight,' Merrily said. 'I'll get over it.'

Part Two

If we want to gauge aright the mind of the community…
we must turn to the oral traditions, the institutions and
practices of the peasant and the labourer. These are
things the law barely recognizes. The Church frowns
on them, ignores them or tolerates them as she tolerates
Dissenters – with scorn and dislike, because she must.
Yet they survive…

E. Sidney Hartland.
Introduction to Ella Mary's Leather's
The Folklore of Herefordshire, 1912

18

A war

She left the Freelander on bare ground at the dead end where a barbed-wire fence restrained the forestry. The temperature had dropped in the night, and the morning was raw. Had to happen sometime. She dragged out her Barbour for the first time this autumn but left the airline bag in the well behind the driving seat.

Now where? Merrily stepped away from the car and looked around. The sky was bright but clouded. The air smelled of smoke. Crows were jeering from somewhere. To her left, a wooden foot-bridge crossed a brook before a steepening path wound up to where the ruins were partly caged by trees. Someone else's tyre tracks curved away to the right, vanishing behind a thorn hedge, and she followed them up to the sign, less visible by day than it had been in the headlights: *Cwmarrow Court.*

A short way up the track was a pair of gates – old wood faded to grey, Gothic loops overhung by thorn and holly trees – and a wooden mailbox hanging from a post like one of those gibbets from which dead crows used to be hung. As she walked over, pulling on her coat, a man in blue overalls and a stained wide-brimmed hat came through a gap between the trees.

'Mrs Watkins?'

His voice was loud, more landowner than workman. He beamed through white stubble, opening the gates for her, extending a big hand.

Merrily pushed her right hand out of a once-waxed sleeve.

'Mr Kellow.'

Was it? She'd Google-imaged Dennis Kellow, the heritage builder, and in all five pictures he'd been big and bronze. This man didn't look that big and his face was stretched and battered-looking.

'We don't' – he pulled the gates to behind her – 'invite traffic. Not since some bloody urbanite claimed he'd ruined his suspension on the track and sent us a solicitor's letter. The compensation culture. Try anything these days.'

'How did that end?'

'On the fire. Now.' He stood looking down at her, rubbing his leathery hands together. 'We haven't met before, have we?'

'Don't think so.'

'It's just that people I haven't seen for years often don't recognize me. Lost a lot of weight. Quite deliberate. Not, you know, a *side-effect* of anything.'

He pulled off his well-worn hat to show he still had hair and quite a lot of it, off-white and brushed back, manelike. He put the hat back and they shook hands.

'Sorry about Adam, m'dear. He's normally very reliable. Bloody hospital exploits his enthusiasm.'

'Right.'

When she'd rung from home, just before nine, to make sure she was expected, Adam Malik had said that unfortunately he was on his way out. Quite rare to be called into the hospital on a Saturday morning, but there'd been a bad crash on a notorious hill on the Leominster road, several badly broken bones. He was so sorry. Would she mind awfully talking to his father-in-law, who actually knew more than he did about this… issue? Merrily thinking, as she left, that Adam Malik hadn't sounded all that sorry that he wouldn't be there.

'Now,' his father-in-law said. 'Would you like some tea or coffee, or should I show you around first and let things just come out in their own way? Don't know how much time you have. Afraid I don't really know the formula for this sort of thing.'

'Oh… well… there isn't one, really. It starts with you explaining what the problem is. Then I see if I can help, and how, and then you decide if that's the way you want to go. Tea, yes, that would be good, thank you, Mr Kellow.'

'Dennis. I'm Dennis. Mellowed, you see.' A short laugh, and then he set off up the dirt drive, where you could see a stone chimney stack above the trees. 'Forced to bloody well mellow by my own—' He stopped. 'Sorry, m'dear, with you not wearing a dog collar, one tends to—'

'If you'd heard what I said the day I dropped a bottle of communion wine on the chancel step…'

He smiled.

'Which church?'

'Ledwardine.'

'Rood screen with apples?'

'Gosh.'

'Merrily, I know them all. Used to drop in unsummoned occasionally and spot problems with the fabric. Make a note of the worst on the back of one of my business cards and drop it in the offertory box. They'd call back, eventually. *"That bad?"* Aghast, invariably. "And where the hell are we expected to find that much money?" I was regarded as the Angel of Death.'

'Don't think I've ever found a card in my box. Plenty of big cracks in the walls, mind.'

'Who, as you know, I almost ran into.'

'I'm sorry?'

'Angel of Death.' He carried on walking, a bit slower this time, through the remains of an orchard, misshapen apple-trees with wizened fruit and blackened cages of mistletoe in their upper branches. 'No time for *that* bastard. Hence the weight loss. Prescribed pills and some dreadful marge that's supposed to lower one's cholesterol – couldn't stand the stuff, so just stopped eating almost everything. Seemed to work.'

'You're over it now?'

'Never been better.'

He didn't look it. *A stubborn man*, Raji Khan had said. *Promised to take it slowly from now on.*

'Another fifteen years should see it right.'

She looked up at him.

'The house,' he said. 'Got to finish the bloody house. To a level. Before I die.'

Dennis Kellow was breathing heavily. He glanced at Merrily and she looked away. The track had stopped rising and outbuildings of wood and stone were shambling out of the undergrowth on either side, some semi-ruined. There was a metal barn with one side missing and an elder tree growing out of it, and a roofless granary supported by steel girders. The buildings were like crippled old retainers, kept on unworked.

'How much land, Dennis?'

'One hundred and two acres. Most of the valley. We let most of it for grazing. There *are* other farms not far away, just can't see them from here. There was once a village. Down there, you can still find the remains of homes, overgrown, some with only foundations, buried in woodland.'

He looked all around, as if searching for signs in the valley's tangle.

'Maybe not a village the way we think of them now, but certainly more than a hamlet.'

The track had opened out into a yard, part cobbled, part tarmac, part baked mud. A dented old Defender and a Mercedes four by four were parked outside a house that didn't look like the kind of house that would ever get finished.

'Kellow's folly.'

He stood staring at it, as if he couldn't believe what he'd acquired: a long, crouching house built of rubble-stone the colours of a muddy fox. Irregular windows, some mullioned, two with oaken vertical bars, a roof of stone tiles all the shades of an autumnal paint chart.

'Most of what you see is fifteenth and sixteenth century. Some of what you *can't* see is thirteenth, possibly earlier. Much

106

of the stone would've come from…' Dennis Kellow half turned, extending an arm. '… that.'

She turned, too.

'Blimey.'

The landscape had locked them in; there was only one view left, intimate and yet awesome, directed to an obvious focal point across the wooded valley. Under a sky like tallow, the remains of Cwmarrow Castle poked like a bony fist out of the trees. Weak sun gleamed like sweat on the distant sawn-off tower. Crows were circling it like specks of soot.

'Already falling into ruins when medieval England became Tudor England,' Dennis Kellow said. 'Old castles became stone quarries for farms like this.'

'How much left?'

'Not much beyond half a tower and a receding wall. That's it now. One of the few things English Heritage gets right is to leave these places alone. Don't let them fall down, but never build them back up. What's done's done.'

'Respect.'

'Yes.' He looked down at her, smiling. 'And hope you get some back.' The smile vanished. 'This is what you buy. Cwmarrow. All of it. The whole place, intact. A medieval microcosm. Something magical.'

'Yes.'

'Can't leave now, m'dear. It's as if my whole life was leading up to this. Still. In spite of everything. Actually, *because* of everything. Can't let it win.'

'It's a contest?'

She looked up at him with concern.

'I think it's more of a war, now,' he said.

'Between you and… what?'

He didn't reply.

19

Hicksville

NEIL COOPER WAS a man in transition. Boxes everywhere in his big old flat, a few of them wooden. Bliss upturned one and sat down on it so as to appear unthreatening.

'So how close *were* you to Tristram Greenaway, Neil?'

'Close?' Cooper seemed to flinch, which was interesting. 'I work— worked with him. I didn't, you know, socialize with him.'

'Know anybody who did?'

'Well, no, he… he didn't talk much about his… his private life. Not to me, anyway.'

Neil Cooper's flat was over a shop in a Victorian building in St Owen's Street, close to the city centre. Though not for long; he'd told Bliss he and his growing family were moving next week to a new house, a few miles away at Hampton Bishop. The wife and kids were staying with the in-laws till most of the furniture was installed. Cooper said he'd spent most of last night at the new place, only came back this morning to collect more stuff, which was when he'd picked up the messages the police had left on his machine. He'd phoned Gaol Street without delay but learned nothing until Bliss had arrived with Vaynor.

Two sash windows were halfway up, street noise blowing in. On a Saturday morning, it was like they were sharing a bus shelter.

'See, right now, Neil,' Bliss said, 'we can't actually find anybody else who was in contact with Mr Greenaway. His parents live out towards Evesham but they seem to be away on some weekend break and none of the neighbours know where. And we don't know who his girlfriend was, although they don't seem to be together any more.'

Cooper looked, for the first time, close to smiling.

'Also, Neil, he didn't seem to have any particular friends in his block of flats or on the Plascarreg.'

Not that this was surprising. Some of Greenaway's closest neighbours on the Plas, most of their friends were their old cellmates. The door-to-doors had found a few people claiming they'd just seen him around. Two neighbours had also seen the woman who'd lived with Greenaway for a while.

'Funny,' Cooper said. 'I thought it was going to be about the skull.'

'I'm sorry?'

'Why you were trying to get hold of me.'

'Neil,' Bliss said, 'this is a *mairder* inquiry.'

Laying on the accent because, just occasionally, it intimi-dated people who'd only heard Scousers on TV where they were often bastards. Cooper wasn't actually looking threatened, just as if there were some things he could tell them but wasn't sure if he needed to.

'OK.' He sat down on a box opposite Bliss. 'Let me just say I'm not, you know…'

Bliss put his head on one side.

'Gay,' Cooper said. 'I'm not gay.'

Bliss flicked a glance at Vaynor as he prepared to skip a ques-tion so Cooper wouldn't think there was something obvious he hadn't known about.

Which he hadn't.

'Neil, was it *widely* known that Tristram Greenaway was gay?'

'Well… Oh God, I mean that's the point. No, it wasn't. Tris was quite… well, he was, you know, he was *very reticent* about it.'

'And why would that be, Neil? Being gay, that's like extra points these days. Even gays in Liverpool come out now.'

Cooper's smile was strained,

'He was born and grew up in Hereford, but he didn't come back after university. He'd worked in the London area for several years, and that's where he came out.'

'He told you this?'

'We had mutual friends in London. I was instrumental in him getting this job. He was nervous about coming back. He thought Herefordshire was, you know, Hicksville? He thought gays simply weren't as acceptable in places like this.'

'Because he hadn't been one, as it were, when he was growing up here?'

'It was nonsense, and I told him so. Times change and most people here are pretty tolerant about most things. Whatever you are, they just let you get on with your life, don't they?'

'Not necessarily on the Plascarreg, Neil.'

'You think this was—?'

'We don't know, that's why we're talking to fellers like you who spent time with him. What about the woman who was living at his flat? Why did you start to smile when I mentioned her?'

'Oh. Well. Her name was Rosemary… something. He'd been at university with her. She'd moved to the city to take up a relief teaching job and needed somewhere to stay. When the job expired, she left.'

'When was this?'

'Not sure. Two or three weeks ago? You see, the thing is, he liked that arrangement. He liked to be seen around with women. If there was a pretty woman around he'd make for her at once. There was a girl here looking for me yesterday, he offered to walk her across town to Castle Green. Just to be seen with her, I imagine.'

Bliss glanced at Vaynor.

'Let's have her name, then, Neil. And anybody else you know who had contact with Tris in the hours before his death.'

'It was Jane Watkins. You'll know her mother.'

'Merrily? That Jane Watkins?'

'Looking for gap-year work.'

'And the lad was flirting with young Jane so he'd look straight?'

'Look, he… he was hoping for a permanent job with us. A strong possibility if Des retired and I got his job… well, Tris was hoping to get *my* job. He realized the competition for it was likely to be fierce and he… you know, if there were any councillors involved in the interviewing process, knowing what some of the older councillors can be like, he didn't want anything to queer his— Oh *Christ*.'

Cooper closed his eyes.

They went back to Gaol Street on foot.

'Well,' Bliss said, crossing St Peter's Square between the church and the raised flower beds, 'that simplifies everything doesn't it, Darth? We can now include every friggin homophobe on the Plas.'

'Is homophobe a big enough word for someone who could do that to a man's face?'

'It suggests history. I mean, I realize it's probably homophobic of *us* to link every gay murder either to the victim's sex life or other folks' attitude towards it, but…'

'Experience.'

'Yeh.'

Entering the Gaol Street car park, Bliss spotted Annie's car. She'd need to decide soonish whether to put a mobile incident room into the Plas for the locals to spray *fuck off pigs* on it under cover of darkness. Waste of money, really. As if your regular Plas people would ever be seen strolling in to see if they could assist. Meanwhile, extra vehicles suggested they were setting up the major incident room upstairs.

'I shouldn't really have left the premises at this stage of the game. I just wanted to see Cooper's reactions.'

'Odd, I thought,' Vaynor said, holding the door for Bliss, 'him thinking it might be about his skull.'

'He was in a hell of a state over it on the night.'

'My initial thought, boss, was it was probably the first major discovery since he'd been in charge.'

'And he's fluffed it.' Bliss nodded, and they went up the stairs. 'Yeah. Could just've been that.'

Air of expectancy in the CID room as Bliss went in. Like it might all be over before it had started. He shook his head, making calm-down, as-you-were motions, noticing that Karen Dowell was wearing this kind of birthday-girl look.

'Found it, boss.'

It was in the centre of her desk. Bliss looked down at its silver shell.

'Greenaway's lappie?'

'Wasn't stolen after all. He'd locked it in his car boot. Maybe just taken it to work with him and forgot to bring it out.'

'Frisked it yet, have we, Karen?'

Like he needed to ask. Nobody had actually appointed DS Dowell as official Gaol Street techie, but nobody ever challenged it. Karen and computers, it was almost unhealthy.

'More or less,' Karen said.

'And?'

'He's an archaeologist.'

'We know.'

'That's it. That's all there is. It's all work. He emails other archaeologists, his favourites bar is full of archaeological websites. And he swaps Tweets with archaeologists, or similar.'

'So you're saying no emails with rows of kisses?'

Karen shrugged.

'It appears to be his whole life. Archaeology, history and allied interests. His bookshelves were full of mainly non-fiction, ancient and medieval history. And architecture and a few historical-type novels. It's like if you weren't an archaeologist he didn't talk to you.'

'Pictures?'

'Lots. Mostly open trenches and bits of bone. Archaeological porn.'

'Let's have a look.'

Bliss went through to his office, followed by Karen, carrying the laptop, and Vaynor. He sat down behind his desk, the sun washing in over his shoulder. Annie had discreetly fixed it for him to get this office because it had a window; his old one was bigger but relied on the kind of artificial lighting that still did his head in due to the brain-stem injury he'd never admit to still struggling with.

'Anything been wiped, do you think, Karen?'

'Not that I can see.' Karen set down the laptop in front of him and came round beside his chair and opened it up. 'If you want to see his last email, it was a couple of days ago. One he sent out to…' Prodding the screen. '… whoever that is.'

info@neogoth.net

'I'll find out,' Karen said. 'Anyway, this is his message.'

Please do not share

You may be interested to know that someone we all hoped to meet one day has turned up. You might not recognize him but you all doubtless remember who he is. If you want to know where he was found I can Draw you a Map. Let me know.

'That's it,' Karen said. 'It's slightly different, as most of his emails are full of references to academic papers and—'

'And he doesn't sign it.'

'No, he doesn't. And he doesn't address anybody in particular. That's also unusual. It's still archaeological, mind. As you can see from the attached picture.'

She scrolled up until the picture filled half the screen. Bliss drew a breath.

'Any reply to this?'

'No, I'd've told you.'

Bliss pulled the laptop round, away from the sunlight. The screen brightened and there was this buggered up human skull with its eye sockets full of soil and shit and stuff, and you could see where the cranium had come apart down the middle and been pushed back together. And its gob was open like it was chewing on a mint. You could even see the mint, the remaining teeth grinning round it.

Bliss tried not to grin back. Karen looked at him, curious.

'This means something to you, boss?'

'I don't honestly know. Might just be coincidence, but Neil Cooper lost an old human skull during the storm.'

'Is one skull important to these guys? Cathedral seems to be built on bones.'

'Let's just eliminate it.'

'I could just email this address, ask them who they are.'

'No, let's not talk to them till we *know* who they are. Neogoth – that's a server?'

'Not exactly btinternet. Could take a while to pin down.'

'Anybody here can do it, it's you.'

'I suppose,' Karen said.

20

Work in progress

'WHAT IS IT, then?' Mrs Kellow said calmly. 'What is it if not an act of violence?'

'Casey—'

'He won't face up to it. It's like it nivver happened.'

Dennis Kellow glared into his lap.

'It's how I deal with it. Is that all right?'

Even in the daytime this was a three-lamp room. A small room from a time before glass. The mean, squarish windows were high up in walls of rubble stone – muscle ribbed by irregular, sinewy beams. Stone floor with worn rugs like old stains. A room where sunbeams would rarely reach the ground.

It seemed more medieval inside than it had from the yard, despite the lamps and the plump-cushioned easy chairs. Merrily had watched Dennis Kellow sinking gratefully into one.

'Coincidence,' he said. 'I'm far from a sceptic, but this was all coincidence.'

'Whatever that means,' his wife said.

Casey Kellow was from New Zealand – way back, the accent fading in and out. She had a long, slender body, long legs, and white-blonde hair that made petals around her small features. Seemed placid and yet hardy and ageless, like someone who bent with the winds. Like a daffodil.

'Stroke,' she said. 'What a nice, calm word that is. Like you stroke a cat.'

Merrily nodded. A stroke was incredible violence, like a gunshot to the head.

'I don't want to talk about it too much,' Dennis Kellow said. 'I do keep saying I need to put some distance between me and it. I'm doing everything I can to make sure I never have another, and that's all there is to say.'

Casey sniffed. He glared at her. She was quiet, he was volatile.

'Well, I bloody *am*! And it helps if I don't have to talk about it like some... old man. Like somebody who... who's reached the age where you need to live near a fucking hospital. It's bad enough—'

He punched his right fist into his left palm. Perhaps he'd been about to say something about his son-in-law, the doctor, being brought to live with them like some ministering angel. Merrily worked on an understanding smile.

'You need to let Mirrily be the judge,' Casey said, 'about how many coincidences you're allowed before it stops looking like coincidence. Need to tell her the whole thing, Dinnis, it's not like she's...'

'You're not the imam, is what she means,' Dennis said. 'Our daughter, Nadya, who used to be Nicole, insisted we talk to the imam, and we were a bit worried about what he might do, OK?'

'Well, I'm not qualified to say how he might've approached it, but I suspect it might not be all that different.'

Was that right? Did Muslims deal with these anomalies in the same way? Did they even experience them in the same way?

'I thought I could live anywhere in England, Mirrily,' Casey said. 'Anywhere in the sticks. Which is probably why we're still together after all these years and all the leaking hovels he's dumped me in. But this is... challenging.'

'You've been over here long?'

'Since art college. Where we met. Both of us ristless and looking for something that didn't exist any more. He thinks this is it. Shangri flamin' La.'

'Came out here as an artist,' Dennis said. 'Turned into a builder. Same thing, really, just heavier. More of a restorer, I suppose. Restoring the big picture.'

They gave Merrily tea and told her their story. One she already knew. Everyone who lived around here knew it. There was a breed of incomers who'd become naturalized and were now close to essential in the sticks. Middle-class young people who had arrived in the post-hippy years, white settlers buying decrepit cottages with a few acres. Sheep and chickens. Some hadn't stuck it, the smallholdings became overgrown, the money ran out. But others had spotted openings, their once-suppressed business instincts beginning to stir. Soon, they were modernizing the hovel, selling it into a rising rural market, moving into a bigger one, flogging that. Discovering a talent for transformation. And then, against all their aspirations, finding themselves becoming millionaires. Secret millionaires, driving old Land Rovers, ashamed to expose their wealth because they were from Off.

Casey Kellow picked up the packet of Lambert and Butler from a small leather-topped table.

'You don't, I suppose?'

'My daughter's trying to convert me to e-cigs. Unexpectedly, they do the business, though I'm enjoying telling her how hard the transition is.'

Casey looked sceptical.

'Wouldn't work it for me, lovey. Too old now. And anyway, what's five a day?'

She lit one, and then Dennis Kellow, out of nowhere, came to the point.

'Nobody in my business rubbishes the idea of ghosts. The kind of places we work in, so many odd things happen that, after a while, you hardly notice them. Not coincidence, but it's no big deal either. I don't know *what* happens, I do know it's never particularly *pleasant*. But I'd never encountered anything that seemed as if it might actually be worth worrying about. Nothing physically harmful, you know?'

'Means he nivver wanted to worry about it,' Casey said.

'I didn't want anything getting between me and the project

in hand, no. Certainly not something I couldn't do anything about.'

There was silence. A big old Scandinavian-type wood-stove sat in the inglenook, all cast-iron solid, no glass, no visible flames. Only the warmth in the room told you it was active. Whatever was happening here, it probably wasn't happening in this room.

'Tell her,' Casey said. 'And don't play it down.'

'Should we go to the room? Tell it there.'

'What's wrong with here?' Casey said.

'I won't give into superstition.' Dennis Kellow sat his mug on the table. 'I'm not going to have another bloody stroke just talking about it. Come with me, m'dear.'

Casey Kellow squeezed her cigarette out between finger and thumb, didn't move.

'Take your coat, Mirrily.'

The upstairs was reached by a half-spiral staircase of stone slabs. The handrail was a rope, thick as Merrily's arm. A low-wattage bulb glowed in a rusting bulkhead cage bolted to the wall at the top. Dennis led the way.

'Back in the day – by which I mean the fifteenth century – the upstairs used to be a hayloft. Then it all got extended. There's a more modern staircase at the other side, accessing the seventeenth, eighteenth-century extension where the Maliks live. Could be worse – means we don't have to meet all that often.'

'I see.'

'It's not like *that*.' Dennis waited for her on a short, ill-lit landing, musty-smelling. 'Not really. He's not a bad chap, Adam.'

'I meant to ask,' Merrily said. 'Your daughter and grand-daughter – are *they* here?'

'They went into Hereford. Aisha has a violin lesson then she meets friends. Nic— Nadya said she'd be back.'

He didn't sound confident about this. Merrily joined him on the landing. To the right was a short passage with a door each side and another at the end. To the left, a passage with a dark velvet curtain across. Dennis jerked a thumb at it.

'Maliks that way. We have two small bedrooms and a bathroom here.'

'Your daughter's a convert to Islam, is that right?'

'What did Khan say?' He reached up to a rusted iron bracket reinforcing a beam, letting it take his weight. 'Odd little bugger. What did he say about us?'

'Not much. He said he was just an intermediary. Because he knew me, slightly.'

'Our vicar talks too much,' Dennis said.

'When you say "our vicar"…'

'Call ourselves Christians on the census forms. Which means, like most of the others, that we never go to church except for the occasional Christmas Eve midnight mass. But we try not to kill anyone or worship graven images. How much *did* Khan tell you?'

'Very little. He said I needed to hear it from you. Or rather Mr Malik. He said the imam—'

'That was all down to Nadya – we called her Nicole, she calls herself Nadya. She… When this became a bit too much to take, she got Adam to go and see the imam in Worcester, not expecting the fellow to say what he said. Bit of a surprise. She thought he'd be able to deal with it himself, keep it in the… in the faith. Never thought she'd be talking like that, she… You probably should know that, for all her adult life, where we'd written *Christian*, she put *atheist*. That was when atheists were still radical. She likes to be radical. Probably gets it from me, if truth were known.'

'She switched from atheism to Islam?'

'Maybe not that simple. Nothing's simple with Nadya. Now…' He walked along the passage to the end door, boards creaking. He brought out some long keys but still had to lean on the door to force it open. 'This is the Castle Room. Work in progress.'

He held the door open. Merrily walked through into a gloomy space with open beams and a floor of wide, warped-looking boards. The only light fell from high in the apex of an end wall. It was a grey light. Two walls were plastered, two were naked rubble stone. The only furniture was a couple of wooden stools and a long trestle workbench with a few tools on it.

'This, I suppose, is the haunted room,' Dennis said. 'Somebody, at some time, had put in a dormer window to let more light in, but when I was working for Kindley-Pryce he asked me to get rid of it. Reinstate that—' He pointed to the slitty aperture in the apex. '—as the primary light source. That was part of the original barn. This room would've been a loft, running the length of the original, early medieval building. I said, you do realize how dark that's going to make it? I remember him beaming at me. *Good*, he said.'

Merrily stood in the centre of the room and felt a familiar tension – in her, not the room. The room had probably been waiting for her with... in old houses, it sometimes felt like contempt. Today, she almost relished it. It might well, after all, be the last. The last time. The last haunting.

Before she'd left home this morning, she'd called the gate-house, left a message on Sophie's machine asking if she could see the Bishop. One to one. Some approach to the truth.

'You all right, Merrily?'

'Bit cold, that's all.'

'Not something I can do anything about right now.'

'Dennis...' Pulling on the Barbour Casey had advised her to bring up here. '... before we go into anything, could you tell me a bit about the previous owner?'

'Kindley-Pryce?'

'I probably should know about him, but I don't.'

'What d'you want to know?'

120

'Not sure. But he seems to have started all this. He employed you, I think. To do something that *you* think needs to be finished.'

'Yes.' Dennis went to lean against his workbench. 'He started it, all right. Poor old bugger.'

He was a curiosity. His dreams had been Utopian, but also medieval. Dennis said he didn't fully understand Kindley-Pryce, but he didn't think that mattered. They had Cwmarrow in common.

'Casey didn't like him much. Thought he was selfish, but she didn't really know him. Casey didn't like him because she thought I'd caught his disease, and maybe that's true.'

Selwyn Kindley-Pryce had been born in London but came, he always claimed, from an old Welsh Border family. He'd discovered the area in his students days, at Oxford, where he became a full-time academic. Early medieval history. Those were the days when property round here was dirt cheap and he'd bought a cottage out near Vowchurch, installed his young wife and their baby son there, while he spent most of the week in Oxford.

'Which *was* selfish of him, I suppose. But he wanted a stake in the area. He'd started what was to become a lifelong study of aspects of local history and folklore. But he and his wife divorced – she found out what he'd been doing with some of his female students.' Dennis laughed. 'Always a ladies' man. Anyway, paying her off meant he had to sell the cottage and he went to America, where there were lucrative opportunities for an English medievalist. His wife moved to Hereford with the child who is, of course, Hector Pryce.'

'Seen the name somewhere…'

'Probably on the side of a bus. Hector Pryce coaches?'

'Ah. Of course.'

Not one of the bigger public-transport firms, but well established.

'He's bigger than that now, for sure,' Dennis said. 'Married Lynne Hamer, widow of Malcolm Hamer, who owned a restaurant in town and crashed his plane. Now he owns all sorts. Pubs, restaurants. I was afraid he was going to develop this place when the old man went, but should've realized, not his style at all. Father and son, very different people. Hector was only too glad to see the back of it.'

'No family rift while Kindley-Pryce was around, though.'

'Doesn't seem to have been. His wife married again, might be dead now. Selwyn returned from America a moderately wealthy man, having heard Cwmarrow was for sale.'

'When was this?'

'Twenty-odd years ago? He'd published several books by then, renewed some connections in Oxford. Bought it all, the Court, the castle, the valley. A romantic, inspired by the medieval microcosm, the enchanted valley with the castle on the hill. But also an expert – history, architecture.'

'What was the house like then?'

'A wreck. But he was fit, prime of life, relishing the challenge. Inspired by his vision.'

Dennis hadn't put lights on in here. There *were* no working lights. He said he'd get to that. Merrily zipped up the Barbour and waited.

'Some of this I don't understand,' Dennis said. 'But I'm just a builder.'

'Who went to art college.'

'A builder with a soul. I want to restore what *can* be restored. Maybe get round a few of the rules for the sake of aesthetics, but no outlandish ambition. Just to live out what's left of my life here and leave it secure in its beauty. But not a visionary like him. He used to say he could see new community rising out of the overgrown foundations of the village. Artistic... creative. A lot of artistic people, writers, poets, musicians would come down for events, small festivals – he installed a few caravans in the paddock at the back for those who wanted to stay. Summer nights of music and storytelling. He loved storytelling, the oral traditions.'

'I've not heard of any of this.'

'It wasn't *advertised*, Merrily. Strictly word of mouth. It was actually a bit ramshackle. But it paid for some of the continuing work on this house, the cost of which he seriously underestimated. I actually think he was in two minds about having people around. Once asked me about floodlighting the castle, then changed his mind because he realized it'd become a tourist attraction. In the end, I think he wanted it for himself.'

'I'm still…' She curled cold hands inside her sleeves. '… not really getting a picture of him, somehow.'

'He wouldn't want you to. He cultivated the mysterious. All a pipe dream, really. He had a few people who were sympathetic to his ideas putting money into it, including his son. But I think that was for appearance's sake. Hector's a very different kind of guy. Hard-nosed go-getter.'

'So… what happened?'

Dennis Kellow may have grimaced, too dark to be sure. He talked about the problems of remedievalizing. Attempts had been made, in various centuries, to modernize the place, but Kindley-Pryce had wanted it closer to its original state. Which wasn't easy, because a listed building was more or less in aspic from the day it was listed, and if it had been listed in the 1970s, you had problems.

'Can't just walk in and strip everything back to the year 1450 or whenever just because the owner prefers rudimentary. We had a battle to be rid of the dormers. Obviously, he never finished it, even with me at work. Let alone uncovered what might remain of the village. Thought he finally had the answer when he met Caroline Goddard. You heard of her?'

'Don't think so.'

'Children's writer and illustrator. Like a creature from folk-lore herself. Hair long enough to sit on. They had a relationship, working and otherwise, and out of it came a couple of books for kids, under the pseudonym Foxy Rowlestone. Which were building substantial sales. All looking promising. But then…'

Merrily looked around the room where shadows were draped like dustsheets.

'He died here? I mean, in the house?'

Dennis Kellow blinked.

'Did I say he died?'

21

Bad guy

THERE SEEMED TO be even more boxes in Neil Cooper's flat. Nothing like moving home to make you realize how much shite there was in your life. Bliss put his phone on a packing case in front of Cooper. The phone was displaying a picture demonstrating that even death didn't get you out of the shite.

Cooper, sitting on an upturned toy box, stared blankly at the picture then at Bliss.

'What *is* this?'

His fair hair was dusty, his face looked stretched. He seemed to have aged since they last saw him, less than two hours ago. The day had aged, too, the sash window shut against an irritable sky and intermittent rain.

'It's a dirty old skull, Neil,' Bliss said. 'But is it *your* skull?'

'What?'

'Your missing skull from the Castle Green – is that it?'

'It's just an image. I can't tell from an image.'

'But you wouldn't rule it out.'

'Francis, it's something I saw once, by lamplight in the middle of a storm. Yes, it could be, but then it might not be. The central fracture to the cranium roughly corresponds, as far as I can remember, and it's obviously come out of the earth. But I can't be certain. Didn't even get to examine it before it vanished. Why are we talking about this... now?'

Bliss exchanged a glance with Vaynor who was standing in the window recess.

'All right, let me ask you another question, Neil. Tristram Greenaway. Could he have taken it?'

'The picture?'

'The skull.'

'Why…?' Cooper shook his head, mouth open, not getting it. 'Why would Tris take the skull?'

'I'm asking, *could* he have? On the night.'

'Well, obviously he could have. He was there, and I'd hardly be supervising him.'

'He have anything with him he could've put it in?'

'He had a… a small backpack, I think. Which he often carried. Kept a trowel, maps, gloves…' He looked up at Bliss. 'Where exactly did you find this skull?'

'We didn't. We've just found a picture of a skull on Tristram Greenaway's laptop. Attached to an email he'd sent out, quite recently.'

'Who to?'

'What does that suggest to you, Neil?'

'I don't know. It doesn't make any sense.'

Bliss leaned back, an arm around a step ladder.

'I'll be honest with you. I think there are things you're not telling us. I thought that the other night when we met on the Castle Green. I'm not an archaeologist, but it seemed to me that your reaction to the disappearance of the skull… I mean, yeh, I realized that was not what you'd want to happen, but it did strike me as just a bit extreme. You must've been tripping over flamin' bones for years around the Cathedral and Castle Green.'

'Not exactly.'

'But you know what I'm saying.'

'Not sure I do, Francis. All skeletons, all graves, are examined and logged and—'

'What use would some old feller's skull be to Tristram Greenaway?'

'I have no idea.'

126

'It was a feller, was it? Not a woman.'

'We're pretty sure it's male.'

'All right. Think about it. Y'see, recalling your… state of agitation, the other night, I'm also wondering how important would it be to you to… gerrit back.'

'*What?*'

Bliss said nothing. Vaynor moved a little closer. He was a big lad.

Cooper had gone pale.

'What are you suggesting?'

Bliss shrugged. Cooper half rose then sank back down again. Nobody stayed cool in the moment of realization that a policeman was one question short of asking him if he'd done a murder.

Bliss sighed.

'Just doing me job, Neil.'

'This is insane. All of this is fucking *insane*.'

'Murders often appear insane, to everybody except the killer.'

'All this pales into insignificance now, anyway. The skull.'

'*What* does?' Bliss said. 'What was clearly significant to you before and now isn't?'

Cooper leaned back on his box, closed his eyes momentarily, breathing in hissily through his teeth.

'All right. Let's deal with this.'

Bliss leaned forward over clasped hands.

Cooper said, 'Do you know what a deviant burial is?'

'*I* have an idea,' Vaynor said.

Bliss shot him a glance. Problem with these Oxbridge bastards was that sometimes they knew too much about everything, didn't ask enough really stupid questions.

'*Deviant* burial, you said?'

'It usually relates,' Cooper said, 'to medieval funerary customs, and it can mean a number of things. In this case, the head not being where you would normally expect to find it.'

'Like connected to the neck?'

'In this case, it had been separated from the body and placed between the legs. The thigh bones.'

'So assuming this was not the remains of either a seriously deformed human being or a medieval yogi…'

'Then it was deliberately put there by a third party. As there was a very large old tree on top of it, we have to assume it had not been excavated and carelessly replaced. Hence, it appears to have been buried that way, thus deviating from the norm.'

'And this is a bit special, is it, Neil?'

'Certainly fairly unusual in this part of the world. It's more common in parts of eastern Europe, although it has been found elsewhere in Britain and Ireland.'

'What's it mean?'

'Normally seen as a religious or ritual thing. To contain the spirit of the dead person. Prevent it coming back from the grave. From this, we might speculate that the body was that of someone who had inspired fear during his lifetime. Someone whom the living might've been glad to see the last of.'

'A bad guy.'

Cooper shrugged.

'And the night of October the thirtieth, this was the last time you saw it?'

'This was the last time I saw a skull which may or may not have been the one in the image you've just shown me.'

Bliss snatched up his phone, tapped the screen.

'Have another look, Neil. Have a *closer* look. Let's try and blow it up a bit, shall—'

'All right!' Cooper almost squirming away. 'Yes, I think it is. I *think* it is.'

'Because?'

'Because… because it looks as if it has a stone in its mouth. You see?'

'Like a mint?'

'Sometimes they put a stone in the mouth to… There was apparently a persistent belief that people determined to return from the dead could… chew through their shrouds and… escape. So a stone, or sometimes a bone would be wedged in the mouth to prevent them… chewing.'

Bliss said nothing. Not a lot you *could* say.

'I realize how stupid that sounds,' Cooper said, 'but it was done for that purpose. Apparently.'

'Right. Well, thank you for that, Neil.'

Sporadic raindrops sounded on the window. This was going to need a bit of thinking about. Bliss shifted on his box.

'All right. Going back to the Castle Green burial, is it fair to say that when you saw it, you were excited?'

'I suppose I was.'

'Bit of a coup, then, a deviant burial?'

'Yes. Not exactly a common phenomenon. Anywhere. Especially here.'

'Does all this mean the skull's worth something?'

'In archaeological terms, as part of an otherwise intact skeleton in a grave, it's extremely interesting. As a skull on its own, its archaeological – and monetary – value has to be minimal. It's the burial that's significant. I've taken pictures of what's left which *suggest* the skull was not in its usual place but…'

'It doesn't count for much without one.'

'Probably not.'

'So the *theft* of the skull kind of robs you of your moment of fame. Makes you look a bit daft. And if Tristram Greenaway—'

'No, that—'

'If Tristram Greenaway nicked the skull, he would've known that.'

'Francis, this is insane.'

Bliss looked up at Vaynor.

'Darth, remind me, did we ask Neil where he was last night?'

'Oh, now, look, this is—' Cooper scrambled to his feet. 'Last night, for several hours, as I may have told you, I was making trips between here and Hampton Bishop.'

'Your new home.'

'Sometimes with my wife… and children, until it was their bedtime. To convey furniture and clothing to our new home. It's a straight road from here to Hampton Bishop and I never deviated from it. Don't you have CCTV or something to confirm that?'

'After bedtime, were you on your own?'

Cooper thought for a moment, tonguing his upper lip.

'My wife's sister was also at Hampton Bishop, and she will remember how many times I appeared with… things. Look, it… it never entered my head that the skull might have been taken by Tristram Greenaway, with whom I was always on very friendly terms and whom I regarded as a serious and able archaeologist. And I still… I still find it hard to come to terms with him being dead, let alone murdered. This… is… a… nightmare.'

Bliss nodded.

'Thank you, Neil. We might wanna talk to you again. So, don't, as they say, leave town.'

They'd come in the car this time, Vaynor driving, so it took longer to get back to Gaol Street. Waiting at the lights near the block a funeral parlour shared with a tattoo bar, Bliss leaned back, stretched his legs. Had a sense of getting somewhere, and in record time. Not sure where, exactly, but causing a bit of stress would very often be productive.

'You don't really think he did it?' Vaynor said.

'I've had stranger results. Though it'll probably turn out to be entirely unconnected with the missing skull.'

'But if Greenaway did have it, where is it now?'

'I'm not *dismissing* it as a connection, but let's not get carried away and overlook something more definitively Plascarreg.' Bliss peered at Vaynor. 'So where'd you learn about deviant burials, Darth?'

'TV, actually, boss. A documentary. Nothing too academic. I think it was on Channel Five.'

'Bloody hell, Darth. Feller like you, from the halls of academe, watches Channel Five?'

'My girlfriend wanted to see it. It was about, er… vampires.'

'Vampires.'

'Real vampires. Or rather, real suspected vampires. It involved superstitions from the Dark Ages and beyond. A fear of vampires seems to have been one of the principal reasons for a deviant burial. Like Cooper said, they were found in places like Bulgaria and Romania, where you'd cut the head off a suspected vampire – post-mortem, presumably – as a way of preventing it from coming out of the grave and… doing whatever they were supposed to do.'

'I thought you drove a stake through the… or is that just a Hammer Horror thing?'

'I think there *was* some evidence of that, but mainly they seem to have cut off the head.'

'Cleaner job, on the whole.'

'Quite.'

The lights greened-up. Vaynor took the hairpin left into Bath Street. The rain was coming down steadily now.

'Vampires.' Bliss shaking his head. 'Be the first one in the playground to dig up a vampire in Hereford. Gerra learned paper out of it.'

Vaynor coughed.

'The first to unearth human remains attesting to the possibility of a suspected sanguinary predator, boss.'

'Yeh, that, too,' Bliss said.

22

Believe it happened

PERHAPS IT HAD been coming on for years, but the worst happened very quickly.

'You'd be talking to him,' Dennis Kellow said, 'and there'd be a point where you were simply not on the same page.'

He walked over to the workbench, picked up a chunky old wood-plane, caressing it.

'Maybe I'd been turning a blind eye to it – *I* didn't want him to have to leave here. And therefore me, too. I've worked in far grander places, but nowhere I'd felt more involved. More… connected. Then the housekeeper got replaced by a full-time nurse because he'd become a danger to himself. He'd wander around at night without lights.'

'How old was he?'

'Not *that* old. Probably not much older than I am now. He refused to accept he was losing it. For a long time. Threatening to clobber the doc. And then he suddenly just gave up, went quietly. Into a home.'

'That must've been awful, especially for a man who… lived by his mind.'

Dennis didn't reply, just stood there stiffly in his overalls, and she wondered if she'd said the wrong thing.

'What happened to… did you say Caroline?'

He grunted.

'She'd come and go. And then she just went. She was still a young woman – was to me, anyway. *You* look like a child.'

'Ha.'

'Wasn't like they were married. She just wasn't there one day.'

'And he's in a home.'

'Lyme Farm, up beyond Leominster. Very expensive place. More like a hotel, but with medical and nursing care. Proper food. I don't supposed he even notices, poor old bugger. Went to see him once. He didn't seem to know me. Frightening.' He paused. 'Casey wouldn't come. Already giving me little memory tests. But that wasn't quite how it went, was it?'

'OK, let me get this right. Even though he'd been here for years before it came on, Casey thinks Mr Kindley-Pryce's dementia might've been caused by something in the house?'

He sat down on one of the stools, hunched against the blade of light.

'Casey doesn't know what she thinks.'

'Who was living here before Kindley-Pryce?'

'Nobody. Not for a long, long time. Derelict for years when Selwyn bought it. Owned for decades by a big farmer from a few miles away, who'd just wanted it for the land. I think he died and whoever inherited it was advised to sell the land and the house and the castle… the whole package. It was on the market for the first time in maybe decades when Selwyn was alerted to it. Outbid some crazy pop star.'

'And he ended up selling it to you?'

'Not initially. He thought his friend Jim Turner was having it. The film producer?'

She shook her head. All these names she vaguely knew…

'Turner was making drama-documentaries for television at the time. Moody stuff, bit like those old Ken Russell biopics. And then, like Russell, he was lured into drama – movies, much more money. Kindley-Pryce… I don't think he was actually a scriptwriter for Turner, but he was certainly some sort of consultant, and Turner would come to the events here and *he* fell under the spell of Cwmarrow. Agreed to buy it from Kindley-Pryce and maintain it just as he wanted, and Kindley-Pryce could visit whenever he liked. And, best of all, Turner would pay me to carry on with the work. Which I was more than delighted to do. Onwards and upwards.'

Dennis turned to Merrily.

'Sale never went through. Bloody Hollywood. Turner got his chance and couldn't afford not to take it. Place had become a bit of a mess again by then. An old house doesn't have to be empty for long before things start to seize up. Hector Pryce asked me if I knew anybody who might be interested. Might be a Philistine, Hector, but he's not a fool. Knew that when prospective buyers got surveyors in and learned how much it was going to take to put it right…'

So Dennis had put in a bid. Silly amount but it was all he could afford at the time, even with selling his own house.

'Turned down, of course. Even I would've turned it down. Hector left it on the market a couple of months, during which metal thieves plundered it. Starting to look derelict again, well on the way to becoming a picturesque ruin like the castle. He came back, offering me a chance to rent, peppercorn if I continued with repairs, and an open opportunity to buy.'

The turning point had come with an offer for Dennis's business.

'I was employing about a dozen chaps – working all over southern Britain by then, chasing contracts – National Trust, English Heritage, Cadw in Wales. I didn't want to retire, as *such* – just tired of endless travelling around. Then Adam and Nadya needed somewhere. Casey was dubious, but it looked like fate to me. I sold the business. We bought Cwmarrow. Realization of a dream. Whoopee.' He glanced at Merrily once and then turned away to peer into a dark corner. 'Maybe it went to my head.'

She followed his gaze into the shadows.

'The stroke.' He sank his hands into the slanting side pockets of his overalls, blew out a loud breath. 'I was so *angry*.'

'Dennis, we can go back down if you like. If you'd rather not talk about it here. I don't want to cause you any—'

'No.' He sprang up and strode across to the door, rammed

134

it shut behind him with a heel. 'Talk about it here.' Advancing on the two stools, picking up one with each hand, setting them down next to the workbench. 'When I'm in here, I can believe it all happened.'

The door, despite its weight, didn't fully close. It slid back out of its frame, perhaps because of the obviously warped and tilting floorboards.

'Were there any old stories about this house, Dennis? Anything to suggest… disturbance?'

'I never paid much attention. You can accept things might exist without becoming obsessed by them. Whole valley was haunted, Selwyn used to say. Haunted by its past. Past was alive. He'd lie here – over there – and…'

'This was his bedroom?'

'Oh, yeah. If you stood on a ladder and looked through the slit you'd see it directly faces the castle. He called it the Castle Room. Slept in a massive old bed where he claimed he'd often wake up to the sounds of the village. The village that wasn't there any more. Wake up at first light, hear the village waking up around him.' Dennis snorted. 'The chink, chink of the blacksmith's hammer, all this.'

'You didn't believe him?'

'He was a storyteller, Merrily. Never stopped telling stories. Couldn't separate reality from whimsy. Especially towards the end.' He sat down again. 'Although I'm starting to believe them.'

He nodded to the second stool and she sat down. The only light was from that slit high in the apex stones and the crack left by the door that wouldn't quite close.

'How did you work in here without lights? After the dormer window had gone.'

'There *were* lights. They kept going out. Bulbs would blow, within minutes sometimes. I stopped replacing them.'

'Was this before you were living here? When Selwyn was here and you were working for him?'

'I didn't work in here after the dormer went until he left. He'd brought his enormous bed and slept here. Not always alone. The lovely Caroline Goddard. Anyway, years later, I finally got round to this room. Working up here one night, resetting some of the floorboards, being careful because of the wires under there. Had a floodlight on an extension from the landing. And it... well, it went out. The lamp that was plugged in outside. Wasn't the bulb. Tested it afterwards. Fine. Just wouldn't work in here.'

'What did you do?'

'Didn't move. It was night. No moon. Didn't want to put my foot down the hole in the floor, where I'd taken a couple of boards out. Kept still. There's a quality of quite impenetrable darkness you get in some old houses.'

'Like now?'

'Darker. Much. It was night-time, getting on for midnight, and I'd switched off the landing lights.'

'Where was Mrs Kellow?'

'In the kitchen, I suppose. You don't know where other people are in this house. Sound doesn't carry the way you expect it to. Sometimes, you're on your own and nobody, as they say, can hear you scream, which...' He paused. '... which I did.'

'Screamed?'

'It probably didn't come out. Wish it had. A scream that swells your whole body and echoes inside your ears, I'm sure that's not a good thing.' Dennis extended an arm towards the corner where the shadows were like stone and then rapidly withdrew it. 'Over there.'

Nothing to see. She got what he meant: normally your eyes would gradually adjust to a darkened room. In here, there were occluded areas, slabs of shadow that stayed solid. Merrily pulled the ends of her jacket over her thighs. Her feet felt numb in her ankle boots.

'A figure,' Dennis said.

'Sorry?'

'Standing there. A figure. Not now. Then.'

136

Dennis's white hair looked translucent, like wax.

He said, 'You don't imagine these things can frighten you the way they do.'

'I do, actually, Dennis.'

'I mean, what *are* they? Nothing. Something in the air, an alteration in the light. It's like I said downstairs – you don't think they can hurt you.'

'Male or female?'

'Hard to say. Male, I suppose. No face. Or not enough light to make it out. It was… I'm not enjoying this.'

'We can go downstairs.'

'No – damn – I won't let it. I won't *let it*.'

Merrily bit her top lip. Didn't like this.

'Powdery,' Dennis said. 'Like talc in the air, and you blow at it and it changes shape. Sorry, I'm not putting this very well.'

'You are.'

'An arm. It did have an arm.' He cleared his throat. 'Extended. And I saw a hand. And a finger. One finger pointing at me. It seemed blurred, as if it was quivering.' He laughed, almost shrilly. 'Or perhaps that was me, m'dear, do you think?'

'It was cold? Colder?'

'If I'd been opened up by a surgeon he'd've found packed ice. When I looked again… No, I didn't *stop* looking, I couldn't blink. I was staring at it the whole time, and then I was staring at nothing. I heard Casey… that's the next thing I remember, Casey's voice from outside the room. From the bottom of the spiral stairs. "Why have all the damned clocks stopped?"'

Merrily sat up.

'We had three working clocks,' he said. 'An antique pendulum longcase clock at the foot of the stairs, an old metal wind-up alarm in the bedroom and a battery-powered clock in the kitchen. When she realized the kitchen clock had stopped, she went into the hall and the hands of that one were stopped at exactly the same time. We found the one in the bedroom later. Same time again.'

'Right.'

OK, do the Dawkins: Casey stopped the clocks.

Why would she? And how do you stop a clock, anyway, without breaking it?

Problem with rational explanations, they were usually so much more far-fetched than the alternative.

'Can't explain this,' Dennis said. 'Other than to say these things happen. Been working in old houses for over forty years. I accept things happen. I didn't think they could cause you harm.'

'Mental states can affect your physical state. When your mind and emotions are unbalanced by something shockingly anomalous… Hell, I'm not a doctor, Dennis. How did you feel? At the time. In those moments.'

'I felt… I don't know.'

She waited.

'Sick,' he said.

'Physically?'

'Emotionally. That's worse. Listen, what I'm telling you next is what Casey will tell you if I don't. A week later, same time or thereabouts, we're upstairs getting ready for bed. Casey's in the bathroom, I'm standing at the little bedroom window. Moonlit night, I'm gazing across the valley at the castle, the moonlight's glancing off the stone. I don't know how long I'm standing there. I can hear Casey from what sounds like a long way behind me but she's actually next to me, and she's saying, "Are you all right?" And I have to tell her I don't feel part of my head.'

Merrily shuddered. It was disturbing in a visceral way, the switch from the numinous to the almost commonplace. She didn't like this story at all. It was never going to be part of the *touchstone*.

'I don't remember anything till the paramedics turn up,' Dennis said. 'So here's the bit Casey would tell you. I can't remember it, but she says that, on the window ledge next to where I'm standing, the alarm clock's suddenly going off. When

138

she stops it by knocking it to the floor there's a reply from the bottom of the stairs. It's the longcase clock down in the hall. Chiming. Loud as a church clock. Or so it seemed. Loud and "triumphant".' He coughed into a fist. 'Casey's word.'

Merrily found her hands plunging down into the side pockets of her jacket, so hard that the poppers sprang open. *What is it*, Casey Kellow was saying softly in her head, *if not an act of violence?*

'First time that clock had chimed in over three years,' Dennis said. 'Always saying we'd get it fixed one day.'

23

Seedbed

Casey Kellow, a grey woollen shawl around her shoulders, followed Merrily to the Freelander, leaving Dennis behind the faded Gothic gates.

'What I presume he told you,' Casey murmured. 'You should know it took me the best part of three months to get out of him what he saw. The figure. The finger.'

A wind was winding into the valley, rattling the trees and putting Dennis Kellow out of earshot, but Merrily noticed that Casey, willowy in the breeze, was keeping her back to him and her voice down.

'Finally came out in the middle of a bloody great row. When men come out with things they immediately regret. Nobody understood him, Mirrily, even the bloody house had turned against him. He started to cry. Been very emotional since the stroke. Still is. Don't you ivver say I told ya that.'

'So until this row – three months after the event – you were both keeping very quiet about what happened that night.'

'He was sick. Had to bring him through that.'

'You hadn't told him about the clocks?'

'No. I was beginning to wonder if it had really happened. The clock in the hall, afterwards I took the pendulum out. The Castle Room, I won't go in there, and neither will he on his own. He won't tell you that. *Look* at me, Mirrily.' Casey parted her shawl. 'Goosebumps. Actual god-damned, flaming goosebumps. We're grown-ups. Modern, grown-up people who know all this is shit, and *look at us.*'

Merrily opened the driver's door, and pulled back the seat to reach into the well, bringing out the airline bag and setting it down at her feet. She looked beyond her, across the clearing to where Dennis was leaning on the gate, chin supported by his hands, white hair fluffed in the wind. Obviously knowing he was being talked about but not looking at them, gazing bleakly across the brook towards the ruins on the hill as if he was staring into his own future.

'Why do you think he didn't want to tell you what he saw?'

'That's pretty obvious. He didn't want me to feel even worse about his beloved house, his beloved valley, his beloved, flaming castle. He *claimed* it was because he thought it was the drugs they'd given him in hospital, false memory syndrome, something like that. And he doesn't talk much about his own problems. Thinks it's his responsibility to deal with them. Especially here. If the stroke pushed him out of Cwmarrow, he'd rather it'd killed him.'

'Mr Kindley-Pryce,' Merrily said. 'What do people say about that?'

'In what sinse?'

'How he was forced to leave a place he loved.'

'I don't have the medical details. We're not family.'

'Came on quite quickly, is that right?'

'Who knows how long it'd been coming on. Sure, sometimes I think about that. When you're alone here, your mind wanders into some weird places. It's a separate world, and it doesn't feel happy. Or lucky. Why'd it fall into ruins? Why did the village disappear? Why did people not want to live here, except for crazies like Kindley-Pryce and... Dinnis?' She smiled, resigned. 'Could I see him in a modern bungalow with a conservatory, passing the time with some light gardening?'

'But even when he recovered from the stroke, you weren't comfortable here, is that right?'

'We thought we were at first. Nadya and Adam and Aisha were here. We were a family – well, maybe a strange kind of family, in two units, but Dinnis could talk to a doctor without going through medical hoops, which he hates. But it wasn't right. If things could break, they'd break. Locks jammed, lights fused. There are parts of the house where you'll suddenly feel unwelcome. Like something has a contimpt for you. Worse sometimes. Autumn's not a good time. It's like Cwmarrow imbraces decay.'

'Whose idea was it to get help?'

'Adam's friend was here one evening, Raji? Adam doesn't like to talk about this stuff. He doesn't disbelieve, he just won't give an opinion on what he doesn't have paper qualifications for. Nadya… follows the teachings of the Koran, for God's sake – that girl, if she goes into something, she doesn't come up for air. Raji, he's some different kind of Muslim, more open to weird stuff.'

'He follows Sufism.'

'I've heard things about him, but I kind of like the guy. He was the one put the idea in my head, that we needed to do something about it. He said if we thought there was something harmful here, then it didn't matter how crazy that seemed, we should talk to a priest. Nadya said she wasn't going to have a Christian priest in the house— this is just so ya know?'

'Sure.'

'Raji says, OK, talk to imam and do what he advises. And y'know what *he* said. But Nadya says no Christian priest is coming in their side of the house. And then… I dunno. Something changed. I think something happened we didn't get told about, and the next thing Adam's phoning Raji. Nadya says, OK, do it, but…'

'She doesn't feel she has to stay for it.'

'No.'

'You see…' Merrily unzipped the airline bag. 'I really do need to work on the whole house.'

'I thought you guys were supposed to have a black bag.'

'And a big hat. What's in here, basically, is a Bible, a specialized prayer book and two flasks of holy water. At this stage, it's not about expelling anything. Partly because we don't know what we're trying to get rid of. It's about bringing light into dark places. But if I can only go into half the house…'

'Jeez!' Casey stamped her foot. 'We're so *dysfunctional*. Adam's more English than I'll ever be, wants to be a countryman, with a chainsaw. And here's Nadya – English born and bred – throwing up these crazy cultural barriers.'

'Well, look…' It was easy to overreact, and sometimes stupid. Equally, it could be dangerous to *under*react, and this bothered her more. 'I don't ever like to leave without doing anything, so how about I do your part of the house. It's a start. A blessing, room by room. At least that'll include the Castle Room. What happens, we say some prayers, sprinkle some holy water. All I'm asking of you is that you go along with it. We have a period of quiet first, where we relax, empty our minds…'

Casey smiled wanly.

'Dinnis doesn't really do that. He finds relaxation strissful?' The smile died on her face like an early sunbeam. 'He tell you about the feeling he had that night, in the Castle Room?'

'He said he felt sick.'

'Just that?'

'Emotionally sick.'

Casey sighed into the wind, dusty with fragments of dead vegetation.

'He thought he'd grown closer to the house. Giving it what it wanted. Restoring some of its heart. And what he got back was this… withering disdain. He doesn't like to talk about that.'

Merrily shouldered the airline bag. By the time they reached the gate, Dennis was walking away back up to the house, retreating like the morning light. The way the day had dulled was fusing everything together, bushes, trees and masonry, so that it looked as if the house had been sewn into the hills.

The longcase case clock at the bottom of the stone stairs was silent and nobody acknowledged it. The Kellows let Merrily lead the way upstairs, with her prayer book and flask. They followed her meekly with the Lord's Prayer, the old version: *Thy* name, *Thy* kingdom come. Ending on *deliver us from evil*, which never resonated more than in a room with the windows shut and all the cupboard doors open.

Occasionally, there would be a sign of something at this stage – something expelled or something lifting.

Nothing. In the Castle Room, the tools stayed on the workbench and the door stayed almost shut.

Outside it, afterwards, she glimpsed something behind the velvet curtain across the left-hand passage and pulled it aside, revealing the edge of a frame, one of a couple, containing a mosaic type design and some calligraphy. The Islamic side of the house.

Merrily paused, glanced from Dennis to Casey.

'We need to get them on board,' Casey said.

'Think of the house as an organism, divided into two.' Merrily gestured at the frames. 'Two faiths. Who knows what effect that might have. I don't.' She needed advice. 'How would you feel about me talking to someone about this?'

Casey looked at Dennis.

'Who?'

'It would be someone outside the diocese. I wouldn't be disclosing your names or the location.'

'Need to ask Nadya,' Dennis said.

'I'm sorry about this,' Casey said. 'Could we call you?'

'Let me finish your side of the house before I leave. What have I missed?'

Windows closed, cupboard doors open. Sprinkles and prayers, sprinkles and prayers. She was finding it easier these days to slip into the optimum state of mind, a quietness that was nothing like trance – the irony of this catching up with her between the kitchen and the sitting room.

Just as you were reaching a degree of competence, someone in a purple shirt came to take it away.

*

144

The Freelander was balanced on a hump of brackeny ground at the end of a passing place in the single-track lane, Merrily leaning against its flank, looking down on the valley, huge old trees on either side. She was on about the same level as the castle ruins across the valley. Cwmarrow Court had vanished. Nothing in sight that was lived in by people.

She'd stopped here to check her phone because there was no signal in the valley, leaving the Court reliant on landlines which, in this part of the world, would often come down in bad weather. If there was heavy snow you could be trapped for weeks.

All kinds of lines were down here. She was guessing she wasn't being told things because there were things they weren't even telling one another. The family, virtually any family, was a seedbed of secrets and lies. Secrets guarded from everyone outside the family, bigger secrets inside it. Not like she hadn't been there with Jane.

And then there was religion. Bring religion into the situation and there was nobody you could entirely trust.

They'd offered her lunch. She hadn't felt hungry. Sometimes, after a blessing, you actually did feel very hungry. She just felt empty, which was different. She got back into the Freelander, took a wrong turning but kept on and eventually finished up on the edge of the village of Dorstone, which was no bad thing; you could take the steep and twisty single-track lane over Dorstone Hill and pick up the road towards Leominster and home.

Near the top of the hill, wooded either side, the phone chimed, making her heart bump in a way it never had before. Oh God. Time to replace the chimes with the blues riff or the barking dog before they were rendered terminally eerie. The chiming and the stroke. Even priests were hardwired for superstition. She really had to talk to somebody about this. The idea of something non-physical inflicting physical harm was outside her experience.

She dropped down to second gear, took a slippery incline to the right and parked close to the exposed Neolithic burial chamber, Arthur's Stone.

Nobody else here; there rarely was. Perhaps there were times of day when Arthur's Stone – actually a rough arrangement of big stones – would look sinister and forbidding, but mostly it made her think of a prehistoric mechanical digger trundling towards the edge of the hill.

She got out of the car and laid the phone on the capstone's tilting table. The phone displayed a four bar signal. The screen said *missed call*. The number was the gatehouse office. She called it back.

'Merrily, where *are* you? I've rung seven times in the past two hours.'

'I… I've been out of signal. It's Saturday. Is there something wrong?'

What was Sophie doing in the office on a Saturday?

'You left a message asking me to make you an appointment with the Bishop. He could see you today.'

'Sorry, I was thinking Monday. The Bishop doesn't usually—'

Or the old Bishop didn't.

'Or rather, he said he could see you before lunch.'

'I never thought. Bernie would've been watching the football.'

'Where did you say you were?'

'Erm, getting a puncture mended.' Dear God, it had come to blatant lies now. 'In… in Leominster.'

'I'll see if it's still possible, but you'll need to make it later. He has a meeting with the Archdeacon in about ten minutes, say an hour for that. I can perhaps get you some time when he comes out.'

'Right.'

She leaned on the stone. Across the Golden Valley, the so-called holy mountain, the Skirrid, had its nose above the horizon, sky and mountain fused by rainclouds. She was sorry she'd asked for the meeting. She was tired. She felt steadied here, didn't want to leave.

Sophie was the person she would normally have told about the pointing finger, the chiming clocks. And couldn't.

'Merrily. When you go in with him…'

'Mmm.'

'Be very careful what you say.'

'About what?'

'About anything,' Sophie said.

24

Appropriate adult

USUALLY JANE DRANK cider. This afternoon, in the Black Swan, it was grapefruit juice, and no explanation.

Years since Lol had given up psychotherapy for full-time music, but Jane… well, you just couldn't help studying Jane. People with kids went on about the joys of parenting ending at about eleven, before the teenage years inflicted some kind of horrific trial-by-combat, but Lol was glad he'd been on the sidelines during the crazy years. Whatever happened for him and Merrily, he and Jane were never going to have a father/daughter relationship grown from loving memories of bedtime stories and bottle-feeding.

'So how's Eirion?' he said, as the Black Swan's posher bar-room filled up around them.

'Oh.' Jane looked into her glass. 'Fine.'

A whoop went up the other side of the bar – somebody scoring on the big-screen TV in the public.

Fine. Where did you go from here? Try to find out what was bothering her – because something was, and badly – or just back away and let it emerge in its own time?

'I was just thinking he always used to come over at weekends,' Lol said.

'Not every weekend.'

Jane's eyes flickered.

They'd met on the square, Jane looking into the window of the bookshop, Ledwardine Livres, Lol just looking around, feeling his way back into the village and hoping Merrily might drive in from wherever she'd gone. She'd talked last night about the Bishop but not so much about Raji Khan or what Khan had wanted. Maybe none of his business. Nor was this, really. He was Jane's friend, that was all.

'Eirion was with you, wasn't he?' Lol said. 'In Pembrokeshire.'

'Just for the first few weeks. Until he had to go back to Cardiff.'

Eirion was entering his second year at Cardiff University. Then he'd go on to journalism college. He was a nice guy, but he'd been Jane's first real boyfriend, and an attractive, curious kid like Jane, living in a society that scorned moral parameters... Lol wondered if she ever felt she'd missed out on a wild youth.

As the bar filled up, background chat rising, they talked about Lol's first production job, at Prof Levin's studio, for mad Belladonna, once iconic. A woman who wanted to work with him as a fellow neurotic. Whom he'd first met, memorably, by candlelight at the top of the church tower at Ludlow. *Who the fuck are you?* Bell had said, with death on her mind. Bell was famous for her recording of 'Gloomy Sunday', the Hungarian suicide song.

'Is it good?' Jane asked. 'The album?'

'Er, depends what you're looking for.'

'Lot of late nights?'

'Coming back here, it's like I'm in jetlag.'

Jane grinned. It was a mature grin. She's a woman now, Lol thought, and I'm not her dad. There's nothing we can't say to one another. Why not ask?

He leaned back, looking at the blue light cast on her face through the square of thick old mullioned glass, working up to it.

'So. Here we are, then. Back within a day of each other. At Hallowe'en. Is that an omen?'

Jane said nothing.

'You do still believe in omens?'

149

She looked uncomfortable.

'Not obsessively.'

Lol stared at her. Jane raised her hands.

'Yeah, I know, whatever happened to Mystic Jane? Look… if she eventually does go to university to study archaeology, ancient history, whatever, she probably needs to wipe the slate clean. Come to it without preconceptions. Avoid looking like a loony. Mystic Jane… cold storage.'

'That's a shame.'

'You reckon?'

'Myths and legends,' Lol said, 'I think they ground us. Connect us to where we are. But then I just write songs.'

Jane sighed. Lol thought, You really don't know where you are, do you?

He took a breath.

'So, Eirion—'

'Laurence!' Another stool was dragged up to their table, a black beanie dropped down between the glasses. 'How yer doing, son?'

'Francis,' Lol said.

Frannie Bliss, the cop, sat down, beamed at Lol, then at Jane.

'Can't stay long, kiddies, I'm on me lunch hour. Well, me lunch twenty minutes today, and I should be having it at me desk under the circs, but I just wanted a quick chat with Jane.'

Jane blinked but recovered fast.

'Sorry about the tag, Inspector. Must've come off. I'll bring it in when I find it.'

Bliss smiled fondly.

'Been across to the vicarage, but there was only the cat in. With this being business, I thought your ma ought to be around. But Lol's probably OK, if he doesn't mind.'

'What – as my Appropriate Adult?' Jane raising her eyes to the beams, lowering them slowly to give him the hard stare. 'You cheeky *sod*, Bliss, I'm nineteen!'

150

'Mother of God,' Bliss said. 'Doesn't time fly?'

'Apparently that's when you get past a certain age. What am I supposed to have done?'

Bliss sighed.

'What a pity it is, Jane, that your first encounter with the law should've involved an officer less soft-shoed and deferential than meself.'

'If you were Annie Howe, I wouldn't even be talking to you now.'

'She's a changed woman, Jane.' Bliss looked sorrowful. 'Word is she's found love.'

'Like with some sad little bloke who gets off on being beaten and whipped?'

'I wouldn't know, Jane. Listen, I believe you went to talk to a certain Mr Cooper, of the county archaeologist's department, the other day. What was that about?'

'And that concerns West Mercia Police... why?'

'Humour me.'

'If you must know, I was offering to sleep with him in exchange for temporary employment.'

Lol flashed Bliss an expression to say this was just Jane being Jane, because it had gone beyond banter. She'd always got on with Bliss, knew her mum liked him, but she was behaving like she might have done a few years ago when she was at the difficult kid stage.

But Bliss was looking wry and patient. Which was also odd. According to Barry, there was a murder investigation on in Hereford.

'Cooper says you met him on Castle Green and you arrived escorted by a guy called Tristram Greenaway.'

Jane shrugged and picked up her grapefruit juice, swirled it around.

'I just knew he was called Tris. What's *he* done?'

'He's got himself murdered, Jane.'

The glass went down hard, Jane searching Bliss's face.

'It was on TV and radio this morning, victim not named because we hadn't talked to his next of kin.'

Jane had slumped.

'Bloody hell.'

'I'm sorry if you and he…'

Bliss was watching her, Lol wondering if he was here because he'd wanted to see Jane's reaction when she heard this guy was dead. Surely not…

'Me and him, nothing,' Jane said. 'That was the first time we'd met, and our relationship lasted possibly twenty minutes?' Mild pain in her eyes now. 'A nice… nice guy. What happened to him?'

'We're waiting for the post-mortem. Thing is, Jane, you seem to have been among the last people to talk to him before he was killed.'

'If you want an alibi, I was with Mum for the rest of the day. I may be wrong, but I think it might be against her religion, covering up a murder.'

'So you didn't know him.'

'I went to the office looking for Coops, and Tris said he was at Castle Green and offered to show me where it was. I suppose I was flattered because he was good-looking. *Very* good-looking. So I didn't tell him I knew the way.'

'You thought he fancied you?'

'It's been known to happen.'

'Course it has, Jane. What did you talk about?'

'I dunno. Not much. I mean, we didn't like hold hands and arrange to meet later or anything like… God, this feels so weird. Was he attacked in the street or something?'

'I'll be upfront with you,' Bliss said. 'We don't know why he was killed, but we don't think it was robbery and we don't think it was random. He was found at home and nothing seemed to have been stolen. Which is why we're interested in his movements on the day he died. Who he met, what they talked about. If he'd said he'd have to dash off because he was meeting somebody.'

'You should be so lucky.'

'I can only ask.'

'I don't know,' Jane said. 'He was very friendly. He didn't actually make any kind of move on me or anything.'

'He was gay, Jane.'

'Oh.' Jane had started playing with a beermat. 'I see.'

'He seem happy, to you?'

'Wouldn't say that. He was very friendly, but I think that was just how he was, his nature. He told me he thought he was going to get a permanent job with the county archaeologist's department because the head guy was expected to take early retirement and Coops would get his job and Tris would get Coops's job, but that's not going to happen.'

'He thought he wasn't going to be around for long?'

'He said he thought that, with all the cuts, the department itself might not be long for this world, but I think he was just being cynical.'

'So not happy.'

'That's the impression I got. Then Coops came over, so he didn't say anything else.'

'He didn't say anything about Neil Cooper?'

'Not really.'

'Neil say anything about him?'

'You think what happened to him was something to do with his job?'

'I don't know.'

'Oh yeah, he told me Coops had found a new grave on Castle Green after this tree came down in the storm. And there were some bones. When I asked Coops, he…'

Lol thought he saw a movement, a shadow crossing Jane's face.

'Go on,' Bliss said.

'He just didn't say much. I was like, Oh you found some bones, right? Thinking there might be a big excavation coming off. And he said, Who told you that? And I said it was Tris.'

'And he said?'

'Oh— and I said, Should he have kept quiet about it? And Coops indicated it was no big deal one way or another.'

'He said the bones were no big deal.'

'Words to that effect. Look, I'm just one of the unemployed. He didn't have to tell me anything.'

Bliss shook his head gently, and Lol wondered what this was really about. Coming out here to talk to somebody who, chances were, wouldn't have anything to tell you... well, that surely wasn't a DI's job. In a murder inquiry, the DI was supposed to sit in his office and coordinate.

Jane finished her grapefruit juice, put the glass down. No more Bliss-baiting, her heart clearly wasn't in it any more.

'Where *is* your mam?' Bliss said.

'She's...' Jane shrugged. 'Dunno. Out doing vicar things.'

Lol said, 'You want Merrily to call you?'

'I'll catch up with her,' Bliss said. 'At some stage.'

25

Agony

SOPHIE'S DOWNCAST EYES said, *I'm so sorry.*

A stark light was pushed into the gatehouse from a white line of sun between tough, gravelly clouds. There were three of them in the office and none was a bishop.

'Bishop Craig's asked me to talk to you,' Siân Callaghan-Clarke said to Merrily. 'As Archdeacon.'

There'd been no women bishops when Siân, ex-barrister, daughter of a Blair-era baroness, had been appointed as the Bishop's head of human resources, or she might well have skipped this thankless phase.

'I mean, rather than as a friend,' Siân said. 'Although I like to think we are these days. Friends.'

She looked up from the visitors' chair, an eyebrow raised, all poise and sleek grey hair. Well, yes, they were better friends now than when Siân had been appointed to coordinate a failed diocesan deliverance panel with the psychiatrist, Nigel Saltash. There was almost trust between them now, but it wasn't wise to count on it; a new regime could alter the whole diocesan dynamic.

'Don't look so mutinous, Merrily. Every bishop has a different way of working. Close the door. Come and sit down. Sophie, could we trouble you for coffee?'

Sophie nodded, moved to the dresser by the sink. If anybody ought to look mutinous it was Sophie – losing control, seeming no longer at home here. Merrily closed the door and went to her chair behind the desk in the window but didn't sit down. The chair wasn't in its usual place, and the desk had been moved forward. Siân turned her own chair to face it.

'Do sit down.'

Merrily wanted to move the chair back against the wall under the window. It didn't look right and it didn't feel right when she sat down.

'Bishop Craig's more into delegation than Bernie was,' Siân said. 'Something we all need to get used to.'

'You mean he doesn't like to break unwelcome news personally. To the shop floor.'

'Oh, it's not my idea of unwelcome news. He'd like you to consider accepting the post of Rural Dean for your area.'

'*What?*'

'Area supervisor,' Siân explained, like she needed to. 'More responsibility. More money.'

'Head prefect,' Merrily said.

She felt numb.

'That's rather unfair.' Siân's expression didn't change. 'You could be next in line for my job, if not here, then somewhere…'

Siân's voice faded. Merrily heard traffic trickling down Broad Street. She felt unplugged. Sophie stood frozen at the dresser, her back to them. The room had dimmed, Merrily sensing those gritty black clouds tightening the narrow line of white.

'What about Mark Shriver? Is he leaving?'

'He's relinquishing the post. With a view to retirement in a couple of years. The Bishop sees you as an obvious successor.'

Did that even seem likely?

'Siân, I don't know what to say. He doesn't even know me. The one time we met, it was like I wasn't here.'

'He might give that impression sometimes,' Siân said, 'but I can assure you he makes it very much his business to know everything.'

'Yes. Evidently.'

'He doesn't make these offers without due thought and consultation. He tells me he's recognized your people skills.'

'Huh?'

'The way you've dealt with people facing… critical situations? Isolated people who often find it hard to discuss their problems. Including certain priests. Martin Longbeach always says he wouldn't have come through his crisis without you, and we both know that country parishes…'

'That mostly you can't give them away,' Merrily said.

Siân didn't deny it.

'With several churches each and fluctuating congregations, rural priests are finding it increasingly hard to cope, and it's not likely to get any easier. Making Rural Dean a vital role.'

'And quite a lot of extra work.'

'It's what you make of it.' Siân smiled professionally. 'Have a think about it. I can see you as a very special kind of agony aunt to the clergy of North Herefordshire.'

How patronizing was *that*?

'However…' Merrily took a slow breath. '… with the deliverance work as well…'

Over at the dresser, Sophie clashed crockery.

Siân was silent.

Lol cleaned out the stove, pulled the *Hereford Times* apart and crumpled it, page by page, into the firebox, adding kindling but not setting light to it. It still wasn't that cold.

He sat on the sofa with his mobile, flicked to his contacts list, which actually wasn't all that long. He still didn't have many friends. Or enemies, come to that, give or take the odd psychiatrist.

The phone asked, *Do you want to call this number?*

He hesitated. This really wasn't his business. Jane might well have told her mother all about it, whatever it was.

But, on balance, probably not, and if he didn't do it now he might regret it later. He called the number, and the call was answered very quickly.

'Lol?'

'Sorry, who's—? Oh God, *Eirion*. Must've put your number in by mistake.'

'Oh.'

'Sorry.'

'Well. That… happens. So, um, you OK, Lol?'

'Bit out of it, you know. Most of the summer went on the kind of tour I never thought I'd have the balls to do again. But… it's been an experience. And the way we have to go these days when everybody thinks recorded music should be free.'

'Yes. Well. Good for you, man. You OK, otherwise? Mrs Watkins… Jane?'

'We just had a drink. In the Swan.'

'You and…?'

'Jane.'

'She came back for the weekend?'

'She's back full stop. The dig wound up. You didn't know?'

Pause. The *Hereford Times* was audibly uncrinkling in the open stove.

'No,' Eirion said. 'I haven't seen her in a while. Not since I left the dig. She… to be honest, she hasn't been answering my calls. Don't suppose she's said… anything?'

'You had a row?'

'You know Jane, even if you've had a row she doesn't not answer your calls. You might get an earful of recriminations, but she doesn't not return your calls. All I've had's a couple of short texts. Just conveying the information that she was OK. That everything was fine.'

Fine.

'*Did* you have a row?'

'No. No, we bloody didn't. It was pretty good, out west. Bit rocky at first. Jane had been worried about not fitting in. They're a pretty tight bunch, archaeologists. She was being careful not to, you know, disclose that she'd only become interested in it through earth-mysteries and ley lines and all that embarrassing old hippy stuff.'

'She's said that to me, too. That she was playing it down.'

'I thought she was being overcautious, after that humiliating experience with the TV guys, but it's always best to go along with her. I was a bit worried about leaving her, but she called a couple of days later to say it was fine. She'd been talking to them more, and there were actually other people on the team who thought like her. So that was good.'

'Right.'

'And the other thing… we'd both heard that these archaeo-logical digs were, like, shagfests, but there was none of that that I could see. The guys were quite protective towards Jane. I mean, I might've been worried about coming back to Cardiff, leaving her there with all these… But I wasn't, I…' Eirion's voice failed. 'Come on, Lol, you must know *something*.'

'I don't. Honestly. Something's possibly not right, but I don't know what it is. She's certainly more serious than usual. But that might just be finding herself out in the big world, looking for work.'

'Suppose I came over there. Do you think…? Shit, Lol, I don't know what to do. Am I, like, failing to read the writing on the wall? The big Dear Irene text?'

Lol didn't know what to say.

'When we first… it was like the first time, you know? For both of us. That's not good, is it, these days, the schoolgirl romance that just… carries on? Like you're an old married couple before you're out of your teens. I had mates at school who…'

'Yeah,' Lol said. 'We all had mates like that. Look, you can… you can find the right one at any time, any stage in your life. You can go away and have a string of girlfriends and then look back ten, twenty years later and realize you gave away some-thing special.'

'She *is* special, isn't she?' Eirion seizing on it. 'I mean, she's not easy, she's quite a complex person, she has these mood swings, but… At college you meet loads of women you might once have thought were amazing and…' He broke off. 'Only, I'm *not*. I'm

159

not fucking special at all, am I? Listen, don't even answer that, just… if you find out anything… even it's going to smash the crap out of whatever bit of self-esteem I'm hanging on to…'

'Sure,' Lol said. 'I will. I promise.'

'If this *is* a way of dumping me… it's not Jane. It's not the Jane I thought I knew.'

She'd very deliberately *not* left the Freelander on the Bishop's Palace car park, not wanting to drive out of there aware of doing it for the last time.

Not that it was going to be. Not quite yet. This was more complicated than a simple dismissal. Closer to assisted suicide.

With the day fading fast, she hurried down to the bottom of the car park by the swimming pool, racing the long-threatened rain, but not quite making it. She slammed herself into the driving seat, big drops hitting the windscreen and splattering on impact like hollowpoint bullets from heaven.

She called Huw.

'Subtle,' he said. 'I underestimated him.'

From the bottom corner of the car park she could see lights coming on downstairs in the Bishop's Palace across the river, the sky behind it a smudge of charcoal.

'He's rewarding me,' Merrily said. 'For having done a good job. Enduring for so long something I hadn't wanted in the first place.'

'Who told you that?'

'Sophie. Afterwards.'

Afterwards, Sophie had told her about a new procedure Innes had mentioned almost in passing. In future, all requests for deliverance advice received by Sophie, from the diocesan clergy or the general public, should be referred to the Bishop who would decide whether it was a valid deliverance issue or *something that could be referred elsewhere.*

'Jesus Christ,' Huw said.

'I feel sorry for Sophie, stuck between two…'

'She'll survive. But this is a bit more serious than I thought.'

'Please keep it to yourself. She's not supposed to have told me.'

'So he's rewarding you…'

'For services rendered. And discreetly offering to relieve me of my burden.'

'Ha!'

'Wished this on myself, Huw. All that crap about deliverance having become a touchstone.'

'Don't be so bloody superstitious. This word "burden", that's *his* word? You've never used it, to Sophie or anybody?'

'Not that I recall.'

'He's stitching you up. Just like every rural dean in the country's been stitched up. Your honourable friend, did she tell you how, every time some priest can't take it any more and buggers off back to the city, you've got to make sure his services get covered till he's replaced? Then you get to arrange the installation of the next sucker. That's when you're not talking some other poor isolated bastard down off his church tower. It's a job as gets more depressing every year.'

'Somebody has to do it.'

'Innes is killing two birds wi' one brick, lass. And he can't even say it to your face.'

'He delegates.'

'He goes behind your back! He's shutting the door on you.'

'There's no *licence* for deliverance. It only exists in the shadows. He could just tell me to go.'

'No he can't, and he won't. Not without good reason. You've been conspicuously successful, right from the start. Wasn't for you they'd never've found out about Hunter and the mad, apocalyptic delusions that put him in purple.'

'I've been lucky… and not *that* conspicuous. And Hunter, that was you more than me.'

'Within the Church you've been talked about. At all levels. Happen your card's been marked, I don't know, but I'll find

161

out. Listen. Do nowt. Keep your nose clean. Let me think about this. Don't talk to anybugger till I come back to you tonight.'

'Right,' she said.

She blew her nose.

She wasn't crying. She sat and gazed into the blur of the lights across the river. Rural dean. Why not? Helping new priests fit into the countryside… she could even be good at that. It wasn't that she couldn't use the extra money, especially if Jane went to university next year. Couldn't begin to see it as a step up. Hell, she was never likely to want to replace Siân as Archdeacon. Not her thing, management. No touchstones there.

It was nearly dark. She watched the strange white vapour from the e-cig, like the ectoplasm in old spiritualist photos. She started to laugh, unhealthily, as the phone chimed – damn, damn, damn, *change it.*

'It's Casey. Killow. Mirrily, I'm thinking we never made a firm date. For you to come back.'

'Sorry, I thought I said I'd call you. If I didn't…'

'Can you come tomorrow? When we're all here? Just turn up. I won't tell anybody you're coming.'

'Thing is, Casey, it's the one day of the week when an entire congregation would notice I was missing.'

All seventeen of them, on a good week.

'Oh. Yeah. You're a vicar. Jeez, this place plays tricks with you. Things you'd dismiss as the sheerest lunacy, they come and live with you. Y'know what they used to say about strokes?'

'I'm sorry?' The lights in the palace were smeared across the windscreen. The rain began sluicing the Freelander like a water cannon. Merrily cut the speaker, put the phone to an ear. 'In what context?'

'No, you probably don't. Words become so familiar, people nivver wonder about them. Where they came from. When it happened to Dinnis, I looked up everything I could find in books, the Net… I couldn't sleep afterwards, just lay there looking at bloody Dinnis. Nivver told him. He'd laugh. He always laughs. Listen, ignore me, I'm an hysterical woman, just come soon's you can.'

'It would have to be tomorrow afternoon, I've services in the morning, and I'd need to be back for seven. We do an evening meditation in the church.'

'No, listen, it doesn't matter. I just thought…'

'Is two o'clock OK?'

'You sure?'

'I'm sure.'

'I tell you, Mirrily,' Casey said, 'I don't believe in ghosts. I think we invinted them to explain rational fears we can't deal with – sickness, loneliness, disorientation, what have you. And then they become so real in our heads the bastards might just as well exist. What's the difference?'

'It's a moot point.'

'I didn't ring you, OK? I don't know you're coming.'

'Of course you don't,' Merrily said.

When she drove away, Huw's voice was crackling in her head like the start of a fire. *Do nowt. Keep your nose clean.*

Yeah, right. Like she could, when there were people in this much mental chaos.

26

Good-looking kid situation

IT HAD A name now: Operation Digger. Not particularly clever, but the operational names came down from headquarters, along with a bunch of boffins setting up shop in the major incident room, three floors up.

When Bliss had got home to his semi in Marden on the Hereford plain, the lamps were on, curtains drawn tight, Annie's car parked, as usual, in the next street. Could be that, by now, somebody on the housing estate had twigged that they had more than a professional relationship, but Bliss couldn't imagine anybody grassing him up. Like the woman next door had said once, he was a useful neighbour to have.

When Karen Dowell buzzed Bliss's mobile, the TV was on with the sound down, coming up to the local news. He'd been interviewed about the Greenaway killing by Mandy Patel from local BBC. They were almost mates now, him and Patel.

'We've got them, boss,' Karen said. 'Thought you'd want to know.'

'The parents? Hold on a sec.'

He put the phone on speaker so Annie could hear, laid it on the long coffee table in front of the sofa they were sharing. As DCI, Annie wasn't directly involved in the inquiry, but she'd read all the reports. She'd pick up on the reference points.

'Hotel in Cornwall,' Karen said. 'Late autumn weekend break. They're on the way home now.'

'But you've talked to them?'

'Mainly the dad, Derek Greenaway. Gays are usually closest

to their mums, but not in this case, it seems. Mrs Greenaway was too upset to talk but not as upset, apparently, as when Tris came out. Didn't want anything to do with him for a few years. They'd not long been back on speaking terms. His dad said she was convinced he'd come round sooner or later.'

'What, find a nice girl and raise a family?'

'Be funny if it wasn't so sad.'

'Only child, is he?'

'No, there's a married sister, also living in Evesham, which is why Mum and Dad moved over there when he took early retirement from the council. New grandchildren, far more acceptable. Anyway, about half an hour after I'd spoken to him, Derek Greenaway rang back. On his own, from a corner of the hotel bar.'

'Good of him.'

'I think it helped him unload stuff he couldn't talk about with his wife. He's a former environment health officer with Herefordshire Council, but I don't remember him myself. Anyway, we had quite a long and productive chat, and that's why I'm calling you. He was concerned to know what line of inquiry we were following. His wife – once the shock had worn off, she was worried there might be something, you know, *sordid*?'

'Perish the thought, Karen.'

'You do have to be of a certain generation for that word to be appropriate any more. Mr Greenaway says that, whatever comes out, he doesn't want his son portrayed as some promiscuous good-time boy, because it isn't that simple.'

'Like he'd know.'

'He described Tristram as being a disappointment to himself? Always disappointed that his life wasn't delivering what it should. It's like a good-looking kid situation?'

'I wouldn't know anything about that.' Bliss flashed a glance at Annie, grinned. 'I was always a weird-looking kid.'

'I had a cousin like that,' Karen said. 'Beautiful kids, people fawn over them, and by the time they're sixteen or so they think that's all you need. That and being good at sport, which Greenaway was as well, according to his dad. My cousin, the rest of us just got consolation prizes for not being him. He went from job to job, married three times. Where is he now? I don't know. Anyway, I digress. Sorry.'

Annie was shaking her head, maybe a little sadly. She was the ice queen of Gaol Street, nobody rambled on to her like that. Nobody ever felt sorry for Annie, Bliss thought. Maybe they would if they knew.

Karen was saying that Tristram Greenaway seemed to have grown up with not so much ambition as expectation, leaving university with an undistinguished archaeology degree, but what did that matter if you had the looks?

'It really never occurred to him he wasn't going to be a star like one of these guys on *Time Team* and *Trench One* and write bestselling books that were like mainly pictures of him looking devastatingly handsome in a hole in the ground.'

'Ugly as sin, some of those *Time Team* fellers, Karen. Part of their appeal.'

'Yeah, well, you know what I'm saying.'

Greenaway had had some good jobs, Karen said, but never seemed to keep them. It was always going to be the next big thing. He was once employed on something screened on the History Channel, with a hint that he might wind up presenting. Bought a house at the top of the market, only to have it repossessed when the show got taken off after one season.

Bottom line: his dad had been secretly bailing him out for a couple of years, and always looking out for him. When the job came up in Hereford. Derek Greenaway heard about it from one of his old mates on the council.

'You're saying his old man got him that job?'

'I don't know. Might just have been a question of Tris having local knowledge from growing up in the area. But he got it and he came back to Hereford, the old hometown. But then... it turned out to be another one like the TV job that didn't pan out as expected. Boss, I'm thinking there are some things Neil Cooper didn't tell you.'

'Go on.'

'Greenaway took the temp post with every reason to believe he'd get Cooper's present job when Cooper was promoted after…' Sound of Karen leafing through notes '… Des—?'

'Des Walters. Expected to get an early-retirement deal.'

'That's the guy. OK. The last time Tristram Greenaway talked to his dad, right? On the phone. Couple of nights before he died. Obviously been drinking and he's terribly upset. Get this…'

Bliss and Annie instinctively closing in on the phone to hear how Greenaway had told Derek what a mistake it had been coming back to Hereford, a town of losers. Telling his dad he was getting out forever this time, because he'd been double-crossed. Been assured that Des Walters was already history, so when Cooper told him Walters was coming back after all…'

'He sounds a bloody sight more upset than he apparently sounded when he talked to Jane Watkins. I reckon he's telling his dad what he thinks he wants to hear, don't you? His old man got him the job with the council, but he still wants to be on TV. Bit of a performer, Tris, don't you think? Still, let's talk to Cooper again, see what else we can uncover. Sit tight, Karen, you're playing a blinder on this one, and I'm gonna make sure the right people know about it.'

'Who, Annie Howe?' Karen's laughter distorting in the phone. 'You think Annie Howe will help reboot my career?'

'Hang on, I think that's me doorbell, I'd better…' Bliss didn't look at Annie. 'Thank you, Karen. Ta very much. We'll discuss the implications at length first thing tomorrow.'

Ending the call and switching off the phone, just to be sure.

'You mean bastard,' Annie said. 'How many opportunities does anyone get to listen to somebody diminishing them behind their back?'

'Didn't want you to get big-headed, Annie. You've always been an icon to that girl. Admires you as a police officer…' Bliss dodging the flying cushion. '… and as a woman. Now just let me think about this.'

They caught the local TV piece on the Greenaway murder. It didn't delay them long.

'A read,' Bliss said disgusted, switching off the set. 'A friggin' *read*. Murder in Birmingham, two minutes plus. Murder in Hereford, fifteen friggin' seconds over a clip of the Plas.'

'When Charlie's Police and Crime Commissioner,' Annie said quietly, 'the Hereford profile will rise accordingly. Sorry. Remind me, how does that phone call from Greenaway senior change things?'

'Well, he's mad at Cooper. Who he now sees as having led him along, maybe deterring him from applying for other jobs he might even have got. And then shafting him.'

'Cooper *didn't* shaft him.'

'All right then, he's blaming the messenger. Either way, we now know Greenaway was seriously pissed off, and that gives us a reason for him lifting Cooper's skull. If only out of pique. *He* gets the elbow and Cooper gets his name in the annals for discovering the first deviant burial in the county.'

'Deviant burial,' Annie said. 'You really like that phrase, don't you?'

'Actually, I do. It sounds like an offence against common decency. "You stand accused of deviant burial".'

'It's not a terrific claim to fame, though, is it? Finding an ancient corpse with its head between its legs.'

'I don't know. And how rational was Greenaway at the time? Was he actually pissed when Cooper rang him up and asked him to come and help out on Castle Green?'

Annie stood up and went to switch off the standard lamp he'd bought in a junk shop to replace the one Kirsty had come back for within a week of leaving him. Now the room was reduced to soft orange from the small table lamp Annie had brought over from Malvern. She came back to the sofa, the light softening her skin.

'So – OK – what's your premise?'

'OK, here's the case for Cooper as the killer. He puts two and two together as regards the skull. He's furious. Goes round to Greenaway's place, says "gimme…" And one thing leads to another. Possible. Both of them are angry now, and no easy way it's going to be resolved. Most murders are not premeditated. Lots of them are over something that appears completely trivial.'

'But when you see the pictures of Greenaway's face… That's extreme rage, Francis.'

'Yeh. That doesn't fit Cooper at all. How about the weapon? Can we afford to dip into the Wye?'

'Where? It's a very long river. OK if he just walked across the road and tossed it in, but…'

'And a lorra silt down there.'

'What about the skull itself? I presume we've been looking for that?'

'Could be in the river too, for all we know.'

Annie was nodding at the phone.

'You realize you've disappointed her again.'

'Karen?'

'She still fancies you, doesn't she?'

'Gerroff.'

'Ringing at night, thinking you might like to go round to her place and discuss the case. Or invite her here.'

'I don't think so.' Bliss shook his head. 'Despite being younger, I've always thought Karen's feelings for me were verging on the maternal.'

'Francis, you don't understand the first thing about women.'

'And don't women love to say that.'

Bliss looked at Annie and she looked back at him. She wasn't wearing the stripy sweater and it wasn't Christmas.

Never mind. He pushed her gently down on the sofa, his right hand sliding under her skirt. Annie shuddered.

Police work. Always underrated as an aphrodisiac.

27

Cunning

JANE HAD LIT a fire, was sitting on the edge of the inglenook in the parlour, listening to music through headphones. Taking them off as Merrily came in.

'Don't let me—'

'No, no, I like interrupting her.'

'Who is it?'

'Laura Marling. Bit smug. Like she knows how good she is. I mean, knowing it is one thing, but *showing* you know it… Lol doesn't. Ever.'

'Maybe that's where he's been going wrong all these years.' Merrily flopped into the sofa, hadn't realized how bone-tired she was. 'I thought… that you'd be seeing Eirion.'

Shouldn't have said that, though she still wasn't sure why. Jane's glance was like broken glass.

'You been talking to Lol?'

'Not since last night. Why?'

'Doesn't matter.'

Oh, hell…

'I may have asked you this before, Jane but *did* something go wrong in Pembrokeshire? Something you haven't told me about.'

'Look.' Jane leaned over and ejected Laura Marling. 'I'm just a bit uncertain about some things. Like digging up the past only to bury it again. What's the point?'

'Unless it's bodies, flower. Bodies should be reburied.'

This wasn't the problem. This was a familiar Jane diversion –

not turning off, just slipping into a parallel lane and you ended up following.

'I can probably think of a full counter-argument,' Merrily said, 'but right now I'm too tired.'

'It just gives *experts* another opening to dream up another unprovable theory about the way people lived or worshipped or whatever. Which always gets discredited within a couple of years by somebody else looking for a book or an academic paper or a bloody grant. We're knee-deep in discarded theories.'

'All adds to the sum of human knowledge. From which we can draw... occasional threads of sense.'

Merrily leaned back into a corner of the sofa, eyes closing. Do *not* be tempted to tell Jane about being offered the post of Rural Dean. Jane would remember how many times her mother had rubbished the race for promotion within the Church. *If this is about money*, Jane would say, *then I'll just forget about university. No problem.* So don't mention it, just quietly turn it down.

And yet... if she turned it down it was unlikely she'd be offered anything again, just awarded more parishes with churches frequented only by sporadic tourists. And would still lose deliverance. If Innes had already decided to dump her this was hardly going to change his mind.

'Neil Cooper's not rung,' Jane said. 'His assistant was murdered, did you know about that?'

Merrily opened her eyes.

'This is the guy who was found at his home, down near the Plascarreg? He worked with Neil Cooper?'

'You knew about that?'

'Heard it on the car radio. They didn't say who he was or what he did.'

'I met him. The day he was killed.'

'*You* did?'

Merrily sat up. Jane told her about the guy who'd insisted on escorting her to Cooper. And about Bliss and Lol in the Black Swan.

'Bliss came here in the middle of a murder inquiry just to talk to you? Why don't I like the sound of that?'

'Lol thinks he came out because he wanted to talk to you. He thought you'd be here. I was just the excuse.'

'Then why didn't he just ring?'

'I've no idea.'

Merrily thinking back to when she was Jane's age. When she thought she wanted to be a lawyer, to get justice for people. Instead, she'd got pregnant and wound up marrying a man whose idea of the law didn't have a lot to do with justice. Would she ever have ended up in the Church if she hadn't felt irredeemably soiled by Sean and his clients? The truth was: probably not. And the awful mixed emotions when Sean's car had piled into a motorway bridge, Sean and girlfriend dead. She'd felt worse about the girlfriend.

'What are you going to do if Neil Cooper doesn't find you anything?'

'I don't know.'

'I mean, not that you have to do anything. You haven't had a holiday, and if Eirion—'

She stopped. Jane was avoiding her eyes.

'We haven't split up, OK? We both just have a lot to think about. He's also working. Weekends, he goes into the *South Wales Echo*. Probably something his dad wangled.'

'I see.'

She didn't, but don't push it. She'd been very young when Sean had died, had thought she should suffer for her feelings: get thee to a nunnery. Not quite so extreme, but she hadn't slept properly for weeks. At that age, emotions ruled, way above reason.

What she said next came out without much forethought.

'Flower, look, how would you— I don't want this to sound patronizing or anything because it isn't, but how would you feel about helping me?'

Jane switched off the stereo.

'Do a couple of funerals? I could probably handle that.'

'Even more exciting... bit of research? In relation to Cwmarrow Castle. Cwmarrow Court.'

It was the only time since she'd come back home that Jane had seemed animated. Looking across the valley at a medieval castle she hadn't known existed. *What is... that?*

'What are you looking for?'

'Who lived there over the years? What happened to the village that used to be there? Anything you can find out, really. Anything that looks, you know, anomalous. You know the kind of thing, by now.'

Jane was looking mildly diverted, which meant she was very interested.

'Why? Can you tell me? In confidence?'

'It's a possibly aggressive poltergeist situation. And there are other problems. The guy there is recovering from a stroke, his wife's clearly very worried about him having another. He loves the house, she's afraid it could kill him, however irrational that might seem. And I know from experience that it's not irrational at all when you're in the middle of it.'

'These are the Muslims?'

'No, these are the in-laws. I haven't met the Muslims yet.'

'You still haven't told the Bishop?'

'I suspect if I did, he'd tell me not to get involved and have someone contact the imam to discuss the politics of the situation. And nothing would get done, and—'

'So you're carrying on with this... doing a foreigner. Extra mural. Clandestine.'

'If you like.'

'Good,' Jane said. 'Excellent.'

'I'm pretty sure there are things I don't know, because you never get told everything – that is, there are things they're probably not telling me – personal things. And other things *they* don't know, which we might be able to uncover.'

Jane leaned back.

'I'm guessing this won't involve remuneration.'

'Your guess is inspired, flower.'

'OK,' Jane said. 'If I'm not getting paid, it won't exactly be patronizing, will it? All right, why not? Makes me feel *kind of* employed. Anything else?'

'There's a man called Selwyn Kindley-Pryce.'

'The folklorist?'

'You've heard of him? I hadn't.'

'You read the wrong books, vicar. He was more of a historian, really. I think he was a history professor somewhere, but he also collected folklore and he wrote books. One was just called *The Cunning*.'

Merrily shook her head. Never heard of it.

'I haven't got a copy,' Jane said. 'Too expensive, even if I'd wanted one. It's like huge and scholarly. By which I mean tedious. They have one in Hereford Library and only the title looked readable. You're saying he had some connection with Cwmarrow?'

'He lived there.'

'Wow. I didn't know *that*. I didn't even know he was from this area. Wouldn't've shoved it back on the shelf so fast. It's a study of folk magic and healing in Britain. Which makes it sound more interesting than it looks. I mean, academically, it was probably the definitive work on the subject, but you wouldn't want to plough through it and get bogged down in all the footnotes and references and appendices and glossaries and stuff.'

'So the title, *The Cunning*, that's cunning folk?'

'Community wizards, hedge witches. Local healers and clairvoyants. I didn't realize there were so many. Up to last century, even. Hundreds of them. The book just looked like a mass of contemporary accounts. Academic, very dull.'

'Except I don't think he was. He was described to me as a storyteller. Loved to tell stories. Toured schools, that kind of thing. And, in later years, wrote children's books with a partner, girlfriend… Caroline…? Can't remember, but the books were written under the name Foxy… something.'

Jane sat up in the sofa.

'Rowlestone?'

'You've come across them? See, I didn't think you had.'

'Because you always monitored what I was reading, which was quite annoying.'

'I thought of it as taking an interest.'

'Bloody hell,' Jane said. 'Foxy Rowlestone. No I never read any. Not even as an impressionable child. Some of the other kids at school did. Before we came down here. It was a bit of a cult thing. Not for very long, because I think it finished after a couple of books. Imagine if Harry Potter had packed in after two books. Might've been forgotten now. But, yeah, very cool for a while.'

'But you were above all that?'

Jane smiled, shaking her head.

'I was about twelve. They'd probably been around a while by then. You know why I didn't go near them? Because I'd found those old pictures of you in your black-lipstick years.'

'It was actually my black-lipstick six months. I was about fifteen.'

'Don't try and squirm out of it, you were a horrible little post-punk with a vampire fetish.'

'Fetish is entirely the wrong word.'

'Anyway, that's why I avoided the Foxy Rowlestone books. There was a girl on the front of one actually looked a bit like you, in a black dress and a cloak. They were like Anne Rice for pubescent kids. Sexy vampires.'

'And set in this area?'

'Not that I recall from the odd copy I flipped through, though we were still up north so I wouldn't've noticed. Actually, I think they were set in one of those mythical places. I know the series ended suddenly, and some of my mates – Michelle, you remember Michelle? – she was quite hacked off to find there weren't any more. I mean, I'd guess they sold pretty well. But then there were the Twilight books and all that stuff to help them get over it. We never run out of vampires, do we?'

'*We?*'

'Well, not me, as you know. Too sophisticated. Vampires are just literary creations from the nineteenth century. I could see that, even then. Interesting, though, all this bollocks coming out of the Golden Valley.'

Merrily told her what she knew about Cwmarrow Court, the village that disappeared, the clink of the blacksmith's hammer in the morning.

'I like that,' Jane said. 'You get these tales of villages in Wales that vanished under the sea and you still hear the church bells ringing when there's a storm. Actually, lost villages in Herefordshire, that's not so unusual either. Just like humps in the ground where there used to be buildings. When are you going again?'

'Tomorrow afternoon.'

'I come along?'

'Well, I'm not sure they'd—'

'No, I mean drop me off before you get to the house, and I'll wander round the valley, maybe check out the castle. I'd like that. They don't have to know I'm even there.'

'I'll think about it. Oh, and there's something else you could look into if you get a chance.'

'You haven't eaten, have you?' Jane said. 'Should I make something? Or if you want to go and spend the night with Lol – I mean *all* night – that's no problem.'

'No, I—'

'Don't go all embarrassed on me, Mum. It was me who wanted it to happen, long before either of you…'

'I know. I'm sorry. Anyway, it's Sunday tomorrow. Early shift.'

Perhaps this was stupid but it felt wrong leaving Lol's bed before first light, creeping back to the vicarage and then off to church for Holy Communion. At the same time, she felt guilty about neglecting Lol, back home for the winter, only to become the recipient of her angst. Putting on her glitter for him, for dinner, and they'd wound up sharing a sandwich. Last night she'd probably looked old. Too old for him, now he'd beaten his past and could face an audience. Oh God.

'Tell you what, flower, if we eat healthy all next week as penance, why don't you go to the chippy?'

'What was the other thing? The thing you wanted me to check out.'

'Strokes.'

'Strokes? You mean like…?'

'High blood pressure. Paralysis. Something Casey Kellow said. I can explain later.'

'They do beanburgers now,' Jane said. 'At the chippy.'

Sunday tomorrow, and she didn't have a sermon. Some parish priests, it was an organized chore; they kept sermon files on their computers, would recycle them, making subtle alterations, preserving the central theme inside a different framework. Others beat their heads on the laptop: what can I talk about that I haven't mentioned yet this year? Going through the news-papers like a desperate columnist, searching for something to be reassuring about.

They'd eaten the beanburgers and chips in front of the fire and Jane had gone up to her apartment in the attic to trawl the Net and her library of weird, second-hand books. Merrily had gone into the scullery where it was too cold to fall asleep, to put together a sermon and wait for Huw. *Don't talk to anybugger till I come back to you tonight.*

She was remembering what Huw had said about Innes and his precocious skills as a preacher. She hated preaching. The Holy Spirit channelled through the minister. How dangerous was it for a priest to assume that what was coming out was God-given wisdom?

The words *Cunning People* were on the screen. From the days when cunning was more about native skills than slyness. The parish priests would have known about the cunning people.

Perhaps some of them had *been* the parish priests. On either side of Offa's Dyke, Christianity and paganism had lain side by side for centuries. Which, she saw now, was no bad thing. Compared with places like East Anglia, there seemed to have been remarkably few witch trials along the Welsh border.

There probably was a reasonable sermon here, about the tradition, in this area, of tolerance, a virtue of increasing importance in an age of polarized fanaticism.

She hit the keys.

By half past ten, she'd more or less nailed it. The print on the screen was starting to swim. The e-cig had run out of fluid. Ethel was under the desk, between her ankles, dropping hints about food. Huw had not rung and she needed sleep. She went to feed Ethel in the kitchen, then rang Huw's machine – by this time of night, it was nearly always the machine. She left a message suggesting they talk tomorrow night, saying she was tired, probably couldn't think straight.

'Time is it, lass?' Huw said.

'Oh.' Hadn't heard him pick up, as usual. Perhaps he always picked up. 'Coming up to eleven.'

'Didn't realize it were that late. I should've called. It were just I thought I'd phone Jenny Roberts.'

'Sorry?'

'Just came into my head to ring Jenny Roberts. Always meant to ring her, see if she were all right. See if I could help. But time passes and you neglect things.'

'Jenny Roberts?'

'Oh aye, I didn't call her that. No need for anonymity now. Ann Evans, did I call her that? Happen I wouldn't've rung her at all if Innes showing up in Hereford hadn't brought it all to mind again. Why couldn't the bugger've shown up sooner?'

'What?'

'Discontinued line. I rang the local rector – different one now. Told me Jenny Roberts were dead. Died two months ago. Found in the Usk at Newport. When the tide went out. Tidal river, the Usk. Happen thought she'd be washed out to sea, never found.'

'Oh God.'

'Her body were in the mud, near the city centre. Couldn't've been more public. Didn't make much in the local papers and nobody told me. But then, no reason why they should.'

28

Smashed faces

USUALLY, THE BRILLIANCE that flashed up in the night was just worthless dream-residue. Bliss knew that, but it still wouldn't let him get back to sleep. Annie was breathing evenly, like all was right with the world, when he slid out of bed. Picking up his phone from the bedside rug, creeping off with it to the bathroom.

Sometime in the early hours this was. He hadn't bothered to check. He sat on the bog's closed lid in his briefs and his slippers and brought up on the phone the picture from Greenaway's lappie. The skull grinned raggedly out of his hand. All skulls grinned. They got the joke about death.

Which never seemed all that far away in the hours before dawn, when time was like a closed telescope. Only moments, in the great schemes of things, since the skull had had flesh and skin and eyes. Before they were smashed in.

Like Tristram Greenaway's. *Beautiful kids, people fawn over them*, Karen said.

Somebody had ripped into Greenaway's meal-ticket face with the claw end of a hammer, or similar. *Could* have been the result of an escalating row over a job, maybe with some X-factor to heat it up. But the damage still suggested malice or envy or rage or bitterness. Somebody whose boyfriend he'd pinched. Or someone who thought – unlike Greenaway himself – that his looks had got him too much too soon. *No more, Tris. Sorry, pal, you're going out looking like a butcher's slab.*

'Warrabout you then, son?' Bliss murmured to the gappy, ruined grin. 'They have claw-hammers in your day?'

This was the face he'd been seeing when he awoke – the dream-residue – with the brilliant idea that he should show it to Billy Grace. Email him the picture. *Just out of interest, Billy, knowing how you like something a bit different. What happened to this feller?*

Two smashed faces eight hundred or so years apart.

someone we all hoped to meet one day has turned up

'You? Why would anyone want to meet you, Steve?'

Bliss had taken to calling him Steve. Steve Skull.

'Cos you're deviant, pal. They had you down as a vampire. They buried you with a stone in your gob to stop you chewing your shroud.'

Shrouds must've been different in those days, more like body bags. Bliss stood up, went over to the window with its view across the darkened estate to grey fields, middle-distant hills. No visible lights.

Not such a brilliant idea at all, really. He went back to the lavvie, sat down with the phone and looked up Billy Grace's email address. Wrote Billy a brief note, saying he'd give him a bell later, if that was all right. Attached the picture and sent it. Nothing lost, except some sleep.

He was about to switch off the phone when a little red thingy signalled a new email, timed 23.35.

Karen Dowell.

Got them. Neogoth.
I'll feed it into the machine first
thing tomorrow, but thought I'd
tell you first.
All closer than you'd think.

It was, too. Bliss smiled. A new direction for tomorrow. Real old-style cop, Karen, in spite of being not yet thirty-five. Didn't turn off when she went home.

Or maybe it was just that she was between boyfriends.

... still fancies you, doesn't she? Annie had never said anything like that before.

He crept back into the bedroom, stood listening to her steady breathing. Could be she'd taken a sleeping pill; she'd admitted once that she used to take them occasionally, without explaining what used to keep her awake.

Charlie?

She hadn't known what Charlie was when she'd joined the force. Well, you wouldn't, would you? Not your own dad, a good man whose race through the ranks in the days before fast-track had been nothing at all to do with his weekly night out at the Masonic hall. A good man who'd be unlikely to boast to his daughter about covering up for a wealthy killer.

Bliss felt the damp and the cold of the night he'd faced-up Charlie in front of Charlie's house and come off worst.

Go home, boy. Go back to Liverpool or wherever it was you crawled from... You got no friends...

Charlie had friends. Charlie always had the right friends.

Bliss stood in the dark, dog-tired and wide awake, wondering where Annie kept her sleeping pills.

29

Rambling in the night

PLEASE. WHISPERING. GET this over.

Cold. Merrily aware of wearing what she wore in bed, the long T-shirt, only even longer and white as a shroud. She felt very small, and the piercing smell of church polish was a thin wire in her nose.

Unknown churches at night, unlit, were seldom welcoming, even to a priest. She most certainly didn't want to be here. She stood behind the back pews, keeping the doors in view. The polish smell gave way to the mould of old vestments.

Smells in dreams – did that happen?

This is a lucid dream, a voice murmured.

Jane used to talk about lucid dreams, how she'd tried to induce them but it never worked. In a lucid dream, you knew you were dreaming and you could direct the outcome.

Your duty to stay, Jane whispered. *See this through.*

But it was not Jane's voice. Why had she thought that?

Let this be over, let this be over, let this be…

A hiss came back in reply, a thin wind from the cavern of shadow that was the chancel behind its knotty rood screen. She felt the hiss on her face, personal and contemptuous. Wanted so much to be out of here. But dreams of this kind always demanded commitment. You were part of a cycle.

There was a moment of silence then a hideous grinding, the *thock* of something dislodging, springing free and then – *oh God, oh, God, oh God* – directly in front of her, huge as the prow

183

of a wooden ship on a stormy sea at night, the great Victorian pulpit rose out of the well of the nave.

Filling her with the level of primeval horror that, once you'd grown up, you rarely felt outside of dreams. Tried to back away, but couldn't feel her feet, could only stare at a mauvish mist above the pulpit, watching it gradually taking the form of a man. He had no face, but his hands were in hard focus, arthritically twisted, knuckles swollen, gripping the pulpit's rim. She knew what would happen next and, as soon as she knew it, it began, one gnarled hand unlocking from the pulpit, rising in a ratchety way, like in an early film, frame by frame, a forefinger extending to point steadily at the centre of her—

She awoke with the scream trapped in her throat.

In the half-lit kitchen, where the clock said five-fifteen, she sat in her tatty dressing gown and drank tea, Ethel watching from her fleecy bed near the wood-stove with its faint pinky ashes. The windows were black.

She was thinking of Huw Owen, and how much this was going to damage him.

Always meant to ring her, see if she were all right... But time passes and you neglect things.

Women and suicide. You only learned about Huw's personal history when circumstances compelled him to tell you. Like his relationship with a woman called Julia. A late flowering. They might have married had she not taken her own life. Not because of anything Huw had done or failed to do, but that didn't make it any better. He hadn't seen it coming. That, to someone like Huw, was neglect.

When the kitchen door opened she twisted round, and Jane stood there, hazy with the hall light behind her, like a dream figure in her blue towelling robe. She was carrying her iPad and the old-fashioned wooden clipboard she still used to make notes on.

'Sorry, flower, did I wake you?'

'Wasn't really asleep. Heard you coming down and you didn't come back up, so…'

'I did look in to say goodnight. Didn't I?'

'Doesn't matter if you didn't. You've obviously got a lot on your mind.' Jane opened up the wood-stove and threw in some brittle twigs from the basket. 'We're not going back upstairs, are we?'

'Only to get dressed, in my case. Holy Communion in under three hours.'

The twigs flared in the stove. Jane stood with her back to it.

'Just I wanted to catch you before you left. That village, Cwmarrow. It seems to have died in about the thirteenth century. Or before.'

'Died?'

'Most of it's in *The Buildings of Herefordshire*. It seems to have been quite a big village in the Middle Ages. Like Ledwardine was a town back then. Cwmarrow was never that big, but it was a definite community. And then it was abandoned. Could've been plague, that's the speculation.'

'Let me get you some tea.' Merrily stood up. 'What about the castle?'

Jane said the castle had been active, until about the fourteenth century, when some castles started to become domesticated, turned into homes rather than fortresses. Not this one. It was a fortress that turned into a ruin.

'The Court was probably a farm from the beginning, providing meat and stuff for the castle and then the village, when it was there. It grew up again, to an extent, but it never really came back.'

'And why was that? Any idea?' Merrily brought the teapot to the table, with a mug for Jane. 'Is it a bit early for toast?'

'I don't feel hungry.'

'Nor me.'

'There's really not much about it at all,' Jane said, 'even on the Net. Quite a few medieval villages have just disappeared. It's surprising how quickly walls collapse and stone foundations get overgrown. Be interesting to have an excavation at Cwmarrow. Geofizz, ground radar. You could probably map out the whole village. I'd like to look.'

'Sure. Why not.'

Be good to have Jane there, it really would. She was so grateful to Jane for coming down, lighting up the stove, leading her out of the ambience of that clinging paranoid dream.

'The Golden Valley's still largely unknown,' Jane said. 'Unvisited. A few miles west and it'd be in the Brecon Beacons National Park. Tell tourists somewhere's a national park and they're all over it.'

'In the shadow of the National Park. There's a film – *Shadowlands*. About C.S. Lewis – Narnia?'

Jane nodded.

'The film was about his last holiday with his sick wife – in the Golden Valley. Too sad for me, flower.'

'The whole area has a little-known history of connections with writers on the surreal and the bizarre. Guy who wrote *Alice in Wonderland*?'

'Lewis Carroll.'

'His brother was the vicar of Vowchurch, so the chances are he came here. Probably picking up some of his ideas. I wouldn't know. Didn't really get on with that book. And there was M.R. James, of course, at Kilpeck and Abbey Dore and… Garway.'

'And there was Selwyn Kindley-Pryce.'

'Also sad,' Jane said. 'Well, at the end. It was happy at first. He was in his element.'

Jane talked about an academic, but also a poet and a romantic. Moderate distinction at Oxford and then professorships at American universities. Well received books, an accumulation of money, and then Pryce returned to England in late middle-age to realize a dream.

Dreams. What attention, if any, were you, as an exorcist, supposed to pay to dreams? The crack of unholy light under the door. When did you put a foot in the door?

Not a problem that need concern a rural dean.

Merrily expelled a cloud of pale vapour and the e-cig glowed green.

'You're sticking with it then?' Jane said.

'What?'

'The e-cig. I mean, really, don't feel obliged. I hate the thought of coming over as, you know, holier than… even holier than thou.'

'You?'

'*Pious.* You always hated that word. I always remember that, from when we first came here. You were like, I *never* want to be pious.'

'It was embarrassing,' Merrily said. 'Determined to be a *new vicar.*'

The flames leapt behind the stove glass and sent a warm flush to Jane's face.

'All those bitter rows. Horrible. I can hardly bear to think about all that now. I just… so totally hated you being a vicar. Dad dead, and you… I was a little shit.'

'A little shit and a pious bitch,' Merrily said. 'Those were the days.'

Remembering when they were sharing a room at the Black Swan, before they moved in here, and she was murmuring her morning prayers at the window, Jane going. *Do you really have to do that in here?*

She looked up, and Jane's eyes were glassy with tears.

'It's weird, Mum. I don't want… change any more. Suddenly, I'm frightened of it. I bought those e-cigs for you and Gomer because I wanted you to, you know, live forever? Like, I realize I'm going to have to leave here at some stage, but I always want to think I can come back and it'll be just like it was.'

Merrily blinked.

'God's sake, Jane, tell me about Kindley-Pryce.'

Jane was pouring herself more tea.

She'd started with Wikipedia.

'A lot of pretty dry stuff there. Like his books. He called himself an anthropologist, which I guess is not as boring as it sounds. But that's, like, the story of his life. The first part of it was boring, but when he came back from America he was a different man.'

'When was this?'

'Nineteen nineties? His wife had died – his second wife, older than him. His first marriage in England ended in divorce. One son. The second wife was from a wealthy Californian family and she'd financed his studies. He collected quite a lot when she went, and he seemed to have decided to make a new start and came back to England and bought Cwmarrow Court... which was falling down, is that right?'

'Close to derelict.'

'Described in Wikipedia as Pryce's folly. He'd just, like, fallen in love with it, and most of his money went on making it fit to live in. When the cash began to run out, he started holding events there. Music and lectures. Kind of upmarket – string quartet stuff. And also traditional folk-singers and fiddlers and all that. And they'd play and he'd tell his stories. There was an article about him in the *Guardian*, which had a quote about him that said...' Jane consulted the printouts and notes in her clipboard. 'Kindley-Pryce claims his discovery of oral traditions has liberated him from the straitjacket of academia. "It's brought me alive," he says. "Even in my advancing years."'

'Sounds like a bucolic idyll.'

'This is him.'

Jane opened up the iPad, brought up a photograph of a man with a face like a brown egg. Either shaven-headed or completely bald. Eyes heavy-lidded as if they were looking down at his own minuscule smile.

'So he had this new girlfriend,' Jane said. 'Caroline Goddard, children's writer, and they created Foxy Rowlestone. I haven't downloaded any of the books yet. I thought I'd see if the bookshop had any.'

'You never know. I'll give you some money.'

'They did OK, those books. A cult following, according to Wiki. But there were only a couple before Pryce and Goddard split. I found some pictures of her. Much younger than him. And then she goes and leaves him, and things are like downhill all the way.'

'Dementia?'

'Horrible,' Jane said.

'Mmm. With the demented, they say that the oldest memories are the last to die. But how can anyone really know? No cure. They don't come back to talk about it.'

Jane said, 'You think his mind, like, vanished into… not so much his own past as the place's past?'

Merrily shook her head, non-committal.

'Can a storyteller's mind disappear into a world of his own imagination?

'Creepy, Mum.'

'Yes.'

Jane pulled a smile together.

'And while we're talking creepy… the other thing you asked me to look up. Strokes?'

'Oh, yeah. I forgot.'

'You won't now,' Jane said. 'Not ever. Stay there.'

She went upstairs, came down with a very old paperback, flopped open on its much-split spine.

'This is just in case you think I'm making it up.'

Pushing the book in front of Merrily. The print was tiny. In this light, she could make out about every third word.

'I keep putting it off, flower. The sin of vanity.'

'New reading glasses?'

'I'll pick up a pair at a chemist's tomorrow. Today. Can't afford—' She bit off the rest about not being able to afford a proper session with an optician and pushed the book back to Jane. 'Would you mind reading it out? Feel free to paraphrase.'

Jane lifted up the book. The cover print was easier: *Katharine Briggs. A Dictionary of Fairies.* Merrily looked at Jane.

'Really?'

'Just a medical term now, for a seizure that leaves part of you paralysed. There's probably a long name for it somewhere, but nobody uses it.' Jane sat down. 'Funny thing, I've started to envy you lately. Who else has a job which allows them to delve into this stuff with a real sense of purpose?'

'Go on.'

'The word 'stroke' actually derives directly from British and Irish folklore and means exactly what it sounds like. *Fairy-stroke? Elf-stroke?*'

'Never heard that.'

'Basically, some unsuspecting human being wanders into a fairy realm – fairy glade, whatever – and the fairies don't like it. Bastards never do. They despise us. So a miffed fairy might put out a glowing finger and stroke the intruder on the side of the head – or anywhere else – and that part of the body immediately becomes like numbed?'

'That is… *really* where it came from?'

'I didn't believe it either.'

'Blimey.' Merrily recalled Casey Kellow on the phone. *Things you'd dismiss as the sheerest lunacy, they come and live with you.* 'You don't think, do you?'

'These old beliefs,' Jane said, 'they're still with us. They're like burned into our ethos. It's all there underneath, just mutates into something that thinks of itself as science.'

Jane's expression was almost one of defiance. Merrily's mouth was dry. Fairy tales. Invented to send children happily to sleep.

She stood up and walked over to the biggest window. A line of purple made the sky look like a Victorian coffin lining.

What is it, then? Casey Kellow had said. *What is it if not an act of violence?*

The line of purple was in the wrong place. There was no spark of dawn.

Part Three

O you who talk so much, instead of so much talking beat
your head and search the secrets…

Farid ud-Din Attar
The Conference of the Birds
(trans. C.S. Nott, 1954)

30

Dark Net stuff

IT WAS THE only remaining shop in a cramped little dirty-brick square called, for no apparent reason, Organ Yard, and its contents spilled out like an old-fashioned eviction on the patchwork of concrete and cobbles. The second-hand stuff, this was: rugs and dark-stained furniture from abandoned churches and chapels. Nice and sad on an autumn Sunday morning.

The shop had a wooden sign swinging from a wrought iron bracket, peeling gilt lettering – probably always been peeling – on matt black.

It said, *The Darkest Corner*

Made Bliss realize all over again what a small city Hereford was. Small but still secretive. It had surely taken him less than five minutes to walk over here from Gaol Street, down an alleyway from Commercial Road, past some shabby warehouses with a view across to the backstreet ruins of the Blackfriars monastery.

Walking inside, out of the light, Bliss remembered suggesting to Neil Cooper that his missing skull might turn up with a cig in its mouldering teeth at some Hallowe'en party.

Or somewhere like this shithole.

As it happened, a human skull was on the counter. Plastic but realistic. You had to look twice, especially in the dim light from a hanging lamp of dirty glass. Bliss tapped a fingernail on the pitted cranium.

'Has a look of you, Jerry.'

In the dimness behind the counter, Jerry Soffley smiled his diagonal smile. He hadn't changed. Long straight hair, eyebrows pencilled coal-black against his white face. All shamelessly out of date, looked like a roadie for the Spiders from Mars. Must be at least four years since Bliss had nicked him for dealing ecstasy from these very premises. Even then, Es had been sliding down the cool person's shopping list.

'Clean as clean, me, now, Mr Bliss,' Jerry Soffley said in his cindery whisper. 'Been clean for over two years and anybody tells you otherwise is probably some old fart from the Chamber of Trade.'

'Yeh, I heard you'd joined the Chamber.'

Soffley sniffed.

'Seemed the thing to do when I yeard we was one of the six oldest surviving businesses in the city.'

'That a fact?'

'I'll name you the others. There's Morris's in Widemarsh Street, there's… wazzat menswear place—?'

'I believe you, Jez. Just like I believe what I can smell is only incense sticks.'

'I'll show you the packet!'

'Never mind.'

Bliss's senses were adjusting to the darkness. To his left was the door to the vinyl room, full of death-metal LPs in gatefold sleeves and a hanging rope with a noose which, if he remembered right, Jerry Soffley used to claim was from a prison in Australia. At the bottom of the vinyl room, he recalled, was a stairwell leading to a small cellar containing an Egyptian stone coffin and part of a guillotine.

Behind Soffley's counter, there was a rack of dusty robes and dark dresses, stickers for brands like Sinister and Necessary Evil. Above them, shelves of wide hats and masks and display cases containing the vicious rings worn by Hell's Angels. If nothing had changed, the rubber kit, chains and stuff were in the cellar.

'Quite quaint in here now, Jerry. You thought of applying for a grant from English Heritage?'

194

'You laugh, Mr Bliss, but Gothic culture don't go away, look. This *is* English heritage. Art, architecture, literature…'

'Tristram Greenaway,' Bliss said. 'Go on… tell me you don't know who I'm talking about.'

Soffley's eyebrows narrowed, making a black bridge over his thin nose. Weighing up his options, probably realizing he didn't have too many.

'All right, yeah, I yeard. Who en't? Come on, Sarge, couldn't be more sorry about what happened to that boy, but I en't seen him in years. Not since he *was* a boy. Fifteen, sixteen?'

'It's "inspector".'

'What is?'

'Me. Got promoted.'

'Nice one. Congratulations. Well deserved. You was always a smart little bastard.'

'Thank you. That was quick, wasn't it?'

'What?'

'You remembering Tristram Greenaway. Just like that. After all these years. If it *was* years. And not days.'

'Aw, fuck *off*, his picture was on the box! Ole picture, from when he was at the Cathedral School. That's how come I knowed who he was. Used to come in regular, with his mates, school uniforms, and I en't seen him since, swearda God.'

'What did he come in for?'

'*I* dunno, it was a long time ago. All sorts. CDs, books – we did more second-hand books, them days. Gothic novels. Bram Stoker, Sheridan le Fanu, Anne Rice. I do remember he'd buy old LPs. He liked the covers. Triple gatefold sleeves. I don't remember what else, but he must've come in a lot, else I wouldn't've remembered his face, would I?'

'So you've had no contact with him since he was a lad.'

Bliss watched Jerry Soffley doing some rapid blinking.

'I never said that. Just I en't seen him. His name's on my mailing list. People who buys from us and sells through us, mail order. I'm saying he just din't come in no more, thassall.'

Bliss looked around at the black and white stills from *Nosferatu the Vampyre*, the framed LP sleeves for Nico and Siouxsie Sioux and other stuff he preferred to think of as before his time. He'd come here on his own, because he was the only one of them who'd ever nicked Jerry Soffley, a trader more streetwise and sly than he looked.

'You doing much business on the Net these days, Jerry?'

'Well, aye. Half my trade's on the Net. Way it goes, now – eBay, specialist goth sites.'

'What about Neogoth dot net?'

Soffley didn't blink.

'Well, yeah, that's us.'

'Us?'

'Me. No secret. Mabbe not the biggest goth ring in the world, but we holds our own. Scores of clients worldwide, different interest groups, public and private, sharing info, what have you.'

'Let's start with the basics,' Bliss said. 'It's a website, is it?'

'Messageboard kinder thing. Special interest. If you're looking for a book or a document or an album or a DVD, souvenir, memento, whatever, you posts your request on the site, and anybody who's got one they want to sell… you know? Was a private thing, but it started to fade off, look. We took it over, in the end, for commercial reasons. Made sense.'

'People buy and sell through you? Gothic kit.'

'Everything. For which I gets commission. Or it might be some'ing *I* can obtain. Could be anything from a holy relic to a signed copy of *Interview with the Vampire*.'

'What kind of people?'

'All kinds. Groups, individuals…'

'But it's a closed ring.' Bliss drawing on what Karen had told him. 'Is that the right terminology? Membership only? That's usually heavy porn, Jezza. Dark Net stuff.'

'Yeah, well, it's not. That's balls, that is. This is just people who wanner talk to each other, rather than the world, about dark and spooky things. Some are quite well known. Experts, celebs. Actors, musicians. Private people.'

'And maybe some of things they're selling they wouldn't want to see on the open market?'

'Long as they en't doing nothing illegal, that's none of my business. Or yours, I reckon.'

'Or what they want to talk about isn't talked about in what you might call polite society?'

'Well, so what? Fetish stuff. Fantasy. Fifty Shades of Shit. Long as no children or animals is harmed, it en't illegal.'

'And you're sure, are you, that this is always the case? Like, if we were to have a poke around...'

'Aw come *on*.'

Jerry Soffley spreading his hands, looking pained.

'So,' Bliss said. 'Tristram Greenaway posted stuff on Neogoth.'

'Not often.'

'Few days ago, he sent you a picture of a human skull.'

'Did he?'

Bliss did a long sigh.

'I'm giving you some leeway here, Jerry. Don't piss me about. When you heard he'd been murdered, the first thing you'd do would be to go into your data and refresh your memory.'

'All right, yeah. He sent me a picture of a manky ole skull. Loads of 'em about. Nobody was interested.'

'How d'you know?'

''Cos nobody come back to me about it, did they?'

'However, that could be because they decided to go and talk to him directly. And wound up killing him.'

'No. Wasn't posted under his name, was it? That's one of the advantages of Neogoth. It goes through me.'

'Exactly. You could tell them.'

'Yeah, well, I didn't.'

'There was an email message with it, right? Indicating that someone out there might be interested to know about the skull.

Greenaway saying that if they wanted to know where he found it he could draw them a map.'

'Some'ing like that.'

'Mean anything to you?'

'Nothing.'

Bliss looked down for a few moments at the black tiles on the floor, the ones at the front with vinyl LPs set into them. Then he looked up, hands behind his back.

'Tell you what I'll do, Jerry. You lend me your computer and write down all the passwords and things—'

'No way!'

'Would save a lorra time, pal, and also, if I have to go to extra trouble to get access, I'm not gonna be well disposed towards—'

'*You*—' Soffley's forefinger came up. 'You think it's easy making a living in Hereford nowadays, you go and count the fucking charity shops. And check out the business rates we pays to them Tory fuckers on the council. I lose people's trust, they stop dealing with me, and word gets round in no time. And anyway...'

'What?'

'It wouldn't help you. Very few of them posts under their real names. They don't want their names all over the Net as lovers of what other folks thinks is weirdo stuff.' Soffley sniffed. 'Anyway, I don't keep my computer yere.'

'I'll expect it here by lunchtime. And if you've tampered at all with any files, my expert will know.'

'This could mess me up bigtime, Frank,' Soffley said sulkily. 'This could make me persona not gratis kind o' thing.'

'We'll bear that in mind. Say two o'clock? I'll send some-body round to pick it up.'

'No! Shit... wait.' Soffley was halfway round the counter. 'How about I just brings it in? Only a laptop. Don't want no bloody coppers strolling in and out like I'm some fucking fence.'

'Perish the thought, pal. I'll tell the desk to expect you by close of play. And don't piss about with the contents because my techie will know, and I'll be very cross.'

He was on his way out when Soffley called him back. Bliss stood still for a moment then turned back to the counter.

'This might sound a bit callous, look,' Soffley said. 'But we all gotter live, right? This boy Greenaway, he have any old vinyl at his place?'

'Vinyl.'

'Only I was thinking, if there's a house clearance, look, I wouldn't mind sifting through any stuff, no obligation.'

'No obligation.' Bliss nodded slowly. 'Very charitable of you, Jerry. I'll see your thoughtful offer is conveyed to Tristram's nearest and dearest. I'm sure they'll be in touch.'

'Ta,' Soffley said. 'Ta very much, Frank.'

'You call me Frank one more friggin' time, pal,' Bliss said, 'and I'll have some lads with a spaniel turn over this place to track down the precise source of that exotic pong.'

31

Unsaid

IN THE MALIKS' lofty living room, where the wind sang in irregular, square iron-framed windows, Nadya was saying she didn't believe in ghosts.

'You think it's all imagination?' Merrily said from a cushion in a window seat. 'Self-delusion?'

Not sure how much she believed in Nadya Malik or the need for the prim blue headscarf – hijab, right? – in a room full of close relatives and one other woman who, even though it was Sunday, had made a point of coming in plain clothes, no collar, no visible cross. Who came in peace.

'Not necessarily, but I don't believe it's anything to do with dead people, either,' Nadya said.

'You personally don't believe that? Or doesn't the Koran…?'

No, no. Shut up. Don't go down that road. Leave the Koran on the shelf.

'I think…' Adam Malik, in a rugby shirt and cream jeans, sat at the other end of the long, cream leather sofa, chin propped up against a fist, looking like he really didn't want to be here. '*I* think, that whatever the Koran may or may not have to say about unexplained phenomena is hardly relevant to us here and now. As our friend—' Adam shifted awkwardly to face Merrily. 'Our friend in Worcester is quite unequivocal that we should put ourselves in your hands.'

Emphasizing this to his wife, Merrily felt.

Nadya glared into her hands folded over the long black skirt.

Born-again Muslim. To her, at this stage, very little in life would be detachable from what it said in the Koran.

Silence seemed louder in this room, probably a former barn attached to the original house, high beams and rudimentary trusses exposed. On an end wall, a carpet-sized hanging had minarets against a sunset seen through archways. Dennis Kellow, sharing a brown leather sofa with his wife, had his back to it.

'I'm simply making my own position clear,' Nadya said. 'I don't expect it to affect anything.'

Merrily suspected that under the scarf her hair was actually very short. Arguably, most men would find Nadya sexier like this, all the emphasis on those full lips, the upturned, very English nose. She wore a high-necked light-blue jumper and she was tall, like her parents, perhaps taller than her husband.

'So if not spirits of the dead,' Merrily said, 'what would be your theory about what might be affecting this place?'

'I would not want to intrude.'

'No, please… it's your home.'

'All right. We might use the word "djinn".'

'Defined as…?'

'Well, a djinn is…'

'What might come out at you,' Dennis said grumpily, 'if you're stupid enough to apply Brasso to some antique Arabic teapot-lamp.'

'Dad, stop it.'

Dennis sat back, feigning chastened. The wind rattled the panes behind Merrily. She could feel a draught on her spine.

'OK, I do know a bit about this. Let me see if I've got it right. In Islamic – or Arabic – legend, a djinn is a mischievous entity, perhaps even malevolent, which may assume human form – even the likeness of someone known to be dead – to deceive people. The essential point being that a djinn is not thought to have human origins. It's a thing of… *smokeless fire*?'

'Well done,' Nadya said.

'Or even a thought form.'

Nadya frowned.

'Now you're going beyond the teachings. We don't do that.'

Merrily said nothing, sliding back into the window recess. The view from here was to the hills behind the house and, beyond them, presumably, the Black Mountains. She'd left Jane out there, exploring the landscape. Hadn't told anyone that Jane had come with her. Hoped – ridiculous, she wasn't a kid any more – that Jane would be careful, come back to the car if the weather turned nasty.

'*I* don't usually bother my little head about these things.' Adam Malik sat up, allowing a hint of his Black Country accent to wander in. 'Being just a mechanic who—'

'Who likes to demean himself,' Nadya said.

'A mechanic who tries to reassemble people. I often think the reason I drifted into orthopaedics is that it's the one form of surgery where you're lucky enough not to see too much of death. Putting people back together and sending them back out into the world, that's me. Less emotionally-challenging than other areas.'

He was maybe thirty-seven, flecks of grey in his tightly trimmed beard, a quiet smile.

'However,' he said, 'here we all are, trying to survive in an increasingly complex world where faith and spirituality are no longer perceived by many Western people as positive influences. Nadya, *no*—' Fending off the hard stare. 'We need to say it. This kind of situation would have been fully accepted by my grandparents, and don't think I'm dismissing it. It's just that in my professional situation I have to be wary of being linked with any—'

'Primitive superstition,' Nadya said.

A lot of cream leather between them now.

Merrily said, 'Your friend in Worcester…'

'We hoped,' Adam Malik said, 'that the imam would relieve us of any need to speculate about the nature of the disturbance.

We didn't think there'd be demarcation lines. He'll be happy to talk to you if you want that, but he understands if you *don't* want it. He says it's a matter of practicality, not politics, if that makes sense to you.'

'Actually, it does.'

'Well, there we are, then. We're in your hands.' He glanced at his wife. 'All of us.'

'All of you,' Merrily said. 'Erm… I was about to ask about your daughter.'

'Upstairs,' Nadya said quickly. 'Doing her homework. She usually does her weekend homework on Sunday afternoons.'

'Does she know about any of this? Does she know about her grandad's experience?'

'Reverend Watkins, she's a *child*. She—'

'I did look into this,' Adam Malik said. 'And talked at length to a neurologist of my acquaintance. It's not unknown for hallucinations to be linked with strokes. Seeing things that aren't there, hearing voices when no one is speaking. There are even accounts of people seeing what they've described as demonic figures. Sometimes in dreams, sometimes not. It can be very frightening. Sometimes this *is* an effect of the prescribed drugs.'

'But that's… after a stroke,' Merrily said. 'Surely.'

'Well… yes. I've discovered no recorded evidence of anything similar occurring pre-stroke. Pre-stroke symptoms tend to be physical. Headaches, impaired vision. Not, however, impaired in *that* way.'

'And…' Merrily looked at Casey. 'If Casey heard the clocks…'

Casey said nothing. Merrily saw the accusatory look that Nadya tossed like a dart at her mother, like it was Casey who'd brought the Anglican Church into the house.

'Has Aisha ever mentioned seeing or hearing anything? Feeling anything?'

'We're not sure,' Casey said. 'However, we're aware that a child – particularly an adolescent child, because I've read about this – may in some ways be more vulnerable.'

'And sometimes,' Merrily said, 'can be seen as the focus for it. Which does need some consideration. Hormones can be linked to all kinds of anomalous—'

'*No!*' Nadya's hand came down on the arm of the sofa. 'I'm not having that. Aisha is happy here. She's settled in at the school, has friends – real friends, Facebook friends. She's a normal girl. She loves the countryside, goes off for long walks. Likes to read, and… and long may that last.'

'And, in between all this…' Merrily hesitated. '… is she following the Islamic faith?'

'She's free to follow whatever faith she wants to,' Adam Malik said. 'Or no faith at all. There's no pressure here. My wife came to Islam some years after we married, with no demands from me, and I want no demands made on my daughter.'

'Although I have to say,' Nadya said, 'when it happened, it gave my life a direction and a structure I would never have imagined achievable, and I'd like that for her, too. As the Church was always meaningless to me, irrelevant to my needs, I could never have imagined that faith could absorb one's life at every level. This is the *energy* of faith. Becoming part of something moving forward.'

Nobody reacted. Nadya gazed into space, wearing a little, knowing smile. Merrily saw Dennis Kellow's big fists tighten. Adam Malik was looking steadily across the big room.

'And what about you?' Merrily asked him.

'Oh, I'm very happy to be here, Mrs Watkins. I'm a convert…' He smiled. '… to the countryside. A convert to the countryside, yes.' He seemed pleased with that. 'And I understand what absorbs Dennis about this old house. It's a unique place, a worthy project…'

'You see, I'm looking for a way in.' Merrily moved to the edge of the window seat, leaning into the room. 'Some way of addressing this in which you're all willing to play a part.'

So many complications, here. So much unsaid. No wonder the girl went for long walks.

And – the worst of it – none of them helped. They let her talk about the various options: the full blessing, the Requiem Eucharist for the restless dead, the exorcism of place for an indefinite but aggressive presence. She didn't feel that any of these was right. She didn't know enough. She had an acute sense of specific things she *did not know*.

At one time – in Canon Dobbs's day, not so very long ago – an exorcism of any kind would demand not merely acquiescence but the active belief of all participants. Attendance at a church service would be required, before and after. And people would go along with that.

At one time. She threw a wordless prayer out into the churchy room, felt it fluttering feebly like a tissue.

'Can we just…? Before we make a decision, can we lay this out? If I say anything anybody disagrees with, just tell me. OK? Let's start with what's been described as a perceptible hostility here. Something Dennis felt. A presence in the Castle Room.'

She looked at Dennis, giving him a chance to deny it, take it all back.

He said nothing.

'And then the stroke.'

Nadya opened her mouth, then shut it again. Casey's arms stiffened against a shudder. Dennis drew a long, unhappy breath that seemed, to Merrily, to be echoed and amplified by the wind outside.

'And I'm getting a bit uncomfortable,' she said, 'about the reluctance to involve Aisha. Who, if she's anything like my daughter at her age – which is not so long ago – will know exactly what we're talking about.'

Know *exactly*?

Was that not the problem? Did any of them even know enough to frame a theory?

She'd never felt more uncertain. Scared of doing something, scared of doing nothing.

32

Foetal

BELOW JANE, THE brown water was wind-whipped through a little, steep-sided gorge before piling noisily under the wooden footbridge.

Noisy like a watermill. Maybe there'd been a mill here at one time. It made sense. Standing on a grassy mound, Jane half-closed her eyes, drew a long breath and held it. She might not have a tiny fraction of the great Francis Pryor's feel for a landscape, but she could at least fantasize.

Go.

Letting the breath out, very slowly, she projected a water-wheel into the scene. The wheel was rough and wooden, a cluster of buildings forming alongside it.

Fragments of autumn dusted her face. She felt the slope of the mound under her boots. She could hear in her head the creak and clank and cistern-hiss of the wooden wheel behind her as she turned her head to look back up the hill to the trees concealing the old farmhouse, Cwmarrow Court.

Do you trust this place?

Amongst the thorn hedges and the brambles between the brook and the Court, she carried on building. Mental Lego.

OK. Hundreds of people must have trusted Cwmarrow in the past – a small, fertile valley with water, what was not to rely on?

So why had they all left, leaving just two medieval buildings facing each other across the brook? Two buildings united by the sharing of stone. Through daylight fading ahead of schedule, Jane looked up at the crumbled ochre walls of the plundered Cwmarrow Castle and the trees below it, mountain ash and silver birch, getting swung across the castle hill by the stiffening wind. Between them, the brook was growling: *Don't come over, don't come over.* The sky behind the ruins was solid, like a board. A barrier. The only movement was the water, like it couldn't race through here fast enough.

Why had Cwmarrow been allowed to die?

Godforsaken.

Good point. Where was God in this place?

Jane came down from the mound and stood beside it, looking all around the valley. If there was a medieval village, there had to have been a place of worship.

Slitting her eyes again, she saw mud where there was grass, conjured a track, a village street winding up from the mill, maybe a ditch down one side oozing animal and human sludge. Small houses of wattle and daub – walls of stiff dung. Strong smells here, but not all of them bad; there would have been orchards, a cider press, fermenting fruit, pleasantly intoxicating on a warm day.

And somewhere a blacksmith would be hammering. There was always a blacksmith, the glow of the forge, a red eye in the gloom. The sound of the hammer which Mum said she'd been told that Selwyn Kindley-Pryce had heard from his bed in the early morning.

Clink clink.

This morning, while Mum was in church, doing the Sunday shift, she'd wandered over to the village bookshop in search of Selwyn Kindley-Pryce and Caroline Goddard. Crucial country proverb: *use it or lose it.*

The shop called – you had to laugh – Ledwardine Livres, was run by the slightly severe Londoner, Amanda Rubens, and her partner, the plump, goblinesque Gus Staines. Gus was there alone this Sunday morning. It was the slow season between the tourists and the Christmas shoppers, and Jane was the only customer. She'd been nervous. *Oh God.*

Gus wore a thick green woollen dress and a chunky necklace not much smaller than a mayoral chain. Jane had told her the guy whose books she was interested in was probably before her time, and Gus had laughed.

'Virginia Woolf? H.G. Wells?' And then, when Jane had tossed her the name: 'Oh dear. Poor Mr Pryce.'

'You *did* know him?'

'Well, not here, obviously. Before I went to London, I used to work part time at what was then the finest bookshop in Hereford. The one that used to be in Church Street? No more beautiful location, just below the Cathedral. Gone now, Jane. History. Like most of the best shops in town.'

Gus was smiling, which didn't mean she was happy. Gus always smiled in the face of life.

Jane said, 'You sold Kindley-Pryce's books there?'

'We *stocked* them. Didn't sell many. *The Cunning* was over twenty-five pounds, which was big money back then, especially here. You learn that there are prices beyond which people in Hereford will not go.'

'And it was a bit dry, I suppose, *The Cunning*.'

'Yes, but then he produced something which we all thought would be of more general interest. It was called *Borderlight*, much shorter and more colourful. An interpretive retelling of legends and stories from the medieval chroniclers. Privately published – I doubt any commercial publisher would have touched it. Still overpriced, but quite exquisite, with lovely, parchment-like paper and pen and ink illustrations by his friend, Caroline Goddard.'

'She was an artist, too?'

'She wrote and illustrated children's books. I have a copy at home... somewhere. I can bring it in for you to look at. Borrow it if you like.'

'That would be fantastic.'

Gus beamed, a happy gnome even though nothing had been sold.

'They wrote some children's books together, for a national publisher, Jane. Under the name... ah...'

'Foxy Rowlestone.'

'Yes. We only learned that Foxy Rowlestone was two local people when it was too late. Maybe we should have guessed with Rowlestone being a village at the end of the Golden Valley. Terribly annoying because the books had sold well even with no local connection. Would have been wonderful to get the two of them into the shop to sign copies. Did you read them, Jane?'

'No. I was a snobbish kid who thought books like that were naff. I was reading, erm, Tolstoy. Why was Foxy's identity hidden?'

'Because they didn't want the *attention*, apparently. Didn't want their readers – teenagers – coming to look for them. And finding their home, which they were using as a setting for the books – the castle on the hill, the village huddled under it and the forest all around where vampires lurked.'

'Cwmarrow was the setting for the books?'

'It was never named. They didn't even say which part of the country it was in – people thought Cornwall or somewhere.'

'Blimey, Gus, think of the lost tourism.'

'So you haven't any in stock.'

'We've *never* had any, Jane. By the time we opened here, the series was over, almost before it had started. And the Twilight books were out by then, from America, totally cornering the young-adult vampire market.'

'But if Foxy Rowlestone had carried on...'

'Well, *possibly*. Who can really say? But they didn't carry on, and it's easy to see why. Ironically, a few years earlier, Mr Pryce agreed to come into the Hereford shop and do a signing, for the self-published book, *Borderlight*.'

'When was this?'

'Ten years or more. Seems such a very long time ago now. A different era. Mr Pryce was...' Gus looked strangely glum. '... charming. Kindly – like his name. Suntanned, wrinkled face like a walnut. He wore a sort of safari jacket. Made me think of one of those Victorian academics who went out to Egypt and places like that to excavate old tombs. There were some people who came in who knew him well. You know, "How are you, Selwyn? You're looking jolly fit…" And within a few years…'

The memory had seemed to throw a shadow over Gus. She put the smile back on and began to gather some local guide-books into a stack.

'Time to put these away. Holidays over, Christmas books coming in soon.'

'Can you still buy the Kindley-Pryce books?'

'Possibly second-hand, but be prepared for some steep prices. I doubt the print runs were very extensive.'

'Only, Mum thought he might be still alive.'

'Then God knows what he's like now. I believe they got him into a home out beyond Leominster. One of these awfully expensive places with private nursing. I believe his son made the arrangements, to get him out of that big house.'

'What about his partner… Caroline?'

'Gone.'

'Oh.'

'Left him. Not terribly supportive of her, was it?'

'She left him because he was losing his mind?'

'Well, she was much younger. What do you do? Spend your best years caring for an old man who can barely remember who you are?'

Jane hadn't known what to say.

'*Yes.*' Gus had become suddenly very solemn, quite fierce. 'Yes, you *do*. You *should*. For better, for worse. In sickness and in health. That includes mental health, or maybe I'm old-fashioned.'

'But they weren't married or anything.'

'They were *a couple*. Marriage is wonderful, but it's essentially a recognition of an existing commitment.'

Jane nodding, finding a tentative smile. Now or never.

'Erm… I haven't really seen you since you and Amanda…'

210

'It was lovely,' Gus said. Augusta Rubens-Staines, as she was now. 'Your mother was kind enough to bless us in church afterwards. Couldn't ask for more.'

'No. Erm, congratulations.'

'Thank you, Jane.'

'Right… well…'

Oh God, this was impossible. Jane had become breathless, turning away, glancing out of the window, across the square.

'Is there something else I can do for you, Jane?'

Cold feet. Her feet had actually felt cold, as Gus smiled her whitest, most accommodating smile. Really nice woman.

No thank you,' Jane said. 'I just… That's fine. I'll look forward to seeing the book.'

She was swaying, transferring her weight from her left foot to the right and back again, Pressure, pressure, pressure. Horribly aware, in the stiflingly strange intimacy of the Cwmarrow valley, of the person she'd been just a couple of years ago. The stupid, arrogant, self-important, self-righteous little bitch. Echoes of the bitter rows with Mum, all the stuff she'd put Eirion through. The *certainty*. How could you be so sure of yourself?

Gap year. Super. Everybody should have one. Sam had said that. In Pembrokeshire, when Eirion had left. *Super chance to find out who you are, Jane.*

Super was one of Sam's words. Sam, the *real* archaeologist, who'd seen the potential in Jane, telling her to read the books of Francis Pryor. Sam who had later said, *More things, Horatio.*

'Leave me alone!' Jane snarling into the wind. 'I don't *know*. I don't know what I am. Nothing's certain. Just get off my back.'

Through tears in free-flow, Jane started to laugh, stamping away through the greasy grass, following the track her mind had made, the village street with the peasant homes and the blacksmith's forge, the hammer banging in her chest. Let it all go. Stop thinking. Stop *thinking*.

Another track had opened up in a corner of her mind's eye, this one ribboning up into the shallow hills that neighboured Cwmarrow Court to the south, mostly bristling with forestry, the kind that got planted on land nobody cared too much about, the kind of coniferous forestry that didn't exist in Britain in the Middle Ages. Anything could be under there.

Zipping up her parka to stop it snagging on the rampant blackthorn, Jane made her way up towards the near-black conifers. There was movement in the eastern sky, small clouds like gunboats on darkening water. At some point, it would rain, hard. The ground was steep and already slippery; the boots she wore were wrong for this.

She stopped halfway up the hill. Turning to look back across the valley, she found she was viewing Cwmarrow Castle from a very different angle, the tower side-on so you could see that most of its back was missing. Like a movie-set tower, just a façade, the truth about the castle exposed: defenceless from behind, impotent, relegated to the role of ornament. The castle wouldn't like that; you could almost feel its bitterness, its resentment. *He don't like that, see,* the local people would say. *He en't happy, he—*

'Uh—'

The castle rocked. Jane was flailing, a heel caught under a root. She went down hard on her bum in the spiky ground, bushes thrashing, a briar whipping up and snagging her hair.

She lay there, winded. It had felt like a physical assault. *We don't want you yere.*

She didn't get up. The light had changed in the sky, the gunboat clouds crowding. On the ground, all the colours had gone, as though the land had bled out. She rolled over stiffly, looking up the hill again, through bushes and saplings. Not far above her was a flat space below the black ramparts of the forestry. A rough plateau, quite extensive, partly covered with gorse. It was hard to see much. Jane reached up shakily, pinching the briar away from her eyes, taking some hair with it. She was going to look like shit.

Right. Gripping one of the slimy rotting tree roots that brought her down, she came to her feet, moved towards the edge of the flat ground, projecting on it a small grey-brown stone church with a timbered bell tower. The kind you found over in Radnorshire. This village would surely once have been in Wales. The gorsey table of land could well be a circular church-yard, an indication that the church had been built on a site of earlier worship. When it fell into ruins the stone would've been carried away for building, over at the farmhouse. If you exca-vated, you might well find foundations. And graves, scores of humble medieval graves, bones upon bones upon bones. Lying under her now, cold and broken.

God deserting Cwmarrow. God watching it die.

The wind blew into Jane's face as she peered across the over-grown churchyard beyond a carpet of crispy, shed leaves, to a pillared temple of conifer trunks which faded back into the deep smoky green where a woman stood.

Jane slid back down, sharply startled, into the brambles and the old nettles and the rotting roots. Twigs crackling in her hair, she edged herself back up the spiky rise to peer through the brambles.

There was no one there.

More things, Sam said. *More things, Horatio.*

Jane breathed out hard. Well, of course there was no-one there. These projection exercises got out of control.

Time to go.

Her hands felt cold and wet from the decaying tree roots, as she dragged herself back up, over the rim of the plateau, into the ground cover, holding her scraped hands inside the sleeves of her parka away from the thorns, like paws. As she came to her knees, a sound like laughter was chopped up by the wind, and the woman was back.

The woman moved in a juddering way as if she was blown along by sporadic gusts.

A briar ripped Jane's cheek as she went back down. In the

grainy half-light the darkness slipped away from the woman like a long coat as she sank into the leaves as if into a pool, and the leaves rose in a cloud and then settled over her thin, pale, naked body.

More things, Horatio.

Jane went foetal in the slimy grass.

33

Homework

THE SILENCE WAS broken eventually by Nadya.

'Does it matter what this is? You wouldn't actually *know* anyway, would you?'

'None of us knows.'

Nadya's expression said, *Speak for yourself.*

Merrily stood up, shouldering the airline bag. A call to Raji Khan tonight might be in order. *Not my place to tell you what to expect*, he'd said. *You should hear it from the people concerned.*

But if these people, some or all of them, had reached an agreement about how much to disclose to her and nobody wanted to step outside it, what was the point of her being here?

'Is it likely,' Merrily said, 'is it at all likely that Mr Kindley-Pryce would be in any fit state to speak to me?'

'Now?' Dennis Kellow going back into the sofa. 'The way he is *now*?'

'I'm just...'

'I rang the home this morning. Thought I should. I always think they're going to say he's dead. The woman there said he had good days and bad days. I don't know what that means. Maybe these things plateau out.'

'Not for very long, Dennis,' Adam Malik said. 'And each plateau is likely to be considerably lower than the previous one. The truth is nobody really knows about dementia. We really don't know enough about the workings of the brain. Whatever kind of dementia this was – and without access to his medical records I'm in the dark here – it can develop slowly or rapidly.

All we can say with any degree of certainty is that people don't come back.'

Merrily nodded.

'And if you're asking whether it might have been affected – or even caused – by something that happened here,' Adam said, 'it's no use talking to a doctor, is it?'

'What about Caroline Goddard? Anybody know where she might be now?'

Nobody seemed to.

'OK. If you ask me what I think I should do this afternoon… from the information I have, it would be to go through the house again, room by room, repeating what we did yesterday. In every room.' She paused. 'Including Aisha's.'

'N—'

Nadya rising up, arms waving, Dennis Kellow leaning aggressively forward.

'Nadya, the kid's not *stupid*…'

'That's not the—'

'Kids like a wall of security they can bounce off. Couple of bricks coming loose, they're the first to notice.'

'I have made it perfectly *clear*,' Nadya said, 'that I don't want her exposed to any of this.'

Dennis's face coloured, but Casey froze him with a glance and then turned to her daughter, head on one side.

'What *you* don't want her exposed to, Nicole, is the idea that a form of religion you despise might actually be effective.'

Nadya was out of the leather sofa, Adam putting out a hand to her, but she squirmed away. Couple of bricks? It was like the air was thick with demolition dust

A silence. Then Adam Malik came slowly to his feet.

'*I'll* go up and talk to her. All right?'

His wife stiffened. He turned away from her, walked across the rich Afghan rug to the stone flags and down to the bottom door and the hall where they'd come in and the back stairs. At the door, Adam turned. His face looked grey with weariness.

'Mrs Watkins, I think you should come with me.'

He didn't look at his wife.

Merrily looked at Dennis and Casey.

'Yes,' Casey said. 'You should talk to her.'

Merrily nodded, walked over to Adam. He opened the door for her and she went through to the dark, woody hall, peered up rough, wooden steps. A paleness dropped from single-pane skylights on the landing at the top.

You're sick.

Jane in the Freelander's driver's seat. The vehicle parked in front of the barbed wire fencing off the forestry. Engine running, heater on boost, its noise blanking out the rushing of the brook. The car doors locked. Would that you could lock out something that was in your head.

More things, Horatio.

She held the phone gingerly, painfully putting in a text. There were cuts on three fingers. She'd pulled several thorns from her left hand. Dipped a tissue in the brook to clean up her face.

She'd seen nothing up there – *nothing*, right? Nothing that was outside of a sick mind that barely remembered the scramble back down from where there might have been a church and now only gorse and leaves.

And white flesh.

White flesh and shivering leaves.

Oh dear *God*. Was this what people meant by a breakdown, malfunction of all the senses?

Or just a refusal to accept the truth.

She read the text back.

Eirion, I'm sorry.
You don't need this.
Should've told you
ages ago. I might not
be who you thought

> I was. I'm sorry for
> wasting so much of
> your life.

Couldn't stand to read it a second time. It was like something done by a kid of thirteen. They just didn't talk like this, her and Eirion. They laughed at people who talked like this. And she'd never called him Eirion, always Irene.

Irene. Jesus. She dabbed with the tissue at her swollen eyes.

Couldn't send it anyway. No signal here.

It was quite a big bedroom, with some light oak beams in its pitched ceiling. Replacements. New beams for old. It was neat for a teenager's room: a three-quarter bed with a lurid red and gold duvet, a black and gold dressing table with cosmetic bottles artistically arranged and a pair of pink headphones. A laptop and a television. Bookshelves and a double wardrobe.

But no teenager.

'She bloody does this,' Adam Malik said, suddenly furious. 'Slips away, in and out of this house like a cat.' He closed the door, stood with his back to it. 'I can't apologize enough, Mrs Watkins. You must be wondering what kind of madhouse you've walked into.'

'Every situation like this I walk into,' Merrily said, 'people are worried they might be going mad. Me too. It's a thin line.'

'I do *not* dismiss these things,' he said. 'I just… As you might have gathered by now, I don't do religion. Or rather I *do* it, to a point. I am not a zealot. And my wife… my wife, I hope to God, will calm down. One day.'

'Dennis says she used to be an atheist.'

Adam Malik sighed.

'I won't say that was what attracted me to her, but it certainly didn't put me off. No, that's— that's probably going too far. I'm just not an extreme person, that's all. I consume Mars bars before major surgery during Ramadan, to keep up the blood sugar. And other necessary transgressions I don't talk about. Though obviously, there's less need for discretion in Hereford.'

'How did your wife feel about coming here?'

'How she talks and how she feels are not always the same. She'll tell you what a sacrifice it was coming to a city with no mosque for the sake of her father... while, in reality, she loves being part of a vociferous minority. Listen, I'm sorry, I shouldn't talk like this. She's just very driven. The pioneer spirit. Like Dennis, and he doesn't see it either. Both of them more drawn to the cutting edge than I'll ever be, and I'm a damn surgeon.'

He laughed uneasily, but he was still shaking.

'She converted because she thought it would please my family. And then she... she'll tell you she realized what was missing in her life.' He opened out his hands. 'Can we leave it there?'

Merrily nodded. She went over to the bookcase, attracted by a name in Gothic lettering on the black spine of a paperback.

'This blessing,' he said. 'She's not here so that can go ahead. Will it calm the atmosphere or what?'

'I don't know.' She looked for his eyes. 'What do you think?'

He said nothing.

'*I* think there's something missing. Something you're not telling me.' She put a finger on the top of the paperback. 'Can I?'

'Of course.'

She drew it out. The cover showed a twilit castle on a wooded hill. It could have been a photograph, messed about with. It was not *quite* like Cwmarrow, but the resemblance was there. A white beam shone from a tower room, softening and broadening out to tint the rooftops of the houses in the village below the hill. The image continued on the back of the book where, on the edge of the beam, a thin, grey shadow hunched, predatory.

The Summoner
Nightlands, Book One

'Foxy Rowlestone,' Merrily said.

'You know who she was, presumably.'

'Just never seen a copy before.'

'I bought her both Rowlestone books,' Adam said. 'Her gran – Casey – was a little unsure, but I saw it as a way of making Aisha feel at home here. She had all the Twilight books. A voracious reader since she was small.'

'And she enjoyed this?'

'You know what they're like, nothing could be better than Twilight. And then after a few weeks and a second reading and a third…'

'So it did make her feel at home.'

'It made her excited. That's her second copy. Only one split in the spine, see? Telling her friends at the new school that she lived in the Nightlands, and of course they all wanted to come and visit. Drove Dennis daft, all these kids. Doesn't happen so often now. Crazes wear off quickly at that age. Though not for Aisha.'

'Even though the books stopped.'

'She's written to Foxy Rowlestone. Twice, I think. Asking when the next one's coming. As thousands of young people do, apparently.'

'She get a reply?'

'Not that I know of. When Kindley-Pryce was taken into care, I don't suppose the lady had the heart to continue. I think she still writes children's books, just not this kind.'

Merrily slid the book back. Most of its neighbours had similar dark spines. Not unusual, kids Aisha's age.

'I'm now sorry I bought her the books,' Adam said.

'Too close? Too scary?'

'Certainly too close, but she's not scared. Like my wife says, she's happy. Talks about writing her own. Continuing the story. As children do. Do they call it fan-fiction? Look.'

He pulled open both wardrobe doors. There was a velvet curtain across one side, and he pulled it back.

'Oh,' Merrily said. 'I see.'

'Bought through the Internet. Whole websites devoted to this stuff.'

'Yes, well…' Merrily fingered the black velvet and the satin. 'It appeals to a lot of kids. I… went through a similar phase. My mother was horrified, but it just… it makes you feel mysterious and exotic. Never think you might look daft.'

The window was high in the wall opposite the door. Cwmarrow Castle gleamed dully from across the valley like a rusting tin can flung into the hill under a sky loaded with rainclouds.

'She's changed,' Adam Malik said. 'She always seemed younger than her age. A bit clingy. To me, rather than her mother. And to Casey and Dennis. Now it's like she doesn't need us.'

'At her age they change. Rapidly. Shockingly, sometimes.'

'I know. I have three sisters.'

'I'm sorry. Is there a boyfriend?'

'No. We're pretty sure of that. And none of the usual adolescent rebellion. We don't quarrel, she just… doesn't appear to need us. She's distant, self-contained, in a quite adult way. As if she has her own life and we're not part of that. Casey says this place changes people and not for the better.'

'But she still reads young-adult books.'

'Are they?'

Adam Malik turned abruptly to the bookcase, ran his hands from shelf to shelf before finding what he wanted near the bottom. Extracting it and pushing the others together to obscure the gap. He held out the book, its cover curling.

'This is her old copy, she won't miss it. Put it in your bag, and if you have chance to read it…'

'OK.'

'I don't think Dennis has read it,' Adam said, 'but I have. I like the countryside. I want to understand this place. Its location is non-specific, but once you know it's about here, you begin to see the effect the place had on Kindley-Pryce. It's Caroline Goddard's writing fuelled by his imagination.'

Merrily took the book. The splits in its spine were like fish bones.

There was a knock on the door before it was pushed open, impatiently, against Adam's shoulder. Merrily slipped the paperback into her airline bag as he stepped away from the door.

Nadya stood with arms folded, glancing around the room.

'Where is she?'

'Evidently not doing her homework,' Adam said.

34

Full broadcast quality

As THEY DROVE out of Cwmarrow, the sky broke. The rain came slanting in and, with it, mist.

Jane didn't seem to be sorry they were leaving. Her hair was wet and her face was scratched and there were mud patches on her parka. The way she used to come home when she was a kid, only then she'd be happy.

'I tripped,' she'd said. 'I tripped and fell. Wrong boots. Don't ask. I'm not hurt, I'm just pissed off about it, OK?'

The village was two or three miles behind them before Merrily realized it wasn't OK. Should've paid more attention, but she'd still been full of the farmhouse. Blessings sought, the sprinkling, the intoning of the Lord's Prayer – Nadya's delivery clipped and efficient.

No resonance from any of it. There was a fog in that house that you could almost see, like it had acquired a dementia of its own. Did it make sense that Kindley-Pryce's failing mind had, in some sense, been absorbing the house's memories?

Or could he have left something behind? Confusion-residue. Fog. Back in the living room, the rest of it over, she'd prayed for fresh light to enter the house, fresh air to blow through it. Feeble, really. Inexact. She felt anxious, and that was not a good way to leave a disturbed house.

And now Jane…

Nothing much remaining of the enthusiasm she'd shown for trying to find a lost village. When Merrily asked her if she'd discovered anything, she'd mumbled something about the possible site of a church, but like what did she know?

They drove around the village of Dorstone, unspoiled, arboreal, its church squat and solid, and over the hill towards Leominster, past the turning to Arthur's Stone, where Jane had always liked to stop, but not today.

After they crossed the Wye at Bredwardine, the mist began to lift, trees, already wintry, standing disconsolate in the fields.

Jane said suddenly, 'What *are* ghosts?'

They hadn't been talking about ghosts. They'd been talking, in a desultory way, about the imaginary village Jane had tried to visualize in the Cwmarrow valley.

'Like, do you know yet? After all your deliverance work, are you any clearer about it? Do ghosts exist *out there*? Or are they only in our heads? Projections of our lowest fears. Anxieties. About death. And life. Why do we never get any closer to answering those questions?'

'Dunno.' Merrily glanced sideways. Jane was animated at last, but not in a good way. Her face was colourless. 'Why do you ask?'

Jane didn't look at her. After a while she started to talk about seeing things that weren't there.

'Don't say your brain can't do that to you. Hallucinations are more common than we think. Most of us see things that aren't there and just dismiss them.'

'Well, yes.'

'And if you're doing that deliberately...'

'How do you mean?'

'If you're concentrating on visualizing something. Like say if you're an artist. If you keep visualizing, like in a meditative state, and you're like interacting with the energies of a place... like, if it's a powerful place... then you could actually be conditioning your senses to start experiencing things that aren't there. Maybe your brain starts doing that on its own. When you're not... expecting it.'

'Jane—'

'And sometimes it mingles with your innermost feelings? Your anxieties. Your obsessions? And you're seeing images you don't want to see? Something the brain constructs from your fears and your deepest anxieties and your... subconscious self.'

Merrily remembered last night's dream, horrible but entirely explicable in terms of negative thoughts before bed.

'Jane...' She slowed the car. 'Are we still talking about ghosts?'

'I think so.'

Something surfacing here. She speeded up. Keep it casual. There had been a time when Jane was experimenting with mental and spiritual exercises. Magic, in other words. The heavy pagan days. But that was over, wasn't it?

'You're saying you were creating a ghost village at Cwmarrow. Visualizing it.'

'Erm... more than that. Adding the sounds and the smells.'

'Putting a living village into a deserted landscape?'

'A medieval village. Pathways, rough housing. The smithy. The church.'

'Did it lead to anything? Did you find any remains of buildings... anything?'

'I told you. There was a flat area that could've been the site of a church. Like a circular churchyard.'

'And... something happened?'

They came out at Kinnersley on to the Leominster road. The pleasant road home, open fields long views. The rain had stopped and the sky was ambered.

'I was just theorizing, that's all,' Jane said. 'Just thinking, like, what if something *had* happened?' Staring through the windscreen at the open road. 'That's all.'

When they got in, the answering machine was bleeping.

When was it not?

'After the meditation,' Merrily said. 'We're going to have a proper meal. No fast food, no crap.' Aware of all the times she'd said that on a Sunday evening. 'OK?'

'OK.'

Jane trying to smile.

'And we'll get Lol round, is that all right? I feel bad about Lol.'

Jane started shaking her head sadly.

'You talk about him like he's just some neighbour who lives on his own and we ought to invite him round occasionally.'

Merrily blinked in the silence.

'I'm sorry,' Jane said.

'Yeah... well...'

Merrily undid her coat, pulling the paperback of *The Summoning* from a side pocket and laying it on the edge of the refectory table. She'd taken it out of the deliverance bag as soon as she'd got back to the car. It might be just an airline bag, but its contents were exclusive.

Jane picked up the book.

'Who gave you this?'

'Adam Malik. He bought it for his daughter. He thinks it might help for me to read it.'

'Rather you than me. Life's well too short for romantic vampires.'

'Let nobody say I don't suffer for my... whatever it is.' The cat door snapped; there was mewing. Merrily dropped her coat over a cane chair. 'Right, Ethel. Food. Forgot to top up the dried before we went out.'

'I'll sort it. Go and deal with the machine, it's getting on my nerves.'

Sophie said, 'I did suggest you rang back after your meditation service.'

'I know you did. I'm just trying to clear the decks because we're hoping to have a decent meal tonight, for once.'

'Tomorrow then,' Sophie said. 'Tomorrow will do.'

'Erm...' Merrily prodded the scullery door to with a foot. 'Somehow, I don't think so.'

There had been three messages on the machine, all from Sophie, asking her to call back. Only the final one had suggested she might leave it now until after the meditation. Sophie didn't like to damage anyone's performance in church. And how often did she ring on a Sunday about something that could wait?

'I've an hour before the meditation.'

Sophie laughed nervously.

Nervously. *Sophie.*

Merrily said nothing.

'I didn't sleep much last night,' Sophie said. 'This is something which… is not the kind of thing I do, you see.'

'What isn't?'

'The Archdeacon's offer to you? Of the Rural Dean position?'

'I'm so excited I've thought of little else.'

'Obviously, that followed a meeting with the Bishop.'

'Obviously.'

'Which took place here. In the office. Our… office. Which the Bishop now regards as his office. His base in the community.'

'Where he can watch his flock milling down in Broad Street.'

'When Siân arrived,' Sophie said, 'the Bishop suggested that I might want to do some shopping.'

'You mean he wanted you to leave them alone.'

'Evidently.'

'No little woman can ever resist an unexpected opportunity for some shopping, Sophie.'

'I almost always sat in on Bernard Dunmore's business meetings. It was part of my job, as his secretary.'

'Celebrated all over the city, and beyond, for her discretion.'

'Don't laugh at me, Merrily.'

Sophie's voice rising, cracked.

'I'm sorry. Never have laughed at you. Never will.'

'I had a fairly good idea what they were going to discuss.'

She would have known *exactly* what they were going to discuss.

'I said a silent prayer. For advice.'

Merrily said nothing. The door hadn't quite shut. She could hear Jane talking to Ethel. There was no noise from outside but in her head she could hear the old briar tapping against the window.

'There was no apparent discouragement,' Sophie said.

'*He* trusts you, then.'

'I… once saw a reporter from Radio Hereford and Worcester interviewing the Dean in the Close. It was an impromptu interview, the Dean had to catch a train and she didn't have her recording device. So she simply brought out her iPhone and recorded the interview on that. I was astonished.'

'A little-known technological miracle,' Merrily said. 'The tiny mic in an iPhone can give you a recording in broadcast quality. Making you wonder why they need all this expensive kit, but then I'm just a vicar.'

'I never forgot that. What the iPhone could do.'

'And, erm… you have one, don't you, Sophie?'

Bloody hell.

'When I'm in the office I keep it in my mail tray. When I went shopping, I didn't take it with me.'

'*Sophie…*'

'Doesn't take much to… accidentally set it recording. I left a flimsy letter half over it. Old-fashioned airmail quality. Hoping the battery was charged.'

It would be fully charged.

'And so it recorded the meeting between Bishop Craig and Siân Callaghan-Clarke. In what would have been full BBC broadcast quality if the phone had been closer to them. But it's still audible.' Sophie paused. 'Disturbingly audible.'

'Right.'

'I was stupid enough to listen to it in full before bed.'

'Oh. Not good, then.'

'Not good at all.'

A silence. Back in the kitchen, Jane was talking again, but not to Ethel. *No*, then, *I don't know. Maybe.* On her mobile perhaps. *OK, I'll try.*

'Merrily, I've been private lay secretary to the bishops of Hereford for more years than I'm inclined to admit. The question of what I'd done being a possible betrayal engaged me for some time in the hours before dawn.'

Yes. It would.

'I've downloaded it to my computer,' Sophie said. 'Having given the matter further consideration, I think I should send it to you.'

'Sophie, I—'

'Don't listen to it until after your meditation. Perhaps even leave it until tomorrow. I'd just ask you not to send it to anyone else. Distrusting the Internet, as I do. If you wanted someone – say Huw Owen – to hear it, you could perhaps ask him to come over. Or take it to him.'

'Right.'

'I shall send it… now. There. Done. My conscience is entirely clear. I was reminded who I worked for.'

Not God. Not directly.

'The—'

'The Cathedral.'

Saying it slowly as if the word itself was empowering, could light up like a chandelier.

She didn't go near the computer.

Jane had made some tea, and they sat at the refectory table, and Jane picked up the paperback, *The Summoner*. Turning it over to see what was standing on the edge of the beam of light from the castle keep.

'Could I read a bit of this, after all?'

'I'd be quite glad if you would, actually, flower. I might whizz through it too quickly, miss something you'd probably spot.'

'No need to butter me up.' Jane laid the book down. 'That was Sophie?'

'Bishop trouble.'

'And you don't have to keep taking this.' Jane's face was expressionless. 'I like it here, and there are a lot of things that still need doing but…'

'Hell, flower, it's not *that* bad.'

'Isn't it?'

'No.'

Merrily stood up.

'Maybe I won't come tonight,' Jane said. 'I'll read some of this crap. Make myself useful.'

She didn't say who she'd been speaking to on the phone. But then why should she?

Upstairs, Merrily changed into the Sunday evening meditation kit: velvety jeans, black woollen top, discreet pectoral cross. No dog collar. There'd been a few moans when she'd introduced the meditation to replace Evensong, but it was working now. Brilliantly, some weeks, and for all the right reasons now that the healing element was on the back-burner, less intense. A time of renewal. Forty people some weeks, and building again with Christmas in sight.

When she padded across to the church to light the candles, bring her chair down to the spot below the rood screen, some of the regulars were already there: Gus and Amanda from the bookshop, Kent Asprey, the GP, Barry from the Black Swan, who came in once a month. Gomer Parry – did he meditate or just ruminate? Some of them were not what you'd call Christians, not what you'd call anything. Which was fine; she'd given up drawing distinctions. It was about a communal spirituality, a calming. A village thing.

Sometimes she imagined she could see the benign shade of Lucy Devenish moving on the edge of the candleglow. Lucy who had been mentor to both Jane and Lol, who had lived in what was now Lol's cottage, her famous poncho draped over the newel post at the bottom of the stairs.

But Lol himself…

She looked from face to shadowed face.

… was not here.

Not that he'd ever been seen a lot in church, having grown up wary of organized religion, thanks to fundamentalist, happy-clappy parents who'd disowned him when he needed them most. His apathy, built on old resentment, hadn't quite gone away. Morning service, the trite hymns, the quavering psalms, the cloying sameness of a grinding anachronism… a sense of wasted hours.

The compromise had been the meditations, growing from an image, a line, a verse. Lucy Devenish had introduced him to Thomas Traherne, seventeenth-century Herefordshire poet and nature mystic. Merrily thought that Lol, having been away so long, would be here tonight. The church filled up, he didn't come.

She stood up, disappointed. Verses from Luke that recalled Traherne would provide tonight's glowing mantra. She didn't really need the book. Gave it to them as Traherne would have done in the seventeenth century, but soft-voiced. The acoustics in Ledwardine church were good at soft.

'The light of the body is in the eye. Therefore when thine eye is single thy whole body is full of light.'

She looked into the core of the furthest candle, in a stone niche beside the vestry door at the bottom of the nave. What did the eye really see? What did the impressionable mind convince the eye that it had seen?

What did Jane think she'd seen in the Cwmarrow valley?

'But when thine eye is evil thy body also is full of darkness. Take heed, therefore, that the light which is in thee is not darkness. So if thy whole body therefore be full of light, having no part dark, the whole shall be full of light as when the bright shining of a candle doth give thee light.'

When she looked up, the candle had become the white sleeplamp in the computer, blooming like a snowdrop, cold in the dimness.

35

Cold case

THEY TOOK THE pizza out of the microwave, sat down to divide it at the breakfast bar. The blinds were down, the lights were dimmed.

'Jerry Soffley,' Bliss said. 'Don't like him. Called me sergeant. And Frank. *Frank*.'

Annie rolled her eyes. He'd told her some time ago about *his* dad, Francis Bliss senior, known as Frank, who'd counted domestic violence amongst his hobbies in the days before it was considered much of a crime. Dead now. Old twat fell off the Liverpool pier head, Bliss liked to say, although it wasn't that simple. What he'd never told Annie was that Kirsty, his wife, had also called him Frank towards the end, knowing exactly what she was saying. Knowing also that it wasn't true, but she could be vindictive, Kirsty.

'He did bring his laptop in, mind,' Bliss said. 'Soffley. Turns out he actually lives above the shop, some squalid little one-bed flat. Used to have a place at Bobblestock. Must be on his uppers.'

'What if he deleted things before he brought the laptop in?'

'To keep Karen out, he'd have to've extracted his hard disk and driven over it a few times, and even then... What bothers me is that he might have a number two lappie tucked away. I really wanna go and see him again, but I need something to nail on him. Don't wanna be accused of goth-bashing.'

'Goths.' Annie frowned. 'I really didn't want us to have to go there. Waste of space, people like that. Fantasists.'

Meaning she didn't understand what drove them. New Age dark. More than just a fashion thing. Annie didn't even understand New Age lite.

'People who post on Neogoth,' Bliss said. 'All right, let's go out on a limb here. Let's suppose that somewhere there's a nutter who wants that skull for what he *thinks* it is.'

'I thought Cooper knew exactly what it was.'

'Yeh, yeh, he does. But it's nuts and bolts to him, it's not, I dunno, *magic*.'

Annie looked pained.

'All right.' Bliss brought up the picture on his phone. 'The stone in its gob, like an Uncle Joe's Mint Ball...'

'A what?'

'Never mind. Under the circumstances – i.e. that he's let it slip through his fingers – Cooper's not gonna big that up for us or anybody. But that stone, that's the best evidence Greenaway has that this is a significant skull. The head of a feller thought to be a vampire.'

Annie sighed. Flicking off the skull picture, Bliss noticed he had an email from Billy Grace, the pathologist, but he kept on talking.

'I got Vaynor to go into it on the Net. Stone in the mouth, not uncommon in a deviant burial. If it's a white stone, it might have significance in a Christian burial as a symbol of resurrection. In a good way – put there to benefit the deceased. This doesn't look like a white stone to me, though it could just've got mucky over the centuries, but let's assume it's not. To some of the weirdos who do their shopping with Jerry Soffley, this feller's a vampire.'

'Have we talked to experts?'

'Yeh, we put in a call to the University of the Undead. Aw, come on, Annie, who's an expert in this kind of crap? Unless, of course...'

Annie sat up.

'No.'

'What did I say?'

'You didn't. Don't.'

Bliss smiled.

'Mrs Watkins does, in the course of her job, run into people with unorthodox beliefs.'

'*No.*'

'I realize you never liked her much.'

Annie reached for the coffee pot, looked at Bliss who shook his head. This wasn't a caffeine kind of night. Annie poured some for herself.

'Francis, look. It's nothing to do with that. I saw another side of her the night you were hurt. More rational than I'd realized. And intuitive.'

'You said.'

'Did I mention that the chief constable and I had lunch with the new Bishop of Hereford?'

'I thought that was just…'

'A social formality. The chief wanted me to go along because his knowledge of Hereford isn't extensive. New Bishop's a man called Innes. New broom. Not like Dunmore. Didn't appear to think we had any mutual interests. More interested in what we could do for him, in relation to church security and the increase in thefts. The chief proudly reminding him about all the stolen statuary we'd recovered and offering to provide advice for the diocese on more efficient locks, burglar alarms, et cetera, et cetera. And I said, without thinking much about it, that we were grateful for the occasional assistance of some of his people, notably Merrily Watkins, in providing information leading to certain significant arrests.'

Bliss put down his phone.

'You didn't tell me about saying that.'

'Why would I? Anyway, it didn't go any further. He brushed it aside. Said he was glad the diocese had been helpful, but any future consultation with any of his staff should be directed through his office.'

'Ah, they all start like that.'

'I think he was serious.'

'So?'

'I'm just passing it on, Francis. Mrs Watkins may not be as accessible to you as she has been in the past.'

'She's me mate,' Bliss said.

'Just be bloody careful, that's all. The chief doesn't like to offend the institutional hierarchy.'

Bliss shook his head in disgust. But, yeh. Maybe it wouldn't be helpful to damage Annie's promotional aspirations. For as long as they were both here.

'You ever feel all the old doors are closing on you?'

Annie didn't reply. He let it go and opened the email from Billy Grace, the reply to his query of last night.

No obvious mystery here, Francis.

Battle wounds. I'd say a bloody big sword, one of those two-handed jobbies. Vertical blow splitting the skull down the middle.

Take out the clay it would probably just fall apart.

Working cold-case now, are we?

Ha ha.

Bliss showed it to Annie; she didn't look impressed.

'What was the *point* of that?'

'Dunno, Annie.' Bliss shrugging uneasily. 'It was the middle of the night. You get daft ideas. Like if you boiled all the flesh off Greenaway's head, right now he'd look not unlike our friend.'

He detected something less positive than disbelief on Annie's face.

'You emailed Grace on impulse while I was *asleep*? With the non-availability of Mrs Watkins, does this mean you're trying to think like her?'

'I'm a maverick.'

'Because it doesn't really make any kind of sense, does it?'

'All right, no,' Bliss said. 'It doesn't. It's not rational.'

36

More

THE FLAT SQUARE package had come in the post yesterday.
Well, Lol knew what it would be and had resisted opening it,
thinking it might be nice if he did it when Merrily was here. An
introduction to a possible future.

Never mind. He risked his bass-string thumbnail slitting
the tape.

Inside, a slim, brown-paper parcel, just over twelve inches
square – wouldn't be the same in millimetres. At its centre,
a Knights Frome Studios card carrying a short message from
Prof Levin.

LAURENCE, I WILL ADMIT THAT WHEN I TOOK DELIVERY
OF THESE, I WAS CLOSE TO TEARS. IF I'D THOUGHT
EARLIER, I WOULD HAVE HAD THOSE IMMORTAL LINES
OF YOURS EMBLAZONED ON THE BACK.
'MOURN THE BARREN YEARS, ALL THE TIME WE'VE LOST.'

Lol slid out the album with the matt sleeve: firelight from
an inglenook, a spindly rocking chair, a guitar – the Takamine,
not the Boswell, which had been indisposed at the time. But
at last you could make out the titles of the paperbacks on the
rug: *Thomas Traherne, Selected Poetry and Prose* and *Select
Meditations*. Impossible to read on the CD cover.

'It's beautiful,' Jane said.

'Yup.' Lol nodding. 'And if Prof wants to claim the barren
years for all the years without vinyl, who am I to object?'

'The first Hazey Jane II album, was that vinyl?'

'Came out in that transitional time, so it was actually vinyl, cassette and one of those new, exciting digital compact discs. Never liked the cover, mind. This is so much more seductive.'

Jane held the LP well away from the stove, probably thinking it was in danger of melting if it got warm. Although actually it might be. It looked fragile and precious; the days of scratches and chewing gum were long gone.

'So, like… will it sound all crackly and intimate when we put it on?'

Ah. Well. Actually, I don't know. Mainly due to not having a turntable any more. Perhaps I'll drive into town tomorrow, see how much they cost these days.'

'I see.' Jane sat down primly on the sofa, pulling off what Lol recognized as her mum's red beret. 'So, to get this right, you phoned, asking me to come over to show me some vinyl we can't play.'

'Well, not necessarily tonight. I was thinking maybe tomorrow. I was actually planning to go to the meditation..'

Where sometimes he'd just sit in a back pew, eyes half open, watching Merrily looking soft and shadowy, the rest of the congregation faded out. Act of worship.

'And, uh… just also wanting to remind you that I was… here.'

'Lol, you said—'

'… in case you needed to discuss anything. Someone to listen. You know?'

'You said there were "a couple of things"…'

'Did I?'

'I thought that meant ASAP, and with Mum out of the way for an hour or so…'

'And you agreed, I think, that maybe there were things you needed to discuss.'

Lol sat down in the armchair opposite Jane on the sofa, with the LP across his knees. Maybe tonight was not a good time for this. Better if they'd both gone to the meditation.

'OK,' he said. 'I happened to be talking to Eirion. On the phone. Eirion, your… can we still use that word boyfriend?'

He watched Jane's head bend in almost a spasm, tangled hair falling forward over her eyes.

He was remembering what Eirion had said about the archaeologists in Pembrokeshire. How Jane had been worried that she'd get sneered at, belittled for her interest in folklore and the crazy twentieth-century hippy theories about the arrangement of prehistoric sites and mysterious energies

All of this dating back to when the TV archaeology programme, *Trench One*, had come to record in Herefordshire and Jane had been humiliated.

Lol thought – they'd all thought – that she'd recovered from that. She was a kid. Kids bounced back. But she hadn't been a kid, she'd been on the cusp of probably the biggest change she'd ever go through, maybe the last time she'd have total freedom to choose what happened next.

This had never even occurred to him before, but suppose she'd only made the decision to go for a university course in archaeology just to *prove* she'd got over it, that she was undamaged. That would be so Jane.

'Eirion said you were worried about not fitting in. At first.'

'True. I suppose.'

'But after he'd left you called him and said you'd found some people with the same interests.'

'That's… an exaggeration. In fact there was just one.'

Her voice sounded dry, almost a croak, but she'd refused anything to drink. She was wearing an old Gomer Parry Plant Hire hoodie, coming apart at the neck.

'Most of the others were even more cynical than I'd figured. And then the worst happened. One of them said he'd seen the rushes for the *Trench One* edition that never got screened. Where Bill Blore takes me apart as somebody who ought to be applying to… to…'

'The University of Middle Earth.'

'They never let it go after that. Little snide remarks. Well, it's not like I can't take a joke, but when it doesn't stop…'

'When it doesn't stop it's become bullying.'

'So you keep laughing, knowing that it's a relatively small world, archaeology, and there could be guys here I might wind up working for or attending their lectures, and I'll always be Mystic Jane from the University of Middle fucking Earth. I just… I wanted out, Lol. Actually cried myself to sleep one night. It was going to follow me around, you know?'

'You can't be alone, Jane, in thinking there's more…'

'Yes you *can*. There are professionals and there are loonies. It's like Mum – there are like hundreds of clergy who think she's bonkers. And that's the bloody Church, which is supposed to believe in the One God and all his… all his sodding angels.' Jane had clearly given up pretending she wasn't crying. 'I'm a mess, Lol.'

'We're all a mess. People who don't think they're a mess are just stupid. Go on.'

Jane smiled through it.

'One day, these guys arrive.'

Guys with dowsing rods. Not kids, middle-aged guys who said they were members of the British Society of Dowsers on a field trip. They were on their way to Carn Ingli, the famous mystical summit in the Preseli Hills. Lol thinking, *Oh God…*

'They've spotted the dig,' Jane said, 'and they'd pulled in to have a look. Normally, I mean, dowsers, I'd be dying to talk to them.'

'Well, it works,' Lol said carefully. 'Doesn't it?'

'Lol, the guys I'm with, they've got geofizz, they've got ground radar. Does that suggest they're ready to believe they could do their surveys so much cheaper with a couple of bent coat-hangers?'

'See your point.'

'They're quietly taking the piss. Leaning on the vehicles, making smart remarks. I was making tea, and...'

'You offered them some, right?'

'How insane was *that*? The looks I was getting, I was close to asking if they could quietly give me a lift back to Milford. But then... Sam comes over and starts talking to them. And like, Sam's pretty smart. Sam is, you know, Dr Burnage? And wrote a couple of books, published by some American university like Yale... serious stuff, you know? And I realize Sam's not being sarcastic, not rubbishing it at all. Thinks it's entirely reasonable to think Neolithic people used to dowse for water sources when they were looking for places to settle. And the fact that blind springs tend to be found under standing stones... there *is* a mystery here.'

Jane's face was reddening, only partly because of the stove. She'd said, *You can't tell Mum any of this... not any of it.* And he'd sworn that he wouldn't. *And especially Eirion...* No, no, not a word. And he wouldn't, although he suspected this was going to be difficult.

'So I, like, tentatively join in with the discussion and one of the dowsers lends me his rods and, yeah, I'm getting reactions. You can feel it in your arms. But I'm still being fairly reticent, saying, gosh that's quite interesting, isn't it? Not revealing how much I actually know about earth energies and stuff.'

Which was quite a lot. Lol knew that Jane had been reading about all this for two or three years. Jane had a wooden box containing two pendulums and a pair of Joey Korn swivelling rods.

'And then Sam stands back, with a little smile and paraphrases Hamlet. Shakespeare. *More things, Horatio, more things.*

'... in heaven and earth, Horatio, than are dreamt of in your philosophy. Talking your language.'

'Sam nailed it. Ancient people, we don't just need to find out what things they made, how they lived. We need to see through

241

their eyes, sense what they sensed... aware that their senses would have been much sharper than ours... accepting that they might well have been aware of things we no longer perceive.'

'That really *is* your language.'

'God, yes. I could've kissed Sam. Never been more grateful to anybody in my life. Rescued me from rock bottom. I suppose I kind of worshipped Sam, like when you have a crush on your teacher.'

She was looking at the floor again, hands on her knees.

'Went to the pub that night, just the two of us, and it was really great. I felt like I was... you know, in the vanguard of something. We talked till we got thrown out. About Hereford and Alfred Watkins and the Straight Track Club. Sam said Watkins was a really significant archaeologist whose contribution had been ignored because it came from instinct rather than scientific methodology. I told Eirion on the phone. He said that was great. Somebody I was in tune with.'

Lol didn't know how to respond. It was clear where this was going, and he felt sad about it, for both of them. He'd known Jane for just a little longer than he'd known her mother, but he wasn't sure that unloading this on him was going to help her.

'It all turned around.' She looked up, bleakly dry-eyed. 'I didn't want it to end. I was learning – or thought I was – that it didn't matter how you came to it, or how you found the commitment. And because I was a mate of Sam's, other guys started to take an interest in helping me, and they'd take me off to the pub and places, and nobody mentioned Bill Blore again.'

Lol could hear Eirion.

We'd both heard that these archaeological digs were, like, shagfests, but there was none of that that I could see. The guys were quite protective towards Jane.

'I thought I'd grown up,' Jane said. 'I thought I'd changed. I was looking back at the waste of space I was at fifteen. Looking back from the adult world. God, how we fool ourselves.'

Lol took off his glasses, couldn't find a tissue and rubbed the lenses with the hem of his sweatshirt.

'If you want to leave them off,' Jane said, 'I'll cut to the chase. On the last night, everybody went to the pub and, like, no way was I going to get pissed, so I stuck to cider. Cider and me, I thought we had an arrangement.'

'Not all ciders are the same.'

'Quite. I knew that better than anybody. So obviously I don't remember getting back to the B and B. Except when I woke up next morning and realized it wasn't my B and B.'

'Sam's?'

He thought she nodded, but maybe not.

'You heard from Sam since you left?'

'We haven't spoken since.'

'So it's over?'

'Lol, it never really started, except…'

She looked back at the floor. Lol sat there with his glasses in his lap, feeling the onus on him to make her feel better.

'Well,' he said. 'You know… I mean, these things happen.'

'There was a text,' Jane said. 'Asking if I'd got Sam's email. Perhaps there was something important in it. I don't know. I'd deleted it as soon as I saw the name.' She paused. 'Dr Samantha Burnage.'

Lol said, 'Oh.'

Jane looked almost relieved.

'It's not just about telling you. I've told Lucy now.'

She looked up. All around the room. As if she might find her there: Lucy Devenish, soul of the village, mentor to Jane, mentor to Lol, living on in the stone and the timber and the applewood smoke.

37

Coffin wood

THERE WEREN'T SUPPOSED to be discussions afterwards, at least not in the church. The deal was that they just left quietly, carrying something away with them. Something positive, you hoped.

But whatever you suggested, there'd always be two or three people who wanted to talk. Tonight, in the porch, Gus Staines, in a long grey woolly, handed her a small Ledwardine Livres carrier bag. For Jane. As promised. No hurry to have it back.

'She *is* all right, isn't she?'

'Jane? She's a bit undecided, I think. About what she wants to do with her life. We've all been there, I suppose. Why do you ask?'

'They grow up very quickly, don't they,' Gus said. 'We forget.'

'I suppose it just doesn't seem very quick to us at the time. Seems to take forever. Sometimes I wonder if we ever do. Grow up.'

Hell, was that even true? One of the worst aspects of being a priest was people expecting you to have a higher level of wisdom.

Merrily hurried out of the lychgate, over the cobbles and back to the vicarage without meeting anybody else. It would've been nice to see Lol hanging around at the top of Church Street, although, even before the call to Sophie, the idea of inviting him over for a meal had lost its momentum. What kind of an item were they, really?

The vicarage was silent, only the smallest lamp on in the kitchen and a note on the table.

Mum, had something to eat.

Gone for a bath and then bed.

With the book.

Tell you about it over breakfast.

That's if we don't meet before dawn again.

love, J

When did they stop being children? Should she go up to Jane, or would that be an old-hen thing to do?

She wasn't tired. If she sat down she wouldn't relax. If she went to bed early she wouldn't sleep. Talking to Jane, sharing a meal would have passed the time. Now there was no excuse.

How was she supposed to sleep anyway, with this hanging over her?

She went through to the scullery and sat down behind the computer, a sleeping monster with one small, baleful white eye. She stared at the blank screen then awoke it.

Ledwardine Broadband wasn't the fastest. Downloading the audio file took over half an hour. She went back to the kitchen and gave Ethel more food, thought about getting herself something to eat and couldn't face it. Made herself a pot of tea.

It was around ten before she switched off all the lights except the scullery Anglepoise, opened the document in iTunes, plugged in the headphones.

'*Sophie's an admirable woman in many ways,*' Craig Innes said into her ears. '*But Merrily Watkins would appear to be her one blind spot.*'

She'd never really listened to his voice before. It was quite high-pitched. A good, fluty preacher's voice. You thought of sheeny new pine. Coffin wood.

'*—not including those who've eventually wound up in psychiatric care,*' Craig Innes was saying.

The quality was startlingly crisp. Innes must have been sitting at Sophie's desk, quite close to the iPhone.

'Hasn't happened to many women. To my knowledge.' Siân's voice more distant, probably from the desk in the window. Her desk. Her former desk. *'Craig, there haven't yet been many female deliverance ministers.'*

'I don't have figures. It's not widely discussed.'

Siân talked about her own, limited experience in deliverance, her conclusion – unexpected – that there was actually quite a significant demand for it, even in what was increasingly perceived as a secular age. After this came a slow, muted hiss, like *tssk, tssk,* that could only be Craig Innes expressing impatience.

'I'm increasingly inclined to think that it's simply a demand we've created. Or have – unwisely – allowed to create itself.'

'Craig, it's a traditional ministry. Admittedly not always monitored, but—'

'But if the only way we can fill pews is by becoming... ghostbusters... what does that say about the Church in the Third Millennium?'

His voice faded over, you could hear his footsteps. He was pacing, angry.

'... if she says no to rural dean...'

'Do you think she's even had enough experience to be a rural dean?' Isn't that likely to cause some resentment amongst the... the lifers?'

'As exorcist, she replaced a man of over seventy!'

'Yes. But a man who was so forbidding and slightly sinister that people – even priests – were often disinclined to consult him.'

'You're saying it was a bad thing, to discourage people from allowing their imaginations to run riot?'

'What I think I'm saying is that Merrily Watkins, with her sometimes hesitant and even rather nervous approach, makes people—'

'And you think that's a good thing?'

'She's been more accessible,' Siân said lamely. 'That's all I'm...'

Silence.

'Like a convenience store,' Innes said.

A longer silence before Siân tried again.

'It might be argued that she brings people to us who... the kind of people who never expected to have anything to do with the Church. And they come to us for help because they're at the very least puzzled and at the worst terrified. And there's nowhere else to go.'

'At best imaginative. At worst, mentally ill. And also—'

'Craig, look, I'm... I'm not sure I'm really the best person for you to be discussing this with.'

'You're the Archdeacon, for heaven's sake! My chief of staff.'

'However, the deliverance minister, by tradition, reports exclusively and directly to the Bishop.'

'Does she? Does she really? My understanding is that she blatantly takes advice from someone outside the diocese. Now. Am I at fault in not wanting the business of this diocese discussed with an outsider who appears to exercise influence over a woman occupying a position I already distrust?'

'Huw Owen.'

'Who lives alone on the top of a mountain with his head in the clouds. I grew up in Brecon, I have many friends there who've had dealings with this man.'

'Craig, surely it's been normal practice for several years in dioceses either side of the border to have priests sent for deliverance training to Huw Owen.'

Pause.

'Who is mad. Who is known to be increasingly and terminally mad.'

It was after midnight by the time she'd listened to the end, replaying some of it and scrawling notes on her sermon pad.

She sat for another twenty minutes drinking industrial black tea before pulling the phone over and letting her fingers find the number on the old metal dial. Waiting until the answering machine kicked in.

Aware that her voice was going to sound robotic. Only way she could get the words out.

'What worries me most,' she said to the machine, 'is that I don't think it's purely personal. Because if it was, I think I'd get a sense of a reason for him to hate me.'

She broke off, clapping a hand over the mouthpiece to take an e-cig hit.

'And yet I surely can't be insane enough to see a wider picture. Can I? You listen to some bits again, you get a sense almost of something, I don't know, almost apocalyptic?' She laughed. 'Oh shit, wish I could erase this and start again.'

'Aye, all right, lass,' Huw said. 'Start again in the morning.'

'Can that machine even work without you?'

'Don't sleep well these nights. Happen it's me age.'

'Where *are* you this morning?'

'On your doorstep,' Huw said. 'Wouldn't want to miss owt apocalyptic.'

'You know what? That's not a word I'd erase.'

'Quite right,' Huw said. 'Get to bed and don't oversleep. I'll be early.'

Part Four

In some cases, with regard to superstitious beliefs, there is a deep reserve to be overcome; the more real the belief, the greater the difficulty.

Ella Mary Leather
The Folklore of Herefordshire

38

FOTD

JANE AWOKE FOR maybe the eighteenth time into the same impenetrable, hurting, darkness.

A lousy, lousy night. Bruises on her thighs, arms, ankles, bruises she hadn't known about until she got into bed, and each one started opening up aching memories of where it had come from. A dusty, dry shower of shredding leaves kept making her cough as she squirmed in and out of dreams. Dry leaves and damp, rotting leaves and slimy long grass which became, on waking, just her own sweat on the ruched and wrinkled undersheet.

She trailed a hand down the side of the bed, groping for her phone on the wooden floor. The phone told her it was coming up to five minutes past four. Wasn't that the hour of the wolf? Or maybe the hour of the grainy white body that she kept trying to turn, oh God, into a naked man.

Jane rolled painfully on to her back, looking for the attic window. Any window. Any way out.

What had she done? Her instinct was to call Lol, call him now, wake him up, hiss into his ear: *You just forget it, you understand? You didn't see me last night, I didn't come round, I didn't tell you anything and we're never going to discuss it again. You just delete this from your memory.*

As if.

She would, of course, have to go back to Lucy's cottage, sit down with him again. She'd have to find answers to his quite reasonable questions: *Did anything happen? Do you even remember?* And then, with hope in his voice, *Could this amount to sexual assault?* Questions she'd evaded, saying she had to go. Needed to get home before Mum came back from church.

What it must have done to him asking her those things. Recalling – as if he needed to, as if every day wasn't tarnished by those memories – the time when, as a teenage rock musician given too much to drink by an older bandmate, he'd wound up in bed with a girl who'd looked at least as old as he was and was probably a lot less innocent. The smashing of his future, his sense of who he was.

But at least it had been a girl.

Oh, come on. Times had changed… dramatically. Gus Staines and Amanda Rubens were a respectable married couple, and quite right too, and she and Sam were, like…

… consenting adults. Unattached, consenting adults.

Had she consented? She didn't know, any more than she knew what she'd seen on the gorsey plateau. If anything.

Jane reached up for the cord and put on the light. Colour bled gradually into what was left of the Mondrian walls, faded red and blue squares between the timber framing. On the floor beside the bed, where the phone had lain, was a book, *The Summoner.*

She wouldn't get back to sleep now. If she'd ever really slept.

In the hours before dawn, she opened the book and entered the Nightlands. Like she'd ever left.

Bliss was at Gaol Street before seven, parts of the pavements slick with the first frost, Dowell intercepting him on the stairs, bulked out in a Scandi-looking sweater.

'How long you been in, Karen?'

'I dunno, two hours, three. Listen, I've found something, Frannie. Well, it might be not be that much, but it's one of the few non-obvious things that pops up on both hard disks.'

'Soffley's and Greenaway's?'

He followed her through the CID room into his own office, where she already had the two laptops opened up.

'Not *quite* the same, one's only initials – that's Greenaway's – but the context suggests we're looking at the same thing. FOTD. Mean anything to you?'

'What *is* the context?'

'It's in a deleted email Greenaway sent to someone called Gordon Barclay-Hughes, who seems to be the editor of one of those Internet magazines read by nutters. Greenaway says he's lost touch with the people from FOTD, especially someone he just calls JT, and can Barclay-Hughes help him out?'

'When was this?'

'Well, that's the point. Night before he died. I only went looking for it because Barclay-Hughes replied today, evidently not having heard about Greenaway's murder. He just says – hang on, I'll— OK, here it is, he says, "Sorry mate, not heard from any of them in years. I assumed that all fell apart way back. I imagine Mr T's far too big for all that now. Cheers, Gordon."'

'You tracked Gordon down?'

'He's in Devon. Totnes.'

'New Age hotbed, Karen,' Bliss said. 'They have public buildings with parking spaces for UFOs. Let's ask Devon and Cornwall if they know him. What's the other reference?'

'That's in Soffley's Neogoth contacts file. Nothing new, and nothing to explain what it is. Just a reference to the Friends of the Dusk. FOTD?'

'Friends of the…?'

'Dusk.'

'That's gorra hint of Dark Web about it, hasn't it?

Bliss looked at Karen She had her plump lips pursed, nodding.

'I do like the sound of Mr T, Karen. I love it when fellers are described as "too big". If there's any childish pleasures left in police work, taking down someone who's too big has to be one of them. And did Soffley let them see the piccy of Steve?'

'Who?'

'The skull, Karen. Go on, make my day.'

'Consider it made, boss,' Karen said.

'I thought it was going to be worse than it turned out to be,' Jane said. 'It's not the usual kidlit fantasy drivel. Where the vampires aren't all bad because there are different kinds of vampires?'

'But they're always sexy.' Mum sounding tired. 'That seems to be a given.'

Maybe she'd slept badly. She was doing her best to look attentive, but she really wasn't all here. She'd made scrambled eggs for them, with wholemeal toast, but was only picking at hers. She was wearing her old grey dressing gown, frayed at the hem and the cuffs, and the slippers with one flapping sole. She looked... God... middle-aged.

Jane wasn't hungry either.

It was seven-thirty a.m.

'The romantic vampire stuff,' Jane said, 'that's been around for most of my life. If I hadn't read *Dracula* and *Salem's Lot* I'd still be looking for a vampire to fall in love with. Although the ones in this book... I don't even know if they *are* vampires in the strictest sense.'

'That's what it says on the back.'

'Yeah, but that's what publishers do, isn't it? Vampires sell books.'

'But you actually finished it?' Mum reached for a piece of toast but didn't do anything with it. 'The whole thing.'

'Yeah.'

'And enjoyed it?'

'I wouldn't quite say that.'

'Why not?'

'I don't know. It's just... dark.'

'You like dark.'

'It's... I don't know.'

'OK.' Mum put down the toast. 'This is very good of you, flower. You want to go from the beginning?'

Hereford was never going to be a city that never slept.

Bliss took Vaynor with him across the zebra, through the sluggish early traffic to Commercial Road, where most of the lights were for security, and into the alleyways leading to Organ Yard, where there were no lights at all.

Above the dark brick courtyard the early sky was ridged like galvanized roofing. Vaynor directed the little light in his phone at the window blinds in The Darkest Corner. The blinds were old and rubbery-looking.

There was nobody around to disturb. Bliss rapped on the glass, raised his voice to the sky.

'Good morning, Jerry. Time to come out of your coffin.'

'I think the premise is,' Vaynor murmured, 'that they go *back* to their coffins at daybreak, boss.'

'Don't be pedantic, Darth. Come *on*, Jerry!'

He shook the door handle and the door opened.

Bliss looked up at Vaynor, stood and thought for a few seconds. Pulled a tissue from a pocket of his suit and wrapped it around his hand before pushing the door all the way.

The light was on inside.

'After you, Darth,' Bliss said eventually, then changed his mind. 'No, all right, he knows me.'

The dirty glass hanging lamp was the brightest light he'd met since the traffic on Commercial Road. Bliss stepped inside, Vaynor just behind him. He blinked, and the smell came for him, aggressively, made only more sickening by the resident cannabis scent.

'Oh, for fuck's sake,' Bliss said quietly.

He didn't move, looked all around the shop. Plastic skull. Rack of dark clothing, hats, album covers, posters. Jerry Soffley's last slanting smile, wide-open eyes like little poached eggs.

Hello again, Sarge. Frank.

Soffley was sitting up against the wall left of the counter, near the doorway to the vinyl room, the state of his exposed teeth indicating that with his very last breaths he'd been sucking in blood and snot from his smashed nose. No need to go too close, you could guess from the state of the wall what the back of the head would be like.

Bliss said, 'Jerry, I never thought. Never entered me head for a minute.'

Thought he'd known exactly where he was going with this case, all his questions for Soffley lined up neat as bullets in a clip: *Friends of the Dusk, Jerry – who? Names. Locations. What are they about? How was Tristram Greenaway involved? Is it a gay thing?*

The shop was no less tidy than it had been yesterday. This wasn't about robbery, any more than Greenaway's murder had been. Bliss was seriously pissed off about this. Why hadn't he entertained the slightest possibility that somebody might think Jerry Soffley knew too much to be left alive?

He came gratefully out of the darkness to find Vaynor leaning back against the exterior wall, the back of his head tilted into greasy old brick, looking up into the clean sky.

'Not your first one, surely, Darth?'

'First one like this, boss.' Vaynor fetched out a bent cigarette and lit up. 'Fast-tracked into CID, if you recall. Due to my record of…' He stared into the smoke. '… academic excellence. Missed out on a lot of dead drunks in back-alleys, motorway carnage.'

He was looking at the end of his cigarette in disgust.

'I didn't know you indulged,' Bliss said.

'Don't. Not much anyway. It's to get rid of the smell. And the taste.' Vaynor risked a glance at the bottom of his trousers and the bits of butchery on his shoes. 'Hadn't we better call this in?'

39

The Summoner

THE NIGHTLANDS. THE countryside in negative. It looks lush and verdant by day but at night, even in high summer, the colours drain away and the trees become skeletal around the village and on the hill where the castle stands.

The village doesn't have a name, nor does the castle.

It's not like Castle Dracula. It's the reverse of all that. The castle is held by a good family with a tradition of protecting the people who live in the village below. You gradually meet the villagers, the baker and the blacksmith. And the Cunning Man who's not as cunning as he used to be.

'The village is surrounded by this thickening forestry,' Jane said. 'Or rather forestry that thickens at night. Even though, at night, its leaves disappear. Night is like winter. That's quite nicely described – only the bad parts, the spiky bits and the thorns remain, and the deeper you go, the harder and tighter it gets and the more all your exposed skin gets cut and slashed.'

At night, the forest becomes limitless, as if it's part of some other sphere of existence or it leads to one.

'You don't have to explain these things to kids,' Jane said.

Thinking how easy it had been for her, with her bruises and abrasions, to realize it all.

'Entering the wood is like crawling through coils of barbed wire. Although Foxy Rowlestone doesn't put it that way because barbed wire hadn't been invented then.'

The book's inside cover had a photo of Foxy Rowlestone sitting on a small knoll by a stream, her face half turned away, her hair in coils, feet hidden in the folds of her long, velvet-looking dress. If Dante Gabrielle Rosetti had been a fashion photographer…

'When's this set, exactly?' Mum said.

'Twelfth century. That's made clear. All the history seems to be accurate. Over twelve hundred years since the birth of your Saviour.'

Jane buttered a half-slice of toast. It still looked too sickly to eat. She was wearing a sweatshirt and jeans, but Mum must've spotted a wince.

'Bruises?'

'One or two. I didn't realize. It's OK, I've applied arnica.'

'You're sure it's OK?'

'Yeah, yeah. Anyway, the Summoner's back. After nearly a century.'

'The Summoner.'

'He comes out of the woods, the Nightlands. He looks human, vaguely. He's stick-thin, skin and bones. And he's part of the Nightlands. Almost like part of the wood when he's in there, so it doesn't harm *him*. Because he's basically a corpse, anyway.'

'A zombie?'

'That word isn't used, thank God. It's post-medieval, it isn't British and it's naff. But kids can work these things out for themselves.'

'You always could.'

'The Summoner… the villagers thought he was history. Hasn't been seen in anybody's lifetime. But they know that when he comes it means certain death, and he gives no warning of his visits. He's suddenly there, in the village, and everybody rushes inside and cowers and waits for his declaration. "I am come," he says, "to call a name." And the villagers are frozen into a state of like breathless terror? On the basis that whoever's name is called will not have long to live. They'll fall ill and die within a few days. Once your name's been called, you don't ever get spared. That's it. Curtains.'

'Bingo from hell.' Mum shook her head. 'Sorry. I'm tired. No, you're right, that's darker than sucking blood because it happens in everyday life, even kids' lives. People you know fall ill and die – relatives, neighbours, and that's genuinely frightening.'

'Anyway,' Jane said, 'the village is resigned to it. The local peasants say that any man with the courage to try and approach the Summoner finds, when he reaches the spot where the fiend was last seen, that he's no longer there. And they'll hear the parting laughter from somewhere deep in the wood, sometimes followed – gleefully – by the name of the man who tried to catch him.'

'So nobody does.'

'Even up at the castle they're helpless. The current knight, Sir William, is away at the Crusades, leaving his wife and daughter with his elderly father, Sir Roland. We're seeing all this through the eyes of Sir William's daughter, Catherine, who's sixteen and about to experience the horror first-hand when the Summoner appears on the castle hill. Calling for her mother, who starts to go pale and anaemic. And so it goes on.'

'What's the intended age group for this stuff?'

'Young adult. Twelve-plus?'

'It's just I'm wondering if this is a metaphor for the Black Death or something.'

'Kids hate metaphor. Besides, the rest doesn't really fit with disease. The Summoner is what's left of this itinerant magician. He'd slink around the towns and villages of the borderland, passing himself off as a healer but all the time he'd be experimenting on his patients in his search for the secret of immortality. Which he evidently found, in a warped way because, despite being killed by one of Sir Roland's ancestors, he comes back, every generation or so. He's older – like, he should've been dead perhaps decades ago or even centuries. He comes back to rejuvenate himself by taking other people's lives.'

'Which *is* a vampire thing, isn't it?'

'But without the fangs and the puncture marks. He's just absorbing their life energy. Which, to me, is scarier. Because it makes more sense.'

'Mmm.' Mum pushed her plate away, held the e-cig up to the lamp, brown fluid rising. 'Go on. I'm still listening.'

'This is the interesting bit. In the past, the Summoner destroyed the village by taking so many people that the others just packed up and buggered off. So the village was left derelict, and it took over fifty years for people to start coming back. And now they're leaving again.'

'I get the connection,' Mum said. 'What I don't get is why kids – girls – apparently loved it so much.'

'I'll explain. Comes down to Geraint, the blacksmith's son, who comes up to the castle to chop the wood and refurbish the weaponry. He's like very strong and handsome, but he's just a peasant, and Catherine's been brought up to have nothing to do with him… so you see where this is going. Especially after old Sir Roland, Catherine's grandad, puts on his rusting armour and goes out to the woods to take on the Summoner and doesn't come back, and then, next night, the Summoner returns, stronger than ever, and calls out the name of Geraint's dad, the blacksmith.'

'No let-up, then.'

'Oh, you really do feel their desperation, Catherine and the blacksmith's son, both bereaved. There's a memorable scene where Geraint forces himself to go into the woods and comes back with Sir Roland's discarded armour and works into the night at his forge putting together a new suit of armour out of the old one. One that fits him, natch. And then he makes a big sword, and— You keep looking at the clock.'

'Sorry. It's just that Huw Owen's coming… I don't know when, and I need a shower. I take it Geraint kills the Summoner?'

'And buries him in the wood. Which you just know is going to turn out to be a mistake. Mainly because you know there's a second book.'

'He's undead, the Summoner. Presumably.'

'Still undead after two books. Still out there. Mum...?'

'Mmm?'

'Remind me who I said lived in Cwmarrow Castle?'

'Erm... the de Chandos family? And then the... Lowry... no... Loudons? I've got it down somewhere. There's not much. Cwmarrow Castle was built at a time when local history doesn't seem to have been recorded much outside of the Domesday Book, especially in a place like this, in the border, so we're reliant on—' Mum jumped up suddenly. 'Oh hell, Jane, I forgot – lot on my mind. Gus Staines gave me a book for you last night. I put it... somewhere.'

'*Borderlight*?'

'Sorry. Would've given it you last night, but you'd gone up. It's on the dresser. Jane... is it easy to find someone on Facebook?'

'Usually. I packed all that in, as you know.'

'I do know, because of all the times you've assured me that it's now strictly for sad middle-aged people. Except ones like me who wouldn't have time even if they wanted to go there. But obviously there are a few million kids still doing it. Would it be easy for you to... you know...?'

'Stalk one for you?'

'Can you do that without revealing your own identity?'

'To an extent. It's not stalking, Mum. Everybody who goes on Facebook is screeching, Look at me, look at me! I *had* planned to go into Hereford and remind Coops I'm available for work, but he's probably got enough on his mind. You'll want me out of the way, right, when Huw's here?'

'I never like to inhibit him.'

Jane looked up at the high window where the dawn sky had a flawless, metallic sheen. It looked cold, the day already unrolling emptily.

'Jane's Bureau of Investigation,' she said. 'We're good but we're not cheap.'

'I'm a priest. We're always broke.'

'What's the name?'

'Her name's Aisha,' Mum said. 'Malik.'

40

Going out normal

FELT LIKE SMASHING his fist into the old brick. He'd fucked up, misjudged this. Made light of it almost – the chickenshit row involving archaeology, egos and a skull called Steve that somehow escalated into a killing.

The cordon tapes were going up, forensic screening on its way, the alleyway already blocked off by the van that would eventually ferry Jerry Soffley to his undignified appointment with Billy Grace.

The nailed-up doors and the barred and boarded windows of Organ yard mocked Bliss like the dead eyes of a suspect who knew only two words: *no comment.*

'Is there no bugger living in *any* of those buildings, Darth?'

Most of all the brick properties overlooking Organ Yard on three sides were hardly well maintained.

'Commercial premises, warehouses, garaging,' Vaynor said. 'No apartments that I'm aware of – but then we didn't know Soffley lived over the shop.'

'What are they? You're a local lad. Anything that opens daily?'

'A furniture shop? Back end of a pub.'

'Pub. That's better. Which one? You lose your sense of direction this end of town.'

Durex suits had taken over the shop, Bliss and Vaynor, unsuited, relegated to the perimeter. It was a fine, cold morning, but Slim Fiddler said bad weather was on the way, Bliss wondering if they'd bring Soffley out before the rain came and the wind. Before the weather turned Gothic.

Could've talked to me, you daft twat, when you had the chance. Some bastards aren't worth protecting.

Greenaway, that could've been rage, this was different. This was much more like hard-man stuff, a cold and intentional killing. This dragged you right back into the Plascarreg Estate. He should have known. He should've seen a thin Plas vein running through this from the start.

He pointed up beyond a grey-painted wall with a door in it, probably to a small yard, rusting metal steps rising out of it.

'What's that fire escape for, Darth?'

'Not sure… no, wait, that'll be the gastro-pub, the Old Coach House? And on the end, that's a gents' hairdressers, I think.'

'Open till late then, the pub.'

'Yeah, but all the windows are boarded up. This is the problem. Nobody looks down on Organ Yard. It's not like that little yard's going to be a beer garden or anything, it's just to accommodate the fire escape.'

'Need to go over that yard, anyway, in case anything got conveniently tossed over the wall. Wonder if any of them have CCTV.'

'Can't see anything from here. No cameras at all in the immediate vicinity, though we'll have pictures of anybody *entering* the vicinity from the front. Not too many to eliminate after closing time on a Sunday.'

'Including Soffley on his way back from delivering his lappie for Karen. 'Let's look at the timeline: my little chat with Soffley, Soffley going to pick up his laptop, bringing it into Gaol Street, returning to his shop. Did someone follow him? That'd be nice, wouldn't it?'

'Or if he met somebody.'

'We need to find out who knew him in town, where he drank. Look, this is significant – he normally has stuff out in front of the shop, second-hand pews and things. Nothing here now. It's all been taken back in, and not put out again. Strongly suggesting this happened after closing time.'

'Or the killer comes just as Soffley's ready to shut up shop and put the lights out. Might just have walked in as a customer.'

'No sign of a break-in, so either Jerry let somebody in or, as you say, somebody followed him in. Sunday teatime, Darth, in Hereford. Nobody to hear you scream. Whoever did Soffley had time. Walk in. Hit him with whatever it was. Door bolted, down with the blinds, finish him off. Wait till dark.'

'Not long to wait.'

'Then slip away.'

'Professional?'

'Looking that way.'

Vaynor squeezed his second cigarette to death between finger and thumb, pocketed it.

'I know how it *looks*, boss, but at the end of the day how sure *are* we that this is the same one who did Greenaway?'

'We're not. Yet. Won't be the same hammer, might not even *be* a hammer. And where we were thinking Greenaway was maybe an argument that got out of hand, this is somebody who wanted Soffley dead, came in with that purpose. But if we assume they *are* linked, this puts the Greenaway killing into a whole new league, doesn't it?'

'Doesn't look like a domestic argument gone wrong any more, I'll give you that.'

'Another thing. Whoever did this probably had the time and the privacy and all the props – hangman's rope in the back room, masks, executioners' hoods with eyeholes, assorted S and M kit...'

'Sorry, boss?'

'To arrange something artistic. But they didn't. Nothing to suggest they didn't just leave him where he fell.'

'It's not *Midsomer Murders*, boss.'

'No, but this... this is almost an insult. Final insult. Bog-standard blunt instrument. Routine. Nothing Gothic. Going out normal. He'd friggin' hate that, Darth. He'd be... mortified may be an inappropriate word, but...'

The front window of the Darkest Corner was full of invasive white light, Durex suits prowling like aliens inside and out. Bliss was aware of Vaynor looking at him strangely.

'I'm not being friggin' whimsical. If it was kids – teenage lads – they wouldn't be able to resist playing around, dressing him up a bit, all the spooky kit in there.'

He felt mad at himself. Sick at what he might, inadvertently, have set Soffley up for. Sad for a poor bastard he hadn't liked and who hadn't liked him either.

Twisted. He felt twisted up inside, uncomfortable. This was going to be a big case now. Extra bodies shipped in from Worcester, probably with a new SIO, maybe Iain Twatface Brent, Worcester-case scenario. Everybody up to the Gaol Street penthouse, computers uncovered, the dogs of war unleashed.

And it was too small for all of that. This was something… not domestic, but certainly prosaic and rational and unworthy of any of the spooky drivel that was going to get sprayed all over the media.

He felt that keenly. He stared around the enclosing buildings, the dumb intimacy of Organ Yard. Glad now that he hadn't ignored the new Bishop and had a quiet word with Merrily Watkins, because the weird bits were just a distraction, not even window dressing.

41

The Hereford Issue

THE BISHOP WAS saying he'd spent some days walking the city streets alone, a stranger, unrecognized. Listening to people, absorbing their concerns. A new moon in the Hereford firmament.

'Pretentious, too,' Huw said. 'I'd forgotten that.'

He was sitting in Merrily's scullery, chair pushed back against the wall, his boots off, his feet in hiking socks up on the desk. He'd been here since half-eight, arriving in plain clothes: worn canvas jacket, no dog collar. What was that saying?

'*This was towards the end of September,*' the Bishop said from the computer. '*I saw some people standing out there looking up at the gatehouse. At this office. Do you know what one of them said?*'

No reply from Siân Callaghan-Clarke.

'*It was a woman. She said, You know what that is? Up there? That's where the exorcist works.*'

'He just made that up,' Huw said. 'The bugger.'

'*Medieval,*' Innes said. '*Over there is the apothecary, next to him the money lender. And, up there, that is the exorcist's office. You see what I mean? Colourful word, medieval, but hardly a propitious one. Suggestive of something half developed. Often describing societies that torture prisoners, publicly dismember petty criminals and use religion like a blunt instrument.*'

'But not necessarily in our own society, Bishop.'

'*Which...*' Innes carrying on talking as if he hadn't heard her. '*... is one reason for my decision to find her somewhere else, less public. I thought the cloisters at first, but there's an increasing* number of tourists trooping around there, and word gets out. And the cloisters are even more medieval. And substantially darker.'

'You'd like to put her somewhere less visible. Or not visible at all?'

'Perhaps a corner of the crypt,' Merrily said.

Huw looked up at her.

'Going to sit down for this, lass?'

She pulled a stool to the other side of the desk. There was a lot more to go, none of it missed by the iPhone which, if fully-charged and not overloaded with data, could apparently record for hours.

'*Don't get me wrong,*' Innes was saying. '*I do believe we have a part to play in the healing of minds, and that we should not deny that. But it mainly amounts to observation, counselling and, when necessary, referral.*'

Pause.

'*Referral?*' Siân said.

'*To an outside agency more qualified to deal with it.*'

'*You mean the National Health Service.*'

They heard the Bishop's grunt, the click of a briefcase hasp.

'*I did say when necessary. While accepting that this is not always a judgement call for us…*'

The sound of leafing through pages before the Bishop read out a very well-known paragraph from 'A Time to Heal', the Church's millennial report for the House of Bishops on the Ministry of Healing, including deliverance. The report was widely seen to have put deliverance firmly in its place – one short chapter. The paragraph's punchline, after references to epilepsy and dissociative and catatonic hysteria, was the suggestion that 'the man with the evil spirits in Acts 19.16' had been suffering from schizophrenia.

Siân said suddenly, '*What about Sophie?*'

'*Oh, Mrs Hill stays here. Mrs Hill is my secretary.*'

'*But Craig, Sophie maintains the deliverance database, deals with aftercare schedules, acts as a sounding board…*'

268

'*Entirely unofficially. And that role will shrink.*'

Merrily turned her face away from the computer. Was this the third or fourth time she'd made herself listen to this?

The final time she'd cut it short. Separated something from the end that she wasn't ready for anyone, not even Huw, to hear.

'*It's inevitable,*' the Bishop said. '*Essentially, how I feel about Mrs Watkins is that she was rather forced into this unenviable role – Hunter ostensibly wanting a young, attractive woman to make it all appear less frightening. But, as we know—*'

'Ha!' Huw swung his feet from the desk. 'How do I stop it for a minute?'

Merrily leaned over and froze the recording. As expected, Huw had identified the detonator.

Hunter. A name you rarely heard in the vicinity of the cathedral, although he was not long gone. Bishop Mick: young, charming, populist, well connected. And possessed of an inner darkness that still remained unapproachable. It would be impossible to believe if you hadn't been there – that the Church, faced with something so primevally explosive, could be so brilliant at defusing it, erecting a blank wall of unlikely but surprisingly effective, politically correct diffidence. *Poor Michael,* they'd purred to one another. *How could we have missed the signs of such emotional and spiritual instability?*

'Remind me,' Huw said. 'Has anybody ever said owt in public about Hunter working the night shift?'

'You know they haven't. Except for one downmarket tabloid which the *Guardian* didn't even bother to mock. The fact that he was so quickly gone... well, that was all that's ever seemed to matter. Besides, realistically, we still don't know how much of it was down to being blackmailed over his... sex addiction. Which, of course, wasn't talked about either.'

'Don't matter, lass. He were playing for the other side. Don't matter why. Don't matter what they said or didn't say, it went deep. *Bloody* deep.'

'And was buried even deeper.'

'Their only consolation was it happened in Hereford. The arse-end of nowhere. And, credit where it's due, they moved fast to put the diocese into a safe pair of hands.'

Bernie Dunmore, suffragan Bishop of Ludlow. Close enough to know something of the situation, old enough to sit on it.

'I'm guessing Innes had been in the wings a long time,' Huw said. 'Dunmore were never really chief-executive material, and he knew that. He happen also knew who was in line to succeed him and said nowt. These things get settled behind closed doors.'

'At my level, we don't even know where the doors are.'

'Dunmore was about buying time, we knew that,' Huw said. 'He hung on longer than expected, but that were no bad thing. Canterbury having quietly set up a working group to deal with what'd become known as The Hereford Issue.'

'You know that for a fact?'

Huw leaned back into a pool of sunlight.

'Once talked to a feller – I'm not going to name him, but I were up north, catching up wi' a few folks. Attending a small dinner party in York, not my scene usually, but I couldn't get out of it. This feller, he used a word from them daft American ghost shows on the idiot channels. Ah, he says, the Hereford *dark portal.* Needs to be sealed off once and for all, don't you think?'

'That was a joke, right?'

'It were said in a way where you could *take* it for a joke.'

'Jesus,' Merrily said.

'What to do about Hereford,' Huw said. 'Do you appoint a deeply spiritual man – High Church, candle-burner, incense-swinger?'

'Too medieval?'

'Or do you go the other way? A low-church hard bastard. Happen there were long, private discussions in back rooms – discussions as never took place. See, wi' nobody talking like this any more, it's easy to forget nowadays what the Church were originally supposed to be about. Don't you think?'

'I think about it all the time. So what did this... working group... come up with?'

Huw smiled.

'Haven't seen the report. If there *was* a report, which I doubt. But the result, of course, is Craig Innes. A bland and pragmatic man on the surface, steel frame underneath. A mixture of modernism and the Welsh Chapel mentality. Not so much a new broom as an industrial Hoover. Gets into the dark corners.'

'Including mine.'

'Especially yours. He's been put in place to wipe out the last traces of Mick Hunter and all his works.'

'I'm still seen as part of Hunter's work and, as such, the Church wants me out?'

'The Church is saying to Innes, Do what you need to, but don't draw attention to it.'

'Because I'm one of the last links with Hunter?'

'*Because*, lass, you know as much of the truth as it's possible for anybody to know.'

'Well, yes, but which I don't talk about because everybody would think I was crazy. Why have they left me alone for so long?'

'Because the Church has always moved grindingly slowly. And of course you've done a good job, handled more hot potatoes in a couple of years than Dobbs stuck a fork into for his entire career. You've made mistakes and a few iffy friends, you've taken wrong turnings. But Dunmore always liked you, even when you made things hard for him. All right, occasionally, he'd be told to give you a prod, like making you work in a committee with that bloody shrink and Siân. But even Siân's come round.'

'I thought so, too.'

Huw folded his arms.

'I just don't know, lass. It's clear he can't just get rid of you, he's got to try and make you bugger off of your own free will.'

'Rural dean...'

'Promotion. A vote of confidence. That's a good start. Go on. Play me the rest.'

271

There were bits they could skip, business unrelated to deliverance. It was clear Innes hadn't wanted to come on too heavy with Siân. The purpose of this meeting was to deal with human-recources issues, including whether the rural dean job should be offered to Merrily – Siân hardly in a position to say no to that.

And Siân had been a barrister, a useful hard wall to bounce his ideas off.

Slowly, Innes unwrapped his bundle, laid out his case against Merrily Watkins continuing to operate as deliverance consultant.

He had everything. Either he'd researched it himself, with the help of unknown people within the diocese, or the putative Working Party had given him a file, which even included an interview Merrily had once done – with the full agreement of Bernie Dunmore – for a national magazine.

'… *where she says…*' Innes evidently consulting a tablet or something. '"*It still amazes me when I meet a member of the clergy who purports to believe in a supernatural God but rejects the possibility of anything else.*"'

A baffled pause before Siân replied.

'*Is there something wrong with that?*'

'*How many ghosts do you find in the Bible?*'

'*It doesn't do ghosts, but that—*'

'*Surely the message from the Bible is that we should disregard the – probably mythological – byways which distract from our focus on God.*'

'*And people who've become trapped in the byways… we don't try to help them?*'

Thank you, Siân.

But his answer was predictable and final.

'*There are people more qualified to help them.*'

And then, of course, he'd talked about the police. It seemed to Innes that she'd almost courted the controversial, becoming so involved with criminal investigators that they now regarded her almost as *their* consultant. Which meant that she was dealing with issues which would not normally come to the Church's attention, with the inevitable neglect of her normal pastoral duties.

He told Siân about his meeting with the chief constable of West Mercia and the head of Hereford CID.

His information, he said, was that Detective Chief Inspector Howe was not well disposed towards Mrs Watkins, although she'd been unexpectedly reticent over lunch. He'd learned much more in a meeting with a group of prominent Herefordshire councillors which had included Howe's father.

'Bloody Charlie Howe,' Merrily said to Huw. 'Innes might've been told everything about me, but it looks like he knows nothing at all about Charlie.'

Innes said it was County Councillor Howe who, in disclosing his discomfort over the relationship, had called Merrily, in a disparaging way, 'a consultant' to the police. Or rather to 'one ambitious detective'. Unnamed.

'*All I'd say to that,*' Siân said, '*is that the police deal with unacceptable behaviour which is often seen as evil, and there're often moral and spiritual choices—*'

'*Evil?*' The Bishop's voice raised to pulpit level. '*If you're looking for evil, I'll point you in yet another direction. There's a—*'

Merrily froze it again.

'I freely confess that this is not going to sound good.'

42

Swallow the pill

AFTER A WHILE, Jane realized she might have made a mistake using her own name – easy to discount the kind of creeps you encountered up some of these online alleys. But then she'd had no reason to think that Aisha Malik was in that deep.

It hadn't taken long finding the kid through the Facebook search box. On the old iMac at her desk under the Mondrian walls, Jane had checked out five Aishas, but only one belonged to the Foxy Rowlestone Appreciation Society.

Which had over thirty thousand members – seriously impressive with the series discontinued. Not that many of them accepted this.

> I dreamed last night that Foxy had finished two more books and one was coming out before Christmas. I'm just putting this down in case it happens. Cos it was a really vivid dream and I've had it twice.

Evidently a heavy-duty mystic.

Jane's membership of FRAS had been approved within ten minutes. She'd looked up the books on Amazon, and they were still getting almost daily reader-reviews, more of them these days coming from adults for whom new editions seemed to have been issued as e-books with starkly monochrome covers. *Probably OK for children*, one reader said, *but it scared the hell out of me.*

On the fan forum, it was only a short scroll to the weird stuff.

Salli B

I've been in psychic contact with Foxy for two years and
she was as shattered as any of us when she found out
at the end of Book 2 that Geraint had become one of the
Undead but she says to think about it and it will make
everything so much better. It's true!

The moderators had left it alone. It was a little late for
spoilers. Still that *was* a gobsmacker. Geraint the blacksmith's
son had really emerged on the dark side? Or had his life been a
necessary sacrifice to enable him to take on the Summoner on
his own plane of existence? And if Catherine was still human
that would pose some interesting challenges for the Book Three
which never happened.

There was a thread speculating on how this would change
things. Like how could Geraint not be a *good vampire*?

'There are no good vampires,' Jane murmured.

Gretel

I keep hearing theres going to be a film of The Summoner
but it never happens! Does anybody knows WHEN?????

Salli B

It doesn't matter. You can make your own in your head
and one night you will be there in your dreams and no
going back.

Jessica

Did u all know that Geraint was REAL? I think I may
have a chance to meet him. I am soooooooo excited
and accept it will be very very frightening at first but that
doesnt matter cos he is so gorgeous.

Jane was shaking her head, although she could totally
understand how vivid fantasies could form, and that fear was

an essential part of it. A dark rite of passage. You had to go through the deepest fear to find the deepest love.

Francesca
I have read this book about six times. At first I had to stop reading at nite because of the dreams it gave me. Id wake up terror strikken all cold and trembling. But soon I was loving the terror. Theres a dark wood near us that I call the Nightlands and Ive spent hours there waiting for Geraint. My stupid parents thought I was out with my mates. Ha ha ha. I can lie in bed now and Im in the wood and he comes to me. Ooooh! Ooooo! Oooooooo!!!

Not unexpectedly, there were posts from kids claiming to be Geraint, posting pictures of guys who were clearly not them. Some claimed to be friends of his, offering to set up meetings with him for Those Who Dare. There were even takers.

I am going to meet Geraint AT LAST. I have sent him my token and I think we are going to Be Together. I have already met him in dreams.

This was more than slightly scary. This was where the creep element came in. You could only hope the obsessive fans would run like hell when Geraint started sending them pictures of his cock.

In another thread, several people were boasting about knowing exactly where the Nightlands were. None of them getting it right, as far as Jane could see.

No word from Aisha. Evidently, she was just a lurker on FRAS. Her Facebook page suggested she wasn't over-fussed about privacy settings, but there wasn't much of her on show. Her friends were other girls of around the same age, her likes were unsurprising: kid bands, fantasy films and Foxy Rowlestone. She'd left many of the personal spaces blank, had posted some pictures of her family, Foxy book covers and fragments of land-scape that Jane half recognized. But all fairly sketchy.

The list of groups she belonged to flashed up different signals. Jane had hit the *join* buttons for all of them, thinking she could get out easily enough, although you could leave a trail.

Too late now. Waiting for her memberships to be approved – it could take minutes or, for more obscure groups, days – Jane stood by the attic window looking down over the hedge, between the shedding trees, to the village, coolly lit by the late-autumnal sun, its painted walls white as freshly squeezed toothpaste between the timbers.

Strange to think that Mum, of all people, had gone through a goth period, which she talked about occasionally, with entirely justified embarrassment: the black lipstick, the vintage albums by Siouxsie and the Banshees. Early teenage decadence. She must have been very young, younger than Aisha. And even more naive.

Or maybe not. It had always been there, the sexuality of vampirism. The love bites that went deeper. It was only *since* Mum's time that it had changed, becoming weirdly innocent. Those Twilight vamps who didn't go all the way. Not for a long time, anyway. Not without true love.

How naive was that.

Jane felt tight inside.

The Fang Forum accepted her within half an hour. It was mildly entertaining, with adverts for pointy dental caps and red contact lenses so you could see the whole world through bloodlight. It also seemed to have become some kind of goth dating agency, with images of vampire weddings and – less healthy – vampire babies in vintage black prams, with little skull mobiles dangling from their awnings, and vampire toddlers who, presumably, had grown blood teeth instead of milk teeth.

Chances were that these kids would grow up entirely normal, taking the piss out of their sad old parents, people like…

... well, like *this.* Image of a couple with red-rimmed lips, middle-aged infants at a face-painting party.

> Me and my fella been drinking each other's blood for over
> 2 years now. It keeps us together. We are soul mates
> in every sense. We live in each other's veins and will
> become one at death.

Jane skipped instructions on how best to leak quantities of blood without severing a significant artery. Also the long discussion about the nutritional benefits of sanguinary exchange, blah, blah, yuk.

And then, suddenly...

Aisha
I have heard Geraint of the Nightlands comes here. I live in his village near Catherine's castle. Can anyone tell me how to meet him?

Carmilla
Anyone can say that.

Aisha
It's true. I live where England and Wales meet. I live in the old house that is all that's left of the deserted village under the ruins of the castle. I walk in the place where the Village once stood below what is left of the Castle where I can hear the roaring of the forge and sometimes see Geraint and his hammer but only faintly.

Uh-oh.

Jane scrolled deep into the site and there were several other references to Geraint and his hammer. Predictable. Close to the kind of crap she might have written years ago. Mystic Jane from the University of Middle Earth.

After Aisha's post, other people on the Fang Forum started posting about Foxy Rowlestone's book, some of them claiming to have seen the Summoner. Jane remembered Lol talking once about the time he'd spent in psychiatric care and how easy it was to absorb other patients' kinks, how easy to accept your own insanity and hold it close with medication. Easier than breaking out. Swallow the orange-coloured pill.

She stood up and went back to the window, watched the village stretching itself into the cool, clear morning. Gus Staines, plump and comfy, was walking past the vicarage gate with her wife, the taller, narrower Amanda Rubens. Off to open the bookshop. They looked like extras from one of those old British films where the colours always seemed washed-out.

Jane turned violently away from the window. Back at her desk, she found a reply to Aisha.

Carmilla
Wait. Wait for the dusk.

And that was all there was. Maybe there was some take-up on one of the other groups that hadn't got back to her. She was still waiting when her phone, over on the window ledge, made the tawny owl noise. Jane came slowly to her feet, walked over and found a text. Businesslike.

Weekend dig in Wiltshire starting mid Nov.
Place for you if you want it.
love, Sam XXXXXX

Jane looked down, between the trees, to Ledwardine square, the white walls brighter than neon between the black oak, but she could taste the sour autumnal air of Cwmarrow as the owl returned. New text. *Not* businesslike. This one was like poetry.

No rules, Jane. New era. All barriers are down. We go where it's fun. We don't have long, take what pleasures we can. Live like the remote ancestors. Alive to the senses.

43

Get rid

UNUSUALLY WITH HUW OWEN in the room, the air was flecked with unrest. It was far from reassuring that he'd sat, unmoved, through the part where Innes had called him mad. Past the age where he'd care. Content to be crazy, nothing he needed to prove to anyone. *No evangelist, me,* he'd said once. *Let 'em find it for themselves, worth bugger-all otherwise.*

'All right,' he said. 'Let's hear the rest.'

Merrily leaned across the desk and tapped the touchpad, releasing the Bishop's crisp tenor.

'*—an old people's home at Hardwicke, down hear Hay. The proprietor's a woman called Mrs Cardelow. Whose son-in-law is one Graeme Spring.*'

'You mean our...?'

'*Canon Graeme Spring.*'

'Spring's a decent man,' Merrily said sadly. 'Not even ambitious. People trust him.'

'*His mother-in-law's perpetual headache is a woman who was living there when she took over. A former Whitehall civil servant, more recently employed in some capacity at GCHQ in Cheltenham.*'

No reaction from Siân, although it was unlikely she hadn't heard of this woman, even as a joke. Which she wasn't.

'*Old but far from geriatric. A woman who could afford her own home but appears not to want one. Apart from a recently acquired artificial hip, she has no disabilities. No interest, apparently, in physical possessions – admirable really. Or would be*' *under normal circumstances. She wants to be looked after. She has a suite of rooms, now, I'm told. Filled, floor to ceiling, with books. All her needs taken care of, so she can continue her studies.'*

Huw looked at Merrily.

'Miss White,' she said. 'Anthea. Who prefers to be anagrammed. Athena.'

'Amongst her studies,' Innes said, *'are the other guests in the home. Especially those close to… what you might call the end of their stay.'*

'The dying,' Siân said.

'That's… not entirely fair,' Merrily said. 'She's been quite a comfort to… some of them.'

'Does tarot readings for the other old ladies in the home,' Innes said. *'Telling them when they can expect to die.'*

Siân tutted once.

'How horrible of her.'

'Plays tricks with people's minds. To exercise her faculties. Also said to be working on her memoirs – not as a civil servant, about which she's always been very discreet, but as an occultist.'

'Perhaps I have heard of her,' Siân said faintly. *'Though never encountered her personally.'*

'Mrs Watkins certainly has. Visiting her countless times, according to Mrs Cardelow.'

'Five, max,' Merrily said. 'Rarely parting on good terms.'

'What one might call, Siân – and I really don't wish to be melodramatic – a rather unholy alliance.'

'I don't think we should necessarily—'

'What you don't think doesn't concern me greatly. I know. I see a possible unholy and certainly unhealthy association. To which my predecessor seems to have turned a blind eye. But I shall not. No such thing as white magic, Siân, only spiritual perversion.'

'What an ambivalent feller he is,' Huw said. 'Fire and brimstone modernist.'

He glanced at Merrily, who shrugged.

'Stop it there, would you, lass?' Huw said.

Because this might take longer, she closed the document. Not much left anyway.

'She's not a friend. That is, we don't socialize. She doesn't *have* friends. Too time-consuming. But...' She sighed. '... the fact remains that she *is* extraordinary. As I've probably said before, she's deliberately offensive and can appear heartless... all right, sometimes she *is* heartless. But her breadth of knowledge is vast.'

'Aye,' Huw said.

'And there are some esoteric crevices I've never managed to penetrate, and so... there *have* been times when I've dragged myself kicking and screaming to Athena's eyrie.'

'I know.'

She couldn't remember how much she'd told him.

'We go where we have to, lass, to get what we need. We weigh one thing against another. Lesser of two evils. What we don't do is avoid them, pretend they don't exist. We go in, eyes open.'

'I suppose.'

Huw pushed a knuckle into his chin.

'This feller Spring... the canon... is he the kind of bloke who'd go to Innes to grass you up?'

'Well, that's it, I wouldn't've thought so. But then I didn't know he was Cardelow's son-in-law. *She's* never mentioned it to me. Miss White disclosed that there was now a canon in the family, but I never followed up on it. Why would I?'

'Why indeed, lass. Nowt wrong wi' an occasional lapse into naivety...'

'That's—'

'Anthea White, she was a proper spook?'

Merrily sighed.

'When people tell you they were in the civil service, you kind of turn off, so it's only recently I found out that she'd worked for the security services, MI5, anyway. It makes sense. She's drawn to secrecy in all its forms. Occult – hidden. She's hardly the first. Occultism, secrets, codes...'

'Means she'll be on somebody's file, won't she? Several files. Happen she thinks an old folks' home's the safest place for her.'

'That's ridiculous.'

'No, it's not. People like her, eyes get kept on them. Files get discreetly passed around. MI5 must've known what she did on the side. Which might even've been useful to them at one time, but once you're out you can be dangerous.'

Merrily stood up, both hands on the desk.

'We're in danger of losing touch with reality.'

Huw didn't move.

'Far from it, lass. The Church of England, by tradition, is part of the British government. The whole reason it even exists—'

'I *do* know why it exists.'

'And the reason it survives. The reason it will still survive when even cathedral congregations are down to single figures. Contacts. Politics. Church and State, notes passed under the table.'

'I hate conspiracy theories. Never really wanted to wind up as a crazy hag howling on street corners.'

'Keep your nerve.'

'I'm starting to feel almost physically sick. It's like I'm walking in my own shadow. You can also hear Innes talking about Jane and her blatant paganism. Where's he got that from? He doesn't know Jane. And then there's my *sexual relation-ship* – not a partnership because we don't live together – with a musician whose past—'

Huw's hands were up.

'All right. I get it. All it means is he has a small but growing coterie of clerical snouts in the diocese, who, between them—'

'*Who?* Who are they?'

Found she was halfway across the desk. She slumped back into the chair, eyes closed.

'No idea, lass. Not my diocese. Don't know who they are, how many of them there are, or if they even qualify as a coterie. But there'll be a few folks on your side as well. Or there would be if they knew.'

'That's so good to know, Huw.'

'Aye, well, in a situation like this, friends tend to be…'

'Reticent.'

'Especially the bloody clergy.'

I just…' She was feeling almost faint, shook her head hard. 'This has come… absolutely out of nowhere.'

'It's not come out of nowhere. I've told you where it's come from. And it makes you just want to pack in, course it does.'

'It does, actually. Yes.'

'Don't. Just bloody don't. I'm not saying you won't get hurt, nowt surer. The Church of England can be like some old-fashioned public school. Bullying is rife. He'll run you to the edge. But you don't go *anywhere*.'

'I—'

'You tell him where he can stick his rural dean offer. You tell him you want to stay with deliverance.'

'What, call his bluff? He's not bluffing, Huw. I won't bother playing the rest, but I'll tell you something else. He said he'd never been to Ledwardine, but I saw him here once with his wife and two of his kids, OK? Having an ice cream?'

She hadn't planned to tell him the rest. It was, after all, not unreasonable considering the income Ledwardine failed to provide for the Church. Dispiriting, but not unreasonable. Huw would accept that. *We bloody suffer. We get extra shit.* It was only when you looked at it alongside the rest…

'He asks Siân if she can explain why it is that a vicarage this big is housing one woman and, as he puts it, one child. A seventeenth-century black and white vicarage which, if sold, would fetch… he puts a figure on it which is probably an exaggeration, but…'

'And where would he put you and the child?'

'The property people have been briefed to keep an eye open for the next semi to come for sale up on what Gomer Parry calls "the hestate". I can't complain. If they'd put us into a semi when we first arrived I'd've been happy enough. I didn't like the idea of a period mausoleum, and it caused me problems. But you kind of stretch out to fill a place, don't you?'

'Just try and give me some time,' Huw said. 'All right?'

'To do what?'

'I don't know.' A very visible pain in his eyes. 'I've never lied to you, lass. I don't bloody know. But it's clear that if you turn down rural dean, if you don't say, Wow thank you, Bishop, how kind, I don't deserve this... then he'll want you off his patch for good.'

'If not out of the job. Who'd want me anywhere else?' She stood up. 'Need to get a glass of water.'

'You're not sleeping, are you?'

'Not much. Awful dreams. Had one last night... no, the night before... that was a composite of Ann Evans... Jenny... her experience in her father's church and... *oh God.*'

She didn't get the water. She sat down again and told him, as she'd known she'd have to at some stage, very slowly about her other problem. How she was working a foreigner – a particularly medieval foreigner – at the indirect behest of an Islamic cleric.

And a drug dealer.

She told him everything. The vanished village that had come to a kind of life in an old man's head. The manifestation/hallu-cination in the Castle Room. The clocks and the stroke. The bloody fairy stroke.

He listened without a word, as she told him everything. Name, locations, history. The screensaver came up on the computer. It was the cover of Lol's CD, *A Message from the Morning*, showing the solid electric guitar he rarely played silhouetted against a purple dawn. Picture by Eirion Lewis. Who seemed no longer to be in the picture himself.

Huw had his head on one side, as if what he'd just heard in one ear might drift away out of the other.

'I didn't make any of that up, by the way,' Merrily said.

'I don't see how you could.'

'No.'

'Dunmore, you'd've told him if he were still Bishop?'

'Probably. I mean, yes.' She smiled, aware that it was a crooked smile. 'It's almost funny, isn't it?'

Huw wasn't laughing. Outside, a wind was getting up. She turned and saw the sky over the church wall had become overcast.

'You need to get rid of it,' Huw said. 'Don't you?'

'Get rid?'

'Get it sorted bloody quick and cover your tracks.'

'How about I just do my best with it? And then go quietly.'

'Merrily…'

'What?'

'I'll not tell you again.'

44

Walks by night

'LOT OF MEDIA on the car park,' Elly Clatter, the police press officer, said on the stairs to the MIR. 'Two murders, we'll need to give them something substantial. And like I keep saying—'

'Elly, for f—'

'It won't go away till you deal with it, Francis. I know these people.'

'Mother of God.' Bliss's mitt tightening around his coffee cup. 'It's a *shop*. What *kind* of friggin' shop doesn't matter.'

'For the red tops, what kind of shop is everything, and they didn't even need to climb over any walls for the picture you'll be seeing in tomorrow's papers.'

She'd shown him her tablet, and Bliss had shuddered. The Darkest Corner website – should he even have been surprised? – was like the front of some missing Black Sabbath album from 1972. No sign of Jerry Soffley, just a dark-eyed witchy woman in a Scottish Widows cloak sitting in a steeple-backed chair in the centre of Organ Yard with a familiar plastic skull in her lap.

He'd had to put someone on to finding out who she was – possibly Soffley's second wife – and paying her a visit before the hacks found her.

'For all we know at this stage, Elly, *she* killed Soffley, and Greenaway's a completely different case. Why don't you get the DCI to talk to the press? That'll give the bastards a scare.'

'Because the DCI says it has to be you,' Elly Clatter said.

For DCI read SIO, which was good, a mercy. Two murders, under normal circs you'd automatically get some Worcester suit, but pressure of work – an outbreak of terrorism-linked, nervy stuff, up at the northern end – had removed the threat. Bliss was working for Annie.

'Boss, surely...' Vaynor loping upstairs, three at a time, behind them. '... given that the nature of Soffley's business is already on the Net, we can hardly hold back on the gothics.'

'I'm exercising me right to play it down, and I'm not gonna link it to the murder by introducing them to Steve. Not yet, anyway.'

'What if they go into Neogoth on the Net?'

'Without Steve, it'll tell them nothing. Definitely no Steve.'

The Major Investigation Room was what used to be the Control Room till all that went to HQ to be run by people who'd never been west of Pershore. Day one in the MIR was always going to remind Bliss of the first day at his comp, aged eleven. Little kid in a hostile crowd, too many kids who all seemed to know one another. Hated school.

Near the back, Terry Stagg was laughing with two retired detectives with beer guts from before Bliss's time. Lot of extra bodies in from Worcester, including civvies and boffins and people who knew how to talk to HOLMES, the Microsoft murder machine. Two linked killings was a three-megabyte problem.

Annie wasn't here. She'd have issues to offload, delegate, make some space for this, so Bliss was still ringmaster.

He kept his briefing short, Karen Dowell, sitting next to him behind an iPad and three bottles of spring water. Apart from the house-to-house, the shop-to-shop and the CCTV search, today was mainly going to be call-centre stuff, much of it based on names pulled from both victims' computers.

He looked from window to window, one featuring a lot of lower roof and all three big city churches, the Cathedral, St Peter's and All Saints, projecting like the prongs of a trident under a darkening sky. Sonia, the CID seagull, was plucking at the remains of someone's sarnie.

'I'm gonna give yer all a key-phrase,' Bliss said. '*Friends of the Dusk*. This is the only significant name found on both lappies. Who are they? What are they? Where are they? Indeed, *are* they? Do they still exist? I'm assuming none of us, apart from Karen, have come across them. Maybe in the distant past? Anybody?'

He glanced over to the beer guts in the corner. No reaction.

Terry Stagg said, 'Is it a gay thing?'

'Soffley, as far as we know, definitely wasn't. Two ex-wives. One we've spoken to who dumped him for serial adultery. Having broken up his first marriage thinking she could change him. So, no, Terrence, gay is on the back-burner. Darth.'

'What's the actual context here? In both cases.'

Bliss turned to Karen, who consulted her iPad.

'Basically, Friends of the Dusk occurs on Soffley's database of Neogoth members. Greenaway, however, mentions what is probably them the day before he died. This is on an email which simply says, quote, "Gordon, do you have a contact for FOTD. I don't want to go through Neogoth, if I can help it. I'd also really like to try and get through to JT, though I accept that won't be easy."'

'But as we now know, he *did* have to go through Neogoth,' Bliss said. 'Because Gordon wasn't able to assist. Replies that he hasn't heard from any of them in years and thinks the group might have fallen apart. He also says, Karen…?'

'"I imagine Mr T's far too big for all that now." Gordon lives in Totnes, Devon, from where he runs – or ran – an Internet magazine. Devon and Cornwall are finding him for us. Quite soon, I hope.'

'So. FOTD and Mr T… JT,' Bliss said. 'Who is he? We're assuming that all this relates to Steve. For reasons as yet unknown, Tristram Greenaway wanted the Friends of the Dusk to see that piccy – which we would really *like* to be of the skull unearthed on Castle Green, but we can't even be certain about that as Neil Cooper says he didn't see it for long enough.'

Bliss uncapped a bottle of spring water. Had too much caffeine today, already.

'Now.' Wiping his mouth with the back of a hand. 'Let's deal quickly with the Hammer Films bit. Because this – although you *don't* reveal it to anybody – is likely to inform a lorra your questions during the long call-centre hours.'

Karen brought Steve up on the screen behind them. Bliss talked for a while about deviant burials and the kind of people who might be interested in one. Bringing up the expected smiles when he let the v-word out.

'So, Francis...' Rich Ford, the uniform inspector, was leaning in the doorway at the bottom of the room, looking unmoved. '... we could be looking for somebody with what you might call a distinctive lifestyle?'

It was rumoured Rich was coming up to his thirty and talking with the brass about pension deals. Already demob-happy.

'No plan at this stage,' Bliss said, to get this shit over with, 'of ringing round the health clinics in search of any bugger with a garlic allergy.'

'But if we're looking for someone who walks by night, Francis,' Rich Ford said, 'presumably—'

'Nor will we be talking to Charlie Howe,' Bliss said.

When Devon and Cornwall came through, Bliss and Karen were down in Bliss's office. A DC Peter Lord in Exeter. She put him on speaker.

'Gordon Barclay-Hughes works in some sort of herbal cig shop. Quite legal, ahem. He's all right, basically. Bit off the planet. Knew Tristram Greenaway, but not about him being murdered. Quite upset, but not *too* upset. Confirms he exchanged emails with Greenaway about Friends of the Dusk, about which he's happy to talk to you. You thinking of coming down?'

Karen looked at Bliss, who wrinkled his nose.

'Might just talk to him on the phone first,' Karen said.

'JT,' Peter Lord said. 'Jim Turner. My son loves his films.'

'Films, Peter?'

'Boy's room's full of DVDs. Actually, I didn't know who JT was either till Gordon told me and I ran him past the kid. Dunno if he's in this country or not. I'll leave that to you.'

'Absolutely,' Karen said. 'Thanks, Peter. Very speedy service.'

Bliss saw she was already tapping Jim Turner into Google. Not a name he was familiar with either. No wiser when the image came up: beardie bloke with a shaven head, his back to a cinema poster. He stood up, reading over Karen's shoulder.

'Let's get Darth in, he knows all about these arty twats.'

Karen did some rapid tapping and scrolling, freshly washed dark hair bobbing away, then sat back, like she'd given birth.

'Look at this, Frannie. We on a roll here or what?'

45

Courting the goddess

HUW DIDN'T STAY for lunch, saying he didn't like the look of the weather. Storms usually came in over the Beacons. There were things Merrily wanted to ask him, but they could probably wait.

She went over to Jim Prosser's Eight Till Late for some feta cheese and fresh salad material. Jane had not come down by the time she was back. She went through to the scullery and bit the bullet.

The woman – very posh – at Lyme Farm asked if she was Mr Kindley-Pryce's niece. Friend of the family, she said. Didn't say which family.

'When did you see him last?'

'Oh, quite a while. I've…'

'You do realize he may not recognize you?'

'I'm prepared for that.'

'Three o'clock?'

'Fine. Thank you.'

Her name and address were taken. She gave the right ones – you could only go so far. She'd already called Foxy Rowlestone's publishers. Their publicity department said Foxy's editor had left some years ago. When Merrily had suggested they must have an address to send her royalties to and pass on fan mail, they took down her number and her email address. She didn't, somehow, expect to hear from them.

She rang Martin Longbeach, currently locum vicar at Underhowle, up near the Forest of Dean. Not around. She left a short message on his machine. Martin had been a member of the aborted Hereford Deliverance Panel, with Siân Callaghan-Clarke and the psychiatrist Nigel Saltash. She'd done Martin some favours. His turn now.

Not that any of it would help.

Over lunch Jane said, 'You going to tell me about Aisha Malik?'

'I've never met her. Only listened to other people talking about her, and that can be misleading. I expect you can tell me a lot I don't know.'

'Well, not much, actually. But it might be confirmation of something.'

Jane opened up her iPad, telling her about the Foxy Rowlestone Appreciation Society and the rather more adult Fang Forum.

'Struck me as crazy, Mum, that series packing in after two books. Foxy was sitting on a fortune.'

'Only half of Foxy was left with a functioning mind.'

'So? From what you say, it's the woman who knew how to write – I mean, for kids. If the old guy had already given her the basics, why couldn't she write more on her own? Even if she carried on giving him a share for doing nothing.'

'That's a good point, actually. If I could find her.'

'Still in the area, you think?'

'Could be anywhere.' Merrily scrolled down. 'Carmilla. Presumably naming herself after Sheridan le Fanu's female vampire.'

'One of the first. Pre-Dracula.'

'I used to have a copy.'

'In your goth days.'

'Didn't last long. As I keep emphasizing.'

I don't know,' Jane said. 'Some people might say that becoming a priest, shamelessly wearing the black kit…'

'Don't start that again. This is the last, is it? "Wait for the dusk."'

'That's when Carmilla seems to start taking her seriously.'

'I wonder why.'

'Because she's given authentic details of where she lives.'

294

'Yeah, but for that to cut any ice, Jane, Carmilla would have to *recognize* it as authentic.'

'I didn't think of that. You're right.'

'And if it was common knowledge in vampire circles she could still be making it up. Anything else from Aisha?'

'There are just hundreds and hundreds of posts, and most of them are complete drivel. However, I did find one other. There might be more, but you spend all day...' Jane pulled over the pad and searched around. 'There you go.'

Aisha

The blood is only the start. Symbolic of something much more powerful. I have a fulfilling relationship across the Divide that goes beyond the blood.

'Mmm,' Merrily said. 'That's a step forward, isn't it? A fulfilling relationship across the Divide. With whom?'

'I've been thinking about this. It's on the Fang Forum so she doesn't spell it out. If it was on the Foxy site, it would be more obvious. It could be mirroring the later situation between the girl in the book, Catherine, and Geraint, the blacksmith. The situation that seems to be hinted at in the second book, when Geraint apparently dies but returns – undead – to deal with the Summoner on his own level. Then I'm guessing we get kind of a Twilight situation where Geraint and Catherine might well develop an interesting relationship.'

'Across the Divide.'

Jane nodded.

'What's your feeling about that? Is it bollocks or is it reflecting something?'

Jane put down her fork, gazing through the lower window at the green and mauve lichens on the churchyard wall.

'I think she has a pretty vibrant fantasy life. I'd say *inner* life, but that might be pushing it. I keep thinking back to when I was doing the pagan thing out there.'

'Courting the moon goddess.'

The look Jane flashed her was momentarily about fear and… *hurt*?

What?

Then it was gone.

'Does that…' Jane's voice was low and flat. '… equate with what you know?'

'I was in her room. We'd gone from room to room. Nadya, her mother, was anxious she shouldn't be involved in this because she said she was happy here, untroubled. But it seemed to me that if hers was the only room that wasn't blessed…'

'Then it would just become a natural focus for… whatever you're dealing with?'

'Yes. Exactly.'

'It might even be *driven* in there.'

'Made a horrible sense,' Merrily said. Sometimes Jane seemed to have an instinctive grasp of deliverance logic. 'I felt that was what Huw Owen would be saying if he knew. Anyway, we went through the Maliks' part of the house – Islamic wall hangings and medical books, quite a plain bedroom, other rooms in the process of being sorted out. Aisha's room – she wasn't there.'

'Where was she?'

'Don't know. She goes for long walks. I'm surprised you didn't see her.'

Jane's eyes flickered.

'That might have been interesting. What was in her room?'

'Usual things. And some less usual. The books… fantasy and horror. And in the wardrobe, amongst the usual, there were some dark, gothic clothes, rather medieval. You've been there.'

'Not like you have.'

'That was a long time ago. Another era. The thing is, where does she wear them? Does she hang out with other teen goths? *Are* there any nowadays?'

'Apart from Jude Wall and his mates, who do it once a year for entirely commercial reasons.'

'Is it cool any more?'

Jane looked over the lichens again, thinking about it.

'If she *does* have like-minded friends, it's not immediately obvious on her Facebook page. Like, she has friends, but none of them seem to have followed her into the places she goes. The people on the Foxy site, there's not much familiarity, not much taking the piss. I think she's... a bit of a loner.'

'Are you OK? The bruises?'

'Not a problem.'

But there *was* a problem, still. If you couldn't spot a problem after nineteen years...

'I'm going to see Selwyn Kindley-Pryce this afternoon.'

'Wow,' Jane said. 'What's your excuse?'

'I'll think of something. Huw thinks I need to sort this, quickly.'

'In case the Bishop finds out. Because it's not official. But if you've told Huw...'

'Huw's my friend, not my boss.'

'And like, what kind of state's the old guy going to be in by now?'

'Mr Pryce? I suppose I'm hanging on to what I was told about him kind of vanishing into his own fantasy world. Maybe he'll let me in.'

'But that was years ago.'

'Yes. I know. But the fact is, he's the last living link to whatever might be happening at Cwmarrow. I don't know. I'm covering all bases, as they say.'

'Bit of a self-imposed ordeal, if you ask me.'

'Not really.' Merrily carried the dishes to the sink. 'I've visited quite a few people with dementia. Prayed with them. It can be quite... Anyway, I have to be there for three.'

'Leave the washing up for me. And then you want me to go back into Aisha's social media? Or I could message her, ask a few—'

'No! Don't go near her. Actually, if you have time...'

'All the time in the world.'

'Maybe you could see what you can find out about djinns.'

'Like genies? Arabic elementals?'

'See, you're halfway there. I'll go and get back quickly. Gales forecast for tonight.'

'Just don't catch his disease,' Jane said.

46

Bloodline

BLISS HAD A picture of Gordon Barclay-Hughes that was probably wrong – wispy beard and a pot belly, for some reason
– but the voice fitted: speed-talk in one of those outer-London
accents that seemed to have infected half the south-east.

'Yeah, yeah, Friends of the Dusk, that was a good name, that
still resonates. But they always sound deeper than they turn out
to be. This was dawn of the Internet, mate. Cranking away on
dial-up, like the old cat's whisker and crystal set days. *Wireless*
again now – everything comes round. Crazy.'

'Who started this, Gordon?'

'The Dusk? It was just there. A few famous people, clever
people, and they was all your mates. Virtual equality, man. Jim
Turner – he was our mate.'

'Where's he these days?'

'Gawd, I dunno. In the sack wiv some starlet? They prob'ly
don't say that any more, showing my age, Gary.'

'Francis,' Bliss said.

'Bloody shame about Trissie. Had an email off of him the
other day.'

'Yeh, that's why I'm calling.'

'Course you are. Bit hyper today. Open up the shop, copper
at the counter, you think, hello, here we are, more round the
back. But, there you go, it was just the one, bearing sad news.'

'To get back to Friends of the Dusk…'

'Tell you how come I was a member, yeah? We had a book
store, me and a lady – gone now, the way of all my ladies. Before

I come to GD, this was – Glorious Devon. Luton, two year lease. We did fantasy books and comics, mainly, and we found there was a lot of interest in vampire stuff – niche market, but a big niche. Which was fine 'cos I always liked that stuff, partic'ly the classics.'

'Contact, was there, between goth shops in the UK?'

'How d'you mean?'

'I mean, did you know one another? Like, did you ever come across Jerry Soffley?'

'Jerry...' Barclay-Hughes was silent for a moment. 'He do the clobber as well? And the music? Still going?'

'Yesterday I'd've been able to say he was. However—'

'He was a character, Soffley.'

'He was murdered last night,' Bliss said.

Sounds of a match being struck close to the phone.

'You're not winding me up or nothin'?'

'I'm sorry, Gordon.'

'Soffley *and* young Trissie?'

'Any thoughts on that, Gordon?'

'You thinking they might come after me? That's what this is about?'

'Why would you think that, Gordon?'

'I dunno. Dunno why I said that. Shock, I s'pose.'

'That the kind of thing the Friends of the Dusk might do?'

'Naw! They was just... enthusiasts. Anoraks. No way...' Pause, Bliss heard smoke being expelled. 'I just looked it up on the Net about Trissie. Beaten to death? Bleedin' 'ell. Whassis about? Soffley, I never met him, but he was well known in the trade. Not many total goth shops around. We used to haunt house-clearances. If we found anything dark, apart from books, we'd buy it, maybe flog it to Soffley, if it wasn't too big for a carrier.'

Bliss listened to a few more minutes of this stuff before asking about Jim Turner, namechecking the feature-length documentary film Karen had pointed out on Wikipedia, *The Bloodline of Dracula*.

'Yeah, yeah, fact and fiction. It's how I met him. You know that bit near the beginning, where all these—?'

'I've not seen it, Gordon.'

'Well, he shot that in our shop. The opening sequence, yeah? All the vampire books and the fans talking about it. We got these mates in top hats and capes and that. He was looking for people obsessed with the undead – what the film was gonna be about originally, and then some people he met, they put him onto the fact that it wasn't just stories. And it wasn't just Transylvania.'

Wikipedia: *Turner spent months tracking down so-called deviant burials, linked to vampire mythology, in the UK and Ireland.*

'And did he know Tristram Greenaway?'

'He'd've met him, yeah. Maybe same day I met him. We was at a party at Selwyn's place. He was wiv this gorgeous lady who wrote the books wiv him. I say it was a party, it was a conference, but it was fun. I think that was when it started.'

'What?'

'Friends of the Dusk.'

'Gordon...'

'Yeah?'

'Could you tell me, in like baby-words, exactly what Friends of the Dusk *is*... or was?'

'Well, it was... the dusk. The edge of night. They was out on the edge.' Pause. 'What do you know about vampires in Britain?'

'Norra lot, but, strangely, more than I did.'

'You ask people which part of England has to do wiv vampires they'll tell you Whitby in Yorkshire, right, 'cos that was where Count Dracula landed? Except he didn't, did he? On account of Dracula didn't bleedin' exist. He was made up, right?'

'Yeh, I knew that.'

'But what if we're missing the point. What if we got better vampire stories on our own doorstep? Which is what Selwyn was saying.'

'Who's Selwyn?'

'I thought you knew. Selwyn Kindley-Pryce was one of the biggest experts in the field. I don't mean like me, I mean proper experts, university guys. Selwyn would tell you it ain't all about fangs and stakes through the heart, garlic, all that shit, and it ain't about Transylvania. The first known vampires were probably British.'

'Are we supposed to be proud of that, Gordon?'

'Part of our heritage, mate. As celebrated by the Friends of the Dusk.'

'How?'

'All sorts of activities. There'd be like weekend festivals at Selwyn's place – amazing place, way out down by Wales, I'd never find it now. Caravans there and yurts and all that, or you could bring your own tent, and there'd be music and lectures and… all a bit hazy. Should I be telling you about this?'

'I'm not drug squad, Gordon. And me own memory's a bit selective, this being a murder inquiry.'

'Yeah. Right. Thanks. So that's why it's all a bit…'

'Inexact?'

''Sackly…'

'Plenty of gear circulating at this festival.'

'Look. I dunno. Might just've been me. I didn't make any purchases there. Usually brought my own. It was all a bit posh, otherwise. One or two titled people – I'm sure I didn't imagine that. Faces I thought I recognized. My lady, who was wiv me, said one bloke used to be in the government.'

'You still in touch with your lady?'

'That was a couple of ladies ago. Don't even know if she's still alive, mate. She was doing smack, last I heard.'

'But Tristram Greenaway was definitely there.'

'Trissie? Yeah, yeah, he was always there. He was just a kid when it started, a baby goth, like a lot of them.'

'So this was before he was an archaeologist.'

'Oh yeah, yeah. I think.'

'And what was your specific reason for being there, Gordon?'

'Well, I had this Internet magazine – one of the first. A magazine of the Undead. Early days of the Net. We was quite exclusive, subscribers all over the planet. We could spread the word.'

'About what?'

'And collect information. About vampire lore. Selwyn was compiling material for a book. Would've been a terrific book if his mind had held out.'

'He was doing drugs, too?'

'Nah, he just drank a lot of red wine, but… no, his mind was moving out, last I heard. Jim Turner, he was gonna make a documentary, a sequel to *The Bloodline of Dracula* only better… bigger. That never happened either.'

'Tristram Greenaway, was he involved?'

'Trissie… he was studying wiv Selwyn and helping out in return. He knew his way around. And I think he was also working for Jim Turner.'

'As what?'

'I dunno, gopher? Little errands. He'd just walk around like he belonged. I don't mean cocky, it was just fascinating for him, obviously, hanging out where it all started.'

'Friends of the Dusk.'

'What?'

Bliss shut his eyes, trying to compose a question that might extract a simple answer.

'I don't think you're getting this, are you?' Barclay-Hughes said. 'Selwyn figured he was living in the actual place where this vampire hung out.'

'Which vampire?'

'The *first* vampire. Centuries before Dracula – who didn't, of course, exist. Selwyn could've cleaned up. Made some serious money out of tourism and that. But he wasn't interested. He was a scholar. He just wanted to *know*.'

'Spell his name for me, would you, Gordon? If you can manage that.'

He didn't trust people who reckoned drugs had done for their memories. A good and unbreakable excuse.

When Bliss brought Karen and Vaynor into his office the sun had been overlaid by a sky like slate, but he didn't put any lights on. They could still do his head in, lights.

Maybe he was a latent vampire.

Vaynor asked him why he was smiling; Bliss said never mind.

'All right, listen up, kiddies. From what I've pieced together from Gordon, Friends of the Dusk is, or was, a group of nutters interested in exploring the roots of vampirism in this country.'

'They're not nutters,' Vaynor said. 'I've been doing some more research on deviant burials found quite recently – early medieval, Anglo-Saxon. One, in Nottinghamshire, where the body was held down by metal spikes, one through the heart. In Ireland, where several have been discovered, one skull had a stone wedged in its mouth, so big it almost dislocated the jaw. All thought to be the graves of people considered to be malevolent or dangerous to the community. The word vampire used several times – in the sense of declining to stay dead rather than imbibing the blood of the living. But, sure, vampire's a good word – even archaeologists recognize that.'

Bliss thought about this.

'So we're back to where we started, and it's making more sense. Greenaway is called out by Cooper to assist with a newly exposed old corpse on Castle Green. He spots the obvious. He's already pissed off, thinks he's been dumped on again, misled by Cooper, so he acts on impulse, lifts the skull. Because he knows – or *used* to know – people who'd love to meet Steve.'

'Friends of the Dusk,' Karen said. 'Greenaway was a member?'

'Greenaway was linked with them from when he was a young lad. A baby goth, as Gordon calls him. Good-looking, personable kid. Gets in with this group – coterie – formed around a bloke Gordon says was a scholar, Selwyn Kindley-Pryce, who lives somewhere… *out towards Wales.* Let's find out who he is. Or was. He held small cultural festivals Gordon says were a bit posh. Surely, some of us *ought* to know about this. Especially those of us who like to describe themselves as local.'

He glanced at Karen, who shook her head.

'Posh festivals sounds like white settlers.'

'Dinner parties,' Vaynor said. 'Cocktails on the veranda. Don't invite the natives, unless you have nobody to serve the drinks.'

'Mother of God,' Bliss said. 'Is *every*bugger here an inverted snob?'

'Still doesn't sound quite right to me, boss,' Vaynor said. 'We still don't know what Friends of the Dusk was *really* about, do we? Sounds a bit airy-fairy. And how organized was it? Was it a proper members' club or just an affectation? Something that sounded mysterious, but didn't amount to much. Or did it really involve celebs and aristocracy with an unhealthy interest in sucking each other's blood?'

'They do exist,' Karen said. 'And I can't imagine it's in any way illegal.'

'For what it's worth, by the way…' Vaynor smiled. '… the Royal Family's apparently distantly descended from Vlad the Impaler.'

'The Russian president?'

Vaynor sighed.

'The medieval east European serial-slaughterer thought to be the model for Dracula. It was in the documentary I told you about. Which was, I'm afraid, insufficiently arty to have been made by Jim Turner.'

Vaynor had spoken to a TV producer called Leo Defford who'd worked with Turner way back. Defford said Turner had made a lot of money very quickly, though it didn't compare with what he was hauling in these days, in the States, where Vaynor had been trying to track Turner down. Unsuccessfully so far; the States could be unhelpful if you were looking for a rich bastard. America loved rich bastards.

'There's one question we've been avoiding,' Vaynor said. 'One person we don't really know about.'

The lad didn't *like* to appear intellectually superior; he just couldn't help himself. Bliss nodded.

'Yeh. Exactly. Who the fuck *is* Steve?'

47

At peace

FROM LEDWARDINE, IT was less than half an hour's drive to Lyme Farm. Into Leominster, skirting the centre and then out again through the old part of town where it splintered into flat countryside and squally rain, getting wetter and squallier mile by mile.

The journey home would be worse, but there was no way she should avoid this. If Selwyn was beyond communication, at least she'd know.

But what if he wasn't?

A quick check on the Net had shown her that, with Alzheimer's, for example, most sufferers died within five years. But this man was still around after more than ten, and not on a geriatric ward.

What if his condition had stabilized – or even improved – after he'd finally let them separate him from Cwmarrow Court?

Disappeared into his own fantasy world, Dennis Kellow had suggested. But surely it was more than that; he'd spent a lot of money *creating* his fantasy world. Obsessively building it around him, literally. *Remedievalizing.*

So if you took him away from the source of the obsession...

Well, who knew?

As she drove out towards the border with Shropshire, the rain stopped, although the wind kept coming at the Freelander in slow wafts from across the fields, to the sound of a barking dog on the passenger seat.

She pulled into the side of a lane too narrow to park in safely.

'Let me call you back, Huw.'

'Where you off?'

She told him and cut the call. A mile or so down the road she blocked a farm entrance but kept the engine running in case a tractor needed access.

'Turn the car round,' Huw said. 'This is mad.'

'I don't think so.'

Deliverance *was* mad, they both knew that.

'I'm telling you, you don't need this right now. You need to be low-bloody-profile, not marching into some posh people's bloody nursing home telling them one of their inmates might be carrying an infection.'

An *infection*. That was a new one

'I don't march anywhere, and I wasn't planning to tell anybody anything that might—'

'Let me handle it. I can take a couple of days off.'

'Oh, Huw, that's—' Merrily flung herself back into the seat. 'I know you're only trying to help, but they came to *me*.'

'Unofficially. Under the table. Khan the dealer? Jesus wept, lass, this is all a bit bloody timely, if you ask me. How do you know it's not a set-up?'

'I *never* know it's not a set-up.'

'Anybody asks, I can say I'm looking into it for a mate and you know nowt about it.'

'But I do know. It's no good, Huw. Please, just, you know… back off… let me try this.'

He was quiet for a moment. Either that or the wind was getting louder.

'All right. Listen. You tell me everything.'

'I will.'

'Every step of the bloody way. I'm covering your back here. Best I can.'

'I know.'

But she didn't know. What did he mean?

'You're still daft, Merrily.'

'Yeah, I know that, too.'

Borderlight was not a slow read, and by mid-afternoon Jane had finished with it and was leaning back from the refectory table, breathing out slowly, feeling almost personally menaced.

She sat for over five minutes with her arms folded, her face upturned to the highest window and the sky of deepening grey. She could almost feel the dusty autumn air around her head and face, brittle fragments of leaves like rapid, stinging thoughts.

It was a horrible story, really. Jane got up to put an apple log into the stove, Ethel moseying over to lie on the mat in front of it.

'You really don't have to look far, Ethel,' Jane said. 'It's all here. The Nightlands, everything.'

Ethel looked up. All cats knew the nightlands.

Borderlight was lying closed on the kitchen table. It was like one of those early books in museums where you could only turn the pages if you wore special gloves. Not the kind of book people bought to read, just to have. It was the size of a prayer book, made thicker by the quality of the tawny pages, browner around the edges to suggest age. The illustrations were mainly engravings – new ones, though you wouldn't think it – and some had been coloured like stained glass. The print was old-fashioned, and the first letters of each story were illuminated.

It was a labour of love.

Love was… did she even know what it was?

Jane put on all the lights in the kitchen, laid the book on the refectory table and photographed several pages with her iPad. All of them were from a single chapter relating to a medieval Latin manuscript *De Nugis Curialium*. Its translators included the great ghost story writer, M.R. James. Who used to stay in the Golden Valley. How things kept coming around in smoky cycles. She needed to break one.

No rules, Jane.

New era. All barriers down.

Jane checked the pictures were OK then slid the book inside the Ledwardine Livres bag and took it into the hall, where she put on her boots and parka and went out by the front door and across the cobbled square, into the driven rain.

This time.

We go where it's fun.

We don't have long...

In this job, as congregations aged, you were increasingly in and out of nursing homes. They'd changed a fair bit over the past few years, after all the public inquiries and exposés. You used to be able to recognize them with your eyes shut, by the smells. Or even, with your eyes open, by the drab furniture.

But places like Lyme Farm, owned by some company in Birmingham, were up there with all the five-star hotels Herefordshire didn't have: a cluster of white cottages inter-linked by lawns and low glassed-in passages like long conservatories.

The downside of spending your last years in a haven like this was selling everything except the clothes you no longer stood up in.

'They'll tell you, it's like being on permanent vacation.' Donna had a cultured possibly Californian accent. 'Like a cruise ship in the fields, one lady said. I thought that was lovely. We're going to put it on our website.'

Donna, sixtyish and slim, wore a dark green dress that could never be called a uniform or an overall but might serve as both. She led Merrily down a wide passage with skylights, past two different hairdressers' shops, a newsagent, a cinema and the entrance to the swimming pool with a wheelchair park.

Enjoy your day, Donna would say to the people they passed, most of them wearing leisurewear and trainers and not all of them old.

'We encourage visitors,' Donna said. 'People enjoy coming here – even young people. They can eat in the restaurant, walk the grounds. And the residents like to see them wandering around. Gives a sense of balance – young and not so young. A sense of social life. It's like never having left the real world but without all those pressures.'

A *sense* of social life?

They came out in a cubical room with a picture window framing a view down the long fields of north-west Herefordshire and across rusting woodland to the Welsh border at its least threatening.

Donna turned left. Merrily followed her down a passageway with triple-glazed windows and a door to a courtyard with dwarf apple trees, a fountain and seating. A overhead rustic sign said, *The Old Stables*.

'Mr Kindley-Pryce has one of our larger apartments – living room, bedroom with en suite and a library.'

'He still reads?'

Donna smiled confidentially.

'Let's say he likes to have books around him.'

'Is he well?'

'Physically, very well, I'd say.'

'And… happy?'

'He's contented. Sure doesn't try to abscond.' Donna laughed lightly. 'His accommodation was customized. We try to make transition easier by accommodating some of the residents' own furniture. They choose a small number of much-loved pieces and we try to furnish around them.'

'That sounds nice.'

'To give you an example, Mr Kindley-Pryce had a very large bed to which he was greatly attached? We took apart a built-in wardrobe to fit this monster into the bedroom but it still didn't work. So – lateral thinking – the living room is now the bedroom, and the former bedroom is his den, what he likes to call his study. We adapt, you see. We're flexible.'

'Wonderful.'

'We think so. We're well staffed, and this enables us to remain unobtrusive, instead of a few people hurling themselves around everywhere. There's a button in every room – not emergency buttons, we don't like that word. Now—'

They'd entered another glassed-in area overlooking the courtyard and stopped outside three adjacent light pine doors, one with a large **3** on it and a white button next to a small speaker. Donna turned to face Merrily who'd come in civvies – the short, belted, dark blue woollen coat, the skirt, the beret.

'—could you remind me of the nature of your kinship with Mr Kindley-Pryce?'

'Erm… none. Friend of a friend.'

Explaining about Dennis Kellow, who'd worked for Mr Kindley-Pryce for years, as a builder, and ended up buying his beloved house. Who often talked about him, wondering how he was getting on.

'Dennis was – you know what men are like, Donna – a little afraid to come and visit him and, you know, see what the years had done to him. I'm more used to it, in my job, so…'

'You're a nurse?'

'Erm, no, I'm…' Sometimes you had to use it. 'I'm in the Church. A vicar.'

'Right.'

'And knowing I was going to be in the area today, I said I'd call in.'

It sounded weak, but it would do. Donna nodded.

'Well, I don't think you'll find this too upsetting. He's remarkable for his age. You'd think he was ten years younger. Comes from not worrying about a thing. Partly, I guess, because of the nature of his disability, but also because he's at peace with the world. I really feel that. At peace with *his* world.'

'Erm, what kind of dementia does he *have*?'

Donna frowned at the word.

'We're not permitted to discuss medical details, Mrs Watkins.'

'No… I'm sorry.'

'He still has quite a few visitors. His son, nieces. Sometimes they take him out for the day. Might not recognize all of them, but they're OK with that.'

Donna pressed the white button. After two or three seconds, a soft voice was in the speaker.

'Hello there.'

'Good afternoon, Mr Kindly-Pryce, it's Donna. With a visitor?'

Odd. Talking to him, she pronounced his name *Kindly*.

A warm chuckle in the speaker.

'Man or woman?'

'It's a lady, Mr Kindly-Pryce.' Donna smiled. 'A young lady. The Reverend Watkins. A friend of an old friend, Mr…?'

'Kellow,' Merrily said. 'Dennis Kellow.'

'Mr Kellow?'

'Ah yes… yes. I know.'

Donna bent her head to Merrily's ear.

'He truly *doesn't* know.'

Merrily nodded.

48

Kingsize

IT PROBABLY *HAD* been part of a stable. You'd accommodate a couple of shire horses in here, no problem. Sections of stone wall had been left exposed in the creamwashed plaster between wide new windows, triple-glazed, and rafters and purlins were uncovered overhead, globular lamps attached to them, switched off.

The furniture, two chairs and a small dining table, was Shaker-plain and functional, and you might have said most of it was modern if most of it had not been the bed.

God...

A big room, but the bed made it claustrophobic. It was beyond kingsize. There were two carpeted steps with a handrail to get you into it, this work of gross art, its stained oak headboard reaching halfway up a buttermilk wall, fat corner posts rising to tiered pinnacles ending in pine-cone finials. Merrily was reminded uncomfortably of the monstrous pulpit in her nightmare about Jenny Roberts.

'My *dear.*'

She jumped. The voice, soft and breathy, came from a deep chair beside the bed.

'How *marvellous* to see you again.'

He was wearing a thick black velvet dressing gown with a red collar, like a long smoking jacket. His lower legs were bare, feet in black moccasins.

'No, please...' Merrily said, 'don't get up.'

But he was up already, a large and bony hand wrapping around hers. Donna waited in the doorway, smiling.

'You're looking… very well,' Merrily said to Mr Kindley-Pryce.

He released her hand, standing quite tall, only a little stooped. His face was vertically fissured like an almond.

He pointed.

'Green chair, please.'

'He wants you to sit there,' Donna murmured.

'Thank you.'

When you sat down, you were looking up at the bed. No matter where you sat you'd be looking up at the bed. It had thronelike status in the room. Because of the bed, she could only see half the window from here, the half full of low, loaded sky.

'Red chair somewhere,' Mr Kindley-Pryce said.

There was. It was leather-covered and behind him, and he lowered himself back into it, his wide mouth settling into a smile. He had a Mr Punch kind of smile that made his face seem longer. The red chair and the green chair faced one another at the side of the bed. She should've brought something for him. Should've asked on the phone what he liked to eat… drink.

'So,' he said, 'all the way from England.'

'Erm…'

'My accent, I guess,' Donna said. 'He spent many years in the States. He sometimes thinks…'

'Oh, I see.' It seemed wrong to lie to him, so she just went for it. 'I've come from Cwmarrow, Mr Pryce.'

Only a moment of incomprehension before his face seemed to light up like a fairground lantern.

'How marvellous,' he said.

'Yes. Yes it is.'

'And how is Sir William?'

'Erm…'

'I'll leave you, then,' Donna said.

Giving Merrily time to remember that Sir William had been a character in *The Summoner*, the knight away at the Crusades.

As the door closed almost silently behind Donna, Merrily felt a sense of vacuum, as if her ears had popped. The triple glazing meant you could see the wind bending trees outside but you could barely hear it. A disturbing sense of separation, as if it was back-projection, a storm with the sound turned down.

She said, 'Sir William who lived at the castle?'

Mr Kindley-Pryce fixed her with eyes like knots in wood. A little glimmering back there.

'I see him in… in…. in clouds.'

'Oh?'

Sometimes they couldn't find the right words. She didn't know what he meant. He was nodding to a slow rhythm, eyes half closed, as if nodding himself to sleep. The rain spattered silently and rolled down the window. Dennis Kellow's voice came back to her.

Slept in a massive old bed where he claimed he'd often wake up to the sounds of the village.

His eyes opened.

She smiled at him.

'Good that you still have the bed, Mr Pryce.'

'Bed?'

'From Cwmarrow.'

'The *bed.*' It had a heavy maroon quilt. He reached up and stroked it. 'Had it all my years.'

'This bed?'

Unless he'd brought it back from America, that couldn't be true. She looked directly into his eyes. You should always try to hold their gaze, Kent Asprey, the Ledwardine doc, had told her once. Let them see they have your full attention.

'Dennis is still working on the house. You remember Dennis?'

He looked at her for long moments, tiny points of light far back in his eyes and no source of light in the room to cause them.

He rose up in his chair, his neck craning, his lips forming a word.

'*Cwmarroooooo.*' He sat back. His mouth opened in hoarse laughter. '*Kee, kee, kee.*'

He seemed still to have most of his teeth. How old was he... eighty-five? Older than that?

Huw was right, she shouldn't've come. She had no medical knowledge. He didn't *look* so bad, but he was clearly far from compos mentis. Whether he was better than he should be after all these years was anybody's guess. There were always anomalies.

She tried Dennis Kellow's name on him again and he repeated it and nodded, but that was all. No sign of recognition. What had she expected? Had she hoped for something revelatory, some sense of an underlife in the Cwmarrow valley, some symptom of... oppression?

Oppression was the safer word. She felt, for an instant, disgusted with herself, with what she'd become, always attuned to the possibility of *otherness*. Why couldn't she have left him alone to be... old?

The bed, though... that *was* oppressive. The bed was a piece of Cwmarrow, a constant, stark reminder that he'd traded a house and a castle, a whole valley, for a beautifully carpeted stairway to heaven.

'Well,' he said. '*Come along...*' He was leaning back in his chair, his long hands gripping the wooden armrests. 'Old man, me. A very... old... man. No time to wait. *Kee, kee, kee.*'

The room was very dim now and the air, quite suddenly, felt both dense and abrasively frigid. But Mr Kindley-Pryce in his dressing gown, the only lights the distant pinpricks in his eyes, didn't seem to notice the cold.

'Going to take off your... your things, are you? Relapse?'

Relax?

She glanced at the door, had the slightly worrying thought that Donna might have locked it from the other side. She really didn't want to, but she stood up and took off her coat, hanging it from a wing of the green chair.

Mr Kindley-Pryce clapped his hands, laughing again, his legs parting the black and red dressing gown and, as she sat down, despite the shadows, she saw too much.

'*Kee, kee, kee.*'

Her head jerked away, and she felt dizzy, the fading light fluttering around her like a cascade of grey moths, carrying his soft voice to her as he reached up and patted the bed.

'*Merr-il-y... Come along.*'

49

Before he was mad

IN THE HALF-LIGHT, she backed into him.

'Steady,' he said.

Merrily, still shaking, spun round and stumbled. His hands closed around her arms and she cried out and looked up at him, frozen. The years had fallen shockingly away, he was younger and stronger, his skin firm and tanned, and his hands had seized her shoulders.

She twisted away, backed away, against a wall with another door in it that opened behind her and she almost fell into the space of what should have been the bedroom, now lined with books and pictures. Grabbing at the air, she saw the old man directly in front of her, still in his red leather chair, knees together under the dressing gown, his eyes blurred, focused on nothing, the bed's headboard rearing up behind him like some wintry cathedral.

'I'm awfully sorry,' the man in the main doorway said. 'Didn't mean to startle you.'

Different voice, more than a hint of Herefordshire, and he wasn't wearing a dressing gown. He had on a dark suit and a tie with a small crest on it. Consternation on his long, smooth face.

'My fault entirely,' he said. 'I should've knocked.'

He held the door open and glanced over a shoulder at the old man in the chair.

'Having his nap. Slip out now, I should. He won't notice you've gone.'

Merrily's legs felt weak. She looked back at Selwyn Kindley-Pryce. His eyes were closed, but something of the smile remained. She went back and grabbed her coat.

In the conservatory area outside, he held out a hand.

'Hector Pryce.'

'Oh…'

What a powerful emotion embarrassment could be, sometimes stronger than fear.

'I'm… so sorry about this.'

'Nobody expects that bed.'

'No.'

He was giving her a way out.

'I expect one morning they'll find him dead in it. Lying in state. Quite a fright for someone.'

'Well—'

'Nice place this, ennit? I think we did well.'

We?

They were standing on stone crazy-paving with what looked like AstroTurf either side, three rustic benches with cushioned seats. Hector Pryce had his hands behind his back. He was fiftyish, with that gym-toned look about him. Shaven-headed and tanned enough to have been abroad quite recently.

'Now,' he said. 'Forgive me. What's so interesting, suddenly, about my poor old father?'

In other words, why are you here? She wanted to say why are *you* here, but then she knew.

'I'm sorry, I'm a bit ignorant. You have a stake in this place?'

'I'm a director of the company.'

'Ah.'

Did the Kellows know this? Probably not.

'We have another spread, over in Warwickshire. More of a gated community there – proximity to Birmingham. This place is more casual. I come in most weeks, stroll around, see how we can improve it even more. We're opening a little theatre next year. For concerts. Be like… what's that place?'

'Glyndebourne?'

'Las Vegas.'

Hector laughed.

It was a long shot, Jane knew that. She really didn't think they'd actually have a copy in the bookshop, she told herself she just wanted to talk to someone about it, confirm that she wasn't imagining connections that weren't there. Needed to trust herself again.

'*De Nugis Curialium*. I've been asked for this before, Jane, though not recently,' Gus Staines said. 'I remember we did once try to obtain an English translation for someone and it proved impossible.'

'M.R. James translated it, I think. Or some of it.'

'Yes, a number of people have, I'm sure, over the centuries, but try to lay your hands on a copy, even second-hand.'

'Oh.'

'It translates as *Trifles of the Courtiers*. Which Map *was* – a courtier to Henry II. Also a cleric. Hold on. Yes, here…' Gus Staines bent to the computer on the counter. 'Canon at Hereford and St Paul's and – oh – almost became Bishop of Hereford in 1199.'

Walter Map, chronicler. Born around the middle of the twelfth century, according to *Borderlands*.

'Although no one is sure, quite, in which year he died,' Gus Staines said, reading from the screen. 'A man from the Welsh border, as his name suggests – not uncommon in the area to this day, as we know, Jane, sometimes spelt with two ps now. Studied at the University of Paris. *De Nugis Curialium* is his main surviving work… stories and anecdotes he'd picked up on his travels.'

'Not *made* up?'

'Was anything entirely made up in those days? Yes, they say Geoffrey of Monmouth and his tales of King Arthur were invented and certainly embroidered, but it all came from stories in circulation at the time. There was something there, to build on. This one… well, Walter Map clearly relished ghost stories, tales of revenants, and this is probably his best known. Although, as you say, not that well known today. Certainly the most sinister, though, as I recall.'

Jane asked if anybody had ever pointed out at the time that Selwyn Kindley-Pryce had clearly used Map's story, as retold in his own book, as the basis for *The Summoner*. Gus put this to her partner, Amanda Rubens, who said she hadn't read it.

'You have to remember,' Gus said, 'that Foxy Rowlestone, despite the name, was never really identified as a local author. As for this…' Picking up the copy of *Borderlight* Jane had brought back, sliding it under the counter. '… it just came and went. Limited edition. I think he just wanted to create a beautiful book to showcase the work of his new friend, Caroline. It was never a talking point.'

'It has to be the source for Foxy, though, doesn't it?' Jane said. 'Could we go through the story – do you have time?'

She saw Gus and Amanda exchange looks as a man and a woman came in with two children.

'What's this about, Jane?' Gus said with her goblin smile. 'Do you mind my asking?'

'Doing some research. For Mum.'

'Let's go in the back,' Gus said.

The room behind the shop was an office and stockroom, not so much for books as the stationery items Ledwardine Livres sold on the side. There was also a sink and a very small woodstove with a whistling kettle on top and a door to a toilet. Cosy.

'Coffee?' Gus said.

'No… no, thanks.'

'Well, sit down, Jane.'

Jane sat on a stool, hands in the pockets of her parka in case they were shaking. Gus went to sit behind the desk, leaned back and scrutinized Jane over her reading glasses.

'You know, the chances of us having a translation of *De Nugis Curialium* were pretty remote.'

'Mmm.'

'I did think you would probably know that. You're a smart girl. I bet you'd already checked on Amazon and found there wasn't one anywhere.'

'No. I didn't. I try to support local shops.'

'Oh, Jane, *really*... Don't tell Amanda I said this, but we're little more than a gift shop.'

Jane's fists were clenched inside her pockets. Gus looked serious.

'What *is* your problem? *Can* I ask?'

'It's stupid. It's naive.'

Gus looked unconvinced, said nothing.

'It's just... when did you first realize you were a lesbian?' Jane said.

Hector Pryce listened, without comment, to her explanation about Dennis Kellow. Told to someone like Hector, a businessman, it didn't sound at all convincing. When she was out of here she'd have to phone Dennis and explain what she'd done.

Add one to the number of times she'd ignored Huw Owen's advice and regretted it.

Hector Pryce strolled over to one of the rustic benches, waved Merrily to the one opposite, sat down with his hands linked behind his head.

'Kellow,' he said. 'Feeling guilty, is he?'

'I'm sorry?'

'Getting that place for a song. We ought to have waited another year. Property market went up. Another year, we'd've had twice what we got from Kellow. But then, it wasn't mine to sell.'

'You were just your father's agent in the sale? I'm not sure how these things work when the property owner is...'

'Not fit to manage his own affairs? Well, I'll tell you. It makes things very, very complicated, Mrs Watkins. Father, he always thought Kellow would be the best man to look after it. Me, I couldn't understand that. Why not hang on till property prices rose again and let it go to somebody with money to burn? 'Cause that's what they do these old places – burn all your money, ennit?'

'Your father seems to have regarded it as his life's work. Maybe Dennis, too.'

'Bloody mad, people who get obsessed with the past. Past is worthless, messes you up. He had a good life in the States, my old man, and he gave it up… for what?' He eyed her. 'So you're a vicar, and Kellow asked you to find out if my father was still alive, did he? Why not come himself?'

'He… told me he came to visit your father once, but your father didn't recognize him.'

'And that surprised him, did it?'

'I don't think he felt comfortable coming back. And he's had a stroke'

'I didn't know that. What's he like now?' He jerked a thumb over his shoulder. 'Like him?'

'He's made a good recovery, but…'

'I 'spect you, as a vicar, would think me a bit heartless if I said it was his own fault. But living in the past, it *saps* you. Me, I got no time for history. Me and that ole cabbage in there, we got nothing in common. He split up with my mother 'fore I could hardly talk, and I made my own way without him. The money he sent, my mother got that. I made my own way.'

'Well, that—'

'Don't get me wrong, we got on all right when he came back from the States. He thought he was quite well off. Bit knocked back when he found I'd more than him. But he's still my father and I got responsibility to him. Even though I thought he was mad even before he *was* mad.'

He laughed. In the picture window behind him, an apple tree vibrated soundlessly in the wind. Something askew here.

'You're obviously making him comfortable,' Merrily said. 'The bed?'

'Oh, aye. He likes old things from his past around. Sentimental stuff. So I get them for him.'

Merrily smiled.

'I'm told he used to lie in that bed and get a sense that the village of Cwmarrow – the vanished village – was still alive, around him?'

He didn't move, but his face altered, became intense, as if something had risen in him like a gas jet. And then he controlled it, leaned back, hands behind his head again.

'You know what it means? Cwmarrow? In the original Welsh?'

'Seems to mean Valley of the Arrow. Which struck me as a bit odd, when the river Arrow's more than ten miles away.'

'They all think that. My father knew the real meaning, though he never talked about it. Didn't even tell *me* till he'd moved out, and I thought, well, he en't rational, but then I looked it up, and it looked right. *Cwm* – Welsh for valley, sure enough. But Arrow – that en't Welsh, is it?'

'Well… sometimes, over time, a Welsh word gets replaced by an English word that sounds similar, phonetically.'

'Aye. Arrow for *Marw*. You know that word?'

'Not sure.'

'Welsh for dead.'

'It means *Valley of the Dead?*'

She tried not to look horrified.

'Now you know.' Hector hunched forward. 'He's always been a dreamer. *Dreamer.*'

'Dreams can be powerful,' Merrily said without thinking.

'Only if you let them. He's a bloody children's storyteller, a fantasist.'

'He was an academic, wasn't he? A scholar?'

'What's your point?'

'I was just… You said you thought old things weren't good. Sapped you. But you don't mind that the bed—'

'He's an ole man, he en't got long, I get him what he wants.'

She felt a coldness. Hector Pryce got his father what he wanted. And yet wasn't there something close to hatred here? Or something closer to fear. Was that possible?

'I'll get Donna to show you out, shall I?' Hector Pryce said. 'Or can you find your own way?'

Obviously she could find her own way, but she looked for Donna, asking three attendants, none of whom had a local accent or knew where Donna was. She hung around by the reception desk. A stick-thin elderly lady with bright red hair came over and asked if she could help.

'Just waiting for Donna, thanks.'

The old lady nodded seriously.

'A very capable woman, Donna. Nothing seems to bother her.'

'So it seems.'

'Have you come to visit a relative?'

'Just a friend.'

'Kindley-Pryce?'

You'd often encounter someone like this in a home for the elderly. Someone – usually a woman – who knew everything, a gleaner and spreader of gossip.

'You're *his friend*?' she said.

'Friend of a friend. It's the first time we've met.'

'Not a niece, then? I thought you might be one of his nieces. *Great*-nieces, more like.' She peered at Merrily, a glaze of contact lenses. 'You do look younger from a distance.'

'Well, that's something.'

'He's the king here, you know,' she said. 'Three apartments to himself.'

'Three?'

'Look at the numbers on the door. Or rather the *shortage* of numbers. One, two, three and three is the only number on a door.'

'His son's a director of the company.'

The old woman scowled.

'It's a glossy funeral parlour, this place. I'll tell you something.' She came close to Merrily. 'You don't want to be here at night.'

'Why's that?'

'I don't come out of my room. Sometimes I leave a light on. Who cares about their bills? We pay enough.'

'Come on now, Jean.' Donna had appeared. 'Jean does our public relations,' she said to Merrily, not smiling, steering her away. 'I'm afraid some of our guests don't care too much what they say or to whom. Privilege of age, I guess. Now you take care on the roads, Mrs Watkins. The weather's not going to be anyone's friend tonight.'

Merrily stopped well short of the electronic double doors.

'When does a person with dementia become too far... you know, too far gone... to go on living here?'

'That's not an easy question to answer. Some people with difficulties are inclined to wander at night, might require extra supervision.'

'Mr Kindley-Pryce does that?'

Donna looked away.

'I guess.'

'Donna... did you tell him my name?'

'You were with me when I spoke to him.'

'That's the only time you spoke to him. You didn't tell him earlier that I was coming?'

'He wouldn't have remembered.'

'Or anyone else?'

'You're in the book. Mrs M. Watkins.' Donna stared at her. 'Is there something wrong?'

'I meant my first name. Did you tell anyone my first name?'

'I don't believe *I know* your first name,' Donna said.

She thought of asking Donna about the nieces and the great-nieces who apparently came to visit Kindley-Pryce. *I get him what he wants.*

She didn't. She smiled and left.

50

What can haunt you

LOL LIKED HER. He'd always kind of liked her. He thought even Merrily liked her more than she thought she ought to. But he was still wary when, for the first time, she rang him.

'How are we, today, Robinson?'

Did you tell her the truth, that you half wished you were back in Knight's Frome working with the crazy Belladonna? He carried the phone to the edge of the desk so that he could see out of the window above the condensation. The glass seemed to be panting in the wind.

'You haven't been inhaling white powder again, have you?'

'I've never inhaled white powder, Athena. When you've been inside a psychiatric hospital and not as a visitor, you start closing doors that have never even been open.'

'How sad,' Athena White said. 'Old beyond your years. How is Watkins?'

'Which one?'

'Is she with you?'

'I'm alone.'

'Ships in the night. As usual. You must be wondering if it's meant, you and her. When you're not staring out of your window at an unlit vicarage, hating God.'

'I don't hate God.'

Lol moved away from the window, dragging the phone back across the desk, and sat down hard. She might just be referencing 'The Cure of Souls', the embittered song he wished he'd never written a couple of years ago, but, when he thought about it, it was most unlikely Athena White had deigned to listen to any of his music.

'Do you ever dream she was out of it, Robinson?'

He didn't reply. Twice this afternoon he'd been across to the vicarage. Monday, traditionally, was a vicar's day off. Nobody in, no car in the drive. Yes, all right, sometimes he'd resented that God and the church were too close, constantly demanding. The magic was in distance: church bells and birdsong.

'She'll never be out of it,' Lol said.

'Perhaps not voluntarily…'

'OK. I sometimes think about it, but I always conclude that life isn't that simple. And maybe isn't supposed to be. There's a side to her that's always going to be there. And if your competition for a woman's attentions is the ultimate ineffable mystery, then— Aw, shit, Athena, what do you *want*?'

'Suddenly, she has enemies, Robinson. Inside an ostensibly benign, venerable organization which actually is possessed of a Stasi-like ruthlessness.'

Merrily had learned that a much younger Athena White had worked for the intelligence services during the Cold War. A mindset that lingered.

'Where are you getting this from, Athena?'

'Don't treat me like an idiot, you know how vindictive I can be.'

Through the remisting glass, Lol saw a hooded figure at his door.

'I want you to listen,' Athena White said.

'I think Jane's outside.'

'Then send the brat away.'

'I'm going to have to call you back,' Lol said.

Your teddy bears – were they girls or boys?
   You mean there are girl teddy bears?
   Good answer, Gus Staines had said.

329

It had, eventually, become ridiculous. Jane laughing through tears she couldn't stop. Tears like the rain on the window.

Did you ever feel drawn to other girls at school?

I liked some girls a lot. There were girls I preferred to hang out with. Girls I wanted to hang out with, and I was quite disappointed when they didn't want to hang out with me.

Not what I meant by 'drawn to', Jane.

Jane threw off her parka, flopped in front of Lol's stove, shivering.

'Can I get you a drink?' Lol said. 'Brandy?'

'You trying to seduce me?'

'I was thinking for the shock.'

'How do you know I've had a shock?'

Lol shrugged.

'There was a time when I kind of wanted you to. Seduce me.'

'Jane, maybe this is not the time—'

'No – listen – it is.' She looked up at him; he looked worried. 'It *is* the time. I had a crush on you – before Mum, obviously, I've never been *that* sick. You with your hesitant, unworldly, damaged—'

'Who've you been talking to?'

'Gus at the bookshop.'

'Bloody hell, Jane, you do like to seek out the most authoritative sources.'

'She was very nice about it. She let me unload everything. She was very patient.'

See, I was playing it cool. Didn't want to comes across as some wispy new generation New Age loony. It was Sam who started talking about it. Pointing up to Carn Ingli, in the Preseli Hills, the most mystical place in Pembrokeshire. If you spend a night up there you're supposed to come down as a visionary. Sam was like, 'Well, why not? These stories don't come out of nowhere, they're crucially important. They should inform archaeology.'

And did you go up there together? To sleep at... where was it?

330

Carn Ingli. No, because that was the night we got pissed and I spent the night in her bed. She wanted to do it the next night, go up there and I thought, Christ, it would be like commitment, like getting engaged or something. So next day I came home. I didn't have to, but I was terrified.

Terrified?

That it was... like a latent thing?

Latent... at nineteen? Oh Jane, you're so funny. All right, Sam. Is she feminine, or...?

She's very attractive. In a very appealing, down-to-earth kind of way. She became my refuge. I wanted to be with her.

'She keeps texting me,' Jane told Lol. 'She's offered to get me into another dig. Which would be great. She's clearly a bit, you know, in love? I think. I mean, how would I know? I'm nineteen years old in the Third Millennium and a complete innocent. I've been with just one guy and... and one woman... *possibly*. An innocent and a complete mental case – *you* can see that, you spent whole years amongst them.' She stopped, looking into his anxious eyes. 'You're going to tell me I'm not, right? That I'm not, at the very least, in the middle of a breakdown.'

'I'm not qualified,' Lol said.

Jane moved away from the stove to lean her back against the seat of the sofa and told him about going with Mum to the place with the ruins and the brook and the mysterious plateau below the forestry, where she'd become aware of the woman in black, and the black had fallen away.

'I hoped it was a ghost. I did *not* want it to be the other thing.'

'What other thing?'

'An image of what was really haunting me.'

'And you didn't tell your mum?'

'She has enough to worry about. Doesn't she?'

'And did you tell Gus?'

'No!'

'Why not?'

'Because it's something that – if it's real, and it might be – Mum might want to know, and if I couldn't tell her…'

'So you're just telling me?'

'I'm just telling you. You're the only person I can trust. And you did a psychotherapy course.'

'I dropped *out* of a psychotherapy course. To learn a fifteenth chord.'

Jane grinned.

'Even Irene knows more than fifteen chords.'

'*Irene?*'

'Slip of the tongue. It means nothing.'

'Listen,' Lol said. 'I have one question, as a failed psychotherapist and former mental patient. This… whatever you thought you saw… have you seen it since… in any form?'

'It haunts me. Makes me shiver. If I've learned one thing, watching Mum dithering and agonizing, it's that ghosts are the least of what can haunt you.'

Merrily called Huw from the gloom of the Etnam Street car park, at the bottom end of Leominster, noticing how few cars were parked under its pine trees in case one should come down in the gale.

'You were right. I shouldn't have gone. If I hadn't gone, I might've given up on Cwmarrow on the basis that there was nothing else I could do. And now I can't.'

'Dementia itself can be frightening, lass.'

He sounded cautious.

'It's frightening to begin with,' she said, 'because you know there's no way back. If you're on the outside, you're terrified you might end up hating someone you love because it's not the same person. Because, increasingly, there isn't a person there at all.'

She'd thought hard about this, reliving it again and again, everything that happened at Lyme Farm, as she drove very slowly back to Leominster, headlights on, under creaking trees.

Reliving it again now, for Huw.

When she'd finished, it was like the signal had gone. She looked up at the wavering pines, matt black on deepening grey.

'Huw?'

'It's a bugger, Merrily. I don't know what to advise you.'

'No.'

'How sure are you?'

'On one level, as sure as I can be. I was expecting a sad, befuddled old man.'

'Arguably, lass, what you've just described to me is a sad, befuddled old man.'

'The difference is in the detail. I assure you I didn't *want* to feel a sense of deep... negativity. What scares me most is the very idea of suggesting that dementia leaves people open to elements of oppression... or worse.'

'It's not the norm, but it's always a possibility, even though, in a case of dementia, the borderline between psychiatry and the other thing is almost unchartable. Were you scared in the other sense?'

'Well... yes. Bit shocked, you know, at what I'd seen. I mean, I do know what one looks like in a state of arousal, but this—'

'Was that arousal displayed in any other way?'

'He was perfectly calm. Nothing... except the lights in his eyes. Coming *from* his eyes. Or from *behind* his eyes.'

'Don't like that.'

'And then the use of the name.'

'Your name.'

'Uttered at exactly the right moment for maximum impact. On me. Just on me.'

'And *you* think he couldn't've known.'

'But I can't prove that, not even to myself. Can't prove any of it. Could just be me. In my state of palpitating insecurity. The worst that anybody's implied is that Selwyn Kindley-Pryce was driven out of his mind by something in the house.'

'In other words, nobody's suggested it might have gone *with* him.'

'No.'

'And what do you think it is?'

'I've no idea. There's no clear history apart from recent history. I was hoping that if Kindley-Pryce had short periods of rationality he might just throw me a clue. But in the end, it was his son. I met his son. I think his son is scared of him.'

'Go home,' Huw said.

'And then what?'

'You *can't* be the only one to've noticed summat. Even if not everybody would draw the same conclusions. Who haven't you talked to?'

'Caroline Goddard. His writing partner. At the very least.'

'If anybody knows, it's likely to be her.'

'She certainly got out fast enough. Despite the obvious financial incentives to carry on. But I don't know where she is, and her publishers have no particular reason to get back to me. I'll keep trying.'

'And keep talking to me, all right? Because we both know where this could end up?'

'Major exorcism? Do you think?'

Which she'd never done, and which…

'And you know what that means,' Huw said.

… which she couldn't do without permission from her bishop.

Dear God.

'Get off home. I'll talk to you later. If the wind hasn't brought down the phone lines and the bloody mobile masts.'

51

Just the one

WHEN SHE GOT back, it was fully dark and the only message on the machine was from Caroline Goddard's publisher.

Mrs Watkins, we've spoken to Caroline and given her your number, but she says her Foxy Rowlestone books are very much in the past and not something she wants to discuss. As you can imagine, she's been bombarded with mail from demanding fans, and she hopes you can respect her privacy. Thank you.

Bugger.

She went back into the kitchen, where Jane was sitting at the refectory table under low lights with her iPad, some printouts, Mrs Leather's book and a pot of tea. She looked up, eyes narrowing as if this was an unwanted interruption.

'We can talk about this now, Mum, or I can—'

'Foxy?'

'And djinns. Just some more things I want to check out. This could be heavy. Or, let's face it, it could turn out to be complete crap. I'm not getting overexcited at this stage.'

Something about her had changed. She was focused in a way Merrily hadn't seen in a good while. Not since before she'd gone to Pembrokeshire, anyway.

'What are you getting?'

'I am getting, at the very least, a renewed sense of purpose,' Jane said, almost grimly, and then brought up a smile. 'Look, why don't you call Lol? Or just go over.'

'Don't you want to eat?'

'Let's eat later. Or, if you're not here, I can get something. Go on. Ring him.'

'Are you—?'

'Go.'

'OK, I will.'

Maybe she did need to find some space. Just for a while. She went back to the scullery, rang Lol and got no answer.

He couldn't be far away, not on a night like this. When she'd got back to the village, his truck had been parked on the square. He'd call back. She sat down and listened to the wind and snatched up the phone before the second ring.

'Merrily?'

'Oh.'

'Martin, it is. Martin Longbeach. I've called several times. Didn't want to leave a message.'

'Right.'

'Some things you don't want to leave messages about,' Martin said. 'Do you?'

'Just give me a second, Martin.'

She laid the phone on the desk, went to close the door, came back and sat down. Switched off the desk lamp, took the call in the dark where she suspected it belonged.

Martin sounding guarded, that was no big surprise. After the unexpected, HIV-related death of his partner, Daniel, he'd done some bad things. Embittered, sacrilegious things that could have got him thrown out of the Church were they to be talked about in the wrong company.

But these were private things, between Martin and God, nobody else, nobody harmed, and if you knew him well enough you didn't talk about them because you'd probably been there, too, or might have cause to visit that same unholy place some-time in the future. He was a kind man, Martin, and a good, if unorthodox, parish priest.

'Right, then.' He sighed down a crackling line. 'Bishop Craig Innes.'

'Have you met him?'

'Well, you know, he hasn't been to see me yet... as Bishop.'

'Meaning you knew him already?'

'Well, we're both from Wales, isn't it?'

'It's a small country, Martin, but not that small. And he was in Swansea and Brecon diocese and then Monmouth, and you're from Cardiff, and neither of you speaks like that. So when did you last see him?'

'Oh, Merrily, I don't keep a diary of these things.'

'Not a scheduled meeting, then.'

'We just ran into one another.'

'Just... out of the blue.'

'He was in the area.'

'Was it this year?'

'Probably. Early in the year.'

'So before it was officially known that Bernie Dunmore—'

'I don't know. I mean, yes. Obviously.'

'One question, Martin.'

Outside, the wind was roaring like a ravenous fire.

'Why aren't you asking me why I want to know?'

Hell, she didn't like to think of herself as the kind of person who called favours in, but—

'Oh, Merrily! You always make me tie myself in knots, you— No, that's not true. I *live* in bloody knots. I should quit this job. If there was anything else I was halfway qualified to do I'd go tomorrow. I would.'

'No, you wouldn't. This is where you belong.'

He was a maverick, but where would the Church be without them? His acceptance of his own weaknesses would always make him sympathetic to people most priests would avoid.

'Martin, I'm guessing you hadn't even met Craig Innes before he came to see you. Before it was even whispered that he might be in the frame for Bishop of Hereford.'

'I'd met him briefly. Once.'

'But he'd… he probably said he'd heard a lot about you.'

'Oh yes.' His voice was parched. 'He did.'

'Did you and he discuss deliverance?'

'Oh, Merrily…'

He was qualified. He'd done the course with Huw. He just didn't do deliverance any more, which was no bad thing by anyone's criteria. For his own sake.

'I didn't *tell* him anything about you,' Martin said. 'I said I didn't know anything to tell.'

'But he asked…'

'Please don't hold this against me. I've been agonizing for months, on and off, see, over whether to tell you. What if I was just stirring the pot?'

'This was before you came here as locum?'

'It didn't seem so important, then. Bernie Dunmore was still Bishop. Rumours of him retiring, but nothing official. *You* didn't know Craig Innes then. Or did you?'

'No. Though when I first saw pictures of the new Bishop, I immediately recognized him from somewhere. Only realizing later that I'd seen him in the village, over the summer. With his wife and kids. And more than once. Checking out the vicarage.'

'Thinking what it might be worth?'

'Of course.'

'When he became Bishop, see, I thought to tell you. But what if I needlessly poisoned whatever relationship you had with him?'

'You think it would have?'

Obviously, the other reason for hesitation would have been because Innes might have learned from one of his *small but growing coterie of clergy* exactly what Martin had done, drunk and embittered, in the chancel of his church after Daniel's death.

'Martin, did he mention Hunter?'

'Oh God. Look, he thought I was a gossip. All this gay-boy stereotype bullshit. He thought wrongly. I am *not* a stereotype.'

'That is true.'

'Then he was very friendly. Said he could see canon material in me.'

'*Loose* canon material?'

'Oh, stop it, Merrily, this is no time for levity.'

'That was hysteria, Martin.'

'He said he understood that I'd done a deliverance course but not followed through. Like himself. We had both, he said, exposed ourselves to the most outdated side of the Church. And the most unnecessarily sinister.'

'Sinister.'

'His word. He clearly didn't expect me to argue with him, and I didn't, feeling I'd learn more if he thought I was on his side. So, when he asked me about serving on the short-lived deliverance panel with you and Siân and a psychiatrist whose name I'm quite glad to have forgotten, I said it was a complete shambles.'

'Which it was.'

'If not in the way he was thinking. And yes, I'm afraid he did ask me about Hunter. He said – and you have to understand that he took a long, circuitous route to this issue – he said it might never be known to what extent Hunter had corrupted the Diocese of Hereford but after Dunmore – which he said was a period, essentially, of interregnum – it would fall to the next Bishop of Hereford to repair the damage. A dolorous task, for someone.'

'Dolorous.'

'His word. Not a task, he said, that he personally would relish.'

'A dirty job but someone had to do it.'

'A job which, given the nature of the corruption, would need to be accomplished, he said, as discreetly as possible. And that anything I told him would be treated with the utmost confidence.'

'Never once saying he might be a candidate.'

'Perish the thought, Merrily. I shall get this over. He said it had been reported to him that Hunter had had carnal relations with a number of women priests in the diocese.'

The phone line crackled harshly. Merrily's head went back.

'And then he said this was doubtless an exaggeration, as...'

In the blackness, the window was a ghostly grey square slashed through with a dark cross.

'... as it was probably just the one,' Martin said.

52

The song with the big cigar

SHE SAT IN the dark, listening to the wind and gazing at the window-cross for... who knew? Did it matter? She just sat there, numbed, thinking how *not surprising* any of this was. Quite a valid assumption, really. Innes hadn't invented it, he'd heard it from someone, perhaps from more than one person because they loved to gossip, the clergy, if terribly discreetly. Maybe it had been doing the rounds for years.

So she just sat, aware of being in the eye of the vicious storm, knowing that one move, any move would throw her into the blast. Sat until she became aware of something else not right, something not happening, the missing sound under the wind.

Putting on the desk lamp, she stood up, walked to the door, throwing on the main lights, blinking against the glare and the thrust of tears, before crossing over to the window. Opening it, careful to hold on to its rim with both hands to prevent it being wrenched away and smashed against the wall.

When she pushed her head into the wind and rain and looked down, the tears came unexpectedly and very quickly.

She looked down again, through her tumbled hair, to double-check, quite aware that in times of stress small things could assume disproportionate significance, before pulling her head back into the scullery and then closing the window, carefully applying the fastener and then the stay, her shoulders shaking as all the lights flickered.

'Merrily?'

She turned round and he was there in the doorway. Jane must have let him in.

He said, 'What's happened?'

She stood there, shaking her head.

'Please,' Lol said. '*What?*'

He looked stricken. He was wearing his old, washed-out *Alien* sweatshirt from his first solo album that nobody bought. She heard herself saying things.

'Tried to call you. You didn't answer.'

'The phone's dead. The lines are down somewhere.'

'Huh?' She moved to the desk and picked up the phone: nothing. 'It wasn't before. Never mind. Where's Jane?'

'She's gone up to her apartment. With some sandwiches. She says she'll tell you in the morning. What she knows.'

'Sandwiches,' Merrily said. 'What a crap mother I am.'

'She's nineteen. I think that's a woman. What were you looking at out there?'

Merrily wiped her eyes with her sleeve.

'There was this old briar we never cut. It used to tap against the window in the breeze. Sometimes when there wasn't a breeze. I used to think it was like a warning of... of something about to happen. Someone watching out. A bit sinister, but not in a bad... Anyway, silly.'

'It's gone?'

'It's still there. On the ground. Broken by the wind. Pathetic, aren't I?'

'No, but...'

'Also, the last call before the phone went down, I learned that the Bishop is of the firm opinion that I was sexually intimate with Mick Hunter and appears not to care who knows.'

Lol stayed silent.

'Obviously it's not—'

'Not something you even need to say.'

'No smoke, Lol.'

'He's looking for a sacrificial lamb?'

342

'Very sensitively put.'

She broke down again and let him hold her until the wind reached screaming pitch and all the lights went out.

The alarm clock's luminous fingers said 3.25 when Merrily awoke, naked and cold, in her own bed.

Evidently still no power, no lights out there, but the wind wasn't so loud, was just skulking around like a tired drunk. She felt around on the floor until she found the long T-shirt and pulled it on.

Lol said, 'What are you going to do?'

'Uh—' She sank back. 'How long've you been awake?'

'A while, I suppose.'

'Not since—'

'No, no.'

'I'm sorry about that. Bit desperate, wasn't it? Like we were on the *Titanic* and we knew about the iceberg in advance. My fault. A bit last-chance saloon.'

'Is it?'

'I'll have to go. I *will* have to go. Sooner rather than later. No point in dragging it out.'

'You can't go. That's as good as admitting it. Something you've been shamefully accused of. And letting the bastard win.'

'The bastard doesn't see it as a contest, and it probably isn't. No, look, it's not going to help anybody, me fighting the inevitable. Most of all, it's not going to help Huw. Huw will damage himself trying to save my arse, and he's much more important than me, in the great scheme of things. He's stronger, he knows more and he can still pass it on and… and we're not going to get to sleep again, are we?'

'We're all right, aren't we?' Lol said. 'I mean us. We could be all right.'

'Yes. That's something, isn't it? We're all right. In spite of everything. We're all right. And we've got Lucy's house. On a mortgage.'

'From where you can stand at the window and watch the new vicar going about his or her daily—'

'No. Don't think I could do that.'

God.

'And you love that house,' she said. 'And this village. So I suppose we're not totally all right after all, are we? Also, the property market was stronger when you got the mortgage to buy Lucy's house.'

'We,' Lol said. '*We* raised the deposit.'

'And by the time we've paid the mortgage off… it probably won't be a negative equity situation, but…'

'Two middle-aged people,' Lol said. 'With a cat in a basket. Maybe in a mobile home, touring the country looking for gigs. And when the gigs run out there's always busking. People leaving tins of Whiskas on the pavement for Ethel.'

'What are you trying to say?'

She turned over to face him directly, but he was already out of bed, struggling into his briefs. Unlike Selwyn Kindley-Pryce – *Oh God* – Lol wore briefs.

'Stay there,' he said.

Dark grey screen, white vertical lines.

They were sitting up in bed; they had Lol's laptop between their knees. She hadn't known he'd brought it or she might have asked why. The battery showed a 75 per cent charge, so that was all right, they could watch funny clips on YouTube.

'Lol, what *is* this?'

'Wait.' He opened a document. 'I didn't tell you about this because I was convinced, for a long time, that it wasn't going to happen. That they'd pull it at the eleventh hour.'

'Pull it?'

'I'm still not entirely convinced. But Prof says they've spent too much to turn back now.'

He clicked on the little arrow. Symbols began to appear on the screen, then a clock, then some stuff about copyright.

344

Then colours. Woodland.

Sound. Crackly footsteps through old brittle autumn leaves, overlaid presently with a familiar nail-strummed acoustic guitar as the camera found faces, a woman and a man, early middle-aged, coats and scarves, and Lol's voice came in, at its most wistful.

Remember this one, the day is dwindling
down in Powell's wood, collecting kindling
smudgy eyes
moonrise
golden.

The camera finding the woman's twilit eyes.

Merrily said, "Camera Lies"?'

One of the songs Lol had written when he was living in Prof's granary. When they were only together in his head.

'The song with the big cigar,' Lol said.

'Huh?'

He froze the picture. Merrily tried to see his eyes by the light from the screen.

'All right, what *is* it?'

'It's a commercial. An epic advert. Enough to fill half a commercial break. A long, costly narrative ad.'

'What's it advertising? Cosmetics?'

'Not exactly, no.'

Lol prodded the pause symbol and it started again. Now you were looking at a village in the evening, lights on the church as the couple walked, hand in hand, past the lychgate.

Here's a moment below the sandstone spire
across the square the scent of apple fires
angel wine, hands entwined
hold on...

'I don't get it,' Merrily said.

345

'This is a version before the lettering went on. It's all lettering, no voice-over.'

'For what?'

The images were coalescing in a kaleidoscope of soft colour as the breathy chorus came in.

I keep sensations in the album of my heart
the crunch of curling leaves, the crackling of the frost
flip the pages on the nights we lie apart
and mourn the barren years, all the time we've lost...

'Barren years,' Lol said. 'All the time we've lost. What's that sound like it's advertising?'

'A fertility clinic?'

'Oh, come on, would I do that to Jane? Mortgages.'

'*Mortgages?*'

'It's not the *most* discredited bank in the country, but a few thousand punters must have no cause to love it. Obviously, I'd rather it was a respectable charity or a nice hybrid car, but where do you stop worrying about the effects you're indirectly having? If you've done the music for a Mars bar commercial, do you get anxious about tooth-decay and diabetes?'

'So what's it actually saying?'

'It's directed at thirty-somethings, maybe forties, wondering whether it's too late to take out a mortgage.'

'Mourn the barren years, all the time we've lost?'

'So make sure you don't lose any more. If you think it's too late for a mortgage, come and talk to us, and we'll be happy to rip you off. Thing is... when I wrote that song I was not hopeful of things working out for us. Or even getting started.'

'I know.'

The song had ended before the last verse and the line explaining the title.

Camera lies...
she might vaporize

in cold air.

He'd written several songs about her, but this was the most despairing.

'That was why I was thinking they'd change their minds about it,' he said. 'Pull the song and replace it with something less negative.'

'Without the last verse, it isn't negative.'

Lol switched off the laptop, explaining how it had come through Prof Levin who'd been doing electronic jingles for an advertising agency. Who seemed to have become his agent. He'd had a song used in a commercial before, which had paid some of the deposit on Lucy's cottage but wasn't screened very often. This, however…

'This is a big-budget commercial, going out on over fifty stations in this country alone. Peak hour. And the bank… it's part of some kind of international conglomerate. We're looking at several countries. Europe, USA, Australia. It's not just the synch rights, it's—'

'What are the synch rights?'

'Doesn't matter. I'm scared to try and work it out in case I'm wildly wrong, but Prof's done some calculations. Each time the ad's screened we get a few quid – different amounts according to the network and the time of day. It…'

He took a breath. His voice came back quite small.

'For a while, it seems, we could be looking at over a grand a day.'

Merrily felt herself pale.

'You and Prof?'

'Each. Well, my share, as writer and performer, is more than his. I don't know. I've never been an expert on… money and stuff.'

'For… how long?'

'Months, probably. Maybe longer. There are apparently plans to keep the tune and change the video.'

'I'm feeling a little bit weak, Lol. Am I right to be feeling weak?'

'Then again, it might not work out. The ad could be a flop, get pulled at any time. But even if it did we'd probably be looking at enough to pay off the mortgage on Lucy's house. And then there's the spin-off CD sales... downloads... It's... it's all a bit ironic.'

'I don't think that's the word. How do you feel?'

'I'm still kind of in denial. The point is, this is one of the few ways comparatively obscure musicians can make money these days. It's not a vast amount compared with what bands were collecting in the golden age, pre-digital. But it's life-changing for me. Us. Possibly.'

'Yes.'

She felt his gaze, his nerves, the fear that something might vaporize in cold air.

'Wanted to tell you as soon as I came back, but circumstances... All I'm trying to say is... if you wanted... needed... to move on... then we could do it, couldn't we?'

She pushed back the duvet, grabbed her e-cig from the bedside table.

'We're really not going to sleep now, are we?'

'Probably not.'

'I'll go down and build up the fire.'

'I'll do it.' Lol sat on the side of the bed. 'Been living with this for days. It doesn't happen to people like me, does it? Then again, I didn't think people like you happened to people like me either.'

'Don't be daft. Who wants someone like me?'

The wind muttered in the trees at the end of the vicarage drive.

'And then there's Jane,' Lol said.

'I didn't want to mention Jane. Not yet. Anyway, Jane is not your problem.'

Merrily paused at the bedroom door, her dressing gown half on, remembering Jane, tearful in the early morning.

Like, I realize I'm going to have to leave here at some stage,

348

but I always want to think I can come back and it'll be just like it was.

Whatever happened now, it wasn't going to be like it was.

'I knew Jane first,' Lol said. 'Before you. I want her as a problem.'

She smiled, went back to the bed and sat down next to Lol, bent across him, touched him.

'Congratulations,' she said softly. 'Well deserved.'

The wood-stove blazed. Two short white candles shone on the kitchen table.

They'd talked for two hours plus. Talked all around it. It felt like whole days had passed since she'd returned from Lyme Farm. Like the world had been upturned in the storm but was far from steady.

Lol finished his tea, picked up his laptop.

'I think I should leave now.'

'Leave?'

'Go home. Give you some space. To decide what you want to happen. What you want me to do. If there's anything I *can* do.'

She looked at Lol. There had never been a time when they'd felt they could decide anything. This money, however much it turned out to be, was his money. They weren't married, they didn't live together. His money, his song. *No*, he'd insisted, *it's your song. If there hadn't been you there wouldn't be a song.*

There was no light in the sky, the wind still prowled. The storm wasn't over. The radio said no let-up until evening.

'I may have to go out this morning,' Lol said. 'To, um… see Prof. Things to organize. I should be back by midday.'

'You have to go? In this?'

'I do have to go. I'm not leaving the county or anything.'

'This county can be a killer in bad weather.'

'I'll drive carefully.'

They held one another in the porch, with the wind whipping past, and then he was gone into the swirling darkness of the village square. She looked up and saw a faint blueish light in Jane's attic apartment. Jane had a battery-powered lamp with a blue plastic shade.

Back in the house, Merrily found her mini Maglite, turned it on and followed the beam through to the scullery where she tried the phone. Still off.

On the edge of the desk was a sheaf of printouts. One word pencilled at the top: *djinns.*

Jane must've crept down with them some time after she and Lol had gone to bed. You had to love her.

She came back to the kitchen and fed Ethel, filled the kettle and put it back on the wood-stove, found the old toasting fork. Sometimes she felt she could live like this for an indefinite period: no lights, no phone, toasting fork.

Actually there was a phone. She found the mobile on the dresser where it had lain all night, switched off because she couldn't charge it unless she went out in the car. She switched it on.

Answering service: three messages, two last night, latest one about twelve minutes ago. All the same person.

'Mirrily, will you for Christ's sake call me back.'

53

Only the start

EVEN IN THE drive, the wind was getting under the car like a big hand.

You'd better just go, Jane had said. *You're not going to be happy if you don't.*

It wasn't yet dawn, but there was enough light to show that Lol's truck had gone from the square. The Freelander rocked as she turned out full into the blast, headlights on. The wind was coming out of the west, the rain was stinging. A vague glow in the Black Swan suggested Barry had fired up his generator.

Old Barn Lane was blacked out and she had to drive around two substantial fallen branches to get on to the bypass.

The first time she'd called Casey back, it could have been too early. No answer, but it showed the line was still active. She'd waited half an hour, reading Jane's notes on the djinn, which were unexpectedly disturbing, then tried Casey again. Nothing.

When you thought about it, people didn't oversleep in these conditions. She'd called back again, leaving a message this time, and that was when Jane had come in, thrusting a slice of honey-smeared toast into her hand.

Just be bloody careful, Mum.

Not much traffic on the roads, apart from Land Rovers and long-distance lorries. Weather warnings had been going out on radio and TV for more than a day now.

She couldn't imagine Lol's journey being all that necessary in the conditions. Outside of a studio, Prof Levin was famously laid-back. What was Lol not telling her? When someone had already given you too much information to process, you tended to ease up on the questions.

As she did, at some stage every morning, she whispered the Lord's Prayer – the traditional version; this was not one of those times when you talked to God like a mate.

'*... as we forgive them that trespass against us. Lead us not into temptation...*'

Bit late for that.

could be looking at over a grand a day.

Insane money, footballers' money. Well, no, not that insane, nowhere near. And then there was tax, doubtless other deductions. And it was only for a period of time, so—

'Oh, f—'

The Freelander bucked; she'd driven over a well-known jagged pothole, invisible because all the potholes were full of rain. She slowed. No point if you didn't get there because you'd ripped a tyre, bent a wheel, or aquaplaned into a tree. If you were dead or quadriplegic, it wouldn't matter too much how many thousands your boyfriend collected for having a song about you picked up to sell mortgages.

Lol had turned up last night determined to tell her about the song with the big cigar – *her* song. Obviously, the good news was supposed to have been revealed over their first proper dinner at the Swan, the night she'd worn the glittery dress. And it would, indeed, have been a wonderfully warm, celebratory night, had it not been the night Raji Khan had arrived to lead her astray. The night before that brief but ominous meeting with the new Bishop.

And now the black clouds were well overhead, the bitter wind was blowing and Lol had arrived, laptop under his arm, to tell her that if – *when* – the worst happened, they would be *all right.*

All right for money.

Because *money mattered.*

'You're not that crass, Robinson.'

Muttering as she drove across Bredwardine Bridge, noting how the Wye had already drowned its little beach. Taking a left by the modest war memorial, and then dropping down a couple of gears for the twisting climb up Dorstone Hill.

It could be a wasted trip, but at least there might be a chance to ask Nadya why, the other afternoon, she'd said, *We might use the word djinn.*

The entity of *smokeless fire.* Jane had found that reference, but also some correspondences that hadn't occurred to Merrily. Jane had divided a page into two columns, one headed *djinn,* the other *faerie* – Jane always used that spelling, less Christmas-tree. The fairies of Celtic folklore tended not to have flimsy gossamer wings.

It was, Jane had discovered, another Jane – Lady Jane Wilde, nineteenth-century Irish poet and connoisseur of fairy tales – who had suggested the word originated not in medieval England but in Persia. The inference was that faerie folk had a lot in common with the djinn. Jane's two columns were filled with cross-references, some underlined, like the fact they both preferred to be <u>left alone</u>, had extremely long lives but were not immortal. That both could grant wishes – note the genie of Aladdin's lamp and Cinderella's fairy godmother – but both could be <u>malevolent</u> and also <u>inflict terrible harm</u> on intruders on their territory.

There were no actual references to strokes or paralysis, but the thought was there, thank you, flower.

Had Nadya been remotely serious, or just showing off her knowledge of Islamic folklore? OK, more than that; there were no fairies in the Bible but to a Muslim, the djinn, whilst unholy, did have its place in theology. No pick'n'mix in Islam.

Approaching the top of Dorstone Hill, with the wipers whipping at the slanting rain, she had one of those flashes of amazement at the insanity of it all: fairies and djinns, a grown-up woman in the twenty-first century theorizing about fairies and djinns and vampires and the fairytale summoner in the Nightlands.

Words. Made-up words in a children's novel. Words for persisting, irritating anomalies which the greater world could safely ignore, because the Church, itself in rapid decline, continued to appoint a handful of eccentric priests to keep them under the table.

And yet... why not?

You accepted it would never be more than a small, obscure, thankless task, but you didn't just walk away from it because of one man, no matter what political engine was powering him. You didn't hobble away to save your bit of credibility, because credibility was the last thing this job was about.

And you acquired responsibilities, more and more of them. Working deliverance, you built up a list of clients. Some of them, you didn't even know they *were* clients until they got back in touch, these people you'd helped or tried to help when they were faced with something that *could not be happening*. And they'd still be there, these ex-clients, until they or you died. So when they came back, saying, *It isn't over*, would you then reply, *I'm sorry, I don't do that any more and it was bloody silly anyway...?*

The phone barked on the passenger seat. Jane? Lol? Merrily reversed a long way, with restricted visibility, into a lay-by big enough to accommodate a tractor and trailer, a naked sapling bending forward to guide her in and slash the car's flank.

One-bar signal, not great.

'Thought maybe you'd dumped us, Mirrily. Couldn't've blamed you.'

'I'm sorry, the phones were off and the power, and I just didn't get your message until this—'

'Anyway, it's all too late now.'

'Wh—?'

'You were right. —malfunctioning household, wrong for each other and in the wrong place. And, Jesus, is this— wrong.'

'You're cracking up.'

'In more ways than I can start to tell ya.'

'Give me a minute.' Merrily getting out of the car, having to fight the wind for the driver's door. She found her way up a track into a small wood, holding the phone tight to her ear under the hood of her waxed coat. 'Any better? This is about as high as I can—'

'You're outside?'

'Yeah, I'm—'

'If you thought we were crazy, it's got a whole lot worse. Adam's taking Aisha to stay with his parents. Nic— *Nadya* agrees it's the best thing. They want her to have medical tests. Me, I wanted you to see the kid, what's happening to her, I said that was what the imam would want, I said call *up* the flaming imam, ask *him*. Adam said finally, yeah, we should wait for Mirrily, but that was last night, and now he's taking her to work with him and Grandpa Malik's gonna pick her up in Hereford and Nadya's gonna follow later with her things.'

'Why?'

'Because something – *no, the hell with what you think, Nicole, I'm gonna talk about this* – something came to a head.'

'There's something wrong with her? She's ill?'

'I don't know. She's sullen and she's hostile and she screams at you to keep out of her private life. Raji was here again last night. He talked to you?'

'No.'

'He talked to Adam. Adam's—'

'Casey, are they still there?'

'It's too late. They'll be leaving in a couple of—'

Listen, if this is any help I'm at the top of Dorstone Hill which is – what? – five, ten minutes away?'

There was silence in the phone, as if the signal had finally gone. Then Casey said,

'Yeah. I'm sorry, too, Mirrily. If only you weren't so far away.'

It meant Nadya was still within earshot.

It meant get here fast.

She drove down the wooded hill until it came out on a crazy bend. Clear, and she was across and down towards the village of Dorstone with its squat church, turning left into a lane that she immediately thought might be the wrong lane, realizing that she'd only travelled *from* Cwmarrow to Dorstone and in better weather than this.

The countryside rumbled around her, alive with storm debris, the Golden Valley not so golden, roughened fields the colours of mould. The temptation was to race under avenues of big trees, get them behind you, but that could be crazy. The signs gave out wrong messages: Peterchurch, Michaelchurch, Urishay. Cwmarrow was too small for signs until you were very close, nobody getting beckoned into the valley of the dead – was that right? Was that *really* right, the valley of the—?

No, wrong. Wrong way.

She backed into a field entrance, turned round in spurts of mud, went back to the last crossroads, tried another lane, this one falling away, sharply downhill – promising, please God, let this be right. The swinging trees were gathering and forming a tunnel – yes – and she saw ahead of her, like a rock formation, the ruin of the castle on its jutting hill. And then…

How quickly these things happened, as if a savage wind could speed up time itself. As she rounded a tight left-hand bend, the castle vanished along with a slab of sky and, when she saw why, she thought there was no way that she wasn't going to die.

'*Oh f—*'

Words torn out of her, not the ones you'd choose as your last, Merrily sitting up hard, both feet down, throwing both hands over her head and face, as the early morning sky turned back into night and the noise was like a cliff-fall and under it Lol's voice, softly: *Remember this one, the day is dwindling.*

Part Five

In each of us is a Hell of serpents. If you make yourself secure against these unclean creatures you may remain tranquil; if not they will sting you even in the dust of the tomb until the day of reckoning.

Farid ud-Din Attar,
The Conference of the Birds
(trans. C.S. Nott, 1954)

54

A peg

IN HIS LAID-BACK, academic way, Vaynor was looking excited. He had a nifty piece of kit to connect a phone to his own digital voice-recorder, and when he played it back for Bliss, in Bliss's office, at just gone eight a.m., the quality was surprisingly good. But then a call to the USA usually sounded better than a call to the other side of Hereford.

'I thought Turner was English,' Bliss said.

'Doesn't take them long to become naturalized. Odd, really, boss, Americans are supposed to love an English accent and when we get out there we just want to sound like them'

'Why is that necessary?' Turner said when Vaynor told him he'd like to record their conversation.

'It's so I can share the information with my colleagues, Mr Turner, and they'll know I'm not misrepresenting you.'

'It's not going to be played in court, or anything?'

'I can assure you it isn't. Although I'm wondering why you'd think it might. Wind up in court, that is.'

'I live in a litigious country, Detective Vaynor, where the police...'

'Sorry, Mr Turner?'

'Doesn't matter. What can I tell you?'

'I'm rather hoping you can tell me about Tristram Greenaway.'

'Who?'

'An archaeologist.'

'Oh... wait. Yeah, OK. I remember him. He did go on to be an archaeologist, then? That's good to hear. How is he?'

'Dead, Mr Turner.'

'OK.'

In the short silence, Bliss looked at his Google image of Turner with a videocam on his shoulder, his close-mown beard a grey smudge. There was a white high-rise building behind his head.

'He was murdered,' Vaynor said. 'It's why I'm ringing. I believe he used to work for you.'

'I didn't hear about that. That he was dead.'

'I don't suppose you would in America. Unless you and he were still in touch.'

'You said murdered?'

'I did.'

'OK...'

'He did work for you?'

'Well, not... That is, he wasn't on the payroll as such. It was just a sporadic holiday job. Used to get a whole bunch of kids who wanted to work in my business in whatever capacity.'

'This was in Hereford?'

'I was living near Hereford, and yeah, for a short time, we had an office in town. Didn't turn out to be a great idea. TV production, you're much safer in London, less of a novelty. We'd have a steady stream of young people – students and out-of-work kids – looking for a future in the glamorous world of television. And Greenaway, he was one of them.'

'But you remember him, particularly.'

'Did I say that? No, look, OK, he was that kind of guy. That is, he made sure you remembered.'

Vaynor kept quiet.

'He was everywhere,' Turner said. 'Keen to learn. Keen to... be remembered.'

'What kind of work did he do for you?'

'Research, I guess. Finding people we could talk to. Finding out what they'd be able to tell us, what they'd say in an interview. This wasn't major interviews, only voxpop stuff. Wasn't a permanent job, but he'd been accepted for some university anyway. I recall letting him do a couple interviews, ask the questions, get people talking. We didn't use the questions, just the answers. You don't see him, you don't hear him. He was… disappointed about that.'

'Thought he'd be a star?'

'Thought he'd be on camera. Wanted to be a presenter. I said, kid, you go ahead with your degree course. TV presenters have a limited life expectancy. Get yourself something to fall back on. You're saying somebody killed him?'

'I'm afraid so.'

'Where?'

'At his home, in Hereford. He was working for the county archaeologist's department on a temporary basis. So he thought he had what it took to become a TV presenter?'

'He was a kid. He thought that what it took was just a nice, white smile, backed up by an engaging personality. I guess he grew up.'

'Mr Turner, we don't think it was a random killing or robbery,' Vaynor said. 'So we're trying to piece together his past. Presumably, you knew he was gay.'

'That still matters in the UK? He didn't make a thing of it. He was whatever you wanted him to be.'

'In what way?'

'He was – OK, I don't like to use this word, but I can't think of another – a flirt. Not just in a sexual way, though I don't doubt the kid would've made his body widely available in the cause of career development. That's unfair, he's dead, I'm sorry. It just got to be annoying, the way he'd keep hitting on you with ideas. You know how many shows come out of ideas from the public? I don't either, but it has to be negligible.'

Vaynor asked a few questions regarding relationships formed by Greenaway. Turner said he wasn't aware of any.

'My information,' Vaynor said, 'is that you and he were both members of a secret society called Friends of the Dusk.'

Turner laughed, a bit nervously, Bliss figured, but that might be wishful thinking.

'*You make it sound like the Masons. It wasn't a* secret *society.*'

'*How would you describe it, sir?*'

'*It was just… like a way of sharing information about something we were interested in at the time.*'

'*Vampirism?*'

'*Oh… look, don't go thinking of guys walking around in capes with their teeth sharpened. This was a special-interest group, kind of academic, and the special interest was finding the origins of vampire lore… specifically in the UK.*'

'*As distinct from Transylvania.*'

'*You got it. There was a man called Selwyn Kindley-Pryce, a one-time university professor over here. A Brit, but spent some years here, at colleges. He specialized in the area where history and folklore crossed over.*'

'The feller who hosted festivals,' Bliss said. 'Now in an old folks' home.'

And unfit to be interviewed, according to inquiries. Advanced dementia. Been in care for years. They'd checked him out last night, and his place in the Golden Valley, now under different ownership.

They listened to Turner talking about this man's obsession with a story from a medieval chronicler who Vaynor had only vaguely heard of but could probably unearth if it was felt to be useful. Bottom line: Kindley-Pryce's insistence that the story was based on fact. That it might be the first really solid European vampire story. And that he was living in the place where what Vaynor liked to call a *sanguinary predator* had taken a large number of lives.

A major obsession for Kindley-Pryce, who'd come back from America to buy the place. A minor obsession for Turner who, at the time, had seen a very saleable documentary film in it.

'*He'd also been co-writing these books for older kids, based on this story, and they used to hold events there, very medieval in atmosphere, very televisual.'*

'And you were a regular guest,' Vaynor said.

'*I'd made this film*, The Bloodline of Dracula, *and I could see something even better. Had everything. A real villain and also a hero in the knight who eventually succeeded in disposing of him in a very Van Helsing kind of way.'*

'You were thinking you'd follow this Kindley-Pryce in his... quest?'

'And we already had all these great visuals from his weekend festivals.'

'Was Tristram Greenaway working with you at the time?'

'*Couldn't keep him away. He'd gotten to be friends with Kindley-Pryce – Selwyn, he, uh, liked young people around. And Trissie, he just wanted to mix with glamorous, important people.'*

'Your film,' Vaynor said. 'It never got made.'

'*It, uh... Few reasons for that. Mainly, end of the day, it was just a story from a medieval chronicle, and medieval chronicles are notoriously full of bullshit. We needed something harder. We needed a peg to hang it on. Selwyn was convinced – from not much evidence – that he was living in the place where the undead guy had done his stuff. He also thought he knew where they'd had to bury the corpse to stop it reanimating, which had to be close to Hereford Cathedral, and he—'*

'Can I stop you there for a sec? Why did he think that?'

'Bloody hell, Darth,' Bliss said.

'*Because the Bishop of Hereford, at the time, was involved. If we could've found the remains, it would've been the biggest thing since they dug up Richard III under a parking lot in Leicester, but the chances of that happening were remote. Selwyn and I had an agreement that if we could harden it up I'd offer a feature-length documentary to the networks. We set up a website to which we could admit people who could be useful, and we called ourselves Friends of the Dusk. Trissie Greenaway was* in the original group. All done under the umbrella of... I don't really understand these Web set-ups, but it was some outfit that could provide security and filter emails.'

'But nothing came of it. Was that the only reason you gave up on the film?'

'You can't wait for ever. I always wanted to move into feature films, movies, and I got a chance over here.'

'A call from Hollywood.'

'Kind of, yeah. You don't say no to the big H.'

'When did you last look at the Friends of the Dusk site, Mr Turner?'

'Don't recall. Don't know if it's still extant.'

'Do you know anything about an email sent to the Friends, via Neogoth, from Mr Greenaway?'

'Hell, no... I keep saying, I gave up on all that years ago.'

'So what would your reaction be if you found out that Tristram Greenaway had posted evidence of a deviant burial a short distance from Hereford Cathedral?'

Pause.

'You're saying he did, Detective?'

'Suppose it was a human skull with a stone in its mouth. Would that be fairly conclusive to you?'

'Shit, you're kidding.'

'And obviously a good image for TV.'

'Well, yeah, but—'

'When were you last in the UK, Mr Turner?'

'I live here now. I'm a US citizen with an office in Burbank. Wife, kid...'

'When were you last over here?'

'In the summer. Briefly. Aw, come on...'

'When did you last see Mr Pryce?'

'Years ago. He's probably dead by now. He had Alz— I dunno, some form of dementia. He was a fucking vegetable. Another reason it was never gonna happen. That side of my life, it's over.'

'So you weren't in touch with Tristram Greenaway? You didn't have an email address or anything for him? Or he yours.'

'Are you kidding? A boy who once ran errands over fifteen years ago?'

Bliss was impressed with the way the lad had handled it. Could see why he was excited.

'One thing strikes me immediately, Darth. He's a TV documentary man. All right, he's making feature films now, but old instincts die hard. He had to abandon his follow-up to *Bloodline* because it wasn't sexy enough, but now it's all lighting up again and he's got a bloody *mairder*. How friggin sexy is that? And he's not displaying any excitement. He's not asking *you* any questions.'

'That's true,' Vaynor said. 'And also... he's lying about something else.'

'Go on...'

'He said he'd had to give up buying this house, the Court, because opportunity was knocking in the States. The call from Hollywood? But the guy I spoke to who knew him, Leo Defford – documentary producer who evidently didn't crack Hollywood – said Turner was out there for nearly two years, doing menial assistant-director jobs before he got anywhere. Defford says he could never understand why he got out of the UK so quickly, but it wasn't for the money.'

'That's nice work, son,' Bliss said. 'We can use that. I don't see him as a suspect in the Greenaway or Soffley cases, but it does look like he's gorra few things to hide. And – this is the point, Darth – it also looks like he has some video I'd *really* like to see.'

'At Kindley-Pryce's parties, ten years ago?'

'You see a better opportunity of gerrin all your suspects on view together in one place? It's like friggin' Hercule Poirot in the library.' Bliss was out of his chair. 'Get back on to him.'

'He'll be in bed.'

'Well, get the bastard *out* of bed. Lean on him. Threaten him. Tell him we'll talk to the FBI and see it gets leaked to the *LA Times* that he's being questioned as part of an investigation into… into *the mairder of a young gay man in England.*' Bliss sat down again, pleased with that. 'I don't give a shit how you do it, but I want a DVD of Mr Pryce's parties on this desk by mid-morning.'

He went up to the MIR to tell Annie. She was with Karen Dowell and the lads going through the CCTV for about half the city. Nobody looking impressed.

'About twenty-five people who might have gone into Organ Yard at an appropriate time. We've identified about half of them, and none looks terribly interesting at this stage. But—'

'When you gerra minute, ma'am, there's something I'd like you to listen to.' What a turn-on it was, calling her ma'am, especially when a case looked like shifting up a gear. 'The parties at this Kindley-Pryce's place, Cwmarrow. We actually think video exists of the Friends of the Dusk at play.'

Annie raised an eyebrow.

'Interesting. Oh… just so you know – Cwmarrow. Traffic are attending an RTC there. Storm-related. Fallen tree.'

'I do hope there wasn't a skelly underneath.' Bliss smiled. 'Anybody hurt?'

'One dead,' Annie said.

55

Grim visitor

THE POWER CAME back before ten a.m. Could've been worse, often was. In case it went off again, Jane was straight up to her apartment and the computer.

She'd awoken several times in the night – probably the wind hammering the house – but each time she'd remembered the story from *De Nugis Curialium*.

Still hadn't found a complete English translation, but she had found what was probably the best modern retelling of the story.

Of all places, it was in a book she'd been dipping into for years, *The Folklore of Herefordshire* by Ella Mary Leather. The reason she'd forgotten was that it wasn't part of the book itself, was only mentioned in the introduction by E. Sidney Hartland who'd been discussing burial anomalies, including...

... the operation of turning a corpse in the grave – that is, turning it so that it will lie face downwards. This is one of the many methods to prevent the restless dead from haunting the living. Mrs Leather records a case at Capel-y-ffin. A ghastlier story, which probably belongs to Herefordshire – at all events, to the diocese – is recorded by Walter Map at the end of the twelfth century, although he speaks of the occurrence as taking place in Wales.

Oddly, it wasn't told by Mrs Leather in the book itself. Tempting to think that was because she regarded it as history rather than folklore, but more likely because it wasn't linked to a specific location.

Jane copied E. Sidney Hartland's version into the computer, highlighting significant bits.

The background had been related to the Bishop of Hereford, Gilbert Foliot. Jane Googled him. An absolutely real person, a monk, appointed to the Hereford diocese in 1148, in the reign of King Stephen. Later became Bishop of London, so he must've known what he was doing.

The man who approached him was an English knight, William Loudun.

Yes! Jane confirmed that Cwmarrow Castle had been in the hands of the *Loudon* family. Presumably the same name.

Hartland wrote:

A certain Welshman who is described by the epithet *maleficus*, by which we may infer that he was reputed to have dealings with the Powers of Darkness, had lately died without being reconciled to the Church. After four nights, he came back every night to the village and called forth singly and by name his fellow villagers. Those who were called uniformly fell sick and died within three days. The village was thus being gradually depopulated.

So far, the story was more or less identical to the one retold by Kindley-Pryce in his *Borderlight* and later appropriated for Foxy Rowlestone's *The Summoner*.

Gilbert Foliot had been dead for more than ten years when, in 1199, Walter Map had *almost* become Bishop of Hereford. But, as Map described himself as a man of the Welsh borders, it seemed unlikely that he hadn't encountered Foliot. Kindley-Pryce hadn't mentioned this, but then why should he? *Borderlight* was less an academic book than a showcase for Caroline Goddard's artwork.

Had Map actually had this story first-hand from Gilbert Foliot? Like why not?

According to Hartland's translation, Foliot suggested William Loudun dig up the body of the summoner and sever its neck with the spade. Both the corpse and the grave should then be 'asperged' with holy water and the body put back.

Didn't work.

The horrible visitations were continued; and soon only a few survivors were left.

And then the summoner – Hartland was actually calling him a vampire by this stage – called out William himself 'with a threefold citation', whatever that was. She'd find out. One day.

But William had had enough.

… sprang up with drawn sword and pursued the fleeing demon even to the grave. He overtook the grim visitor just as he was falling back into the earth, and clove his head down to the neck… From that hour, the persecution ceased.

Now that was interesting. Took Jane back to last night's research into the djinn. She rechecked. The sword. Both djinns and fairies were said to be repelled, weakened, damaged by iron. Why? It was just there, in universal folklore. It had been speculated that it was because human blood contained iron and therefore connected with human life-energy. Anyway, iron was magical. These threads just went round and round.

So what was the *maleficus*: vampire, djinn, or… something else?

OK…

On the Net, she'd found nothing approaching a complete translation of the story, but there were samples of it. Like this alleged direct quote from Gilbert Foliot, as he attempted to explain the nature of the summoner.

Peradventure the Lord has given power to the evil angel of that lost soul to move about in the dead corpse.

Lost soul implied what was left of the *maleficus*, but *evil angel* suggested something more elemental and demonic.

It suggested possession. A possession beyond death.

This aspect was not discussed in Kindley-Pryce's version in *Borderlight*, but he did take it a little further, saying that Bishop Foliot had invited William Loudun, partly as a way of safeguarding his community, to remove the body and the head from its original grave and bring it to Hereford, where it would be reburied 'in suitable fashion within sight of the Cathedral but not within its sacred precincts.'

They had hands-on bishops, didn't they, in the Middle Ages?

So... Cwmarrow. *Was* this the place? The name Loudon certainly fitted.

Hartland said Map had identified the place as being in Wales. It was likely that Cwmarrow had been in Wales in medieval times – certainly Welsh-speaking. Even now, it was only a few miles from the border.

The village that disappeared would fit the Map story. It would be interesting to try and find descendants of the last people who had lived there into the nineteenth century. Had anything happened to disturb their sleep, make them feel oppressed? Had there been illness, bad harvests, poverty?

She didn't know enough. So much research to be done. Kindley-Pryce, historian, folklorist, anthropologist, must surely have set it all down somewhere.

As for the summoner... the *maleficus*...

It was all around. Jane went back to Ella Mary Leather, looked up the case at Capel-y-ffin, just over the Welsh border in the Black Mountains, that Hartland had referred to in his introduction. Took a long time to get to Capel-y-ffin by road but, as the crow flew, it was barely six miles from Cwmarrow. Mrs Leather quoted a man from nearby Longtown.

I know what I have sin (seen), I helped myself to turn a man in his grave up at Capel-y-finn; he come back, and we thought to stop him but after we turned him he come back seven times worse... No use of him (the preacher) tellin' *me* there's no ghosts.

Was he ever confined to his grave? The book didn't say.

Six miles away... it wasn't much. And even closer... another kind of summoner. Mrs Leather recorded the alleged experience of a man known as Jack of France, 'an evil doer and a terror to all peaceable folk,' who this time was a victim.

One night, the Eve of all Souls, he was passing through the churchyard, and saw a light shining in all the windows of the church. He looked in and saw a large congregation assembled, listening apparently to the preaching of a man in a monk's habit, who was declaiming from the pulpit the names of all those who were to die during the coming year. The preacher lifted his head, and Jack saw under the cowl the features of the Prince of Darkness himself, and to his horror heard his own name given out among the list of those death should claim. He went home, and repenting too late of his evil deeds, took to his bed and died.

And this was at Dorstone, the nearest large village to Cwmarrow.

Suddenly, Jane felt driven, the way she hadn't been for quite a while. It wasn't about archaeology, it was about something bigger, and bigger, too, than anthropology. These stories lived, they were part of the living countryside. In the early years of the twentieth century they were being told to Mrs Leather by people who *remembered*.

Jane was back at the window, looking down on the ancient black and white houses, her hands on the oak in the wall, harder than old bone.

None of this was over. She could still feel her own mixed-up horror at the sight of the woman in the dead leaves at Cwmarrow. Who might well have been this Aisha who had crowed on Facebook about a relationship across the Divide, where the blood was only the start.

Jane felt a shivery kind of energy in her spine.

The Welsh stuff, Eirion might know. Suddenly, she really wanted to call him. *See* him. Like in the Biblical sense. Whatever had happened between Sam and her, while drunk… whatever had happened, she wasn't going to find out she was pregnant, was she?

And no way was she going anywhere near Wiltshire.

Something flared in Jane like sunlight. She started to laugh. Couldn't stop.

She threw herself on to the bed, hugging the pillow, bouncing up and down with this insatiable insane mirth. Heard the phone ringing loudly downstairs like it was joining in. So it was back.

Jane came off the bed and ran down two flights of stairs, grabbing the phone in the hall just before the machine could kick in.

'Ledwardine… vicarage. Sorry, out of breath.'

'Mrs Watkins?'

A woman with quite a small voice.

'She's not here.'

'Will she be long?'

'I'm not sure. I'm sorry. I'm her daughter, if that—'

'No. I'll call her. I'll call her again.'

'Can I give her a name?'

'Well, just… just tell her it's Caroline, would you?'

The line went dead.

56

Blame

THERE WERE TWO cops, one female, one male, both reassuringly overweight.

'Don't look, lovey,' the one called Patti said. 'Come on, try to breathe slowly.'

But it was too late. She swallowed a mouthful of wind and rain, but it wasn't enough. Something contracted inside and she turned away and threw up into the hedge.

'Come on.' Streaks of blood in Patti's blonde hair. 'Best you sit in our car, there's an ambulance on the way.'

'I don't—'

'Oh yes, I think you do.'

With her waxed coat torn and one side of her face wet and smarting, she let Patti guide her away to the edge of the field, and she looked back once, had a sense of smoky, spent violence around the twisted metal, branches clawing the air. You never realized how monumental and vital each tree was until one came down. Maybe a hundred years of growth and now it was windkill.

And killer. She closed her eyes, and it was imprinted on the screen of her eyelids like an old photo negative, the great tree bending like a crane on a building site, slowly but not that slowly.

What were the odds against this in a normal world?

The Freelander was a couple of years too old for airbags. She remembered keeling over on the seat with her hands over her head, feeling the car crushing around her like big boots were standing on it. She remembered that the driver's door had jammed. She remembered squirming across and grabbing the handle of the passenger door then lying back and pushing at it with both feet. A scraping and rending of metal, as a gap was forced, and then her feet had been in the branches, one shoe hanging off, and she must have lost consciousness then, not sure for how long.

More police were visible down towards Cwmarrow. And other people you couldn't see from here. She could hear a woman wailing.

'They're not letting them come any closer,' Patti said, 'for obvious reasons.'

'Could I perhaps…?'

'No way, lovey. I don't want them seeing anybody's blood.'

Merrily put a hand up to her face. It came away slippery.

The wind was quieter. The crows were up around Cwmarrow Castle.

'Looks like he was in a hurry,' Patti said. 'If the tree hadn't come down when it did, it begs the question, would your two cars simply have collided head-on?'

'I don't know. I didn't even see him coming.'

'Country roads are the worst. You just don't ever go fast on country lanes. They were made for horses and carts. Tarmac's just cosmetic.'

'He wanted to be a countryman,' Merrily said.

Patti looked at her, curious, and said nothing.

Merrily moved towards the Freelander's side of the tree.

'Woah,' Patti said. 'Don't touch anything.'

'Can I get my bag? I need… nicotine.'

'We'll get it.'

Merrily nodded, stepped away. She was sure she hadn't even seen the Mercedes coming up from Cwmarrow. She knew now that the Freelander had become wedged under one of the bigger branches, its windscreen smashed by another, on which she might easily have been impaled. The Mercedes was skewed under the main trunk, as if the driver had swerved as the tree came down. One headlight was still on, the other was like a shut eye on the side that was pancaked. The driver's head had been out of his side window, and that was what she'd seen before she threw up: the face and the head of Adam Malik, hanging off, almost severed.

She spun round.

'Where's the girl? Was there a *girl*?'

'With her mother and her gran,' Patti said. 'You asked before.'

'Did I?'

'We think she might have a broken arm. She got out by herself. She'll go in the ambulance, too.'

'That's her dad in there,' Merrily said.

'I've seen him at the hospital, a time or two. And he came out to a crash on Dinmore Hill. Took off a woman's leg to save her life. He was a good man. He cared.'

'Yes. Yes, he did.'

She felt disconnected, incapable and so cold inside and out.

'He'll be missed,' Patti said.

Merrily looked down the narrow road to where he would be missed most, and back at the Mercedes crushed under the tree, not more than an arm's length from the bonnet of the Freelander on the other side. For a darkly glowing moment, she saw both cars as low-worth, expendable pieces in some cosmic chess game, sacrificed for some hideous victory.

She was shaking.

'We'll want a statement from you, Mrs Watkins,' Patti said. 'What you can remember. Why you were here. Formalities. Shouldn't take long. Nobody's at fault here. Act of God, as we used to say.'

'Yes,' Merrily said. 'Blame God.'

Patti stood looking at her, hands on her big hips, yellow waterproof flapping but otherwise unmoved by the wind.

'You're a vicar, aren't you?'

'At present.'

Jane tried 1471, but the woman on the phone had taken the trouble to conceal her number.

Twice, she'd been sent into the hall by a ping from the phone, as if it was about to ring, but it hadn't. The way she was feeling today, there was something ominous about it.

tell her she'll be called.

called forth singly and by name

Stop it! For Christ's *sake*.

She spun away from the phone, as the doorbell rang, as if the two were linked: *summoners*. She glanced out of the hall window, and he was looking directly at her from the shelter of the porch.

Mum had left by the back door. The front door was still locked and bolted; it took half a minute to get it open.

He wore a short brown overcoat with a velvety collar and a tired, tilted smile, and like no way was she going to be intimidated. It was another part of pulling herself together.

Right then.

'Good morning, Mr Khan,' Jane said.

'Ms Watkins.'

'Mum's out.'

'Damn.'

'I'm sorry.'

'Any idea when she might be back?'

'Not really.'

'I don't suppose another chap's been? I'm rather later than I expected, due to the conditions.'

'No. Nobody.'

'Oh. Well. I'm very sorry to have bothered you. It's… Jane, isn't it? I suppose I shall have to try to reach your mother… somehow.'

'Always worth phoning first,' Jane said. 'Can save a lot of time.'

'Indeed it can. I shall call ahead next time. Or she may like to telephone me, if you can convey that—'

'Did you get your car fixed? I mean the bodywork.'

He looked at her in silence for a few beats and then a smile twitched into place.

'I did. In fact...' His hand went to an inside pocket, came out with a narrow, buff envelope. 'This is some money I received to pay for the repair. Quite inadequate, but a touching gesture. I was going to return it.'

Jane grinned.

'Jude Wall? No, Dean, right?'

'Is that the older one? The money was left for me at my Hereford office, without an address. Or a name, come to that. Luckily one of my staff recognized him and knows where he lives... roughly.'

'He'll be gone by now. Has a job and so does his mum. Some days Jude even goes to school. Erm... you came all this way for that?'

'Well, not really, but...'

'But you're returning Wall's money?'

'As a way of conveying to him that he remains in my debt.'

Wow. Jane felt her eyes widening. Either his tongue was well into his cheek or this guy was shameless.

'Is that saying what I think it's saying?'

'And what do you think it's saying, Jane?'

'I think it might be saying that you might, like, approach him or his brother one day with, erm, an opportunity to repay what he owes you. And if he doesn't...'

Raji Khan laughed, sliding the envelope back inside his coat.

'What imagination! Tell me... I'm curious. There was an attempt to inscribe on my car a word that looked like "children". I couldn't, for the life of me, think what that might refer to.'

'Oh, I can tell you that. When they were here, in the porch, trying to blag some money, you did actually refer to them as children. They were offended.'

377

'Ah!' His hands came up. 'Of course. A matter of respect. My goodness, how discredited that word has become.'

'They're just kids. When Dean saw what they'd done, he was… not at all happy. He was like… well, the words *shit* and *scared* come to mind.'

'Gives me no pleasure at all to inspire such an adverse reaction.'

'I bet it doesn't.'

He looked almost affronted.

'Tell you what,' Jane said. 'To save you another journey, how about *I* give Wall his money back?'

'You'd do that for me?'

'*Oh* yes.'

Raji Khan peered at her, hands clasped over his chest. Then he looked back up the drive. Obviously still waiting for someone, or hoping Mum would drive up. He looked back at Jane, wry smile.

'You know, Ms Watkins, there's something about you which, in spite of my instincts, I do rather admire. You have your mother's…' He separated his hands, made small motions with the fingers. 'If not more so.' He took out the buff envelope. 'You *really* want to do this?'

Jane thought of the weight of gritty history between her and Dean Wall, right from when she and Mum had first arrived in Ledwardine and he and his mates had come after her and poor Collette Cassidy in the churchyard at night.

'It would give me no end of pleasure, Mr Khan,' she said.

'It wasn't so hard after all,' Vaynor said in Bliss's office. 'I told Turner that at present we were looking for a killer, that was all. Indicating that other issues might be overlooked if we feel we've been assisted in our principal task. Was that all right?'

'You didn't record that, did you?'

'No, I didn't, boss.'

Bliss nodded.

'When's he sending?'

'Karen's dealing with it, and that computer guy from Worcester. There are some download firms that can get it done quickly, once the compatibility problems are sorted. Might still take a few hours, though, for him to dig it out. He says.'

'I'll run this past ma'am first,' Bliss said, 'but I'm thinking it might not be a bad idea, when we've had a look at it, to screen it for the masses in the MIR. Few fellers in there who might recognize faces that were before our time.'

'Let's just hope nothing goes wrong.'

'Put it this way, Darth. If Turner says it got deleted during the process, tell him you'll be taking steps to have him extradited. Now go and supervise. *What?*'

Vaynor had stopped in the doorway, looked back at Bliss over a shoulder.

'Mrs Watkins is outside. She's not looking for you, is she?'

Bliss was on his feet.

'She's looked better,' Vaynor said. 'Quite a big dressing on her face.'

'You're saying she's hurt?'

'May be wrong, but I think she was involved in that accident on the Cwmarrow road. The fatal?'

Bliss moved past him, rapidly down the stairs and out into the weather, looking round urgently. Finally locating Merrily Watkins with Mills and Calder from Traffic, up against their blue and yellow car. Mother of God, if he hadn't been told he might not have recognized her. Forget the facial dressing and the ripped Barbour, she looked bloody rough.

'Oh, Merrily, Merrily.' Strolling over, dead casual. 'Just look at the state of you.'

Calder looked at him, with suspicion.

'This incident at Cwmarrow?' Bliss said.

He waited. Come on… a place he'd never heard of and it had come up twice? Darryl Mills shook his big head.

'Nothing for you, boss.'

As a former detective and not a bad one, he'd know.

Patti Calder said. 'Mrs Watkins came into town with us, Frannie, to make a statement, and she's without transport. We're giving her a lift home.'

'Patti,' Bliss said. 'There's a lorra mad bastards out there, driving without due care and attention in seriously *advairse* conditions. Why don't you and Darryl go and pull a few over. *I'll* give Mrs Watkins a lift home.'

Merrily looked at him then down at her shoes, nodding. He waited while she shook hands with Patti and Darryl, thanked them and then she followed him to the Honda. By the time they were halfway to Ledwardine, it was easy to understand why she was having new doubts about the existence of a benevolent supreme being.

He, on the other hand…

57

A fence

'I'M NOT MAKING too much of this, Merrily. Not even calling it coincidence. It's just nice to discover we're on parallel lines here.'

'We are?'

All the lines she could see stretching out ahead of her were buckled and twisted.

Bliss had pulled into a lay-by that had become a picnic place because of its view of Cole Hill, behind which Ledwardine was sunk. It had stopped raining; the wind was still irritable but no longer worth a warning on the radio news.

'I don't question it any more,' Bliss said. 'That's your territory, and sometimes I'm glad there's a fence. Considering the subject matter I was gonna have a word couple of days ago. Would've tried harder if I'd known there was common ground.'

'I don't know that there is. You're investigating the murders of two people I'd never heard of until they were murdered. Jane talked to one for about twenty minutes but hadn't met him before. That doesn't make it common ground either.'

'The shared focus, Merrily, is a place called Cwmarrow. In a context in which you tend to see things I don't.'

'You have more confidence in me than I do. It's not that I don't *want* to help… I'm just not in the best of places right now.'

She felt uncomfortable, restricted, caged. The dressing over her right cheek felt like a huge swelling caused by toothache. It didn't hurt that much, there'd been no glass in the cut. The paramedics had applied the dressing at Cwmarrow after she'd refused to go to A and E. She'd left soon afterwards in the police car without seeing anyone from Cwmarrow Court. Which was probably sensible but felt like cowardice and left a raw ache stronger and more insistent than shock.

'Well, yeh,' Bliss said. 'I do realize that almost gerrin' killed…'

'Well, I wasn't. It wasn't pleasant, my car could be a write-off, but compared with what happened on the other side of the tree…'

She shook.

'It was an act of God, Merrily.'

'Why do people keep—?' She rocked back into the headrest, letting her eyes close. 'Never my favourite phrase. It's washing our hands and backing off.'

'You knew him. Feller who died. The doctor.'

'I was on my way to see him. And his daughter. Particularly his daughter.'

'Why?'

'I'm sorry, Frannie, but you don't need to know that.'

'All right. You went to see an elderly feller called Selwyn Kindley-Pryce yesterday. Is that correct?'

She opened her eyes and turned her head towards him.

'Who told you that?'

'Presumably some management person at the home where he lives, when one of my team rang to ask if he was up to being interviewed. Seems he isn't. Seems he's been three sheets in the wind for years.'

'Why would you want to interview him?'

'Friends of the Dusk,' Bliss said. 'Heard of them?'

'Who are they?'

'It was a group of people interested in the British vampire. Or, more specifically, the Hereford vampire. Make any sense?'

'It… Oh God, it may be. Never heard of the Friends of the Dusk, though. Sounds vaguely Masonic.'

'You know anything about the gatherings that Kindley-Pryce had at his place?'

'I know he needed money for restoration, so he hosted festivals involving music and poetry and discussions about local folklore. For which people presumably paid.'

'I should tell you that Victim One, Tristram Greenaway, was connected with the group. As was Victim Two, Jeremy Soffley, though to a lesser extent.'

'I didn't know that.'

'So why *did* you go to visit the old feller?'

'Because, it had been suggested that— See, this is going to sound like complete crap to you—'

'Merrily, how long've we known each other?'

'All right. People ask me to "exorcize" places. They have no idea what it means, but it sounds final. Like I can just go in and say the magic words and everything's back to normal?'

'Whereas you need to know what you're dealing with.'

'In order to condition the response, yes. OK. In confidence…'

'Yeh, yeh.'

'A guy there, at Cwmarrow, his wife believes that whatever they're sharing the house with may have caused him to have a stroke. Kindley-Pryce left the old house because he'd – perhaps quite quickly – developed dementia. Places, in my experiences, can damage people.'

'True enough. Radon gas. Proximity of pylons…'

'Not a huge step to toxic history. I just needed to be sure there was nothing Kindley-Pryce could tell me. In one way or another.'

'And was there?'

'I… If it doesn't make sense to me, it wouldn't make sense to you. Not going to burden with you with something I'm not sure about. Especially as it doesn't relate to either of your victims or… the Friends of the Dusk. Who I knew nothing about.'

Bliss thought about this, gazing out at conical Cole Hill across the flurrying fields.

'What are you doing this afternoon?'

'Feeling sick.'

'I've some video coming over from the States, shot by a man called Jim Turner who—'

'He was going to buy Cwmarrow Court from Kindley-Pryce.'

'Aha. Yes.'

'Pulled out and went to America?'

'Very quickly, it seems. We were wondering why the appeal of the house seemed to have waned for him.'

'You've spoken to him?'

'We have. He was going to make a documentary about the hunt for the old feller's Hereford vampire.'

'*Was* there a—?'

'We'll get to that. He'd already shot some film, video, at one or more of these weekend festivals, which we've asked him to send us electronically. If you feel you're up to it, I'd like you to come in and view it, probably this afternoon. Because, as I keep saying, you're quite likely to spot something – or somebody – that I'd miss the significance of.'

'Ah.'

'What?'

'It's not about whether I feel up to it. Just that if you want to do this officially, you'll need to make an approach to Sophie in the Gatehouse. Sophie then consults the Bishop, and the Bishop – I'm just guessing here, Frannie – tells you, via Sophie, to sod off. Only in more civilized, episcopal terminology.'

'Yeh, I'd heard he was a bit of a twat. What's his problem?'

'Take too long to explain. Suffice to say he strongly disapproves of exorcism in the Church. And seems to want me out.'

'Out?'

'Out of the job, possibly out of his diocese. This is absolutely not me being paranoid.'

'That's ridiculous, Merrily. It's the fuckin' *Chairch*!'

'Don't get me started.'

'Mother of God.' Bliss gripped the steering wheel, both hands. 'All right, one thing, then I'll leave yer alone. Simple question. Deviant burials. What do you know about them?'

'I know what they *are*. To an extent. Why?'

'When the tree blew down on Castle Green the other week, some bones were found underneath. Basically, a skeleton with his head between his legs and a stone in his gob.'

'I didn't know about this.'

'You're not supposed to,' Bliss said. 'In fact I haven't told you.'

'A stone?'

'Between his teeth. To stop him chewing up his shroud, apparently. I call him Steve, though we've not actually met yet.'

'Or to stop him speaking.'

'Yeh, that would work. If he could speak.'

Merrily sat up.

Bliss said, 'What?'

'Stop him summoning.'

'Just tell me in baby talk what that means.'

'You need to talk to someone who's more of an expert than me. And who doesn't need permission from the Bishop and would react very badly if she thought she did.'

'You very nearly smiled then, Merrily. Yeh, that would be all right. As long as it's not Jane.'

'You just have to be honest and upfront with her.'

'As distinct from me normal furtive, lying self?'

'If we go back to the vicarage now and you give me five minutes to go in and explain why I look like I've just been discharged from a women's refuge... I'll let you in. Back way. Park on the square.'

58

Timeless beauty

MERRILY WATCHED BLISS assembling a handful of people he called trusties in his office. She was sitting at the back under the window, wearing jeans and a dark green hoodie, no dog collar, no visible cross. She'd removed the dressing and replaced it with a single pink plaster over the deepest cut. She watched and said nothing.

'I've gorra warn you,' Bliss said to everybody. 'It's arty stuff.'

He meant shot from oblique angles, sometimes against jagged spears of light from window slits or sconces on the stone walls or feeble flames from what DC Vaynor said were rush-lights. He meant that faces were shadowed and unclear and you didn't hear any voices because Jim Turner had applied a music track at some later date: pipe organ, Vaynor said. Occasionally you'd get a glimpse of people playing instruments that looked like plumbing debris.

'There.' Karen Dowell touched the screen with a fingernail. 'That's Greenaway, isn't it?'

Karen had organized a small TV and DVD player and Bliss had pushed the desk up against the door to stop anyone he didn't trust getting in. Although Annie Howe was already here.

'He looks about twelve,' Bliss said.

Tristram Greenaway, fresh-faced and winsome, was in a dark silk shirt and tight jeans. He was serving drinks. Someone had evidently pinched his bottom. He spun round, still holding his tray, and then grinned. David Vaynor calculated he'd be about seventeen and still at school.

'Anybody else we know?' Bliss said.

Two people mentioned Hector Pryce. He had more hair then and a well-trimmed beard. He seemed to know a lot of people and drink a lot of wine. Merrily thought she recognized a former canon from the Cathedral, pink-cheeked and excited, and quite ill now, so she said nothing.

'I presume we've all noticed the obvious?' Bliss said.

Murmurs.

'Look,' he said. 'They're everywhere.'

The video switched to a sequence showing Selwyn Kindley-Pryce sitting in a straight-backed rustic chair with a large book open on his knees. He looked, Merrily thought, like an actor. A handsome, mature, distinguished actor with an actor's tan. People, mainly young women, were sitting around him on and between bales of straw in what she thought was now the Maliks' lofty sitting room.

'Who,' Vaynor asked, 'is *that*?'

A woman was standing between two stacks of bales, an elbow resting on one. She wore a long, sleeveless black dress. Her hair was swung over one shoulder, and you couldn't see where it ended.

'That's what you call timeless beauty,' Vaynor said. 'If you saw her in a painting from two hundred years ago…'

'Steady, Darth,' Bliss said.

The video froze on her. Caroline Goddard, Merrily thought, looking across at Bliss. When she'd gone into the vicarage alone, Jane had told her about a call from a woman identifying herself as Caroline. The same reclusive Caroline whose publishers had claimed she didn't want to talk to a vicar on the Welsh border? Merrily had passed this on, in confidence, to Bliss. Caroline was important now. She would have answers.

'And that's it,' Karen Dowell said. 'That's the lot. We should have some more by tonight, but apparently it won't be that much different.'

'There's a word for what I think we've just seen,' Bliss said.

387

'Probably wasn't a decade ago, Francis,' Annie Howe said.

She wasn't a timeless beauty, Annie, but she didn't set your teeth on edge any more. Something in her life had altered, Merrily thought, not for the first time this year. Didn't seem to bother her that it wasn't as obvious as it would once have been that she was the senior officer here.

Vaynor said, 'Do you want to see it again, boss? Ma'am? Or do you want me to get the retired blokes in?'

'The gerries,' Bliss said. 'Yeh, let's move the desk and wheel the gerries in. But first, let me just tell you about a minor breakthrough. An expert has confirmed what we thought about Greenaway's attempts to market Steve. Let me just...' He leaned into his laptop. 'In case anybody's forgotten...'

He brought up an email, ending with

You might not recognize him but
you all doubtless remember who
he is. If you want to know where
he was found I can Draw you a Map.

'We didn't spend too much time trying to work out what Greenaway meant by drawing a map, but it looks like we should've done. The clue is the use of the capitals.'

Bliss told them in some detail what he'd learned from Jane about Walter Map, suggesting Greenaway had also typed the word 'draw' with a capital D to muddy the water.

'So what's that tell us, Darth?'

'Tells us Greenaway's convinced he's found the final burial place of the allegedly undead medieval evildoer. He's probably hoping it'll be seen by Jim Turner or by someone who can pass it on to Turner.'

'Because Trissie has just learned he has no future with the Herefordshire county archaeologist's department. He's ready to strike a deal. Or maybe even *desperate* to strike a deal, depending on his financial situation.' Bliss looked around the room. 'Anybody see any flaws in that?'

'But he's nicked it,' Karen Dowell said. 'It's a stolen skull. How's he going to explain that away?'

'He's not gonna be too worried about *that*,' Bliss said. 'Let Turner deal with it. We've gorra look at this from Trissie's position. It's the biggest thing that ever happened to him. The realization of a dream.'

'He's up there with the gods of archaeology,' Vaynor said.

'And therefore less cautious than he might normally be,' Annie Howe murmured. 'Consequently, more vulnerable.'

'Annie's right,' Bliss said. 'He—'

Annie? Merrily saw Karen Dowell throw a glance at Bliss, who looked down at his keyboard.

'Anyway,' he said. 'They'd be giving the skull back to Cooper at some point. Having paid for whatever tests've been done on it. Win-win, all round.'

'In fact when you think about it…' Vaynor was on the edge of his chair. 'There could even be a facial reconstruction. Imagine that. The face of a medieval vampire.'

'Alleged.'

'Walter Map's black magician – alleged,' Vaynor said. 'I bet Turner's wondering even now if it couldn't work for him. With the additional frisson of a double murder. What's the betting?'

'Depends what he got up to at Cwmarrow Court, in between filming,' Bliss said. 'Doesn't it? Let's get one of the techies to go through this again, see how many faces we can bring out of the shadows. Let's get stills of everybody. *Everybody*. And then let's talk to Turner again.'

The streets were drying off. The wind had retreated into the hills. Merrily had been offered transport home, but said she needed to do some shopping first, if that was OK. She needed to rest, separate herself. Recover. Think.

She'd told Bliss there were no faces she recognized in Turner's film, apart from Hector Pryce, who'd declared disinterest in his father's pursuits. *Bloody mad, people who get obsessed with the past. The past is worthless, messes you up.*

It was only a few minutes' walk from Gaol Street, across St Peter's Square to the complex of short, narrow streets leading to Castle Green.

She felt she needed to see it, the last resting place of the *maleficus* – allegedly. Jane had told her roughly where it was in relation to the remains of the castle moat and the tall monument commemorating Lord Nelson.

Merrily sat down on a bench. The green enclosure, the river on one side, the Cathedral on another, was all about defence, physical and spiritual. She tried to relax into it.

Gave up and rang Jane.

'Caroline called again.'

'Oh. How did she sound?'

'I said I hadn't heard from you since you'd left for Cwmarrow, and it was like she didn't know what to say next. I said could I get you to ring her when I heard from you? No, she didn't want that. So I gave her your mobile number. However—'

'She hasn't called.'

'No, but it doesn't matter. After the second call, I thought, I wonder if she's forgotten to conceal her number this time. And sure enough, the old 1471…'

'Flower, you're uncanny.'

'I've put it in an email. And yes, it *is* a local number. Let me know if it hasn't come through.'

'I will. Thank you. I don't know what I'd—'

'Oh God, don't go down that road,' Jane said. 'Just keep me in the picture. And get back ASAP. You need to sleep. Recover.'

'No call from either of the Kellows?'

She'd rung twice. No answer.

'Nothing,' Jane said. 'But stay in touch.'

She still sounded animated, involved. Something really *had* lifted.

'Jane… Lol. Does Lol know about the accident?'

'I haven't seen him. Do you want me to go round?'

'No. If he doesn't know, let's not worry him needlessly.'

'Don't switch your mobile off,' Jane said

Merrily sat with the phone in her hands, realizing she'd been gazing all through that conversation at a patch of ground where new sods had been laid.

She walked over. The bank of the River Wye was ahead of her, the Cathedral to the right. A vampire's grave underfoot. Allegedly.

No mention of fangs and blood, but that was all nine-teenth-century veiled eroticism. The methods used by the revenant *maleficus* to drain the life from his victims had not, unless they'd been lost in translation, been specified. It had been perceptive of Jane to underline the theory put forward by the bishop, Gilbert Foliot: *Peradventure the Lord has given power to the evil angel of that lost soul to move about in the dead corpse.*

She was still walking around the grave, trying to make some metaphysical sense of the term *evil angel*, when the phone barked.

She took a breath.

'Merrily Watkins.'

'Are you really all right, Merrily?'

Sophie.

'Yes. Thank you. I'm really all right.'

'The hospital said your injuries were superficial.'

'You rang *the hospital*?'

'What was I supposed to do?'

'You were supposed not to have known.'

'Everybody knows. It's a small city.'

'God.'

'I thought you were perhaps avoiding me.'

'Sophie, I left a message thanking you for… for what you did. I didn't like to go into details on an answering machine. But I am so very grateful.'

'So grateful you're keeping things from me.'

'I just didn't want to compromise you. And I still don't.'

Sophie said quickly, 'The Bishop would like to see you.'

'Now?'

'Now.'

'What about?'

'He hasn't told me.'

'He knows about the accident? That I was there?'

'I don't know.'

'Right.' Merrily stared across at the top of the Cathedral tower pushing at the blank sky. 'Well, if he's not prepared to say what it's about, you'd better tell him I'm busy right now and I'll be in touch. Sometime.'

In the hush, she felt her heart leap like a frightened deer. Sophie's voice remained steady, its tone unaltered.

'It's *the Bishop*, Merrily.'

'Yes. You said.'

'And you want me to tell him you're busy? Without further explanation.'

'Yes.'

'You do know what that's going to sound like?'

'Yes. Yes, I do.'

59

Pulse

THE OTHER OLDIES had gone back to the MIR, leaving Bliss and a man called Bryan Fry. A detective sergeant, retired about a year before Bliss came. Always meant to have a chat with him sometime. Fellow northerner and all.

He was about seventy, bristly white hair and a moustache. Bliss asked him where he was from.

'Southport.'

'Posh,' Bliss said.

'Posher than Birkenhead. Time for a pint, lad?'

'Don't drink much any more, Bryan. Since me head injury.'

'I heard about that.'

'Alcohol – bad news now. Half a pint, I'm legless. Well… head aches, you know. It's improving slowly. But I'll buy you one.'

'Not round here,' Bryan Fry said. 'Let's not advertise this, in case it comes to bugger all. I've still got mates from the old days.'

This sounded worthwhile. Bliss always liked it when they didn't want to talk in front of anyone else. They went to the Spread Eagle, a cavernous old pub, top of King Street, not far from the Cathedral. Bliss bought Bryan Fry a pint and got himself a Pepsi. They sat near the door, on their own.

'It's all bloody different, now,' Fry said. 'Everything's different, and it's changed so bloody fast. Folks talk about the eighties like it was the Dark Ages. I wouldn't last two weeks these days, me. I'd come out with summat I didn't realize was racist or sexist and that'd be it. Can't even call a bloke a fat bastard these days.'

Bliss nodded.

'Obesism. Frowned on.'

'Them girls,' Bryan Fry said, 'in your video. Not what you'd call paedophilia, is it? Just a bit of young fluff.'

'Young fluff,' Bliss said. 'Long time since I heard that.'

'Historic sex abuse. No such thing then. Little girls lined up outside rock stars' hotel rooms. Grooming was about horses.'

'Those were the days, eh?' Bliss said, encouragingly.

'Hey, now I'm not saying *that*, lad. *I* didn't play around. Family man, me, and grabbing all the overtime I could get. But it went on. It went on bloody everywhere. When it was on offer it didn't get turned down much, you know what I mean? And you know the only time it ever became a police investigation?'

'When one of them got murdered?'

'You're not as young as you look, are you? Aye. When one got murdered. And if it was a murder in what we now call an *ethnic community*, well it wasn't a real murder, was it? Didn't make much in the papers either. And don't get me wrong, I'm not saying that was *right*, I'm just saying that was how it *was*. Seems a long time ago now.'

He sank a portion of his pint.

'Well, sure, you'd get a bit of a flap every now and again. Remember satanic child abuse? So-called. Little kids and people in devil masks burning black candles? How long ago was that, now – end of the eighties, beginning of the nineties? All balls. Hysterical social workers. Discredited. Waste of police time.'

Bliss wasn't sure it *had* been a total waste of police time, it just hadn't led to convictions. But he said nothing, let Bryan Fry get on with it.

'Here's the thing, Francis. Woman came into... I can't honestly remember which station it was, but this'd be ten, fifteen years ago. From London. Eastender type. Bit loud, bit *common*, as they used to say. Had a feller with her, but he didn't say much. Reckoned her daughter had been kidnapped by vampires. Well…'

'Yeh,' Bliss said. 'I can imagine that starting a major inquiry. How old was the daughter?'

'Fourteen, fifteen, sixteen, I forget. I wasn't involved, but I remember it. Johnny Flynn had a look at it – he left the force years ago, no idea where he is now. The woman said her daughter and a bunch of other kids had been into these vampire books – kids' books, that's all. And they were going to get together and go and meet this lad who was supposed to be a vampire. And the other kids backed out, and she's ended up going on her own, not telling her mam, and she hasn't come back. Georgia Welsh, her name, I remember that.'

'And the lad who was a vampire?'

'He'd written to her. That's what her mother said. He'd written to her and of course they had to destroy the letter. The mother said it was after they wrote to the writer of this book, who turned out to be two people, living in a spooky old house in the wilds. Young woman, old feller, neither with fangs, I remember Johnny Flynn saying that. He'd gone for a chat. Oh, they said, they got hundreds of letters all the time. Sent stock replies. No, they didn't remember any Georgia Welsh, why should they?'

'And that was that?'

'That *was* that, Francis. The old feller was well connected. And his son was Hector Pryce, new on the Bench, drank with senior police. Johnny Flynn wasn't happy, I do remember that. He thought it was a funny set-up, these two. Just a feeling, you know? But this was *then*, and it turned out Georgia Welsh's mother was on the game and had form for robbing a regular client while he was sleeping it off, so Johnny just got told to forget it, and I don't think we ever heard from her again.'

'You don't know if the girl turned up?'

'I don't, lad. There was never much of a hunt, I know that.'

'And this was definitely Kindley-Pryce's books they were reading? Foxy Rowlestone?'

'Just come out, I think. My kids were a bit too old by then so I wouldn't know. See, I didn't know until today that old Pryce was linked to this, but when I saw the video, all these young girls... well... made me think, that's all. Made me remember. That's what we're here for i'n't it? To remember.'

'Well, thanks, Bryan.'

'Not *crime*, though, was it, Francis? We've only quite recently started seeing crime there. That's the thing. If nobody died, it wasn't bloody crime.'

He finished his beer, declined another.

Bliss said, 'Charlie Howe – was he still in charge?'

'Bit of an elder statesman by then, but still going strong.'

'I didn't miss him on that video, did I?'

'No, lad.'

'But it would be him who called Johnny Flynn off.'

'Probably would.'

Back at Gaol Street, he went straight up to find Annie.

Her office was a lot bigger than his but with fluorescent lights and no proper window. His head throbbed lightly in anticipation of worse to come, Annie hissing at him before he'd got the punchline out.

'Francis, no. No, no, *no.*'

Bliss shut the door, put his back against it.

'We need to at least ask.'

'He hates you.'

'Then let's not destroy anyone else's professional relationship with the bugger.'

'You do remember what happened last time, I take it.'

'He humiliated me. And then I came to talk to you, and you were wearing the stripy sweater—'

'Stop it.'

'—and in the end it turned out to be the best Christmas in a long time. For me, anyway. And I would like there to be another. After we sort this.'

'You'll get nothing out of Charlie,' Annie said. 'Charlie is a clever man. Even cleverer than you, not being weighed down with lapsed Catholic guilt. He certainly has more in his personal history to protect. And more to gain.'

'He thinks the further he rises, the further out of reach he's gonna be. Not any more, Annie.'

'My advice is to wait. Just see what happens.'

'No… listen… nothing's gonna happen if we don't move now. These old coppers, they're still living back in the day. It's like Jimmy Savile – the cops were his *mates*. He's shagging everything that moves and, by all accounts, a good few who've stopped moving, and the old cops are like, Good old Jim, eh? What a bloody character. Now I'm not saying Charlie…'

'I'm glad you're not saying that.'

Annie's eyes were cold. He'd gone too far. He felt his left eye close, the old numbness easing down like a garden slug from the edge of his forehead. He came away from the door, laid both his palms on the desk.

'Think about it. What's best here? Me… or a bunch of ambitious scalp-hunters from another Force?'

'You know,' Annie said. 'That that will never happen.'

60

What to believe

IT WAS INTIMATELY beautiful in the chantry, like sitting inside a richly-decorated stone mushroom, but it didn't hold too many good memories. This was the scene of her bleakest meeting with Bernie Dunmore. All those questions she hadn't wanted to ask but had known she'd have to, about his time as a Freemason.

This was where he'd said, *I'm going to retire, Merrily.* Sitting just there, sweating into his purple shirt. Awful. Leaving her with the persistent fear that she might have had a role in the breakdown of his health.

And now he'd gone, and it felt so much colder in the Cathedral. Even in the gloriously cosy late medieval Chantry Chapel of Bishop John Stanbury. Perhaps even colder in here, and yet...

'This is one of my places,' Caroline Goddard said. 'Been coming here since I was a kid. I feel safe here.'

She'd insisted they talk in the chantry. Anyone could walk in, but nobody would.

They'd met in the Cathedral's north porch. Caroline's phone number had the Hereford prefix, 01432, and her voice had the remains of a local accent.

'I don't know what I can tell you,' she'd said. 'Already, I just want to go home.'

Her voice, as Jane had said, was small and childlike.

It had been a shock to meet her so soon after seeing the woman in the Cwmarrow video with her Pre-Raphaelite hair and what David Vaynor had called her timeless beauty. She was still slim, but her hair was mainly grey now and she'd unwound a white scarf to show that it ended around the collar of her shapeless blue fleece. Her face was unlined but pale; she wore no make-up, no jewellery. She could have been a nun on a solitary holiday.

Wouldn't say where she lived, only that it was in the city, a flat in a modern block, very central. She said she shared it with a widowed sister. Saying she'd once lived with a man for a while, but it hadn't worked.

'This was after Selwyn Kindley-Pryce?' Merrily said.

'I never lived with Sel. I *spent nights* with him. In the early days. Until I couldn't. Any more.'

'I'm sorry, I didn't mean to…'

'I Googled you. I don't talk to fans or academics doing a PhD on metaphysical fiction for children or something. I'd instructed my publishers to tell nobody where I lived. But I recognized your name so I Googled you. I've always wanted to talk to somebody. But there was nobody who would even understand what I was talking about. Even now I'm not sure…'

She looked up, finding Merrily's eyes, her expression somewhere between fearful and imploring, Merrily wanting to give her confidence, not yet sure how to go about it.

'And now I'm afraid. I'm afraid of what's happening here. You're an exorcist. You… look a bit young for it.'

'I'm not that young.'

'I wanted to talk to you on the phone first, to be sure. And then it started to look like you were dead, too, and I panicked. Too much death.'

Caroline looked down at her hands which were around a small, white prayer book.

'I get frightened very easily these days.'

But this was the woman who wrote *The Summoner*. Merrily felt the phone shuddering in her pocket and ignored it.

'You don't write for children now?'

'I write for younger children. Under different pen names. They don't pay much, books for young children, and you have to write a lot of them, but it keeps my mind fluid. I have the mind of a child, everybody says that, as if it's a virtue. "She writes through the mind of a child." Well, that's all right. You come to accept that it isn't necessarily good to grow up. Now.' She turned to face Merrily. 'Who did die at Cwmarrow, please?'

'It was a man called Adam Malik. A doctor. He was the son-in-law of Dennis Kellow, who I think you might remember.'

'The builder. He bought the house, didn't he?'

'And was having problems there.'

'What kind of problems, please?'

'He had a stroke. Which was preceded by some poltergeist phenomena in the house. And an apparition of a pointing figure. Does that make any sense to you... as someone who lived there?'

'That's why you wanted to find me, is it?'

'It's my job. I'm trying to help them.'

'As an exorcist. I read about that. It was on the Internet. My sister works with someone who lives near that house on the estate at Aylestone Hill where the murder was. They said you did a mass there, at night. Is that right?'

'It was a Requiem Eucharist for someone who had died there. Another example of how the history of a place can affect people living there now. Only I couldn't find much about the history of Cwmarrow. Except what was in your novel. *The Summoner.*'

'I don't like to talk about that.' Caroline swung her white scarf back around her throat. 'It's not a happy story. I didn't want to write it.'

'It... seems to be based on the writings of the medieval chronicler Walter Map. Who doesn't actually mention Cwmarrow. So it all seems to come back to Selwyn Kindley-Pryce. And you.'

Caroline drew back into the carved stone wall. Stone like the icing on a milky chocolate cake.

'I was just the writer, you must know that. He wasn't a writer, he was an academic. He couldn't find little words for things. Only big words.'

'He wrote a book called *Borderlight*...'

'*I* wrote that. It was the first book I wrote for him. And I did the drawings, pen and ink, so they'd look like old engravings.'

'And didn't he tell stories? Like in the oral tradition?'

'He still couldn't *write* one. Anything he said in his lovely dark brown voice sounded wonderful. He must have wowed everyone in America. But as soon as he tried to write it down, it came out all stilted and pompous. Don't you believe me?'

'I honestly don't know what to believe any more.'

'You've been hurt. I've only just noticed. Your face. Was that when the tree fell?'

'Part of it fell on my car. If I'd been driving slightly faster I might well be dead.'

'This man who died...'

'It was an accident.'

'You think that was an accident?'

'Put it this way, I didn't see anyone with a chainsaw.'

Stop it, don't get clever.

'If you're an exorcist,' Caroline Goddard said, 'then you must believe in evil.'

'Yes, I do.'

'The Summoner taking life to prolong his own. That's evil, isn't it?'

'Yes. Definitely.'

She had a sense of this woman being out on a high ledge and trying not to look down.

'*Was* there a Summoner?'

'There *is* a Summoner. These things don't go away. I've always known that, since I was a little girl. My dad was a farmer. The kind who sees the countryside as his private factory. Doesn't see cows, only beef. Doesn't notice the sunrise over the hills. Never could see what I saw. When I read stories, as a child, about fairyland, I thought I'm living in it. This is fairyland. And my dad – he just wanted me to help him kill the poor turkeys. I ran away twice and had to be brought back by the police.'

Caroline sat gazing at the triptych over the little altar, the centre picture a Madonna and child with golden haloes. The frame was intricate, wooden and Gothic, with soaring spires.

'I'd been writing stories all my life. In my head, mostly. I was eighteen when I started sending them to publishers. Stories for children set in the fields I knew. Did the illustrations. I was twenty-two when my first novel was published. Paperback original. That was a magic time. I was living with a boyfriend in a caravan. The publishers asked for a picture of me, and they thought I looked… right, I suppose. They commissioned two more books and by the time I went back to the caravan the boyfriend had gone, so I sold it.'

Never made a fortune, she said, but it was a living wage. Her name was Caroline but not Goddard. That had been chosen for her by the publishers a year before she'd met Selwyn Kindley-Pryce at a fantasy convention. He was not long back from America and they had him as a guest speaker because so many fiction writers used his books for research. He came over and they had a few drinks and ended up spending the night together.

'He must've been – what – thirty years older than you?'

'It never really occurred to me. I suppose he was the gentle father I never had. Soft-spoken and incredibly fey. Sophisticated, worldly… and yet otherworldly. I was sure he could tune into my thoughts. Yes, I was enchanted, Merrily – can I call you Merrily?'

'Of course.'

'A lovely name. A name out of fairy tales. I'm coming to the conclusion that you are a good person. Which is not invariably the case with the clergy. Some of them railed against my books, even before *The Summoner*, because of the elements of paganism. Well, paganism is colourful and fun, but it doesn't deal with evil in the same way. That's why I keep coming back here.'

She looked up at the chantry's foliate walls and ceiling as if she wanted to hold them tightly around her.

'So you were writing Kindley-Pryce's stories... and you were...'

'I was his lover, but I didn't live all the time at the Court. I had a little cottage in Dorstone, with my writing room and my studio and my cats. So I was happy to stay there. It was relief from the...'

She went rigid for a moment and then let her shoulders fall.

'He didn't encourage me to go and live with him. I don't think he liked cats. And, to be honest, he... he exhausted me. Physically. Emotionally. I was always exhausted when I came back from Cwmarrow. Whatever form of energy made him into a sort of superman, even at his comparatively advanced age... it was making me feel old before my time. Still in my twenties.'

'You didn't like it? The place, I mean.'

'I loved it, though I'm not sure it loved me.'

'That's more or less what Dennis Kellow told me.'

'Most of all...' She leaned forward. '... I *didn't like the story*. Sel planned it, chapter by chapter. My job was to make the characters real and human so they would appeal to young readers. Especially Geraint. All the girls had to love Geraint. That was the key ingredient. He kept throwing pages back at me. "No, no, make him more... exciting." I said, there are things you can't *say* in a book for children, even teenagers. He said, "You'll find a way". Am I telling you what you wanted to know, Merrily?'

'Yes, I think you are. Thank you.'

Caroline smiled.

'It all started to take on an organic life of its own. Sel believed in it totally because he was a magician, and I had to—'

'Hang on a sec. When you say magician?'

'He just was. He could do things that quite scared you,' Caroline said. 'You didn't say no to him. He was gentle at first, but very dominant. I knew I was being controlled. And that seems all right at first, having all your decisions made for you. But it drained you after a while.'

'Friends of the Dusk?' Merrily said. 'Can I ask you about that?'

'Oh, well…' Caroline bit her upper lip. 'I'm not sure what that meant.'

'Was it just a name for the people who came to the festivals?'

'I don't know.' Caroline looked past Merrily towards the open doorway. Footsteps and voices echoed from the nave. 'I wasn't there all the time.'

Caroline was pressing herself into the corner, waiting until the footsteps had receded.

'There were two kinds of festivals. The public ones, where we'd talk about the books, the Nightlands, and there'd be music. And the others.'

'The others… young fans would come to them, too?'

'Young female fans. I believe. And some male.'

'How would they get there?'

'All different ways. Some would get the train to Hereford and Selwyn's son, Hector, he had a bus company, and a bus would bring them to Cwmarrow.'

I get him what he wants.

Thoughts started twisting and curling feverishly like the knots and whorls of the chantry stone. She couldn't separate them. There was something crucially important here; she wanted to rush out into the open air of the Cathedral Green and chase it down and then come back and put reasoned questions, but Caroline wouldn't come with her, or wait. She had to go for it now.

'To what extent was Hector involved?'

'I don't really know.'

'He doesn't… didn't like his father, did he?'

'No.'

'But he could, quite reasonably, have kept away from Selwyn. Wasn't as if he'd even known him long. He hadn't seen him since he was…'

She fell silent. Caroline's smile had become just a little unearthly.

'Caroline, tell me…?'

'People said it was misleading how alike they looked because they were so different – Sel so gentle and Hector so abrupt and aggressive. But they *were* alike. In other ways.'

'Women? Girls?'

Caroline's laughter was hoarse and mirthless.

'They should all be exorcised. There's a job for you.'

'Who?'

'He needs to be taken out of them. They think they want him. They're always so excited. They think they're entering another world, but it's not what they think it is. It's his little… dirty world.'

'*Who?*'

'The fans. Lots of them.'

'What happened at the other events?'

'I don't know. I wasn't there.'

Merrily took in a slow breath.

'What do you *think* happened?'

'I don't know, but I think it went on happening… after they'd left. He'd found a way in. Maybe he's still doing it. I don't know.'

'From where he is? From Lyme Farm?'

'I don't know.' Caroline looked confused. 'I think he needs Cwmarrow.'

'Do you think there's something… something left at Cwmarrow?'

'*He's* there. When he wants to be. He can be anywhere he wants to be. It's something he's always been able to do.'

'He? Do you mean Selwyn Kindley-Pryce. Or… the Summoner? The *maleficus*?'

Caroline was hugging herself, shaking. Merrily had never felt closer to the dark heart of the job, felt it pulsing away. Here, in front of an altar, the haloed mother and child. *I'm increasingly inclined to think that it's simply a demand we've created*, Craig Innes said. *Or have – unwisely – allowed to create itself.*

'Caroline, listen, it's a funny job, mine. You have to consider things that could get you laughed at. Sometimes, I just have to sit for a moment and think, well, I'm a vicar. And there are many thousands of us, and we like to think we work for this huge, benificent supernatural force, and here's me…'

She stopped talking, aware of Caroline Goddard laughing quietly. Rocking slowly in the old wooden pew, kneading the prayer book inside her woollen scarf. When she looked up, Caroline's eyes were unblinking.

'Thing is, Hector can't get away. He's been seeing his father all his life.'

'Seeing?'

'All his life.'

'But… Hector was here. His father was in America.'

'What difference does that make?'

'Hector told you this?'

'Selwyn told me. How he'd visit his son. Hector never came near me. He didn't really like women.'

'I'm sorry?'

'What are you going to do with this, Merrily, please?'

'I don't know.'

She was feeling so very cold, the chantry no longer cosy; its intricate, organic stonework seemed to be flexing like a map of muscles.

'I suppose I'm going to take advice,' she said. 'I'll try to keep you out of it.'

'You can tell who you like as long as I don't have to speak to them. Some people I just can't talk to, because they don't believe in anything. They'd think I was mental.' Caroline looked into the chantry's small, quite modern stained-glass windows, their colours beginning to dull. 'I'll have to go soon. It's getting dark. My sister'll be worried.'

'Why will she be worried?'

'Because he's still out there.' Caroline stood up. 'The killer.'

Merrily didn't move, looked up at her.

'You mean the killer of Tristram Greenaway?'

'I saw his picture on the TV. I didn't even know he was back in town.'

'Tristram?'

Caroline breathed in hard, leaned her back against the richly carved stone and let her breath out slowly.

'To me, he'll always be Geraint,' she said.

61

The cloaked

SHE CHECKED IN at the desk at Gaol Street, but they said Bliss had gone out. It was dark now, all the lights on, a lot more cops around than usual, inside and out. The lights weren't very bright but they hurt her eyes and she felt very tired and confused and wanted to go home and think about all this. But the DCI was at the door to the stairs.

'Come up.'

Annie Howe, wearing a dark suit, looking not happy. Leading Merrily up to CID and through to Bliss's office.

'You *didn't* go shopping, did you?'

'Ended up meeting Caroline Goddard. Though I didn't know that was going to happen when I left here. If there'd been anybody with me, Annie, it's unlikely she'd have said a word. She's... eccentric. Lives in town but won't say where. I don't think she's using her own name, and she looks nothing like the woman in the video.'

'You're sure it *was* Caroline Goddard?'

'Without taking a DNA swab, yes, I'm sure.'

'All right.' Howe pulled out a chair for Merrily and sat on the edge of Bliss's desk, an open notepad in front of her. 'What can you tell me?'

'Well, I'm not sure how much you—'

'I'm the SIO, Merrily. I know everything. And while I'm not a lapsed Catholic and have never worked in Liverpool – or indeed *been* to Liverpool – I think I can have a vague stab at grasping whatever you're trying to say.'

'OK.' Merrily shrugged. 'Tell me when I reach the elements you don't want to go near.'

'Anything non-corporeal I simply tune out.'

Better, perhaps, not even to go into any of that. She talked about Caroline's relationship with Kindley-Pryce, how they'd slept together on an irregular basis, but not cohabited. How Caroline was dominated and not – if you believed her – given partner status, on any level.

'Now why do we think that was?' Howe said. 'Given that, at his age, you'd imagine that a bit of local arm-candy with waist-length hair would be quite a flattering addition to his… ménage. Also, as they were working together, quite intensively…'

'I think she did most of her writing at her own cottage. As for him, although the age gap is about thirty years, perhaps – and this can be surmised from the video – perhaps he'd been given access to even… fresher fruit.'

'Yes, we did see the tree on the DVD.'

'It was the time, wasn't it? Thousands of teenage girls either side of the Atlantic drawn towards the… the apocryphal world of the undead. *Buffy*, *Twilight* – had *Twilight* started then?'

'I've no idea. Perhaps I need to look all this up. In the meantime…'

Extending an open hand. Merrily nodded.

'OK… part of my job is to monitor semi-spiritual social patterns. I remember reading about million-copy print-runs of romantic vampire novels aimed at young adults. Teen hysteria. This is some years after it started, so I'm not saying the Foxy Rowlestones were doing that kind of business – I didn't actually know about *them* – but if the series had carried on they might well have done. I was given the impression the series stopped because Kindley-Pryce's mind was going and Caroline hadn't the heart to carry on.'

'What is Ms Goddard actually saying?'

'She was walking all around the subject. Trying to be helpful but obviously anxious not to bring anything down on herself. Truly, I think there's a lot she didn't know. A lot she didn't *want* to know. Didn't want to be exposed to. And Kindley-Pryce wouldn't want to scare her off.'

'What did scare her off, if not his dementia?' Annie said. 'I mean, I doubt that would make him easy or at all pleasant to work with. What kind of dementia does he have? All we tend to hear about is Alzheimer's disease.'

'I don't know. There must be medical records. The doctors who look after Lyme Farm would know.'

'Hmm.' Howe made a note on her pad. 'Was all this pre-Internet?'

'No, but not a great deal was happening social-media wise when it started, I'd imagine.'

'So if we're looking at – let's not dress this up – abuse of readers, young fans, it's the books themselves that were doing the grooming?'

'In a way, yes. Not a word that was in use in a sexual context, when this started. But, yeah, there was no need for grooming, the magnetism was there – the glamour, the romance, the mystery. And this sense of the clandestine, the cloaked.'

'You do seem *very* informed about all this.'

'Because I've been there. Well, not *there*, but… for a short time – though not as short as I've assured my daughter – I was a bit of a teenage goth. Black T-shirt, black nails, black lipstick, spooky music, Anne Rice novels… I'm not sure there *was* any young-adult gothic romance back then but if I'd read *The Summoner* at fifteen I might well have fantasized about baring my throat for Geraint, the blacksmith, under a full moon. There. Said it. Caution me.'

Annie stared at her.

'And *I* was supposed to be quite intelligent,' Merrily said. 'Hormones can take you to some dark places. And nowhere darker – perhaps – than Cwmarrow. It seemed significant to me that Caroline was urged by Kindley-Pryce to make Geraint, the male lead, the heart-throb, increasingly appealing in a sexual way. Which had to be done subtly to get published – the vampire in the Twilight series is a vegetarian, for heaven's sake.'

'So if the Friends of the Dusk were preying on young readers, fans… how does this work?'

'I don't know. But I *can* tell you about the bait. Jane did just a cursory search of the Net – the Foxy Rowlestone Appreciation Society – still active – and something called the Fang Forum, ostensibly for adults. She found members claiming they'd been to the Nightlands, as it's called in the books. And others saying they'd actually seen Geraint.'

'How would they know where to go?'

'Some came in on the train and Hector Pryce coaches would ferry them to Cwmarrow.'

'Interesting.'

Caroline says that people who wrote to Foxy Rowlestone – or *certain* people who wrote – would receive a circular or an email package which might include a photograph of Geraint, half in shadow but every bit as good-looking as they could wish for.'

'You're saying…' Annie screwing up her eyes. '… that this Geraint, on some level, existed?

'*Geraint* on *no* level existed. And yet… Oh God, I need to think about this.'

'Just tell me what you know of the facts.'

'The only fact I have is that the shadowy Geraint in the picture was Tristram Greenaway.'

'Goddard told you this? Kids who wrote in were all receiving pictures of *Greenaway*?'

'*That* was the nature of his employment, while still at school, by Kindley-Pryce. He was also in charge of sending the fan pictures off. Nice Saturday job if you can get it. Whether he'd be instantly recognizable is debatable…'

'Was that it? Or is it possible he was involved… further?'

'If he was gay, he couldn't have been all *that* involved.'

'Unless there were a few boys writing in. Can't be ruled out, Merrily.'

'I suppose not.'

'But I can see what you mean about all this being confusing. It wouldn't, of course, necessarily be criminal behaviour unless the girls were under-age. The ones on Turner's film could all be over sixteen. What happened after the photographs of the... the shadow-Greenaway were sent off or emailed? What happened next?'

'I don't know that either.'

'Well, I think I can speculate,' Annie said. 'I think the correspondence would move to a different level. Less public. Perhaps using the Neogoth network, if Bliss has mentioned that to you. They don't want to ask for trouble, so they would prune the list to isolate the most enthusiastic... or fanatical, or... needy...? Still strikes me as astonishing that this could go on in the Herefordshire countryside, for so long with so little leakage. But then, if we consider the industrial scale of sexual abuse of girls by Asian gangs in the north and even Oxford, over years, with no action by the police...'

'I think,' Merrily said, 'that you're looking at something much smaller, if more intense and more... well, more occult. Do you see what I'm—?'

'And that in itself is another can of worms. I imagine police and social services were still nursing their wounds over the satanic child-abuse fiasco.'

'The girls involved... I'd suggest that they don't see themselves as having been sexually exploited as much as... initiated. If finding the Nightlands wasn't made easy for them, that would only add to the excitement... and the commitment, the need – the *desire* – to maintain secrecy. They'd be feeling like the chosen ones. And once they got there... a place that's remote, deeply atmospheric and just sufficiently forbidding, in an enticing way... to somehow bridge the gap between Tristram Greenaway, who doesn't, with girls, and Selwyn Kindley-Pryce who—'

412

Merrily's shudder made the chair move.

'There could have been use of drugs,' Annie said soberly. 'To make it all more... almost hallucinatory. Very easily administered.' She levered herself from the desk. 'Where's Goddard now?'

'In the city, somewhere. Wouldn't give me her address. I don't honestly think she'd make a great interviewee. Not for the police. She's all over the place.'

'That would be for us to decide.'

'Sure.'

It was a police matter now. Whoever killed Tristram Greenaway and the other guys, that was no business of hers.

'All right.' Annie Howe opened the door, held it back. 'Why don't you go home and get some sleep? I'll organize a car. I think I need to get hold of Bliss. ASAP.'

Waiting outside, she felt cold and lost. An unmarked car drew up next to her, to take her home. The driver was nobody she recognized.

62

A flogging

CHARLIE HOWE WAS so very friendly that, but for the call from Annie, Bliss might well have cut his losses and walked out.

'Only just talking about you, boy.'

'Who to?'

Charlie tapped his nose.

'Take a seat, Brother Bliss.'

Bliss hesitated. Last time, he hadn't even got out of the rain outside Charlie's tall, brick home on the main road out of Leominster. Now he'd been ushered into the home office: two desks, filing cabinets, dense black carpet and matching soft leather chairs. Bliss chose the one that didn't swivel.

'Just surprised you took so long, boy.'

Charlie sat in the swivel chair next to the roll-top desk. He never changed: the short, stiff white hair over an indestructible leathery face that just got more lived-in and comfortable, like an old biker jacket. He wore a waistcoat and had an old-fashioned pin through his shirt collar.

'To congratulate you, right?' Bliss said. 'On your candidature for Police and Crime Commissioner.'

Charlie beamed.

'Oh, that can wait till I'm elected. No point in wasting it till you can't afford to offend me any more.'

'Actually, Charlie,' Bliss said, 'it wasn't about that at all. OK if I offend you about something else?'

Charlie reached across the desk and snapped on the brass desk lamp, aimed the tubular shade at Bliss.

414

'This better not be a waste of my valuable time, boy.'

'In that case, I'll get straight to it. Let's look back towards the end of your era as head of CID. A new millennium soon to be dawning, all fresh and free of graft and backhanders, brown envelopes, all the stuff that gave the twentieth century such a bad reputation.'

Charlie said nothing. Bliss talked about historical sexual abuse, how the term had taken off after revelations about Jimmy Savile, the BBC TV personality who helped out in hospitals and helped himself to the patients and anybody else unlikely to complain about being groped by famous hands. Charlie looked irritated.

'And?' Charlie said. '*And?*'

'Georgia Welsh,' Bliss said.

'Not a name I know, boy.'

'Mother arrived from London saying she'd been abducted.'

'By aliens?'

'Vampires, actually. A DC called Johnny Flynn was asked to look into it.'

'Flynn. Aye, I remember Flynn. Wasn't Irish. And, oh, yes, now it does come back to me. A woman with form for robbing a punter. A drunk, a fantasist. Fully investigated. Entirely baseless.'

'You ever heard of Friends of the Dusk?'

'Punk rock band?' Charlie swivelled lightly. 'See, I don't get where you're coming from at all. I had nothing to do with any of this ole shit. That girl, it was run past me as a formality, look. Like dozens of others every week. And, as I recall, she was over sixteen and so able to leave home. And, if my memory don't fail me – and it *don't*, Brother Bliss – she turned up.'

Bugger.

'And you didn't think to talk to her?'

Charlie put a hand behind an ear.

'Do I hear the sound of a very thin straw getting clutched?'

'Here's another name,' Bliss said quickly. 'Hector Pryce.'

'In what connection?'

'Mate of yours?'

'He was a smart young magistrate. A mate of all of us.'

'You still see him?'

'Now and then.'

'You know about Hector's old man entertaining young ladies – *very* young ladies – at his secluded home in the western hills? Readers of his kids' books. Like Georgia Welsh.'

'Selwyn? The distinguished, retired academic, now in a nursing home?'

'Now in *Hector's* nursing home.'

'So?'

'Charlie, in connection with the murder inquiry you've doubtless heard about, we – that's your daughter, who's heading up the inquiry – and me are looking at serious evidence of historical abuse of women and children, ten or more years ago, at Selwyn's rural retreat, Cwmarrow Court. One of those things that just emerge when you're investigating something else. We think young fans of the books were being invited to linked events at Cwmarrow Court and the ones who were most keen would be invited back to more exclusive functions.'

'Well, good luck with that inquiry.'

'Could be big, Charlie, could be wide-ranging. Could be that nobody who had a toe in the pool will walk away. They go on and on, these inquiries and allegations keep coming out of the woodwork for years and years.'

'And? Scuse me if I missed it, Brother Bliss…' Charlie folding his arms. '… but you don't yet seem to have pointed a stubby little finger in my direction.'

'It was your era, Charlie.'

'End of.'

'And not a whisper? Word is Johnny Flynn would like to have carried on with that investigation.'

'What, even though the girl'd turned up?'

'Lot of other teenage girls passing through the Cwmarrow Valley. Didn't you think to talk to any?'

You could almost hear the small creak in Charlie's leathery face.

'You know what, boy? I should throw you out and lodge a complaint. But I'd hate to think there was anything personal that might damage our relations in the future. Or cause you to become obstructive during my election campaign.'

Charlie was entirely relaxed now, came languidly to his feet and strolled over to one of his filing cabinets.

'See, when I got a whisper of this, I didn't believe it. Could've decked the bloke who told me, even though he was an old friend. You know what it's like when you learn something that disgusts you.'

Charlie took out a laminate file, tossed it on his desk.

'Go on, Brother Bliss. Open it.'

Bliss didn't touch the file.

Charlie laughed and went back to his swivel chair.

'I'll do it for you, then.'

There were half a dozen photographs in the file. Big ones, blow-ups. Charlie took one out, held it up. Bliss saw a woman in a cream trench-coat and hat, getting out of a car in a parking bay, a shop front lit up in the background. Charlie took it away and put it face down on the desk, revealing the second photo in the pile: same woman, face visible, on a doorstep.

A sequence. The sixth picture had been taken from across the road, through the big front window. It showed the woman in the trench coat standing with her arms around a man who looked just slightly shorter. His face wasn't visible, but that wouldn't be important.

Charlie made a little amused noise.

'I gather you've started drawing your curtains sooner now. Well, too late, boy. *Too late.*'

'Charlie, this is—'

'See, I knew there was somebody. I started dropping hints.

Anne was given every opportunity to tell me who she was seeing. Not a word.'

'Like it's any of your business.'

'I didn't like that. I thought it might be worth hiring a private inquiry agent.'

'You wouldn't do that, Charlie. You'd look up a discreet ex-copper who owed you one.'

Charlie didn't smile.

'It was sheer disbelief when I first saw these. *Sheer disbelief.* I had to confirm it. Driving past Anne's block and saw your car. That bad night. Hurricane Lorna. Parked up a short distance away, rang her up and said I'd be calling in. Sure enough, out you come within minutes, scurrying into the storm. I remember thinking, terrible driving conditions. Good night to get himself killed. But we can't have everything, can we?'

Bliss said nothing. Sat and took it like a flogging. Thinking hard and coming up with more of nothing. Watching Charlie's mouth turn down in distaste.

'I won't need to tell you how very disappointed I was in Anne. Even after I thought, how far would this little man sink to get at me? I knew you were hurting, look, after our last chat. So… love, is it?'

'Don't use words you don't understand.'

'And you, boy…' Charlie's finger came up. '… will see just how much that word means to Anne when one of you's invited to go on the transfer list. Not just out of the division, out of West Mercia. Hereford's two most senior detectives in and out of one another's beds and keeping it secret? I don't think so, Brother Bliss. Mabbe one of you gets out of the Service, and *I* think that'd be you. Annie wouldn't go. Her life now, the Job. Something to prove.'

'She's still your daughter, Charlie. Remember?'

'Only nominally now, Brother Bliss, since her descent to a ratty little Mersey mongrel. But…' Charlie's mouth smiled.

'… it don't need to come to that, do it? We can all be friends. Distant friends, but friends nonetheless.'

'Yeh, right.'

Bliss's mouth felt like the bottom of a ditch in July.

'Meanwhile…' Charlie brushing the air with a hand. '… get out of my house, there's a good boy.'

Bliss got out.

He was sweating. Sweat was even worse than rain. Driving back to Hereford, he felt too close to crying. What if Charlie was right? What if there was nothing between him and Annie that didn't depend on them being coppers? Meeting furtively like they were undercover, lying in bed in the early hours, talking about crime, how sick was that?

63

Darker glasses

THE WIND HAD gone. Nothing moved at the top of the vicarage drive except for the night clouds, quite slowly. Merrily thanked the cop and got out and, feeling dizzy, held on to a young sycamore as he drove away.

Images were shuffling like picture cards in her mind: a crushed head and a skull with a stone in its mouth, trees and bone and the ravaging wind. Meaningless, pointless connections, alongside a terrible new thought about how she might have killed Adam Malik.

Jane had the door open, came to take her arm – she looked *that* bad? She saw big writing on the notepad by the phone in the hall.

'No.' Jane putting herself in front of the hall table. 'Don't try and call anybody. The insurance guy rang about the car. They've taken it to a garage in Hereford. They'll be in touch on whether it's a write-off, but its age says yes. Now come and eat. *I'm* cooking.'

'You're my mother now?'

'Not planning to be anybody's mother,' Jane said briskly. 'Not ever. I thought you'd got that message. Go and sit down. It'll be crap, but you'll be too tired to notice.'

She made it through the omelette. Like all Jane's omelettes, it was the texture of a bathroom mat. She said how good it was. She sat and inhaled vapour and was starting to tell Jane about Caroline Goddard when the doorbell rang.

Jane switched out the lights, went to peer through the hall window and came back whispering.

'Up the back stairs. Don't argue. Without a car, he doesn't know you're here. I'll get rid of him. *Go!*'

'Never mind.'

Too tired to move, anyway.

Jane didn't leave the kitchen. She went over and made tea, although he'd shaken his head. He wore a sober suit and a black tie. No velvet, nothing eccentric. He sat down well away from the lamp, telling them he'd had a meeting in Worcester lasting most of the afternoon, so hadn't heard the news until he came out.

He pushed fingertips into his forehead.

'I do apologize for burdening you.'

'Not a burden, Mr Khan.'

'You may not be saying that when I've gone.'

'Depends how long you're here,' Jane said.

'My daughter's renowned for her tact.' Merrily laid down the e-cig. 'You've probably heard I was there. Part of what happened.'

'I can see you were there. I'm so sorry. I hope you're not too—'

'It's superficial. The pictures in my head are far, far— Look, it's awful, it's unbelievably awful. I didn't get it right. If I'd pushed harder to see Aisha the last time I... but who am I to demand anything?'

'Easy to play *what if*, Mrs Watkins.'

'The worst thing that occurred to me – just now, on the way back – did he see my car ahead and slam the brakes on? Thus arriving directly in the path of the tree when he might have got through before it was down. His car was at an angle. I thought he must've swerved to avoid the tree, but you wouldn't, would you? The tree's going to cover the entire road and both hedges... But you *would* swerve, while braking hard, to avoid an oncoming vehicle on a single-track lane.'

'Mum, for Christ's sake—'

'Act of God,' Khan said, 'was the phrase used at the hospital.'

'Act of Allah,' Jane murmured, quite bitterly, into the kettle hiss. 'Only fair to share the blame in these situations.'

Khan sighed.

'In the eyes of Islam, Christianity and Judaism, there's only one God. Though it appears that some people see him through darker glasses than others. At the moment, I myself might as well be blindfolded.'

'How's Aisha?' Merrily said quickly. 'Do you know?'

'They thought at first an arm might be broken, but now they don't think so. Mrs Watkins, as Jane may have mentioned, I came early this morning, when you were presumably...'

Merrily looked up at Jane, who did a helpless, too-much-happening thing with her hands.

'I... braved the storm and went over to talk to Adam last night. He was in... turmoil would not be too strong a word. Bothered about things he hadn't told you. Trying to be cool and sensible and rational, while Nadya...'

He broke off. The sweat-glaze on his forehead was the first sign of distress she'd ever seen him display.

Jane delivered the tea, thankfully not Earl Grey, to the table.

'Things I need to do,' she said. Tactfully. 'Back in a few minutes.'

'I was at Oxford with women like Nadya,' Raji Khan said. 'Radical in every possible way. Supported the Palestinians against the Israelis in any given situation. Saw the honourable side of the Taliban. Nothing so wrong with that, until it becomes a rigid mindset and one loses a sense of balance. She wasn't popular in the Worcester community. People were suspicious of her. Some of them laughing at the idea of a jihadi seed in an English ornamental garden.'

Merrily could see her now, in the Maliks' sitting room. The prim blue hijab.

'My feeling,' she said, 'was that Nadya had a problem with religion. Any religion.'

'You're right, of course. More conversant with the Koran than Adam ever was, but that doesn't mean she believes in God. Or… any lower spiritual manifestation.'

'She introduced the djinn…well, not as something she believed in, but as a superior Islamic answer to primitive Western superstitions about ghosts. Spirits of the dead, *pfft*…'

'Yes. Precisely. She believed that what happened to her father was an hysterical product of overwork, obsession and his fear of growing old. He simply didn't want to admit that the house was too much for him. Nadya wanted to bring in an ordinary building firm to modernize it as much as was permissible under listed building regulations and have done with it.'

'I didn't know that.'

'Another source of tension. Adam was the peacemaker. But when he… when something happened to *him*…'

Merrily sat up.

'You're talking about before the tree—'

'It's why he wanted to talk to me last night. He asked me where you lived. It was his intention to try and see you. Today. On his own.'

'To say… what?'

'In fact, we agreed to meet here. He wasn't due at the hospital until mid-morning. I was a little late. Not that it would have made any difference. I suppose he was already dead by then.'

'But why did he…?'

'To ask your advice. About what he'd glimpsed, on… it must have been Sunday. After you'd left. The bulbs had blown on the landing. Dennis had given him two bulbs to replace them and he went through to the stairs – the wooden stairs, not very old, that go up from the Maliks' side of the house. He had a flashlight. It wouldn't work. He told me he looked up and, where the newel post was, at the top, saw a very faint shape. Not bright, but quite distinct. Pointing. At, ah… him.'

Raji Khan pushed the fingertips of both hands into his forehead again. He hadn't touched his tea.

Think. Was he making this up?

Why would he?

She was wide awake now after the meal, two mugs of tea, the vape stick.

'I gather you've been assisting the police,' he said, 'in connection with the two Hereford murders.'

As if he'd felt the need to allow this madness to assimilate, Raji Khan had simply changed the subject.

'Who told you that?'

'I tend to gather information on my travels.'

'Mr Khan, I've had enough evasion for one day. Who told you?'

Khan blinked.

'I serve on committees, dealing with youth, diversity and other boring but worthy issues. The police are often involved, I know some of them quite well. Others I avoid. In Hereford, mainly.'

It was a source of some annoyance to Frannie Bliss that Khan seemed to be protected at some exalted, probably headquarters level, perhaps as an informant. Which wouldn't be linked to the drug trade. In fact, the nearer you got to Birmingham, the closer it might be to intelligence about terrorist activity.

'There are, I regret to say,' he said, 'two sides to many of us. If you'd told me at university that I'd become a, shall we say, entrepreneur, I should have been insulted. It began, I suppose, when, as a student, I worked at weekends, for Hector Pryce.'

'You worked for *him*?'

'I organised music events at Hector's pubs. Always that joy in music. Even the kind of junk Hector wanted was better than not working with music at all.'

And so it came out. How he'd known about Cwmarrow *before* Adam Malik went to live there, intrigued because it appeared so alien to Hector's world of transport, catering, downmarket entertainment and... other less visible enterprises.

'When Hector married Lynne Hamer after her husband was killed in his plane, he acquired two restaurants,' Khan said. 'Neither doing well. Lynne hoped he'd bring them round. Instead, he sold them and quietly put the money into an escort agency and a massage parlour in outer Birmingham. Both of which quickly made money, which he used, gradually, to buy another restaurant and two pubs. So he was respectable and Lynne was happy.'

'I didn't know any of that.'

'Of course you didn't. Had it been known about, would Hector have become a magistrate? It's my understanding that he quietly retained interests around Birmingham. Useful for entertaining wealthy friends. But then… I, too, have mixed, on occasion, in disreputable company. Two sides, Mrs Watkins.'

'Why are you telling me all this, Mr Khan?'

He sat back, at the shadowed end of the refectory table.

'As I said, there's a side of me that mixes happily with the most senior police. But if I went to the police at any level it would have to be passed back to Hereford and those I tend to avoid.'

'Bliss?'

'You, however, are in a safer position, not least because of your profession.'

Huh.

'You're saying you want to use me to pass some information to Bliss?'

'I'm a Sufi. We look within ourselves and act accordingly. The path we're offered can be circuitous. I think the police should be investigating the possibility that Hector Pryce might have knowledge of these two murders.'

'Wh—?'

'Soffley – I knew him. Once worked in Hector's shadow business. His own, in Organ Yard, was overlooked by Hector's pub, the Old Coaching House. With his shop on its last legs, Soffley, I suspect, would not have been above asking for financial assistance. In return for continued silence.'

425

'You think he was blackmailing Hector Pryce? Over the massage—?'

'No, no, no. That's nothing. No, no. I think, over the killing of Tristram Greenaway.'

Merrily took a hit on the e-cig, watched him through the white vapour. Knowing Jane would be outside the door, listening.

'Mr Khan… cards on the table time. Tristram Greenaway was employed – whether he was actually paid or not I don't know – by Selwyn Kindley-Pryce to represent the hero of Kindley-Price's vampire novels. To set young girls' hearts aflutter.'

Khan smiled.

'Young girls. And older men.'

'Oh.'

Caroline: *Hector never came near me. He didn't really like women.*

'Two sides to everyone,' Khan said.

'You *knew* this?'

'I don't think Hector knew it himself – or admitted it – until he encountered Greenaway. A young man on the make. You don't seem surprised.'

'Like you, I get around. Was Hector's… ambivalence… widely known about?'

'*Heavens,* no. His wife wouldn't have known. I only know myself because I was the recipient of a tentative overture… immediately withdrawn when there was no reciprocity. This was after Greenaway had left Hereford, leaving Hector in… there was an element of denial. When I mentioned Greenaway once, Hector's reaction conveyed… oh, perhaps even hatred. For corrupting him, leading him from the straight and narrow. I often wondered what would happen if Greenaway were ever to return. And when I learned about the damage inflicted on a once pretty face…'

'You think he was capable of that?'

'There's always been a burning resentment inside Hector. A sense of repressed violence. But that's only my opinion.'

She was silent, would not tell him what might well have brought Pryce and Greenaway face to face: the dark grail of the Friends of the Dusk.

Steve Skull.

Some minutes later, Jane returned from her apartment. Raji Khan greeted her with a smile.

'And have you given Mr Walls his envelope yet?'

'I'm saving it,' Jane said. 'I want to be able to enjoy the moment.'

'Of course,' Mr Khan said. 'Enjoyment is important.'

When he'd gone, Merrily phoned Bliss on his mobile from the scullery. He was at home. He sounded frayed.

'No name?' he said. 'You're giving me this with *no name attached*?'

'Think of it as one of those Crimestoppers calls where you can leave information anonymously. But you're getting it from me, so at least you know I'm not, as the Book says, bearing false witness.'

'Oh, Merrily,' Bliss said. 'And me thinking I might gerra night's sleep.'

64

The Second Death

IT AWOKE HER twice in the hours before daylight, the way a moaning wind does, or heavy rain. But there was neither wind nor rain and no birdsong, although this was what it most resembled, maybe the hollow, repetitive dawnsong of the wood pigeon.

Merr-il-y... Come along.

Again and again until her eyes opened, and she saw a long hand, made of light, patting the bed, close to her left thigh.

She didn't scream or whimper or squirm away because it was a dream and your own screams always awoke you. Instead, in the dream, because she'd been here before, she didn't move but instinctively whispered the Lord's prayer, with the old-fashioned, not-mates words. Soon afterwards, she awoke, cold and numb, to find the duvet pulled to the other side of the bed so that her legs were uncovered.

Not good.

She sat on the side of the bed in cold air that made her face ache and could only mean a heavy frost, and said the Lord's Prayer again, then went to the window and said it again and again and again until the words had become a moving belt passing through her body from her solar plexus, through her breast and over her head and down her spine, between her legs and back again, and she went back to bed and slept until Jane came in with tea.

'You OK?'

The sky in the window behind her was a flawless, shocking blue.

'Thank you, flower.' She sat up. 'Yeah, I think so.'

Merr-il-y... Come along.

Her elbows went back, hard, into the headboard. Jane's head spun, as if something had flitted past her.

'I... was going to give you until midday. Huw's on his way.'

'What time is it?'

'Coming up to half-eleven?'

'Oh my God.' Pushing the duvet away. 'You're kidding.'

'You were knackered.'

A bunch of calls on the machine about parish business, including a baptism next Saturday. She dealt with them on autopilot. *Yes... I think so... Sure, no problem... I'll check... Is it OK if I get back to you?* Then Sophie called, toneless.

'It's not good news, Merrily.'

'No. I don't suppose it is.'

'The Bishop wants to see you. Formally. At ten tomorrow morning.'

'Where?'

'Here.'

'Be nice to see the old place again.'

'Yes, it's changed quite a bit.'

'Chair gone?'

'Oh, yes.'

'My pens and notebooks and stuff?'

'There'll be a bag waiting for you. I also have to tell you that, as you failed to reply to it, the offer of the post of Rural Dean has been withdrawn.'

'So it's not all bad news, then.'

'I shall see you tomorrow. That's assuming...'

'Oh, yes. I'll be there. Be cowardice not to turn up. Sophie—'

'I have to go.'

Not alone, then.

429

It was no place to work any more, was it? A reason to tell yourself not to be upset.

Huw tossed his canvas shoulder bag into a corner of the hall, followed Merrily into the kitchen, pulled one of the cane dining chairs over to the wood-stove.

'Colder.'

'Yes.'

'Let's not dress this up, lass. We need to talk about a word I'd normally avoid like a Wetherspoon's pub.'

She didn't say the word either.

'Big subject, Huw.'

'Not when you get rid of the shit. And there is some.'

She stayed on her feet. Didn't even remember what she'd said to him last night. She'd rung him after Bliss and another failed attempt to get an answer at Cwmarrow Court. She'd called him from the middle of a thickening mental mist.

'Thank you, by the way,' she said. 'Thank you for coming. I don't say that often enough.'

He ignored it.

'It's not what you think. And yet, in a way it is.'

'Vampirism. There. Said it. Did you say you might be bringing someone with you?'

'I said I were working wi' somebody. Someone who knows more than me about these things.'

'Not sure who that was.'

'I didn't say. But it's a friend of yours who you seem reluctant to regard as a friend on account everything in your theological training argues against it. But that's the Church for you. Self-protection. Let's keep the industry to ourselves.'

'Oh God, you can't mean— You don't *know* her.'

'*Didn't* know her. Been an illuminating couple of days, Merrily.'

'I bet.'

'Woman who runs that home dines out on Anthea White stories. And now a Hereford canon as her son-in-law, "Oh, you must know Merrily Watkins, Graeme, comes here now and again. And always to see Miss White." And then here's Graeme Spring in person, amiable clergyman, chatting to the residents… with the exception of one, who's clearly the subject of some of these chats. How long you reckon before Anthea started to smell a whole bag of rats?'

'She worked in Intelligence during the Cold War, so probably not that long.' Merrily stood at the window, looking out across the grass at the lichen on the churchyard wall, myriad in the sunshine. 'I think, in her provocative way, she was trying to get me to talk about Innes. Couple of weeks ago. I didn't know what she was on about. And how the hell do *you* know all this?'

'Let me go back to the beginning. She called me. She wanted to talk about you.'

Merrily spun round.

'*She* called *you*?'

'Not much she doesn't know about you, lass. Or me, come to that. Long days to fill in an old folks' home.'

'Were you in touch with her when I played you Sophie's recording?'

'Couldn't say owt. Couldn't trust you to leave the ole girl alone.'

'To do what, for heaven's sake?'

She'd begun to feel surrounded from above, prodded like a specimen on a lab mat.

'Might be pushing it a bit to say she's fond of you. Then again, happen it wouldn't. Nowt she could do about Innes, except menace her fellow inmates into silence, but she saw into the dark heart of this Cwmarrow business straight off. Anyroad…' Huw slipped out of his boots, stretched out his hiking socks to the stove. 'I drove over to see her. Walked in, dog collar and all.'

'That would've got straight back to Innes. Mad bastard from Brecon sniffing around.'

'I do like Anthea. Morally flexible, like everybody who ever worked for the government, but it's her immortal soul on the line, not mine.'

Merrily gave up, sat down.

'We talked at length about vampirism,' Huw said. 'I hadn't known about Walter Map and *De Nugis Curialium*. She did. Had it on the shelf in the original medieval Latin. Could even translate some of it. An eye-opener. Summat there, you know. All folk tales, Merrily, there's *summat there*.'

In the Walter Map story, there was a crucial line, Huw said.

Jane, of course, was already on to it. Jane had committed it to memory.

'"Peradventure the Lord has given power to the evil angel of that lost soul to move about in the dead corpse."'

'Lass is right,' Huw said. 'That's the essence of it. Somebody here knew what he were talking about. Might've been Map himself, but I do like to think it were Bishop Foliot. Good to think bishops in them days had their fingers on the spiritual pulse rather than the illuminated spreadsheet. You thought about what it means?'

'Looks like possession,' Jane said. 'Evil angel – demon?'

She'd been sitting quietly at the bottom of the table. Huw didn't seem bothered.

'We reckoned, me and Anthea, that it were more personal than that. "The evil angel of that lost soul." It's part of *him*. It's a clear pointer to what folk like her call The Second Death.'

He looked at Merrily who shrugged lightly.

'I'm not going to knock that. I never have.'

'Go on.'

'It argues that when the body dies, the soul continues to inhabit the astral or spiritual body for a short time – hence all those bereavement apparitions seen by the widowed partner or a close relative or friend, of the loved one… simultaneous with or soon after death. In order to cut all its earthly ties, move on, the soul needs to undergo the all-important *second* death. Leaving the astral body – and the earth – behind. Sometimes, maybe through some obsessive attachment to a place or a

432

person or a memory, it will hang on, causing problems for the living. This generally does tie in with my experience of trying to deal with psychic disturbance.'

'But what if it doesn't *want* to move on?' Huw said. 'Happen wants to keep its body functioning. For which it needs to appropriate the life energy of others. Sometimes symbolized as life *blood*.'

'So what Foliot means by the evil angel,' Jane said, 'is this man's own spirit…'

'The etheric double, as it's sometimes called. Evil because of what it does to hang on. Becomes a predator. Absorbs the energy of the living. Works his way through the village.'

'Summoning people, one by one,' Jane said. 'And they like… they just submit to it? When they're called, they come…?'

'It's a way of illustrating summat else about what, at some stage, we started calling vampires. All right, it's exaggerated, this tale of Map's, and simplified. It's a medieval chronicle, they didn't do psychoanalysis. It's good and evil and nowt in between. He's a *maleficus*. A black magician. Well, that's just words. Happen he's just a heretic who employs his knowledge selfishly. Could be a rogue monk, anything. But he reckons he's led a sinful life, and the message he gets from the all-knowing Church is that he's going to fry in hell for all eternity. He doesn't want to *go*. He feeds on his neighbours' energy to avoid the second death.'

Jane leaned forward across the table.

'But why do they let him in?'

'He's dominant, lass. We've all known people who can make you do things for them and go *on* doing things until you become ill. People who, if you spend too much time with them you feel completely drained. Some old people get like that. Emotionally demanding. And children. I want this, I want that. They want everything you've got. That's a kind of vampirism. That's the summoning.'

'Can't argue with that,' Merrily said.

433

'It's a workable theory. It's evil, but – and this is rare in our line of work – it's a form of evil we can fully understand if we apply ourselves.'

'And we should apply this to Selwyn Kindley-Pryce?'

'Anthea White thinks we can. Old girl got quite excited about it.'

'So why are you – you know – speaking for her? Why aren't we going to Hardwicke to get this from her direct? I'm saying go to Hardwicke because she won't come here.'

'She's not there.'

'She's always there.'

'She's at Lyme Farm.'

'Huw!'

'The lad took her. Lol. One of Lyme Farm's little earners is providing relief stays, anything from a couple of nights to a couple of weeks, so carers can have a holiday. Lol's dumped his old mum there for a night or two.'

'Oh, you are *kidding*...'

'Anthea's idea. She's paying. I'm bloody glad she didn't come to me, you can get a weekend in the Ritz for less than Lyme Farm charges. But... you're a worthy cause, lass. And if it makes you feel better, it's hardly just about you, is it?'

'Huw, I just...' Merrily was up and pacing. 'I really don't like this at all. I've never known Miss White leave The Glades, and I don't like her being there, with *him*? OK, he's demented, but in his case we don't know what that means, do we?'

Huw spread his hands.

'I had a dream about him last night,' Merrily said, collecting a sharp glance from Jane. 'Twice. Maybe more times. Is that me, or is it him? Or can a memory lodge like some kind of parasite in your subconscious? I don't know. I'm well out of my depth. Not scared to admit that.' A new thought froze her. 'Where's Lol?'

'He took the owd lass over there and came back. Supposed to collect her tonight.'

'Where's he now?'

'At his house. Waiting to hear from Lyme Farm about picking her up. Said I'd happen go with him.'

'Huw… what is she *doing*?'

'Would you think I were irresponsible if I said I didn't really know?'

'Actually, yes, I would. She's an old woman. If we follow your theory all the way, what we have there is a man in the advanced stages of dementia, his mind gone to mush, so that all that's left in there is… is…'

'The evil angel,' Jane said.

65

Boyfriend

MID-AFTERNOON, LOL came round. Sheepish, uncertain.

'I'm sorry. I wanted to tell you, but... Athena... you don't, do you? You just don't.'

'No.' Merrily pulled him into the kitchen. 'She's fascinated and frightened me at the same time, for so long...'

Taken her a long time to admit this even to herself. And now, for the first time, she was frightened *for* Miss White. In the way she'd so often been frightened for Jane. A girl and an old woman with no brake pedals. Although even Jane...

She watched her daughter busying herself with tea and coffee, sandwiches and cake, emergency rations. There'd been a crisis here, something Jane hadn't wanted to talk about, something she'd dealt with on her own and had come through. There was a new quietness in Jane – Merrily, who knew nothing, feeling obscurely proud of her. The way she was staying on the fringe, only speaking when she thought there was something she could genuinely contribute.

Merrily had told them – why not? – what she'd learned from Bliss and also Caroline Goddard, which led to speculation from Huw about the grooming of young girls for sex, how that related to vampirism.

'Oh aye, they'll come looking for it. They'll come looking for this Geraint, the young lad, and they'll get middle-aged men, and old men. And they'll let it happen, just like those thousands of kids in Yorkshire. The element of domination mingled with the allure of a forbidden world. I'd like to think if I were still up north I'd've spotted it, but happen I wouldn't.'

'Aisha,' Merrily said. 'This worries me a lot.'

She was aware of Jane wanting to say something and yet *not* wanting to. Jane who had only encountered Aisha on the Internet. But even that was closer than Merrily had managed, the way the Maliks had kept her out of sight.

Lol said, 'Huw, I keep wondering if we ought to go up there now – Lyme Farm. Just to be ready.'

'How long's she booked in, lad?'

'Till tonight.'

'We should wait. It's only half an hour or so.'

'Did I tell you about the camera?'

'Camera?'

'She asked for a camera, to take with her. A video camera. I borrowed one from Prof Levin. Took this old handbag to Prof and he fitted it with this tiny little camera she could operate from a pressure point.'

'Once a spook?'

'She seemed to know exactly what she was doing. I was just the driver.'

'We'll wait for the call, eh?' Huw said.

'I need to make one, too.'

Merrily got up and went through to the scullery.

One more try.

'We'll be leaving, Mirrily.' Casey Kellow had picked up on the second ring. 'Maybe somebody'll take the house for peanuts, or maybe we just sell the land. Doesn't matter, does it? Some things you just can't win. Some places are not meant to be lived in. You can't take on history.'

They're bloody mad, Hector Pryce had said, *people who get obsessed with the past. The past is worthless, messes you up.*

The Kellows were in hell. They'd come to the house to collect some things, and then they were going back to Worcester, to stay in a hotel. Adam's funeral – Muslims did it quickly, but there had to be a post-mortem. They didn't know what the schedule was. It was all a nightmare.

'How's Nadya?'

'Very stoical. Very quiet. Keeping away. Staying with her in-laws. We went over there. It was difficult. Strained, tearful. Nothing any of us could say. But at least Aisha's safe now.'

Was she? If you followed this madness all the way, you might wonder why Adam had died and Aisha had not. You might wonder what lived in her.

'Casey, what happened when they took Aisha away?'

'Why did I know you were gonna ask that? The paramedics had to sedate her to get her into the ambulance. She was hysterical. She was… crazy. Maybe it had just come home to her about her dad.'

'Yes.'

Or maybe something more complex.

'The paramedics were great, saying no problem, they'd seen all this before. I don't think they had.'

'Casey… please tell me this. It can only help, I promise you. Why did they keep her hidden, the Maliks? Why wasn't I ever allowed to see her?'

Loud silence in the phone.

'We thought it was a boyfriend, OK? We thought she was going out to meet a boyfriend. Maybe some boy… man… with a car, who'd be waiting for her out there, when she slipped away. She did that. She'd slip away.'

'Adam told me.'

'When we talked about it – and we didn't talk about it much, because her mother refused to – I'd say, why don't you follow her? I think Adam tried to. Wasn't easy. She had all this dark clothing. If you asked where she was going – well, you know what girls can be like at that age. You asked once, you didn't ask again. Even Nadya was a little scared of her. Sometimes her face… it was… too old for her. Like the face of a mature woman who'd... been round the block, you hear what I'm saying?'

'Didn't anybody at her school...?'

'Mirrily, she wasn't *like* that at school! Even here, not all the time. Sometimes. *That's* why Nadya didn't want you to see her. Because she knew what you'd think, someone in your job.'

'Not necessarily, we—'

'And Nadya thought that was insane because Nadya's an atheist masquerading as a Muslim.'

'What about Adam?'

'He talked to shrinks he knew. Imaginary boyfriend, they said. She had pictures from the Foxy Rowlestone fan club, of this guy from the books. Photos. Some model. She'll grow out of it, they said. She'll meet a real boy, and it'll all be history. Platitudes. Adam was afraid it was gonna turn out to be something midical – that's how Adam thought – reasonably, because she was complaining of hidaches, refusing to go to school. He'd arranged for some tests at the hospital. Yesterday. She was refusing to go. There were... scenes. Her dad... she... it was awful, distrissing... she rakes his face with her nails as they're getting her into the car. Nadya slams the door, he drives away. You know the rest. I think if he'd got her out of the valley, it would've been... I don't know. I don't *know*...'

Casey was sobbing hard. Merrily thought to say stuff about the usefulness of prayer at a time like this and couldn't.

'Casey, can you—?'

'I can't do anything!'

And then she was gone, and Lol was in the scullery doorway.

'Miss White's been on the phone to Huw. We're leaving now.'

439

66

Hereford Gothic

'WE'VE LOVED HAVING Mrs Robinson,' Donna said. 'She's made us laugh so much.'

Athena White was sitting in a window seat across from the reception area, kittenish in mohair, gazing placidly into the dusk with her handbag on her knees.

Lol went over. Athena reached up and patted his face.

'Darling boy.'

They'd come in Huw's Land Rover, driving into a short and savage November sunset, streaks of it still winding like molten wire over the horizon of low Welsh border hills.

'I've made so many friends,' Athena said. 'In such a short time. I'd quite like to say goodbye to some of them. Would that be in order, dear?'

'Of course,' Donna said, her eyebrows almost joining when she saw Merrily. 'Mrs Watkins? Here again.'

'Friend of the family,' Merrily said. 'Would it be OK if I...?'

'I guess. But I'm not awfully sure that Mr Kindley-Pryce...'

'I don't intend to bother him today.'

'Well, I'm not—'

'Come, Watkins,' Athena said.

There were muted lights in the passageways; in the big windows a dark orange sky, an afterglow on the fields on the Herefordshire side. Merrily, the airline bag over a shoulder, Huw and Lol, carrying his laptop, followed Athena White into a side passage and through a modern Gothic door into a plain little chapel with a couple of dozen wooden chairs either side of an aisle at the top of which was an altar covered with a green cloth with gilt edges.

Athena relieved Lol of the laptop.

'Robinson, would you mind awfully standing outside? If anyone wants to come in, tell them there's a... body in here in a coffin or something. They hate to be reminded they're in the departure lounge. No... let's leave the lights out, shall we?'

Huw moved away from the switches and shut the door, leaving Lol on the other side of it. Athena put down her bag on the altar, reached inside and pulled out the camera, about the size of Merrily's old Zippo lighter, a lead with a USB plug and her glasses.

'Don't look at me like that, Watkins. Most of the old biddies at The Glades are techno-savvy these days, even if they waste their hours on social trivia. This...' She bent over Lol's laptop. '... is all rather simplistic compared with the devices one was called upon to operate in my youth, however... I'd be grateful if one of you could help me find the right socket for this.'

She stepped away, but not before Merrily had noticed that her fingers had been fumbling because her hand was shaking. No wonder she hadn't wanted the lights on.

When the camera was connected, Athena let the laptop boot up on the altar then pulled out a chair, set it in the aisle and sat on it, arranging her skirt.

'Take your seats. Don't... don't worry, you won't be viewing his death. Although it would not, in all honesty, worry me in the slightest.'

'Anthea—'

'Do sit down, Owen. Watkins, would you mind awfully... operating the thing for me. It seems to be a... Mac. Or something. I'm more used to Windows.'

'Athena, are you—?'

'Just *do* it.'

Merrily crouched to one side of the altar so she could reach the laptop's pressure pad without blocking the view. Huw Owen pulled up a chair next to Athena's as a man's white-shirted midriff came up on the screen. White. He would be in white, wouldn't he?

'Stop it there for a moment,' Athena said. 'I should tell you the circumstances under which this was filmed. This morning, he came looking for me. He left his room to come and find me. I saw him coming along the passage, looking faintly disoriented in the sunshine.'

'How did you know he were looking for you, owd lass?' Huw said gently.

Athena scowled, her eyes near-black in the dull light of the autumnal dusk through tall leaded windows.

'I tried the nearest door – unmarked – and it opened. It was a white-tiled room containing just a chair and a table and a hospital trolley. I had a sense of death, I suppose. Perhaps an intermediate storage place for people who died in one of the lounges. It had a frosted window. I put my bag on the table, hoping to God the camera was pointing the right bloody way, and waited. He came in, and I leaned against the trolley. Oh, I felt quite dizzy for a moment, I said. Coming on with that sort of dithery, old-person nonsense. He looked quite disoriented, out of his quarters.'

Merrily said, 'Why did he come looking for you? If that's…'

Athena White did her tiny squeaky laugh.

'Because I'd gone to him, the night before. I probably suggested to you, rather boastfully, Watkins, that I do it all the time. In fact, I can't remember the last time, so it was much harder than I'd expected, performing to order. I was quite nervous – hadn't expected that.'

Merrily looked at Huw. He'd put on his reading glasses.

'Found it surprisingly difficult,' Athena said, 'holding the peripheral state between sleep and wakefulness. And then allowing the vibrational stage to continue for long enough to achieve separation.'

'Oh,' Merrily said, dismayed. 'I see.'

It had come back to her, from that afternoon at The Glades with Hurricane Lorna on her tail.

Don't trivialize breathing. I enjoy my breathing, in all its infinite varieties. Along with occasional astral tourism, it's all I have left.

'It's not an exact science, Watkins. And I'm hardly a master or a yogi. It was simply a matter of letting him know that *someone was here.* There's always a low-level paranormal vibe in old folks' homes. He'd pick that up. Question of rising above it to a level he'd notice. I'd visualized his quarters, his door with the number on it, the smells, the ambient sounds, the general atmosphere. Awoke this morning quite exhausted, with an unlikely memory of a huge bed, entirely out of proportion to its surroundings. Anyway, he'd come. What an extraordinary-looking man he is. Face like wood.'

Merrily didn't look at Huw. Anyone here could have told Miss White about the bed.

'And you talked?'

'Oh, yes, as you'll see. Dementia is not a perpetual condition. There are moments of clarity. I'd even wondered, as I'm sure you had, if *his* dementia might have been something of a misdiagnosis. Or even a scam. One can be labelled as demented by one's GP, especially if it's not Alzheimer's. Hospitals and scans and all that are very easily avoided.'

'It's true,' Huw said. 'A doctor can make a diagnosis based entirely on clinical findings, memory and cognitive tests. Especially if he's your mate.'

Athena shook her head.

'No, I do think it's the real thing, Owen, if less advanced than one might have imagined – I'd expected him to have the responses of a radish, but no. There was a kind of electricity. The only way I can describe it. I think, from what Owen told me, that you noticed that, Watkins. Anyway... observe.'

On the screen you saw him sitting down, but he was quite close to the camera so the top half of his face had been cropped.

'*Who are you?*' his mouth said.

'*Athena, my name.*'

'*Goddess.*' His mouth twisted into amusement. '*Goddess? You're* an old bag.'

'*Goddess of wisdom, Selwyn,*' Athena said. '*Forget the goddess bit. But dismiss the wisdom at your peril.*'

His mouth opened and you heard him breathing. It was loud and hollow, like a yawn, the almond cracks in his face stretching.

'Freeze that, Watkins. You hear that? That's *not* his breathing. Not *his* breath.'

Merrily felt the cold snaking around her legs like a spectral cat, moved away from the altar.

'I can hear why you're saying that, owd lass,' Huw said. 'but—'

'We're not going to *prove* anything here, Owen. Proof is entirely subjective. I'm just telling you what I *think*. Make it continue, Watkins.'

Merrily touched the pressure pad and Athena's voice emerged.

'*Where were you last night, Selwyn?*'

He answered at once.

'*Where I live.*'

His voice was all breath now, his mouth wide open.

'*Where's that?*'

'*You know.*'

Merrily wished she could see his eyes but was also glad that she couldn't.

Athena said, 'The phrase "phantasm of the living" is often used for a situation when someone might appear to be in two places at once. Quite often it's no more than a longing, on the part of the viewer of the apparition, to see a particular person, loved one, whoever, and, lo, the person manifests.'

'Aye,' Huw said, 'I've encountered that. Usually unreliable.'

'And then there's the question of projection.'

'We touched on it this morning. When we were discussing the Second Death.'

'Projection is hardly high occultism, Owen, it happens with astonishing regularity, even if some people aren't even aware of it, or are in complete denial. Or regard it as a vivid dream. But, yes, the connection with the Second Death is obvious. It's an intermediate state and is usually reached through one – in my case, the state on the very rim of sleep where one must hold oneself. Fall asleep and you have to start all over again.'

'Or it could be an illusion,' Merrily said.

'Or could indeed be an illusion. Even a *folie à deux* type illusion. Such as might have occurred last night when I lay in my room convincing myself that I was entering his room – not wanting, I should tell you, to remain there long – and he convinced himself he'd seen me.'

The old girl smiled sweetly. Merrily said nothing.

'Tell us what you think he does.'

'Hard to say precisely. I would probably suggest he falls back into his own psychic construction. He's decided that the Cwmarrow valley, with its vanished village, should be where Map's malefactor roamed, picking off his neighbours to allow him to go on living his half-life. Because that's all it can ever be. But half a life, it might be argued, is better than death, especially if you're in fear of what might happen afterwards. You go on taking life in the hope of escaping retribution.'

'Or that's the theory,' Merrily said.

'I'm not going to *argue* with you, little clergyperson. You're perfectly free to reject my opinions – as that's all they can be, this side of mortality.'

'I… I'm sorry, Athena. Really, I'm grateful for what you're doing. I'm just…'

Huw came to her rescue.

'You say a psychic construction. That he's decided the Cwmarrow valley was the home of the *maleficus*.'

'It might not be. It doesn't matter. He's spent years walking that place and visualizing and storing it in his subconscious mind. I imagine all he has to do sometimes is close his eyes and he's there. The sights and sounds and smells and whatever erotic extras he uses. He may always have had the ability. If you study, as I have, the accounts of astral projection you'll notice time and time again the sexual element. He probably doesn't even know he's harnessing that. Especially now...'

'What's the bottom line? How come he can do this?'

'Possibly through the *maleficus* itself. He becomes fascinated by Walter Map's exercise in Hereford Gothic – a vampire story which is perhaps not fictional like *Dracula* or *Carmilla* – and he goes in search of what remains of the *evil angel* of the nameless predator. His quest is fuelled by his enormous sexual appetite. Did you know he raped a cleaner?'

'Here?'

Merrily stepped back. The dusk had turned to night. The only light was the quivering screen.

'Or so it's *said* by some of the inmates. People do tend to talk to me. A young cleaner – just out of school – left the staff with a hefty lump sum.'

'It might be nonsense. He's a rather sinister presence. Do you want to see the rest?'

Huw opened his hands in assent. Athena activated the recording, the camera still on Selwyn-Pryce, the voice hers.

'Must be strange, Selwyn, for a man like you, with a fondness for female youth, to have a son with more diverse tastes.'

No reply. Bloody hell, you had to admire her.

'When did you first become aware of Hector's bisexuality? Obviously, as you weren't around when he was growing up, you wouldn't be aware of it coming on. But surely you must have noticed his more regular visits to Cwmarrow and how they coincided with the occasions when Tristram was there. Young Trissie?'

Had she told Huw about this on the phone last night? May well have done. And he'd passed it on, perhaps very early this morning, to Athena. God, she picked up on things so fast...

That yawning breath came again.

'*He was never the same again after Trissie, was he?*' Athena said on screen. '*The boy would have encouraged him. An influential man in Hereford. Rather amoral, Trissie. Eye to the main chance. Would've dropped Hector like a stone when an offer came in from the satellite TV people in London. Was that when Hector started coming to you for boys? Boys loved your books, too. And then, when he discovered Trissie had returned to Hereford and wanted to meet you all again, what did Hector do to the face which had tormented his dreams all those years ago? What's the matter, Selwyn?*'

The picture stuttered, an explosion of pixels, and then the man in the white shirt was extending an arm, his breath coming in spurts.

'*Kee, kee, kee.*'

The finger pointing.

'*Kee, kee, kee... Athena... White...*'

The screen went black.

Huw's voice was gentle.

'Why did you switch off there, owd lass?'

'I didn't,' Athena said.

'Oh.'

'I did, however, in keeping with the tradition, attempt to make the sign of the cross and found I... found I could not.'

'Ah,' Merrily said.

She pulled the laptop and the bag and the wire from the altar. Brought out the airline bag.

'Will a blessing cause offence?'

'Perhaps not,' Athena said.

In the last of the light, a glimpse of both her veiny hands quivering in her lap.

67

Invitation

ALL THE LIGHTS were on now, four hanging globes.

Merrily helped Athena back to her chair. You could feel the relief coming off her like steam. Or was that imagination?

'You weren't expecting it, were you?'

Athena scowled.

'Of course I was, you silly girl. I only brought you in here to make you feel at home. Little *clergyperson*.'

Her mascara had spread down her cheeks. She was trying desperately not to shake.

Laying on of hands. Probably the first time she'd ever touched Athena White.

'OK.' Merrily finding she was breathing hard, close to panting, but it wasn't hollow, it was nothing like a yawn. That had been the giveaway, that had brought the cold out of the screen. 'He hasn't been in here, to your knowledge?'

'Last place he'd come,' Athena said.

'Right. Huw?'

'I'm convinced, lass.'

'I haven't had a chance to tell you, have I, about Aisha. I suppose I wasn't sure how much of it I believed. It's a funny time, adolescence and the years that follow.'

'You have to believe it,' Huw said. 'While you're doing it, you have to believe it totally. *You* know that.'

'I do.'

'It's what he does. If he thinks he can do it, he can. It's about will power, self-belief. Tremendous, self-generating inner

448

world. Like Crowley. He could do it. Love is the law, love under will.'

She told him about Aisha. What Casey had said. *Like the face of a mature woman who'd... been round the block.*

'There's a bond now,' Huw said. 'She doesn't have to be in the valley. If he wants her, he'll find her. And he'll make her ill. And if he keeps on wi' it she'll die. And after that she won't rest and the cycle goes on.' He lowered himself to look into her eyes. 'That's what you have to believe, lass, if we're going to do this.'

She nodded. She unzipped the airline bag, took out the prayer book, the Bible, the holy water, the wine, the wafers and laid them on the altar.

'Right then, Huw. Let's get Lol in. And then you can give me communion.'

'And then you want to do it.'

'Mmm.'

'The major E? You? Or me?'

'Yes. Me. It's my patch,' Merrily said.

Athena White kept out of it. Well, you couldn't expect her to make too many concessions. But Lol... for the first time since they'd been together, Lol knelt before an altar, as if he was at last prepared to open himself to a wider plan. He was doing it for her, of course, but that didn't matter. He looked up and she caught his eye.

The light of the body is in the eye. Therefore when thine eye is single thy whole body is full of light.

She smiled. She hoped to God that the sense of high calm was not an illusion.

When it was over, Huw produced a thin paperback book from his canvas shoulder bag.

'I don't know whether to give you this or not, lass.'

'What is it?'

It looked old, decades old. You couldn't tell whether its cover was yellow or just yellowed.

'First published 1972 when it were all the rage and the Church decided we should go for it. With rules. But you can see from the title what it were still called, back then.'

EXORCISM

EDITED BY

Dom Robert Petitpierre.

THE FINDINGS OF

A COMMISSION

CONVENED BY THE

BISHOP OF EXETER.

EXORCISM

'Pre-deliverance,' Merrily said.

'Seen it before?'

'Actually, I may have.'

'The deliverance handbook's over three times as thick, good in its way, but essentially it walks all round major exorcism.'

'Which is what's needed here.'

'A major? Oh aye.'

'You sure you don't want—?'

'*No.* I've faced Kindley-Pryce – it – before. It knows my name, Huw.'

'That might not be…'

'Come in with me, though?'

'Oh aye. Try and keep me out. It's not a one-priest job, this.'

'He's an old man. An old, demented man.'

'No. You don't say that. You don't *think* that. It's something inside an old man's body and his corroded mind. And it were invited in. Don't forget that. This is not oppression, this is invitation. *Invitation.*'

'Right.'

She took off the hoodie, positioned the pectoral cross on her cotton top.

'After you,' Huw said. 'You know the way.'

Lol stayed behind in the chapel, with Athena.

Walking slowly down the passageway, muted lighting, the night in the glass walls on either side, she read from the booklet.

FORMS FOR EXORCISM OF PERSONS.

The difference between an exorcism and a blessing was the resistance.

The fight.

I command you, every unclean spirit...

Too generalized?

I command you, O Evil Spirit, through God the Father Almighty and through Jesus Christ his Son and through the Holy Spirit the Paraclete, that you depart...

Evil. Just a word.

Not just a word.

'Damn,' Merrily said, carrying on walking, the airline bag over her right shoulder. 'I forgot to phone Bishop Craig to check if this was all right with him.'

'Do not laugh,' Huw said. 'Don't you *dare* laugh.'

She didn't laugh.

The last time.

The last Deliverance.

The Old Stables. Three doors, only one with a number on it and a white speaker grille.

Man or woman?

Kee, kee, kee....

They stopped. The door was ajar. Merrily glanced at Huw, who lifted a hand, and not in benediction. Presently, Hector Pryce came out, looking at them with no surprise. Donna must have called him, told him who'd arrived. He'd had plenty of time to get here from Hereford while they were in the chapel.

'Dead,' Hector said.

As if to illustrate his point, he held a human skull, yellow and brown and coming apart in his hands around a crooked grin. *He's getting it out of there*, Merrily thought, as Hector kicked the door fully open behind him.

'See? Old man's gone. Somebody seen him off, look.'

An overhead light had turned the whole room into a Victorian engraving of a classical funeral, the great Cwmarrow bed an ornate tomb, Selwyn Kindley-Pryce its rigid effigy. There was an acrid stench of funeral. Death and earth.

'I just found him,' Hector said. 'Thought he was having his nap before tea.'

A buff-coloured pillow, creased, lay beside the head of the corpse. But the eeriest thing was Hector's face: flushed with relief, excitement and a delight only half suppressed. Was he glad he'd done it... glad that someone else had done it... *fooling himself* that someone else had done it?

'Gone, eh?' Huw said.

She could see his grey eyes wondering *where*.

68

The door

SHE WAS THERE again, under the gatehouse arch, just as she'd been on that very first day.

Welcome to Deliverance Tower.

Almost the first words to Merrily from Sophie, the Bishop's secretary, who had been waiting to open the door to the stone steps curving up to the gatehouse and the interior door, which the new bishop, Michael Hunter, had decreed should have a gothic **D** on it below a black cross.

He'd also decided there should be a Hereford deliverance website and that Merrily should have meetings with the director of social services, various mental health charities and the police. Bishop Mick: nothing if not ambitious for the Church's loony spooks.

Of course, she'd got rid of the D as soon as it could be done without causing offence. Telling Sophie that deliverance should be low profile.

And that was how she'd go out.

This morning, she'd parked near the swimming pool again. She was wearing her best woollen coat and a black skirt. She'd come an hour early, wanting time and space to consider what she'd say to Craig Innes but then deciding not to consider it at all. What was the point? There were more important issues.

Bliss had phoned last night to say that Hector Pryce was still angrily denying he'd put the pillow over his father's face, insisting the old man had been dead already. Claiming he'd seen a Land Rover coming down the drive from Lyme Place when he'd arrived. Evidently not Huw's old Defender, which hadn't moved.

Hector was protesting his innocence so hard, Bliss said, that he'd almost coughed to the other two killings. Only a matter of time, Bliss kept saying, sounding weary.

Bliss. Funny thing, walking across the wet and empty Bishop's Meadow not long after eight, Merrily had felt sure she'd seen him walking ahead of her, but then it seemed unlikely because he'd been hand in hand with a woman who was a little taller and bore a superficial resemblance to...

She'd tried to close the gap between them but they'd gone.

Couldn't have been.

She'd need to talk to Bliss later, to wind up her role in this on a note of suitable lunacy. Athena White was demanding that the body and head of Selwyn Kindley-Pryce should be separated. No spades necessary, simply a question of making sure they were donated separately for medical research. Different places, certain provisos. Presumably, only Hector could authorize that. Athena said he might not need to be leaned on too hard.

The whole Cwmarrow situation, the legacy of the *maleficus*, the role of falling trees... it was never going to make total sense. But when did these things ever?

As for the Land Rover leaving Lyme Place... Dennis Kellow had a Land Rover to which other members of his family had access. But then, no more common vehicle hereabouts.

Don't ask. You are not a detective. Within an hour you will no longer be a deliverance minister. You'll no longer be officially obliged to try and explain the inexplicable, or guide people away from it or help them live with it.

So here she was, coming around the benign, sandstone Cathedral under a sober sky, spotting Sophie under the gatehouse. She'd miss Sophie, most of all.

Hold the image, make it into memory, file it next to Day One. Sophie hadn't changed, except that she'd usually worn her white hair in a bun, back then, but this morning it was down and straggly, and that was not normal.

Nor was the way she was standing with her winter cardigan displaying a patch of red the size of a poppy around the abdomen.

God...

Merrily began to run towards her and couldn't run fast enough, could almost see herself running in slow motion, recalling all the misfits drawn to a Cathedral, the mentally disturbed, the coke-heads, once a man with a gun who said it was a cry for help.

Merrily was running to Sophie, like she hadn't run since she was a child running to her mother, so hard she couldn't feel her legs moving, until she tripped and it was only Sophie who stopped her from falling.

Sophie's face was pale.

'Merrily, what—?'

'Are you—?'

'Just came out for a breath of air, Merrily.'

Merrily fighting for her own breath. Couple of weeks of vaping could hardly wipe out the effects of twenty years of cigs.

'I... thought for a minute it was blood.'

Sophie looked down at her cardigan.

'Oh dear,' she said. 'It *is* blood.'

She opened the door to what had been Deliverance Tower.

'You'd better come up.'

The Bishop's new chair – a chair of light grey leather – had its back to the window overlooking Broad Street. Not quite where her own chair used to be but close enough and well-spattered, like Sophie's cardigan, with fresh blood.

Huw Owen was standing next to it, wearing as close as he ever came to full kit: white dog collar, black shirt, with an old but proper suit. He had his head held back, a handful of sodden, reddening tissues around his nose.

'Don't *think* it's broken, Sophie.'

He straightened up, and blood ran around his mouth, into his beard and his dog collar. He saw Merrily and grinned, looking insane.

'All right, lass?'

'Huw— Jesus *Christ*—'

'Bit of a nosebleed. Dry up in a bit.'

'Where's the Bishop?'

'The Bishop left,' Sophie said. 'When I saw you coming, from the window, I thought I'd better go down and see if he was still here, but he… must've gone through to the palace. He… fell on the steps. Fell against the door.'

Merrily looked at Huw. He was still grinning through the blood on his teeth.

'And you fell into the same door, did you?'

'Could say that, aye.'

'To be more accurate,' Sophie said, 'the Bishop walked into what would become a heated discussion.'

Huw sniffed.

'Involving a number of topics… related to his past ministry. You know the kind of thing.'

'Jenny Roberts?'

'Aye, Jenny Roberts were one of them, obviously. His abominable treatment of you another.' He dragged another handful of tissues from the box on Sophie's desk. 'Way I see it, Merrily, we can be too subtle about these things. Could've delivered a sermon, but what bloody use would that've been?'

'What?'

'He's a bishop, but a bishop's a man. Wi' a man's pride. You can wind a man up to breaking point. Well, *I* can. When I'm in the mood. And if I know what kind of man I'm dealing with. Like a man wi' a history of playing contact sport? You keep prodding him, waiting for the moment when he breaks, when he loses it. When he lashes out without quite realizing what he's doing. *Bam.*'

'He hit you? The Bishop actually hit you?'

'Now, see, what's important, lass, in these situations, is making sure the other feller's fist is the *first to land*. And because you're expecting it – happen you've actually *prayed* for it - you know exactly how you're going to react when it comes. You say another quick prayer – well, more of an apology in my case. I'm not a very physical man, as you know. I'm a man of peace and a bit of a wimp, but after what I said to Innes, *I* would've hit me.'

He sat in the bloodied chair. His laughter suddenly seemed very emotional.

'When Huw arrived,' Sophie said, 'the Bishop suggested I might have some more shopping to attend to. I was halfway down the stairs when I realized I must have forgotten my shopping list.'

Huw laughed, snorted more blood, put his head back again.

'I came off worse, I'll not deny that. He's a good bit younger than me, and I were crap at rugby. But I were ready, see? This is the crucial point. Just had to get that one punch in, and then he could do what he liked to me after that.'

Sophie pointed to the iPhone on her desk.

'It was a quite disgraceful episode. If I was the Bishop I'd be taking it further. On which basis, I felt I should obtain photographs which could be used as evidence to support any charges the Bishop might choose to bring against Mr Owen.'

Huw screwed up the used handful of bloody tissues and tossed them into the waste bin.

'He hit me first. No way round that. Well, I'm an ugly bugger at best of times. And at least I don't have to appear in the Cathedral in the full purple kit, *wi' a matching eye*. Thing about falling into a door, is nobody ever believes it.'

He picked up Sophie's iPhone and dropped it into his jacket pocket.

'Some bugger's nicked Sophie's phone. Can't trust anybody these days, though happen they'll send it back. But what if Innes doesn't see sense and them pictures wind up on the Net? Press'll be down on it like a dog at dinner time.'

Huw put a hand on Merrily's shoulder.

'Come in on Monday, same as usual, I would. See what happens. Or what doesn't.' He walked lightly to the door. 'Ta-ra, lass.'

Notes and closing credits

IT DIDN'T SURPRISE me a lot when I discovered that the first convincing British account of something predatory and undead should have originated on the Hereford/Wales border. After years of saying I was NEVER going near a vampire, I had either to keep pretending I hadn't read it or consider how it might echo (credibly).

Should you wish to check it out, Walter Map's account of Sir William, Bishop Foliot and the summoner is retold in several books, from *The Secret History of Vampires* by Claude Lecouteux to the whimsical *Herefordshire Folklore* by David Phelps (The History Press 2009) which (like Kindley-Pryce's version) suggests that the beheaded corpse might have been buried close to Hereford Cathedral. The short, chilling version by Edwin Sidney Hartland remains where Jane found it, in the introduction to Ella Mary Leather's *The Folklore of Herefordshire*.

The village of Cwmarrow might be harder to find but virtually all its significant features can be found in the Golden Valley, in an area between Vowchurch and Dorstone.

Thanks to Mairead Reidy, who divined and dispatched all the right books.

Clerical consultants were the Revs Jason Bray, Peter Brooks, Liz Jump, Sue Richardson and the late, seriously lamented Kevin Wilkinson. Also thanks to the Rev. Nicholas Lowton, who runs things up by the Black Mountains, for his enlightening parish magazine article 'On being a Rural Dean', which includes the key sentence, *The first the new Rural Dean knows about it is when he receives a letter from the Bishop inviting him to be Rural Dean and thanking him for agreeing to take the role on.*

In attempting to tune into her surroundings, Jane must have been recalling Francis Pryor's monumental work *The Making of the British Landscapes* (Allen Lane 2010).

Way back, Jeanine McMullen gave me a copy of Katharine Briggs's classic *A Dictionary of Fairies* (Penguin, 1976) which discusses the fairy stroke, as does Patrick Harpur's *Daimonic Reality* (Viking, 1994). Another informative volume was *The Vengeful Djinn* by Rosemary Ellen Guiley and Philip J. Imbrogno (Llewellyn 2011). Thanks again to Dion Fortune who never fails to come up with something. And Robert A. Monroe's *Journeys Out of the Body* (Souvenir Press, 1972) is probably the most convincing account of astral projection ever published. I'm sure my late grandma, May, would have agreed.

Thanks also to…

Tony Hazzard, writer of many classic songs, on how TV commercials can change your life… or not.

Mobeena Khan (no relation to Raji) who answered lots of questions about non-fundamentalist Muslim life.

The archaeologist Jodie Lewis on the excavation of human bodies, buried deviantly and otherwise.

The Rev. Strachan McQuade (channelled) on… let's not go there.

Philippa May and Paul Rogers at the *Hereford Times*.

Dr Jamie Monaghan, on the diagnosis of dementia.

Dai Pritchard on building technicalities.

Tooki Proctor on Antipodean linguistical pitfalls.

Tracy Thursfield, for magical guidance.

Caitlin Warrior for Internet esoterica.

On the publishing side,

Sara O'Keeffe, Louise Cullen, Liz Hatherell and…

My wife and most ruthless editor, Carol, for spotting all the structural flaws, and then pointing the way forward… which was not, as usual, the direction in which I was heading.